DANGEROUS LIAISONS

"One challenge. To the death. Here in the city. I don't think you can quarrel with that."

"I only quarrel on commission," Richard St. Vier said lightly.

"I saw you fight off two men at Lord Horn's party. It's a mystery to everyone still, what the whole thing was about." His one eye glinted sharply; Richard took the hint, and returned it: "I'm afraid I can't tell you that. Part of my work is to guard my employers' secrets."

"And yet you let them employ you without any contract."

Richard leaned back, entirely at ease. "Oh, yes, I insist on that. I don't like having my business down on paper in someone's drawer."

"Sixty royals," the man said, "half in advance."

Richard took his time as he brought the goblet to his lips. "I don't take money on an unnamed man. — Is it a man?" he added abruptly, somewhat spoiling the effect. "I don't do women."

The other man's lips quirked. "Oh, yes, it is a man. It is a man of some importance."

MORE PRAISE FOR *SWORDSPOINT*

"There is more going on when two of Kushner's characters sit and talk for a few pages than in some whole trilogies. Witty, sharp-eyed, full of interesting people and fascinating conversation, Kushner's first novel is a delight."   —*Newsday*

"An elegant, talented, and vastly enjoyable novel."
                                                      —Samuel R. Delany

"If you have even an ounce of interest in the interplay of sharp swords, and sharper tongues, then *Swordspoint* is for you."   —Charles de Lint

"A tale as witty, beguiling, and ingenious as a collaboration between Jane Austen and M. John Harrison. In short, *Swordspoint* is a well-nigh faultless first novel."   —*Interzone*

"Charming, exciting, and ironically provocative, rather as though Georgette Heyer had turned her hand to fantasy. I enjoyed the book immensely."   —Peter S. Beagle

"A scintillating gem ... witty, wicked, fascinating, beautifully written—and unique."   —Joan D. Vinge

SWORDSPOINT

•a•melodrama•of•manners•

ELLEN KUSHNER

TOR
fantasy

A TOM DOHERTY ASSOCIATES BOOK
NEW YORK

SWORDSPOINT

Copyright © 1987 by Ellen Kushner

Published by arrangement with Arbor House Publishing Company

A Tor Book
Published by Tom Doherty Associates, Inc.
49 West 24th Street
New York, N.Y. 10010

Cover art by Thomas Canty

ISBN: 0-812-51771-7

Library of Congress Catalog Card Number: 87-11483

First Tor edition: July 1989

Printed in the United States of America

0 9 8 7 6 5 4 3 2

For the Other One

Man desires that which is Good.
                    Plato

'We all have faults,' he said,
'and mine is being wicked.'
                    James Thurber,
                    The Thirteen Clocks

In the end . . . everything will be found
to be true of everybody.
                    Lawrence Durrell,
                    Balthazar

SWORDSPOINT

† † †

Chapter I

Snow was falling on Riverside, great white feather-puffs that veiled the cracks in the façades of its ruined houses, slowly softening the harsh contours of jagged roof and fallen beam. Eaves were rounded with snow, overlapping, embracing, sliding into each other, capping houses all clustered together like a fairy-tale village. Little slopes of snow nestled in the slats of shutters still cosily latched against the night. It dusted the tops of fantastical chimneys that spiralled up from frosted roofs, and it formed white peaks in the ridges of the old coats of arms carved above the doorways. Only here and there a window, its glass long shattered, gaped like a black mouth with broken teeth, sucking snow into its maw.

Let the fairy-tale begin on a winter's morning, then, with one drop of blood new-fallen on the ivory snow: a drop as bright as a clear-cut ruby, red as the single spot of claret on the lace cuff. And it therefore follows that evil lurks behind each broken window, scheming malice and enchantment; while behind the latched shutters the good are sleeping their just sleeps at this early hour in Riverside. Soon they will arise to go about their business; and one, maybe, will be as lovely as the day, armed, as are the good, for a predestined triumph. . . .

But there is no one behind the broken windows; only eddies of snow drift across bare floorboards. The owners of the coats of arms have long since abandoned all claims to the houses they crest, and moved up to the Hill where they can look down on all the city. No king rules them any more, for good or ill. From the Hill, Riverside is a tiny splotch between two riverbanks, an unsavoury quarter in a prosperous city. The people who live there now like to think of themselves as evil, but they're really no worse than anyone else. And already this morning more than one

1

drop of blood has been shed.

The blood lies on the snow of a formal winter garden, now trampled and muddy. A man lies dead, the snow filling in the hollows of his eyes, while another man is twisted up, grunting, sweating frog-ponds on the frozen earth, waiting for someone to come and help him. The hero of this little tableau has just vaulted the garden wall and is running like mad into the darkness while the darkness lasts.

The falling snow made it hard for him to see. The fight hadn't badly winded him, but he was hot and sweaty, and he could feel his heart pounding in his chest. He ignored it, making for Riverside, where no one was likely to follow him.

He could have stayed, if he'd wanted to. The swordfight had been very impressive, and the party guests had been well entertained. The winter garden party and its outcome would be talked about for weeks. But if he stayed, the swordsman knew that he would be offered wine, and rich pastry, and asked boring questions about his technique, and difficult questions about who had arranged the fight. He ran on.

Under his cloak, his shirt was spattered with blood, and the Watch would want to know what he was doing up on the Hill at this hour. It was their right to know; but his profession forbade him to answer, so he dodged around corners and caught his breath in doorways until he'd left the splendours of the Hill behind, working his way down through the city. It was breaking dawn when he came to the river, flowing murky green under the Bridge. No one waited there to challenge him, so he set his foot on the stone, ploughing through snowdrifts and the messy trails of other late-night workers who'd come before him, until he'd put the river safely between himself and the rest of the city. He stood now in Riverside, where the Watch never dared to come. People knew him here, and wouldn't bother him.

But when he opened the door to his landlady's, there was a considerable crowd assembled, all wanting to know about the fight. Other Riversiders had been on the Hill too, that night, burgling houses and collecting gossip, and already the rumours had begun. The swordsman answered their questions with as much civility as he could muster, suddenly awash with exhaus-

2

tion. He gave Marie his shirt to wash, and climbed the stairs to his own rooms.

Less than an hour earlier, Marie the whore and laundress, who also rented out rooms by the week, had lain snoring lightly in the arms of a dear client, unaware of the impending excitement. Her friend was a sailor turned coiner, whose wooden leg leaned handily against the headboard. He was her fifth and last of the night, and she, not as young as she once was, slept through the initial pounding on her shutters. The sailor stirred uneasily, dreaming of storms. When the knock came harder, Marie bolted up with a cry, then shrieked at the cold outside the blanket.

'Marie! Marie!' The voice through the shutter was muffled but insistent. 'Open up and tell us all about it!'

Marie sighed. It must be St Vier again: every time the swordsman got up to something they came to her to find out the details. This time, it was annoying to admit, she didn't know — but then, she didn't have to tell *them* that. With the laugh that had always made her popular, Marie got up and unbolted the door to the house.

Her sailor huddled in a corner of the bed while her friends trooped in, taking over the room with the ease of familiarity. It was the right room for socialising, having been the front parlour when the house was a noble's town house. The cherubs painted on the ceiling were flecked with mould; but most of the laurel-leaf moulding still framed the walls, and the fireplace was real marble. Marie's friends spread their wet cloaks out on the gilded escritoire, now missing all its drawers, and over the turquoise velvet chair no one could sit on because of the uncertainty of its legs. Lightfinger Lucie coaxed the fire to a blaze, and Sam Bonner produced a jug of something that made the sailor feel much better.

'You know,' said Sam ponderously, 'your St Vier's gone and killed a duke this time.'

Sam Bonner was a former pickpocket with an unhandy taste for the bottle. He'd been repeating the same thing for half an hour now, and his friends were getting tired of correcting him. 'Not the *duke*, Sam,' one of them tried again. 'He's *working*

3

for the duke. He killed two *swordsmen*, see, in the duke's garden.'

'No, no, in Lord Horn's garden. *Three* swordsmen, I heard,' another asserted, 'and from a very reliable source. Two dead, one wounded, and I'm taking odds on whether he'll live till morning!'

'Done!'

Marie sat on the bed with the blankets wrapped around her feet, letting the betting and the squabbling swirl around her. 'Who's dead? – Lynch – de Maris – Not a scratch on him – Horn's garden – Hired St Vier? – Not St Vier, Lynch – Wounded – Dying – Who's paying St Vier? – Horn – the duke – the devil – How much? – More'n *you'll* ever see –'

More people trickled in, adding to the clamour. 'St Vier's been killed – captured – Five to one –'

They barely noticed when another man came in and silently took a place just inside the door. Sam Bonner was roaring, 'Well, *I* say he's the best dam' swordsman in the whole dam' city! No, I'm lying – in the world!'

The young man by the doorway smiled, and said, 'Excuse me. Marie?'

He was younger than most of them there; dark-haired, of average height, his face dirty and stubbled.

'Who the hell is that?' Sam Bonner growled.

'The best dam' swordsman in the world,' Lightfinger Lucie answered with pardonable malice.

'I'm sorry to bother you,' the swordsman said to Marie, 'but you know how the stains set.' He took off his cloak, revealing a white shirt ugly with blood. He pulled the shirt over his head, and tossed it into a corner. For a moment the iron tang of blood cut through the smells of whisky and wet wool. 'I can pay you next week,' he said. 'I made some money.'

'Oh, that's fine with me,' Marie said with off-handed airiness, showing off.

He turned to go, but they stopped him with the shouting of his name: 'St Vier!'

'St Vier! Who's dead, then?'

'De Maris,' he answered curtly. 'And maybe Lynch, by now. Excuse me, please.'

4

No one reached out a hand to stop him as he walked through the door.

The smell of frying fish made the swordsman's stomach lurch. It was his young gentleman, the University student, wrapped in his scholar's robe, hovering like a black bat over the frying pan in the ornamented fireplace.

'Good morning,' St Vier said. 'You're up early.'

'I'm always up early, Richard.' The student didn't turn around. 'You're the one who stays out all night killing people.' His voice was its usual cool drawl, taunting in its nonchalance. The accent, with its crisp consonants and long vowels, took Richard back to the Hill: for a moment he was once again crouched amid the topiary of the pleasure garden, hearing the same tones ringing on the air from the party guests. 'Who was the poor soul this time?'

'Just a couple of swordsmen. It was supposed to be a duel with Hal Lynch, I thought I told you. Our patrons set it up to take place at this crazy garden party of Lord Horn's. Can you imagine, having a party outdoors in this weather?'

'They would have had furs. And admired the landscaping.'

'I suppose.' While he spoke, the swordsman was cleaning his sword. It was a light, flexible duelling weapon of a sort only he, with his reputation and his reflexes, could carry around Riverside with authority. 'Anyway, Lynch got started, and then de Maris popped out of the shrubbery and started coming at me.'

'Whatever for?'

Richard sighed. 'Who knows? He's Horn's house swordsman; maybe he thought I was attacking his master. Anyway, Lynch stepped aside, and I killed de Maris. He was out of practice,' he added, polishing the blade with a soft cloth. 'Lynch was good enough, he always has been. But our patrons wanted it past first blood, so I think I killed him. I *think* . . .' He scowled. 'It was a clumsy stroke. I slipped on some old ice.'

The young man poked at the fish. 'Do you want some?'

'No, thanks. I'm just going to bed.'

'Well, it's revolting cold,' the scholar said with satisfaction, 'I shall have to eat it all myself.'

'Do that.'

5

St Vier passed into the adjoining room, which contained a clothes chest that also held his swords, wrapped in oil cloth, and a large, heavily carved bed. He had bought the bed the last time he had any money; seen it in a Riverside market stall full of odds-and-ends retrieved from the old houses, and fallen in love with it.

He looked at the bed. It did not appear to have been slept in. Curious, he returned to the front room.

'How was your night?' he asked. He noticed the pair of wet boots standing in the corner.

'Fine,' the scholar answered, daintily picking bones out of his fish. 'I thought you said you were tired.'

'Alec,' said Richard. 'It really isn't safe for you to be going out alone here after dark. People get wild, and not everyone knows who you are yet.'

'No one knows who I am.' Alec dreamily laced his long fingers in his hair. His hair was fine and leaf-brown, worn down his back in the long tail that was the defiant emblem of University scholars. He had been in Riverside since autumn, and his clothes and his accent were the only signs of where he had come from. 'Look.' Alec's eyes, turned to the window, were dark and green, like the water under the Bridge. 'It's still snowing. You can die in the snow. You're cold, but it doesn't hurt. They say you get warmer and warmer, and then you fall asleep. . . .'

'We can go out later. If anyone is trying to kill you, I'd better know about it.'

'Why?'

'I can't let them,' the swordsman said; 'it would ruin my reputation.' He yawned. 'I hope at least you had your knife with you.'

'I lost it.'

'Again? Well, never mind. I can get you another when the money for the fight comes in.' St Vier shook out his arms, and flexed them against the wall. 'If I don't go to sleep soon, I'm going to start waking up, and then I'll feel rotten for the rest of the day. 'Night, Alec.'

'Good night, Richard.' The voice was low and amused; of course, it was morning. But he was much too tired to care. He placed his sword within reach of the bed, as he always did. As he drifted off, he seemed to see a series of white images, scenes carved in snow. Frosty gardens, their branches lush with white roses and crystal thorns; ladies with floating spun-sugar hair escorted by ivory gallants; and, for himself, opponents with long bright swords of clear and gleaming ice.

Chapter II

By midday, most of the nobles on the Hill could be counted on to
be awake. The Hill sat lordly above the rest of the city,
honeycombed with mansions, landscaped lawns, elaborate gates
and private docks on the cleanest part of the river. Its streets had
been built expressly wide and smooth enough to accommodate
the carriages of nobles, shortly after carriages had been invented.
Usually, mornings on the Hill were passed in leisurely exchange
of notes written on coloured, scented and folded paper, read and
composed in various states of dishabille over cups of rich
chocolate and crisp little triangles of toast (all the nourishment
that ought to be managed after a night's revelling); but on the
morning after the garden duel, with the night's events ripe for
comment, no one had the patience to wait for a reply, so the
streets were unusually crowded with carriages and pedestrians of
rank.

The Duke of Karleigh was gone from the city. From what
anyone could discover, the duke had left Lord Horn's party not
an hour after the fight, gone home, ordered up his carriage
despite the snow, and departed before dawn for his estates in the
south without a word to anyone. The first swordsman who had
fought St Vier, a man named Lynch, had died at around 10 that
morning, so there was no asking him whether Karleigh had hired
him for the duel, although the duke's abrupt departure upon
Lynch's defeat seemed to confirm that he had. St Vier had
disappeared back into Riverside, but whoever had hired him was
expected to step forward momentarily to claim the stylish and
elegant victory over Karleigh. So far, no one had.

Meanwhile, Lord Horn was certainly making enough of a fuss
over the use his gardens had been put to, never mind the loss of
his house swordsman, the impetuous de Maris; but that, as Lady
Halliday remarked to the Duchess Tremontaine, meant precisely

what it was supposed to mean. Horn was doubtless trying to coast on the notoriety that the event had given his otherwise unremarkable party for as long as possible. Both ladies had been there, along with most of the city's great aristocracy, many of whom Karleigh was known to have quarrelled with at one time or another.

'At least', said the Duchess, tilting her elegant head, 'it seems to have rid us of my lord of Karleigh for the rest of the winter. I cannot commend his mysterious opponent too heartily for that service. Odious man. Do you know, Mary, how he insulted me last year? Well, it's just as well you don't; but I assure you I shall never forget it.'

Mary, Lady Halliday, smiled at her companion. The two women were seated in the sunny morning room of the Halliday townhouse, drinking tiny cups of bitter chocolate. Both were clothed in billowing yards of soft, exquisite lace, giving them the look of two goddesses rising from the foam. Their heads, one brown and one silver-fair, were perfectly coiffed, their eyebrows finely plucked. The tips of their fingers, round and smooth, peeped continually through the lace like little pink shells.

'So,' the duchess concluded, 'it's no wonder someone finally got vexed enough to set St Vier on him.'

'Not *on him*, precisely,' Mary Halliday amended. 'The duke was, after all, warned in time to find himself another swordsman to take the challenge.'

'Pity,' the duchess growled.

Lady Halliday poured out more chocolate, musing, 'I wonder what it was all about. If it had been anything clever or amusing, the quarrel would not be kept such a secret – like poor Lynch's last duel, when Lord Godwin's eldest hired him to fight Monteith's champion over whose mistress was prettier. That was nice; but then, it wasn't to the death.'

'Duels are to the death only when one of two things is at stake: power or money.'

'What about honour?'

'What do you think honour buys?' the duchess asked cynically.

Lady Halliday was a quiet, shy young woman with none of her friend's fashionable talent for clever chatter. Her voice was generally low, her speech soft – just what men always claimed to want in a woman, but were never actually drawn to in the drawing room. However, her marriage to the widowed Basil, Lord Halliday, a popular city aristocrat, was said to have been a love match, so society was prepared to credit her with hidden depths. She was, in fact, by no means stupid, and if she answered the duchess with ponderous slowness it was only that she was, as was her habit, weighing her words against the thoughts behind them. 'I think that *honour* is used to mean so many different things that no one can be sure of what it really is. Certainly young Monteith claimed his honour to be satisfied when Lynch won the fight, while privately Basil told me he thought the whole thing a pointless exercise in scandal.'

'That is because young Monteith is an idiot, and your husband is a sensible man,' the duchess said firmly. 'I imagine Lord Halliday is much more pleased with this fight of Karleigh's; at least it accomplished something practical.'

'More than that,' said Lady Halliday. Her voice had dropped, and she leaned out a little over the furbelows of lace toward her friend. 'He is immensely pleased that Karleigh has left town. You know the Council of Lords elects its head again this spring. Basil wishes to be re-elected.'

'And quite rightly,' Diane said stoutly. 'He is the best Crescent Chancellor the city has had in decades – the best, some say, since the fall of the monarchy, which is generous praise indeed. Surely he expects no difficulty in being re-elected?'

'You are kind. Of course the city loves him ... but ... ' She leaned even closer, her porcelain cup held out of harm's way. 'I must tell you. In fact there is a great deal of difficulty. My lord – Basil – has held the Crescent for three consecutive terms now. But it seems there's a law that no one may hold it for four straight terms.'

'Is there?' said the duchess vaguely. 'What a shame. Well, I'm sure that won't matter to anyone.'

'My lord is hoping to put it to the vote in spring. The entire Council may choose to override the law in the case. But the Duke of Karleigh has been quietly approaching people all winter, reminding them of it, spreading all sorts of nonsense on the danger of too much power in the hands of one nobleman. As though my lord would take that power – as though he *could*,

when he expends all his strength just keeping the state together!'
Lady Halliday's cup rattled on its saucer; she steadied it and said,
'You may see why my lord is pleased that Karleigh's gone, if only
for a month or two.'

'Yes,' the duchess said softly; 'I thought he might be.'

'But Diane – ' Suddenly Lady Halliday seized her hand in an
eloquent hissing of lace. 'It may not be enough. I am so
concerned. He *must* keep the Crescent, he is just beginning to
accomplish what he set out to do; to lose it now, even for a term,
would be a terrible set-back for him and for the city. You hold
Tremontaine in your own right, you could vote in Council if you
chose. . . .'

'Now, Mary . . .' Smiling, the duchess disengaged her hand.
'You know I never meddle in politics. The late duke would not
have wished it.'

Whatever further entreaty Lady Halliday might have made
was forestalled by the announcement of two more guests, the
Godwins, who were shown up with the greatest dispatch.

It was unusual for Lady Godwin to be in town in winter; she
was fond of the country and, being past that time of life when
social duties required her presence in the city, spent most of her
time with her husband overseeing the Godwins' great house and
estates at Amberleigh. The responsibility of representing the
family's interests in the city and on the Council of Lords fell to
Lord Godwin's heir, his only son Michael. Lord Michael's name
was surrounded with the pleasing aura of scandal appropriate to a
young noble who did not need to be too careful of what was said
about him. He was an exceptionally attractive young man, and
knew it. His liaisons were many, but always in good taste; they
might be said to be his distinguishing social excess, as he
eschewed those of gambling, quarrelling and dress.

Now he escorted his mother into the room, every inch the
well-groomed, dutiful son. He had attended parties given by the
duchess and by the Hallidays, but was not well enough
acquainted himself with either lady to have visited her privately.

His mother was greeting her friends with kisses, all three
women using each other's first names. He followed her with a
proper bow and kiss of the hand, murmuring their titles. Diane
of Tremontaine said over his bent head, 'How charming to find a

11

young man willing to call upon ladies at a decent hour and in conventional fashion.'

'Barely decent,' Mary Halliday amended, 'with us still in our morning clothes.'

'They are so lovely, you ought never change them,' Lydia Godwin was saying to her; and to Diane, 'Of course: he was very well brought up – and the city hasn't altered his breeding, whatever his father might say. I can trust you, can't I, Michael?'

'Of course, madam.' Automatically he answered the tone of her voice. He had heard nothing since the duchess's comment, acid and piquant. He was surprised that a woman of her stature knew enough about his adventures to be able to make such a pointed remark, and was impressed with her audacity in making it in front of the others. The women were talking now, of the season, of his father's grain estates, as he swept his long-lashed gaze over her. She was beautiful, delicate and fair, with the true aristocrat's fragility that all fashionable city ladies strove to affect. He knew she must be closer to his mother's age than to his own. His mother had allowed herself to run to plumpness. It made her look comfortable; this lady looked entrancing. Suddenly Diane was meeting his look. She held it for a moment, unperturbed, before turning back to his mother and saying, 'And now, no doubt, you are disgusted with yourself for having missed Horn's winter ball! I nearly had a headache myself at the last minute, but I'd already had the dress made, and where else is one going to wear white at this time of year? Poor Horn! I've heard that someone is saying that it was he himself who hired *both* swordsmen, just to entertain his guests!'

'Not a very kind "someone",' put in Lord Michael, 'considering how his house swordsman teamed up with Master Lynch against St Vier – '

'Who still contrived to win!' his mother interrupted. 'I do wish I'd seen it. I hear it's harder and harder to hire St Vier to fight for anyone.' She sighed. 'Swordsmen are getting so above themselves these days, from what I hear. When I first came to the city, I remember, there was a man named Stirling – one of the richest men on Teviot Street, with a big house and gardens – *he* was a swordsman, one of the greats, and he was paid accordingly. But no one had to *ask* him who he felt like fighting

12

that particular day; you just sent him the money and he did the job.'

'Mother,' Michael teased her. 'I never knew you had such a passion for swordplay! Shall I hire you St Vier for your birthday?'

'Now, who will he fight at Amberleigh? Don't be silly, my darling,' she said fondly, patting his hand.

'Besides,' Lady Halliday said, 'chances are good that he doesn't *do* birthdays.' Her friends looked startled at this pronouncement, coming from her. 'Well, you've heard the story haven't you? About Lord Montague and his daughter's wedding?' To her dismay they said they hadn't, and she was obliged to begin: 'She was his only daughter, you see, so he didn't mind the expense, he wanted to hire the best swordsman there was to take the part of the guard at the altar . . . It was only last summer, you *must* have . . . Oh, well – St Vier had fought for Montague before, so he had the man up to his house – well, in his study, I imagine – to ask him properly, so no one would think there was anything shady going on – you know all you need before a wedding's people getting jumpy over swords – so Montague offered him the job, purely ceremonial, he wouldn't even have to *do* anything. And St Vier looked at him, pleasantly enough, Montague told us, and said, "Thank you, but I don't do weddings anymore."'

Lady Godwin shook her head. 'Imagine. Stirling did weddings; he did Julia Hetley's, I remember it. I wanted him to do mine, but he was dead then. I forget who we got instead.'

'My lady,' said Michael, with that impish grin she had always found irresistible, 'shall I take up the sword to please you? I could add to the family fortunes.'

'As though they needed adding to,' the duchess said drily. 'I suppose you could save yourself the expense of hiring a swordsman to fight your inevitable romantic quarrels, my lord. But aren't you a little old to be able to take it up successfully?'

'*Diane!*' his mother gurgled. This once he was grateful for her quick intercession. He was fighting back a blush, one of the drawbacks of his fair complexion. The lady was too personal, she presumed upon acquaintance with his mother to mock him . . . He was not used to women who did not care to please him. 'Michael, you are a perfect goose even to think of such a

13

thing, and, Diane, you must not encourage him to quarrel, I'm sure his friends are bad enough. Oh, yes, no doubt Lord Godwin would be delighted to hear of his heir taking up the sword like any common street brawler. We saw to it that you had all the training you needed when you were a boy. You carry a petty-sword nicely, you can dance without catching your legs in it, and that should be enough for any gentleman.'

'There's Lord Arlen,' Lady Halliday said. 'You can't say *he's* not a gentleman.'

'Arlen is an eccentric,' Lady Godwin said firmly, 'and notably old-fashioned. I'm sure no young man of Michael's set would even consider such a thing.'

'Surely not, Lydia,' the exquisite duchess was saying consolingly. 'And Lord Michael a man of such style, too.' To his surprise she smiled at him, warmly and directly. 'There are men I know who would go to any lengths to annoy their parents. How fortunate you are, Lydia, in having a son you may trust always to do you credit. I am sure he could never be any more serious about taking up the sword than something equally ridiculous ... University, for instance.'

The talk turned to notorious sons, effectively shutting Michael out from contributing to it. Another time he might have listened avidly and with some amusement as they discussed various of his friends and acquaintances, so that he could store up anecdotes to repeat at card parties. But although no trace of it showed in his pleasant bearing and handsome face, Lord Michael was feeling increasingly sullen, and wondering how he might possibly leave without offending his mother, whom he had promised to accompany on all her calls that day. The company of women, making no effort to include him, made him feel, not so much as if he were a child again – for he had been a very fetching child, and adults had always stopped to notice him – but as though he had wandered into a cluster of foreigners, all chattering with animation in another language; or as though he were a ghost in the room, or a piece of useless and uninteresting furniture. Even the alluring duchess, though clearly not unaware of his interest, failed to be entirely concerned with him. At present, for example, she seemed to be much more taken with a series of stories his mother was telling about one of his lunatic cousins.

14

Perhaps he might see her again soon, in better circumstances – only to renew the acquaintance, of course; his current lover's possessiveness he found exciting, and was not yet ready to give up.

Finally, they returned to the more interesting question of whether Lord Horn had had anything to do with the fighting in his gardens. Michael was able to say sagely, 'Well, I hope the suggestion will not get back to Horn's ears. He's liable to become offended and hire himself another swordsman to take care of the rumour-mongers.'

The duchess's fine eyebrows rose in twin arcs. 'Oh? Are you intimately acquainted with the gentleman and his habits?'

'No, madam,' he answered, covering his discomfort at her challenge with a show of surprise. 'But I know him to *be* a gentleman; I do not think he would readily brook the suggestion that he had intentionally set two swordsmen against one, whether in private quarrel or to please his guests.'

'Well, you're probably right there,' she conceded; 'whether he actually did so or not. Horn has been so careful of his reputation these last few years – he'd probably deny stealing honey if his fingers were caught in the jar. He was much more agreeable when he still had something to occupy his time.'

'Surely he is as busy now as any nobleman?' Lady Halliday asked, sure she was missing some vital connection. Lydia Godwin said nothing, but scowled at her knuckles.

'Of course,' Diane said generously, 'you were not yet come to the city then, Mary. Dear, how gossip will trip us up! You will not know that some years past Lord Horn was the reigning beauty. He managed to capture the eyes of Lord Galing, God rest him, who was at the time gaining power in the Council, but didn't quite know what to do with it all. Horn told him. They were a strong combination for a while, Horn with his ambition, and Galing with his talent. I feared – along with my husband, of course – that Galing would be made Chancellor. But Galing died, not a moment too soon, and Horn's influence has faded. I'm sure it galls him. It's probably why he insists on giving such showy parties. His star has definitely fallen: he lacks the coin for further extravagant purchases. Not, of course, that Lord Halliday would wish for any distracting influence!'

15

Mary Halliday smiled prettily, her colour reflecting the rose ribbons on her cap. Lady Godwin looked up and said a trifle brusquely, 'Why is it, Diane, that you seem to know the single most unpleasant story about everyone in the city?'

'I suppose,' she answered blithely, 'because there are so many unpleasant people. How right you are to stay at Amberleigh, my dear.'

In despair Michael thought: If they start on about the family again, I shall fall off my chair. He said, 'I've been thinking, actually, about Karleigh.' The duchess favoured him with her attention. Her eyes were the frosty silver of winter clouds. He felt a delicate shiver as they brushed over him.

'You are quite sure, then,' she said, in a low, melodious voice, 'that it was the duke who hired Lynch?' It was as though she had said something quite different, for his ears alone. His lips were lightly parted; and at last he saw, looking at her, his own beauty reflected there. But before he could answer, his mother cried, 'Of course it was Karleigh! Why else would he leave town first thing this morning, making no excuses to anyone – unless he left a note for Horn apologising for the use his garden was put to . . .'

'Not his style,' observed the duchess.

'Then it is clear', Lady Godwin said triumphantly, 'that he *had* to get out of the city. His man lost the fight! And St Vier may still be in the pay of his opponent. If Karleigh stayed, he might have to keep hiring other swordsmen to go up against St Vier, until he ran out of money, or talent. And then he'd be up against St Vier himself – and then, you know, he'd surely be dead. The duke doesn't know any more of swordplay than Michael, I'm sure.'

'But I am sure', the duchess said, again with that strange double-edged tone, 'that Lord Michael would know what to do with it if he did.'

Something fluttered at the base of his spine. Resolutely he took control of the conversation. He turned directly to the duchess, speaking assertively, summoning all the confidence of a man used to having his opinions heeded. 'As a matter of fact, madam, I am *not* sure that the Duke of Karleigh hired Lynch. I was wondering whether it were not just as likely that he had hired St Vier instead.'

16

'Oh, Michael,' said his mother impatiently. 'Then why would Karleigh have left town when his man *won*?'

'Because he was still afraid of the person who did hire Lynch.'

'Interesting,' said the duchess. Her silvery eyes seemed to grow bigger, like a cat's. 'And not altogether impossible. Your son, Lydia, would seem to have a far more complex grasp of the situation than any of us.'

Her eyes had turned from him, and the mocking disdain was back in her voice. But he had had her for a moment – had her interest, had her seeing him entirely. He wondered what he had done to lose her.

The door to the morning room opened, and a tall, broad-framed man came in unannounced. A sense of exertion and the outdoors hung about him: his dark hair was ruffled all over his head, and his handsome face was high-coloured by the wind. Unlike Michael, with his tight-fitting, pastel costume, this man wore loose, dark clothes, with mud-splashed boots up to his thighs.

Mary Halliday's face transformed with brightness when she saw him. Being a good hostess and a well-mannered woman, she stayed seated amongst her guests; but her bright eyes never left her husband.

Basil, Lord Halliday, Crescent Chancellor of the Council of Lords, bowed to his wife's company, a smile creasing his weathered face.

She spoke to him formally. 'My lord! We did not expect you back so soon as this.'

His smile deepened with mischief and affection. 'I know,' he answered, coming to kiss both her hands. 'I came home directly, before even going to report to Ferris. I should have remembered that you'd have company.'

'Company is delighted to see you,' said the Duchess Tremontaine, 'although I'm sure Lady Halliday is more so. She wouldn't admit it, but I believe the thought of you riding out to Helmsleigh alone to face a cordon of rebellious weavers unsettled her equilibrium.'

Halliday laughed. 'I was hardly alone. I took a troop of City Guard with me to impress them.'

His wife caught his eyes, asking seriously, 'How did it go?'

'Well enough,' he answered her. 'They have some legitimate complaints. Foreign wool has been driving prices down, and the new tax is hard on the smaller communes. I'll have to take it up with my lord Ferris. I'll tell you all about it, but not till afterward, or the Dragon Chancellor will be annoyed for not having been the first to hear.'

Lady Halliday frowned. 'I still think Ferris should have gone instead. The Exchequer is his concern.'

He sent her a brief glance of warning before saying lightly, 'Not at all! What is a mere Dragon Chancellor when compared with the head of the entire Council of Lords? This way they were flattered, and felt that enough attention was being paid to them. Now, when I send Chris Nevilleson out to take a full report, they'll be nice to him. I think the matter should be settled soon.'

'Well, I should think so!' said Lady Godwin. 'Imagine some pack of weavers raising their shuttles against a Council order.'

Michael laughed, thinking of his friend riding out to Helmsleigh on one of his fine horses. 'Poor Chris! Why do you assign him all the most unpleasant tasks, my lord?'

'He volunteers. I believe he wishes to be of service.'

'He adores you, Basil,' Lady Halliday said brightly. Michael Godwin raised his eyebrows, and the colour rushed into her face. 'Oh, no! I mean . . . he admires Lord Halliday . . . his work . . .'

'Anyone would,' said the duchess comfortably. 'I adore him myself. And if I wished to advance to any political power, I should most certainly station myself at his side.' Her friend smiled gratefully at her over the rim of the chocolate cup behind which she had taken refuge. And Michael felt, in consternation, that he had just been measured and found wanting. 'In fact,' the duchess continued blithely, 'I have been grieving over how seldom I see him – or any of you – when not surrounded by other admirers. Let us all dine together privately a few weeks from today. You have heard of Steele's fireworks? He's sending them off over the river to celebrate his birthday. It promises to be quite a show. Of course I told him it was the wrong time of year, but he said he couldn't change his birthday to suit the weather, and he has always been uncommonly fond of fireworks. They will entertain the populace, and give the rest of us something to do. So we're all to dust off our summer barges and go out on the river

18

and enjoy ourselves. Mine will certainly hold us all, and I believe my cook can put together a tolerable picnic; if we all dress up warmly it won't be so bad.' She turned her charming smile on Basil Halliday. 'I shall invite Lord Ferris, my lord, only if you two promise not to spend the whole evening talking politics. . . . and Chris Nevilleson and his sister, I think. Perhaps I had better include a few other young men, to ensure that Lord Michael has someone to talk to.'

Michael's flush of embarrassment lasted through the chatter of thanks. He was able to cover it by straightening his hose. A fall of lace cuff brushed his cheek as the duchess stood by his mother saying, 'Oh, Lydia, what a shame, to have to leave town so soon! I hope Lord Michael will be able to represent you at my picnic?' He stopped before he could begin to stammer something out, and simply rose and offered her his seat by his mother. She sank into it with a willow's grace, and looked up at him, smiling. 'You will come, will you not, my lord?'

Michael squared his shoulders, sharply aware of the close fit of his jacket, the hang of his sleeves. Her offered hand lay on his like a featherweight, soft, white and elusively perfumed. He was careful only to brush it with his lips. 'Your servant, madam,' he murmured, looking straight up into her eyes.

'Such manners.' The duchess returned the look. 'What a delightful young man. I shall expect you, then.'

Chapter III

Richard St Vier, the swordsman, awoke later that day, in the middle of the afternoon. The house was quiet and the room was cold. He got up and dressed quickly, not bothering to light the bedroom fire.

He stepped softly into the other room, knowing which floorboards were likely to creak. He saw the top of Alec's head, nestled into a burlap-covered chaise longue he was fond of because it had griffins' heads carved into the armrests. Alec had built up the fire and drawn the chair up close to it. Richard thought Alec might be asleep; but then he saw Alec's shoulder shift and heard the crackle of paper as he turned the pages of a book.

Richard limbered up against the wall for awhile, then took up a blunt-tipped practice sword and began to attack the chipped plaster wall with it, striking up and down an imaginary line with steady, rhythmic precision. There was a counterattack from the other side of the wall: three blows from a heavy fist caused their remaining flakes of paint to tremble.

'*Will you shut that racket up*?' a voice demanded through the wall.

Richard put his sword down in disgust. 'Hell,' he said, 'they're home.'

'Why don't you kill them?' the man in the chair asked lazily.

'What for? Marie'd only replace them with some more. She needs the rent money. At least this bunch doesn't have babies.'

'True.' One long leg and then another swung out from the chaise to plant themselves on the floor. 'It's mid-afternoon. The snow has stopped. Let's go out.'

Richard looked at him. 'Anywhere special?'

'The Old Market', said Alec, 'might be entertaining. If you're still in the mood, after those other two.'

Richard got a heavier sword, and buckled it on. Alec's ideas of 'entertaining' were violent. His blood began to race, not unpleasantly. People had learned not to bother him; now they must learn the same about Alec. He followed him into the winter air, which was cold and sharp like a hunting morning.

The streets of Riverside were mostly deserted at this time of day, and a thick snowcover muffled what sounds there were. The oldest houses were built so close together that their eaves almost touched across the street, eaves elaborately carved, throwing shadows onto the last flakes of painted coats of arms on the walls below them. No modern carriage could pass between the houses of Riverside; its people walked, and hid in the twisting byways, and the Watch never followed them there. The nobles drove their well-sprung carriages along the broad, sunlit avenues of the upper city, leaving their ancestors' houses to whomever chose to occupy them. Most would be surprised to know how many still held deeds to Riverside houses; and few would be eager to collect the rent.

Alec sniffed the air. 'Bread. Someone's baking bread.'

'Are you hungry?'

'I'm always hungry.' The young man pulled his scholar's robe tighter around him. Alec was tall, and a little too thin, with none of the swordsman's well-sprung grace. With the layers of clothes he had piled on underneath the robe, he looked like a badly wrapped package. 'Hungry and cold. It's what I came to Riverside for. I got tired of the luxurious splendour of University life. The magnificent meals, the roaring fires in the comfy lecture halls. . . .' A gust of wind whipped powdered snow off a roof and into their faces. Alec cursed with a student's elaborate fluency. 'What a stupid place to live! No wonder anyone with any sense left here long ago. The streets are a perfect wind-tunnel between the two rivers. It's like asking to be put in cold-storage. . . . I hope they're paying you soon for that idiotic duel, because we're almost out of wood and my fingers are turning blue as it is.'

'They're paying me,' Richard answered comfortably. 'I can pick up the money tomorrow, and buy wood on the way home.' Alec had been complaining of the cold since the first ground-frost. He kept their rooms hotter than Richard ever had, and still shivered and wrapped himself in blankets all day. Whatever part of the country he came from, it was probably not the northern

21

mountains, and not the house of a poor man. All evidence so far of Alec's past was circumstantial: things like the fire, and the accent, and his inability to fight, all spoke nobility. But at the same time he had no money, no known people or title, and the University gown hung on his slumped shoulders as though it belonged there. The University was for poor scholars, or clever men hoping to better themselves and acquire posts as secretaries or tutors to the nobility.

Richard said, 'Anyway, I thought you won lots of money off Rodge the other night, dicing.'

'I did.' Alec loosed one edge of his cloak to make sweeping gestures with his right hand. 'He won it back from me next night. In fact I owe him money; it's why we're not going to Rosalie's.'

'It's all right; he knows I'm good for it.'

'He cheats,' Alec said. 'They all cheat. I don't know how you can cheat with straight dice, but as soon as I find out I'm going to get rich off Rodge and all his smelly little friends.'

'Don't,' said Richard. 'That's for these types, not for you. You don't have to cheat, you're a gentleman.'

As soon as it was out he knew it had been the wrong thing to say. He could feel Alec's tension, almost taste the blue coldness of the air between them. But Alec only said, 'A gentleman, Richard? What nonsense. I'm just a poor student who was stupid enough to spend time with my books when I could have been out drinking and learning how to load dice.'

'Well,' St Vier said equably, 'you're certainly making up for it now.'

'Aren't I just.' Alec smiled with grim pleasure.

The Old Market wasn't old, nor was it properly a market. A square of once-elegant houses had been gutted at the ground floor, so that each house opened at the front. The effect was like a series of little boxed stage sets, each containing a fire and a group of Riversiders crowded around it, their hands stuffed under their armpits or held out to the fire, engaged in what could only loosely be termed marketing: a little dicing, a little flirting, drinking, and trying to sell each other stolen objects, shifting from foot to foot in the cold.

In front of one of them Alec suddenly stopped. 'Here,' he said. 'Let's go in here.'

There was nothing to distinguish this one from any of the others. Richard followed him to the fire. Alec's movements were languid, with a studied grace that the swordsman's eye recognised as the burden of feverish tension held in check. Other people noticed it too, though what they made of it was hard to say. Riverside was used to odd-looking people with odd moods. The woman nearest Alec moved nervously away, yielding her proximity to the fire. Across it a short man with a rag twisted around his sandy hair looked up from casting dice.

'Well, look who's here,' he said in a soft whine. 'Master Scholar.' A long gleam of metal slid from his side to his hand. 'I thought I told you last night I didn't want to see your face again.'

'Stupid face,' Alec corrected with airy condescension. 'You said you didn't want to see my *stupid* face *around* here again.' Someone giggled nervously. People had edged away from the dicer with the drawn sword. Without turning his head the man reached his free hand behind him and caught a small, pretty woman's wrist. He reeled her in to his side like a fish on a line, and held her there, fondling one breast. His eyes above her head dared anyone to react.

'That's good,' Alec said with lofty sarcasm. 'I used to know a man who could name any card you pulled from the deck without looking.'

'That's good.' The man mimicked his accent. 'Is that what they teach you at University, scholar, card tricks?'

The muscles tautened around Alec's mouth. 'They don't teach anyone anything at University. I had to learn to recognise people with duckshit for brains all by myself. But I think I'm pretty good at it, don't you?'

The girl squeaked when her captor's arm crushed her bosom. 'You're going to be gone', he growled at Alec, 'by the time I count three.' Spit flecked the corner of his mouth.

Behind them the voices were murmuring, 'Six says he's gone by two . . . by three . . . Six says he stays. . . .'

Alec stood where he was, his head cocked back, considering the other down the length of his nose. 'One,' the man counted. 'Two.'

'*Move*, you stupid clown!' someone cried. 'Brent'll kill you!'

'But I have to stay and help him,' Alec said with polite

23

surprise. 'You can see he's stuck for the next one. It's "three," ' he told him kindly. 'The one after "two".'

Brent flung the girl aside. 'Draw,' he growled, 'if you've got a sword.'

The thin man in the scholar's robe raised his eyebrows. 'What if I haven't?'

'Well.' Brent came slowly around the fire with a swordsman's sure step. 'That would be a shame.'

He was halfway to the scholar when a bystander spoke up. 'My fight,' he said clearly, so everyone heard.

Brent looked him over. Another swordsman. Harder to kill, but better for his reputation. 'Fine,' he purred in his insinuating whine. 'I'll take care of you first, and then finish off Mister Scholar, here.'

Richard slung his cloak around one arm. A woman near him looked at his face and gasped, 'St Vier!' Now the word was out; people were jostling to see; bets were changing. Even as they pressed back to the walls to give the fighters room, the spectators were agitating; a few slipped out to fetch friends to watch the fight. Newcomers crowded across the open house-front.

Richard ignored them all. He was aware of Alec, safe to one side, his eyes wide and bright, his posture negligent.

'There's your third for today,' Alec said pleasantly. 'Kill him.'

Richard began as he usually did, running his opponent through some simple attacks, parrying the counterattack almost absently. It did give the other the chance to assess him as well, but usually that only served to unnerve them. Brent was quick, with a good swordsman's sixth sense for what was coming next; but his defence was seriously weaker on the left, poor fool. Enough practice on some good drills could have got him over that. Richard pretended he hadn't noticed, and played to his right. Aware that he was being tested, Brent tried to turn the fight so that he led the attack. Richard didn't let him. It flustered Brent; trying harder to gain control, he began to rush his counters, as though by coming in fast enough he could surprise St Vier into defence.

The swords were clashing rapidly now. It was the kind of fight spectators liked best: lots of relentless follow-through, without too much deliberation before each new series of moves. The

24

woman Brent had been holding watched, cursing slowly and methodically under her breath, her fingers knotted together. Others were louder, calling encouragement, bets and enlightened commentary, filling each other in on the background of the fight.

Through his shield of concentration Richard heard the voices, though not the words they spoke. As the fight went on and he absorbed Brent's habits, he began to see not a personality but a set of obstructions to be removed. His fighting became less playful, more singleminded. It was the one thing knowledgeable spectators faulted him for: once he knew a man he seldom played him out in a show of technique, preferring to finish him off straightway.

Twice Richard passed up the chance to touch Brent's left arm. He wasn't interested in flesh wounds now. Other swordsmen might have made the cut for the advantage it would have given them; but the hallmark of St Vier's reputation was his ability to kill with one clean death wound. Brent knew he was fighting for his life. Even the onlookers were silent now, listening to the panting men's breath, the scrape of their boots and the clang of their swords. Over the heavy silence, Alec's voice drawled clearly, 'Didn't take long to scare *him*, did it? Told you I could spot them.'

Brent froze. Richard beat hard on his blade, to remind him of where he was. Brent's parry was fierce; he nearly touched St Vier's thigh countering, and Richard had to step back. His heel struck rock. He found he was backed against one of the stones surrounding the fire. He hadn't meant to lose that much ground; Alec had distracted him as well. He was already so hot he didn't feel the flames; but he was determined to preserve his boots. He dug in his back heel, and exchanged swordplay with Brent with his arm alone. He applied force, and nearly twisted the sword out of the other man's grasp. Brent paused, preparing another attack, watching him carefully for his. Richard came in blatantly low on the left, and when Brent moved to his defence St Vier came up over his arm and pierced his throat.

There was a flash of blue as the sword was pulled from the wound. Brent had stiffened bolt upright; now he toppled forward, his severed windpipe wheezing with gushing blood and air. Alec's face was pale, without expression. He looked down at the dying man long and hard, as though burning the sight into his eyes.

Amid the excitement of the fight's consummation, Richard stepped outside to clean his sword, whirling it swiftly in the air so that the blood flew off its surface and onto the snow.

One man came up to Alec. 'That was some fight,' he said friendlily. 'You rig it?'

'Yes.'

He indicated the swordsman outside. 'You going to tell me that young fellow's really St Vier?'

'Yes.'

Alec seemed numbed by the fight, the fever that had driven him sated by the death of his opponent, drugged now to a sluggish peace. But when St Vier came back in he spoke in his usual sardonic tones: 'Congratulations. I'll pay you when I'm rich.'

There was still one more thing to be done, and Richard did it. 'Never mind,' he said clearly, for those nearby to hear. 'They should know to leave you alone.'

He crossed to Alec by the fire, but a tiny woman, the one Brent had held, planted herself in front of him. Her eyes were red, her face pale and blotchy. She stared up at the swordsman and began to stutter furiously.

'What is it?' he asked.

'You owe me!' she exploded at last. 'Thhh-that man's ddd-dead and where'll I find another?'

'The same place you found him, I expect.'

'What'll I do for mm-money?'

Richard looked her up and down, from her painted eyes to gaudy stockings, and shrugged. She turned her shoulder in toward his chest and blinked up at him. 'I'm nice,' she squeaked. 'I'd work for you.'

Alec sneered at the little woman. 'I'd trip over you. We'd keep stepping on you in the dark.'

'Go away,' said Richard. 'I'm not a pimp.'

She stamped her small foot. 'You bastard! Riverside or no, I'll have the Watch on you!'

'You'd never go near the Watch,' said Richard, bored. 'They'd have you in the Chop before you could open your mouth.' He turned back to his friend. 'God, I'm thirsty. Let's go.'

They got as far as the doorway this time before Richard was stopped by another woman. She was a brilliant redhead of alarming prettiness, her paint expertly applied. Her cloak was of burgundy velvet, artfully draped to hide the worn spot. She placed her fingertips on Richard's arm, standing closer to him than he generally allowed. 'That was superb,' she said with throaty intimacy. 'I was so glad I caught the ending.'

'Thank you', he replied courteously. 'I appreciate it.'

'Very good,' she pronounced. 'You gave him a fair chance, didn't keep him on the hook too long.'

'I've learned some good tricks by letting them show me what they can do first.'

She smiled warmly at him. 'You're no fool. You've got better every year. There's no stopping you from getting what you want. I could – '

'Excuse me,' Alec interrupted from the depths of boundless ennui, 'but who is this?'

The woman turned and swept him with her long lashes. 'I'm Ginnie Vandall,' she said huskily. 'And you?'

'My name is Alec.' He stared down at the tassels on her hem. 'Who pimps for you?'

The carmined lips pressed into a thin line, and the moment for a biting retort came and went. Knowing it was gone, she turned again to Richard, saying solicitously, 'My dear, you must be famished.'

He shrugged polite disavowal. 'Ginnie,' he asked her, 'is Hugo working now?'

She made a practised moue and looked into his eyes. 'Hugo is always working. He's gone so much I begin to wonder why I stay with him. They adore him on the Hill – too much, I sometimes think.'

'Nobody adores Richard,' Alec drawled. 'They're always trying to get him killed.'

'Hugo's a swordsman,' Richard told him. 'He's very good. Ginnie, when you see him tell him he was perfectly right about Lynch's right cut. It was very helpful last night.'

'I wish I could have seen it.'

'So do I. Most of them didn't know what was happening till it was over. Alec, don't you want to eat? Let's go.' Briskly he steered a way back onto the street, through the blood-flecked snow. Sam Bonner rolled boozily up and past them, forgetting his objective at the sight of the velvet-clad woman standing abandoned in the doorway.

'Ginnie, lass! How's the prettiest ass in Riverside?'

'Cold,' Ginnie Vandall snapped, 'you stupid sot.'

Chapter IV

Lord Michael Godwin had never imagined that he would actually be escaping down a drainpipe, but here it was, the stuff of cheap comedy, clutched in his freezing hands. In fact, all of him was freezing: clever, quick-thinking Olivia, with not a moment to spare had flung all evidence of his presence – which was to say, his clothes – out of the window, and instructed him to follow. He was wearing only his long white shirt, and, ridiculously, his velvet hat, jewelled and feathered, which he had somehow contrived to snatch off the bedpost at the first knock on the chamber door.

He made a point of not looking down. Above him, the stars shone frosty and remote in the clear sky. They wouldn't dare to twinkle at him, not in the position he was in. His hands were freezing on the lead pipe of the Rossillion townhouse. He'd remembered it as being covered with ivy; but the latest fashion called for severity and purity of line, so the ivy had been stripped last autumn. Just above his hands Olivia's window glowed temptingly golden. Michael sent out a desolate haze of frosty breath, and began letting himself down.

He ought to be grateful for the escape, he knew that, grumbling as he collected his clothes from the frozen ground, resisting the desire to hop from foot to foot. He shoved his feet into his boots, crumpling the doe-soft leather, even as he still hunted for his stockings. His shaking hands made it unusually hard to fasten the various catches and laces of a nobleman's evening dress – I should always remember to bring a bodyservant along on these expeditions, he thought whimsically; have him waiting right below the appropriate window with a flask of hot wine and gloves!

Olivia's window was still alight, so Bertram was still here, and doubtless would remain for hours yet. Blessed Olivia! Lord

Michael finally managed to squeeze out the benison between chattering teeth. Bertram might have tried to kill him if he'd found him there. Bertram was the jealous type, and Michael had been leading him a dance all evening. He had a moment of panic when he discovered that one of his monogrammed embroidered gloves was missing; he imagined the scene the next day, when Bertram found it perched jauntily among the ailanthus branches under the window: *Hello, my angel, what's this doing here? Oh, heavens, I must have dropped it when I was checking the wind direction....* Then he discovered it, stuffed up one of his voluminous sleeves, lord knew how it had got there.

As dressed as he was going to be, Michael prepared to disappear. Despite all the wool and brocade he was still shivering; he'd managed to work up quite a sweat upstairs, and the sudden plunge into a winter night had turned it to ice on his skin. He damned Bertram roundly, hoping his turn in hell would be one long slide down a perpetual glacier. A sudden shadow fell over Michael as Olivia's curtains were drawn. Now only one slim arrow of light fell across the powdery lawn, where one curtain stood away from the window. Perhaps Bertram had gone – or, perhaps he was still there. Michael smiled ruefully at his own folly, but there it was: one way or the other, he had to go back up the pipe and find out what was happening in Olivia's room.

It was much easier climbing with gloves on, and the soles of his soft boots adhered nicely to the pipe. He was even quite warm by the time he reached the tiny balcony outside the window. He rested there, grinning with exertion, trying to breathe quietly. He heard a hum of voices inside, so Bertram hadn't left yet. Michael edged closer to the window, tilted his velvet cap to one side, and one of the voices became distinct:

' – so I asked myself, why do we dream at all? Or isn't there some way of controlling it? Maybe if we got someone *else* to repeat the same thing over and over, as we were falling asleep....'

The voice, low and passionate with just the hint of a whine, was Bertram's. A lighter voice made answer, but Michael couldn't catch Olivia's words; she must be facing away from the window. Bertram said, 'Don't be ridiculous! Food has nothing to do with it, that's only a scare put about by physicians. Anyway, I know you had a light supper. Did you pass a pleasant evening?' Olivia's reply ended on a rising intonation. 'No,' said Bertram rather savagely. 'No, he wasn't there. Frankly, I'm disgusted; I wasted hours in a cavernous room that felt like an ice cave and smelt like a barn, because I thought he would be. He *told* me he would be.'

Olivia made soothing noises. Michael's chapped lips quirked helplessly into a smile. Poor Bertram! He pressed his dripping nose with the back of his hand. He was probably going to catch a cold from all this, which would not only serve him right, but also provide a convenient excuse for his absence from his usual haunts that night. Prophetically, Bertram was saying, 'Of course he'll have some excuse, he always does. Sometimes I wonder whether he isn't off with someone else.' More soothing noises. 'Well, you *know* his reputation. I don't know why I bother, sometimes. . . .'

Suddenly, Olivia's voice came strikingly clear. 'You bother because he's beautiful, and because he appreciates you as none of the others have.'

'He's clever,' Bertram said gruffly. 'I'm not sure it's the same thing. And you, my dear,' he said gallantly; both of them near the window now, two long dark silhouettes staining the curtains, 'are both beautiful and clever.'

'Appreciative,' Olivia amended. And then, more softly, so that Michael had to guess at all the words, 'and not quite beautiful enough.'

Bertram's voice grew at once less distinct and louder; he must have turned away, but was practically shouting, 'I won't have you blaming yourself for that! We've been over this before, Olivia; it's not your fault and I don't want to hear you talking like that!'

It had all the marks of an old argument. 'Don't tell me that, tell your father!' Her well-bred voice retained its rounded tones, but the pitch was shriller, the tempo faster, carrying through the glass with no difficulty. 'He's been waiting six years for an heir! He'd have made you divorce me by now if it wasn't for the dowry!'

'Olivia – '

'Lucy has five children! Five!! Davenant can keep his bedroom full of boys, nobody cares, because he does his duty by her . . . but you – '

31

'Olivia, stop it!'

'You – where is your heir going to come from? Michael Godwin? Well it's going to have to come from Michael Godwin because we know it isn't going to come from anywhere else!'

Oh, god, thought Michael, hands pressed to his mouth; *And there he is out on the balcony.* . . . He looked longingly at the ground, not at all sure now that he could manipulate the drainpipe again. He was stiff and chilled from crouching there in one position. But he had to get out of there. He didn't want to hear any more of this.

For the third time that night he hooked his legs around the drainpipe of the Rossillion townhouse, and began to work his way down it. The pipe seemed slipperier this time, perhaps smoothed from his earlier passings. He felt himself losing his grip, imagined falling the ten feet into the shrubbery. . . . His upper lip prickled with sweat as he eased his grip to hunt for surer anchor – and one booted foot swung wildly out, and collided with a window shutter in a desperate rattle and a conclusive thump, shattering the stillness of the winter night.

He thought of shouting, 'It's only a rabbit!' His feet hit the ground achingly flat, and he staggered to his knees in the low bushes. A dog was barking frantically inside the house. He wondered if he could make it to the front gate in time to pretend that he had just been passing by and heard the noise . . . but the front gate would already be locked at this hour, his feet remembered, making with all speed for the orchard wall, which Bertram had mentioned needed repairing.

The dog's bark rang crystalline in the cold air. Past the skeletons of pear trees Michael saw a dip in the wall, surmounted by crumbling mortar. It wasn't that high, just about at eye level. He flung himself at it, arms first to pull his body over – and the mortar gave way, crumbling beneath him as he slipped neatly over it like a salmon over a dam.

The wall was considerably higher on the other side; he had just enough time to wonder when he was going to stop falling before he hit the ground, and rolled the rest of the way down the embankment to the street, where he was nearly run over by a carriage.

The carriage stopped, its horses registering protest. From

within a furious voice, male, shouted out fierce expletives and demands to know what was going on. Michael rose to his feet, fishing for a coin to fling at the driver so they could both be on their ways. But the occupant of the carriage, too impatient to wait for an answer, chose that moment to step out and investigate.

Michael bowed low, out of politeness and a hopeless desire to hide his face. It was his mother's old friend, Lord Horn, who had kept New Year's with them in the country almost ten years ago, when he was only 15. Heedless of his driver's sputters of explanation, Horn snapped, 'Who's that?'

Over the increasing noise of the barking dog and the men's voices on the other side of the wall, Michael said as clearly as he could, 'I'm Michael Godwin. I was walking home, and I fell in the street.' He swayed slightly. 'Might I – '

'Get in,' Horn ordered. On shaking legs he hastened to obey. 'I'll take you to my house,' said Horn, slamming shut the door, 'it's closer. John – drive on!'

The inside of Lord Horn's carriage was dark and close. For a while their breaths still steamed white. Michael watched his own with weird detachment as it emerged in rapid little puffs from his mouth, like a child's drawing of smoke coming out of a chimney. As the chill left him, for some reason he started to shake.

'Not the night to pick for walking home,' Horn said. He handed Michael a little flask of brandy from a pocket in the wall. The exercise of opening and drinking from it steadied him a little. The carriage jogged regularly over the cobbled streets; it had good springs, and the horses were good. Michael's eyes grew accustomed to the dark, but still all he could see of the man sitting next to him was a pale profile against the window. He remembered Horn when he'd visited Amberleigh, a handsome blonde with lazy blue eyes and pale hands. And there was his adolescent's envy of a green coat of crushed velvet with gold braid. . . .

'I hope your mother is well,' said Lord Horn. 'I was sorry to miss her on her visit to the city.'

'Very well,' said Michael. 'Thank you.' He had stopped shaking. The carriage turned into a drive, and pulled up before a shallow flight of steps. Horn helped him out of the carriage and

33

into the house. He had no chance to glimpse the notorious winter gardens in the back.

A fire was already lit in the library. Michael sat in a heavy upholstered chair, while his host rang for hot drink. The firelight brightened Michael's russet hair to polished copper. His eyes were large, his skin still pale with shock. Lord Horn sat down and pulled a low table up between them. He sat with his back to the fire. Horn's features were in shadow, but Michael could discern a highbridged nose, wide-set eyes under a broad brow. Hair fair and light as swansdown made an aureole about Horn's head. An ornate clock over the mantel ticked the seconds loudly, as though proud of its place. If you did not immediately notice it for its gilded curves and figurines, you could not miss the noise it made. Michael wondered if it would be appropriate to comment on it.

'You've taken your family's seat in Council, haven't you?' Lord Horn asked.

'Yes.' To avert the next question Michael explained, 'I'm not often there. It's tiresome. I only go when there's some question directly bearing on Amberleigh.'

To his relief, the older man smiled. 'I always felt the same. Bore. All those gentlemen, and not one pack of cards amongst 'em.' Michael grinned. 'You have other things to do with your time, I think.'

The young man stiffened at the insinuation. 'Someone's been telling you tales.'

'Not at all.' Horn spread one jewelled hand on the table between them. 'I have eyes.'

Michael wondered if he should let Horn believe that he'd been reeling-drunk in the street. He'd be a laughingstock if it got round: that sort of behaviour was for green boys. 'I hope', he said with a convincing and heartfelt sniff, 'that I am not getting ill.'

'So do I,' Horn said smoothly; 'but pallor becomes you. I see you have your mother's fine complexion.'

With a jolt, Michael realised what Horn had been trying to do for some time now. Now that he knew it, he became aware of the eyes fixed hotly on him from the shadows. They burned a flush of colour into his own face.

'I understand', said Horn, 'how you might be very busy

indeed. But one always finds time for the right things, don't you find?' Mutely, Michael nodded, aware that the betraying firelight was strong on his features. Fortunately Horn slid his hands to the arms of his chair and rose to stand before the fire, his back to Michael. Now, for the first time since his drop from the drainpipe, he let himself think of Olivia.

He'd always felt sorry for Bertram's wife. She was a beautiful woman. Bertram was fool to ignore her as he did. Michael liked Bertram, with his strange ideas and fierce possessiveness. But he didn't think he'd like to be married to him. When Olivia had approached him with her awkward, naive flirtation, Michael had been flattered, for her reputation was chaste. He'd believed then that she had read his sympathy and attraction to her, and was responding in kind. He'd believed, as he was touching her with his expert hands, kissing her white throat and being so careful not to put her in danger, while she made caution almost impossible with her moans and digging fingers, he'd believed that she wanted him.

She hadn't wanted him. His sympathy and desire, all his tenderness, expertise and charm, were nothing to her, only made her job easier. She hadn't wanted him, she had used him for his sex to get back at her husband and to father an heir.

Horn wanted him: for his youth, his beauty, his ability to please and be pleased. Horn should have him.

He came up behind Lord Horn, sliding his hands onto the man's shoulders. Horn took his hands and seemed to wait. Touched by the formality of their moves, Michael turned him in his arms and kissed his mouth. He tasted spices. The man had been chewing fennel seeds for his breath. The expert tongue flicked eagerly. Michael pressed closer. 'Lydia's eldest,' Horn murmured. 'You *have* grown up.' With nothing between them but the costly fabric of their clothes, Michael felt the man's need, twin to his own. Over the roar of blood he heard the ticking of the clock.

A polite knock broke them apart like a nutshell. A roaring breath of mixed lust and annoyance tore through Horn's flared nostrils. 'Come in!' he called gruffly. The door opened to a liveried servant carrying a tray with steaming mugs; behind him another bore two branched candelabra, fully lit. Horn stepped forward irritably to hasten their office, and the light caught him full in the face like a mailed fist.

For a moment, Michael could only stare. Slackness had invaded the carefully tended skin, blurring the fineness of Lord Horn's features. Little folds hung like someone else's laundry from the sharp lines of his face. What had been uniform ivory skin was turning sallow, except where blood-vessels had broken along his cheeks and the sides of his nose. His blue eyes had faded, and even the lustre of his hair was dimmed like old summer grass.

Michael gasped, and choked on his breath. The handsome man in the green velvet coat was gone, swept back to his youth in his mother's garden. Olivia had thrust him into the arms of this revolting stranger. The mug shook so badly in Michael's hands that hot punch spilled over his knuckles onto the carpet. 'I'm sorry – terribly sorry.'

'Never mind,' Horn growled, still annoyed at the interruption, 'sit down.'

Michael sat, paying close attention to his hands.

'I was with the Duchess Tremontaine,' Horn was saying in a loud voice meant for the servants. It would not do to be caught hurrying them. 'Charming woman. She extends me such courtesy. Of course I was a close friend of the late duke's. A very close friend. I am to dine with her on her barge next week, when Steele sends up his fireworks.'

The liquor, and the effortless inanity of the conversation, were soothing Michael. 'Are you?' he replied, and was shocked at the weakness of his voice. 'So am I.'

The servants finally bowed out. Horn said, 'Perhaps we are destined to become better acquainted, then,' his voice heavy with innuendo.

Michael sneezed violently. It was timely but unintentional. He found himself genuinely relieved to realise that he really did feel horrible. His head ached, and he was going to sneeze again. 'I think', he said, 'that I had better go home.'

'Oh, surely not,' said Horn. 'I can offer you hospitality overnight.'

'No, really,' said Michael, as miserably as he could. 'I can see I'm going to be no fit company for anyone tonight.' He coughed, praying that Horn's persistence would not outlast his courtesy.

'Pity,' said Lord Horn, flicking an invisible bit of thread from his coat into the fire. 'Shall I order you up the carriage, then?'

'Oh, please no, don't bother. I'm just a few streets away.'

'A torchman, then? It wouldn't do to have you falling again.'

'Yes, thank you.'

His wet overclothes were brought steaming from the drying fire. At least the water was warm. He walked home, tipped the torchman, and climbed the stairs to his bedroom with a candle, leaving his clothes in piles on the floor for his servants to find. Michael slipped between cold sheets in a heavy bedgown, a handkerchief balled in his fist, and waited for sleep to overcome him.

Chapter V

The next day came cold and sullen. Layers of grey cloud blanketed the sky. From Riverside the effect was oppressive: the river roiled yellow and grey between the banks, swirling darkly about the struts of the bridge. Above it stretched the city's warehouses and commercial buildings, interrupted only by patches of dirty snow. Richard St Vier got up early and put on his best clothes: he had an appointment in the city to pick up the second half of his payment for the Lynch fight. It was a substantial amount, which only he could be sure of carrying back into Riverside unscathed. He was to meet someone, probably the servant of the agent of the banker of the noble who'd hired him, in a neutral place where the money could be handed over. Both St Vier and his patrons appreciated the formalities of discretion in these matters.

From the Hill the view was quite another matter. The distant rivers glittered, and houses sent up cosy trails of smoke. The sky stretched out forever in rippling layers of silver, pewter and iron, over the domes of the Council Hall, the University walls and ancient Cathedral towers, on across the eastern plain and into the tiny hills.

Michael Godwin awoke at noon, having slept a round twelve hours, feeling remarkably fit. He coughed experimentally, and felt his throat, but the cold that last night had threatened to overwhelm him seemed to have vanished

Just then his manservant came in to rouse him. Michael had forgotten his promise to dine with his friend Tom Berowne that afternoon. There was just enough time to dress and wash. His dry, clean, nicely pressed clothes felt remarkably luxurious after last night's escapades. He put the memory behind him and went whistling out of the door.

Dinner was predictably excellent. His friend's cook was

legendary, and Lord Thomas was full of gossip. Some of it, gratifyingly, was about him. Bertram, Rossillion's son, had lost 30 royals gambling in a popular club last night, and as he left the table had been heard to damn Michael Godwin.

Michael shrugged angelically. 'I wasn't even there. Felt a cold coming on, and stayed in all evening with a hot brick. Oh, much better now, thanks. Poor Bertram!'

He was in no hurry to get home. There might be a note waiting from Bertram, or, worse yet, one from Lord Horn. What a lot of trouble from one night! Of course he would run into Bertram sooner or later. Better make it sooner and turn up at the club tonight after supper. He could tell Bertram pretty stories, and take him home with him. Horn, on the other hand . . . hadn't he mentioned the duchess's barge supper next week? It was too bad, but maybe he'd better miss that one. Horn didn't have the air of a man who knew when to give up. But the image of the duchess intruded itself between Michael and his resolves: her silvery eyes, her cool hand . . . and the voice that mocked and possessed and promised. Perdition take Horn. He couldn't refuse her invitation!

To draw out his walk Michael chose the distracting route home, along Lassiter's Row, where elegant merchandise was displayed before each shop to tempt the wealthy pedestrian. But there was little to distract today. Although the snow had been cleared, merchants were leery of setting much out in the cold, and few people were out walking. His thoughts turned again to the duchess. He'd never heard of her taking any lovers; but she was beautiful, a widow . . . he should have asked Tom whether there were any rumours . . . Michael stopped, half meaning to turn around and return to his friend's, when an odd sight caught his attention.

A man was being ushered out of Felman's Bookshop by old Felman himself with the kind of pomp usually reserved for nobles with enormous libraries. But the man enjoying these favours hardly looked like a book-collector. He was young, athletically restless, anxious to depart. No noble of breeding would show such ill-ease before servile homage, however gross; and no noble would be caught out in a pair of such undistinguished boots, topped by a brown cloak of old-fashioned cut whose edges verged on the shabby.

Michael let the stranger make his escape before he descended on the bookseller.

Felman nodded and smiled, agreeing that, no, it was not the sort of fellow you'd expect to find in his establishment. 'My lord will scarcely credit it to hear who that was. That was the swordsman St Vier, sir, purchasing a volume here.'

'Well!' Michael was properly astonished. 'What did he buy?'

'What *did* he buy . . . ?' Felman ran pink fingers through the remains of his hair. 'I offered him many fine illustrated volumes, sir, such as might be suitable, for I like to think I know how to mate each customer to the appropriate work; well, sir, you will scarcely credit what he *did* buy: a scholarly volume, sir, *On the Causes of Nature*, which is in great demand at the University, being the subject of much discourse these days, I might even say disagreement. I only had the one volume, sir, very handsomely bound indeed; if you would like to order another I can oblige, although the binding will of course take some time. . . . '

'Thank you,' Michael said automatically, making his excuses as he headed for the door. Hurried by an impulse he did not quite understand, he went down the street after the swordsman.

Lord Michael caught sight of the swordsman a few streets down, and hailed the brown cloak imperiously: 'Sir!'

St Vier looked quickly around, and kept walking. Michael broke into a run. As his footsteps neared, the swordsman was suddenly against the wall with his cloak flung back, hand gripping his sword. It was not the sword a gentleman would wear, but a heavy, undecorated weapon whose stroke would almost surely kill. Michael skidded to a halt in the slush. He was glad no one was there to see this.

'My – Master St Vier,' he panted. 'I wondered if – if I might speak with you.'

The swordsman's eyes were, incongruously, the deep lavender colour of spring hyacinths. They raked Michael up and down.

The man hadn't dropped his guard; his hand still held the pommel of his ugly sword. Michael wondered what on earth he was doing with this fellow. Something of his mother's complacent laughter and the duchess's piquant scorn moved him closer to the swordsman. They thought he would have nothing to do with the profession. His mother was sure of it; and something in the duchess seemed to despise him for it.

St Vier seemed satisfied with what he saw; his hand relaxed as he became briskly businesslike. 'Do you want to talk out here?'

'Of course not,' Michael said. If he wanted to talk to the man, of course he would have to take him somewhere. 'Why don't you go along with me to the Blue Parrot for some chocolate?'

Why don't you go along . . . He sounded as though he were talking to an equal. St Vier seemed not to notice. He nodded, and followed Michael back up the street toward the cafe. Michael had to lengthen his stride to match the swordsman's. The man's presence was very *vivid*, at once sensual and aesthetic, like a fine blood-horse. He didn't match Michael's idea of a swordsman: there seemed nothing coarse about him, or surly, or even humourless.

'I'd better say now that my fees are high,' St Vier said. 'I don't want to put you off, but it usually has to be something pretty serious.'

'Yes, I've heard.' Michael wondered if he realised just how extensively his fees were discussed on the Hill. 'But I don't really want anyone challenged right now.'

'No?' St Vier stopped walking abruptly. 'If it's not about a job, then what do you want?'

He seemed less curious than annoyed. Quickly Michael said, 'Of course, I'm willing to pay you for your time, at your usual rates. I'd like you to . . . I'd like to learn the sword from you.'

The swordman's face closed with indifference. Later, Michael realised it was the same bored impatient look he had been giving Felman. 'I don't teach,' was all he said.

'Please believe that I'm in earnest.' What was he saying? He had never been anything of the kind. But the words came spilling out: 'I realise it's an unusual proposition, but I would make sure that you were properly recompensed as befits your skill and reputation.'

Barely concealed distaste showed on the swordsman's face. 'I'm sorry,' he said, 'I don't have time for this.'

'Wait – ' Michael stopped him from turning on his heel. 'Is there anything I could do to . . . '

For the first time St Vier seemed to soften, looking at Michael as though he saw a person behind the massed signals of breeding and grooming. 'Look,' he said kindly, 'I'm not a teacher. It has nothing to do with you. If you want to learn, there are plenty of others in the city who will teach you. I only do my own work; you can reach me in Riverside if you want me for that.'

'Will you . . . ?' Courteously Michael indicated the cafe a few doors down, determined to salvage some dignity.

The swordsman actually smiled at him. There was charm in it, unlooked-for humour and understanding. 'Thank you, no. I'm really in a hurry to get home.'

'Thank you, then; and good luck.' He didn't know if that was the appropriate thing to wish a swordsman, but the man didn't seem to take offence. It occurred to Michael later that St Vier had never asked him his name; and he never found out what the book was for. But he made enquiries that day, and the next, until he finally found himself a teacher.

Alec was mending a sock. His hands were bathed with the grey light from the window, and his stitches were tiny and careful.

'You should let Marie do that,' Richard said, hiding his surprise.

'It's a skill I learned at University. I don't want to lose it. I might need to earn a living some day.'

Richard laughed. 'As a tailor? Look, get yourself some new socks; get yourself ten pairs, get them in silk. I've just been paid for the Lynch job. We're going to be very comfortable, as long as it lasts.'

'Good,' Alec grumbled. 'We need more candles.'

'Beeswax,' said Richard giddily, 'of course. The best there is. Look, I've been shopping uptown.' He took out a brown paper parcel and held it out to Alec. 'A present. For you.'

'What is it?' Alec made no move to take the package.

'Well, it's a book,' Richard said, still holding it. 'I thought you might like it.'

Alec's eyes widened; then he converted the expression into a raising of the eyebrows. He fussed with the sock. 'You idiot,' he said softly.

'Well, you've only got the three you brought with you. And they're almost worn out. I thought you might like something

42

new.' Feeling a little awkward, he began undoing the brown paper himself. It released the rich smell of leather. The binding alone, Richard thought, was worth the price: burgundy leather with gold tooling, gilt-edged pages; the book was as beautiful as a rug or a painting.

Alec's arm shot out: his hand closed on the book. 'Felman's!' he gasped. 'You got this at Felman's!'

'Well, yes. He's supposed to be good.'

'*Good* . . .' Alec said in strangled tones. 'Richard, it's . . . he's . . . they're wall decorations for noblemen's libraries. He sells them by the inch: "Do you have Birdbrain in red leather?". "No, sir, but I have him in green." "Oh, no, that won't go with the rug." "Well, sir, I do have this lovely work on the mating habits of chickens in red. It's about the same size." "Oh, good, I'll take that one." '

Richard laughed. 'Well, it is beautiful.'

'Very,' Alec said drily. 'You could wear it to Chapel. I don't suppose you know what it's about?'

'Natural philosophy,' he responded promptly, 'whatever that is. The man said you might like it. He seemed to know what he was talking about. I could have got you *The Wicked Uncle, or, True Love Rewarded* or *The Merry Huntsman's Guide to Autumn Deer Droppings*. But he said this was what everyone was reading now.'

'Everyone where?' Alec's voice was stiff, the Hill accent pronounced.

'At University.'

Alec went to the window, placing his long palm against the cold glass. 'And you thought I would be interested.'

'I thought you might be. I told him you went there, to the University.'

'But not that I'd left.'

'It was none of his business. I had to tell him something: when he thought it was for me he tried to sell me a book of pornographic woodcuts.'

'At least they would have been of some use to you,' Alec said acidly. '*On the Causes of Nature* – the new translation. They've just lifted the ban on it after fifteen years. Have you any idea – no, of course you haven't.'

With a languid motion he turned from the window. The glass was freshly streaked with blood. His palm was scored with the mark of the darning needle.

Richard's breath caught. But he had faced dangerous opponents before. 'Come on,' he said; 'let's go down to Rosalie's and pay off all our debts. I've been drinking on credit for the past six weeks. You can bet gold against Greasepole Mazarene; he'll have hysterics.'

'That will be pleasant,' Alec remarked, and went to collect his cloak and gloves.

Chapter VI

He'd had tutors all his life, Michael realised; men who came to his home and taught him, courteously and slowly, what it was appropriate for him to know. Even when he was 8 they were deferential, the University scholars whose best hope for social promotion was as tutors, the masters of their various arts. Suddenly he was glad that St Vier had refused his offer. After a series of discreet enquiries in unusual places, Michael finally lit upon Master Vincent Applethorpe's Academy of Swordsmanship.

For a professional swordsman, the threat of termination is always present. The romantic ideal, of course, is to die fighting, young and still at one's peak. For practical purposes, though, almost any swordsman cherishes the dream that he will live until he first notices his precision slipping, by which time he will have built his reputation high enough to be able to resign gracefully from the active life and be welcomed into the household of some nobleman eager for the prestige his distinguished presence will lend. There he will be required only to do light bodyguarding and to give the occasional lesson to the noble's sons or men-at-arms. The worst thing that can happen – short of being crippled – is to run a school.

Everyone knows that the truly great swordsmen are trained by masters, men who appear out of nowhere, on a country road or in a crowded taproom, to single you out for their exclusive training. Sometimes it is necessary to pursue them from town to town, proving your worthiness until they consent to take you on. Only thugs resort to the schools: common sorts who want an advantage in a street brawl, or to impress a lover; or servants eager to impress an employer for promotion.

The name Vincent Applethorpe was not one that lived in legend.

It should have. Applethorpe had been a brilliant swordsman. In his best days he would have given St Vier a good fight. But his name had been erased from the public lists too early in his career for his last fight to be made a public tragedy. Quite early on his arm was slashed in a gorgeous, unchancy bit of rapier-and-dagger work. The wound festered, and rather than lose his life he lost his left arm. He very nearly lost both: only the intervention of concerned friends, who carried him to a surgeon's while he was in a drunken stupor of pain and the fear of gangrene, got him under the knife in time to save his life. The choice, for Applethorpe, had not been an easy one. If he had died, he might have been remembered for his early triumphs. Swordsmen appreciate a glorious death. But inglorious examples of what really happens to one whose skill has failed him at the crucial moment, those they prefer to forget.

There has been no great one-armed swordsman since Black Mark of Ariston, who lived two hundred years before Vincent Applethorpe was born. Black Mark's portrait hangs in the halls of Ariston Keep. Sure enough, one sleeve hangs ostentatiously empty. Swordsmen are full of the stories of his exploits. The portrait, however, shows a man of middle age, his hook-beaked face an impressive mass of furrows. And privately they'll admit that you need both arms for balance, sometimes even for the tactical advantage of switching hands. He couldn't have lost that arm until after he'd made his name as a swordsman. But the stories go on getting wilder.

Ironically, Vincent Applethorpe had grown up in the southern hills, within sight of Ariston Keep. He'd never given it much thought, though, until he came home from the city half-dead in the bottom of a wagon. His sister was running the family farm, and he was supposed to be there to help her with it. Instead he took to disappearing frequently on long walks. He went to the Keep, and would stand for hours on a hill above it, watching the people go in and out. He never tried to get into the hall himself, just stood and thought about great one-armed swordsmen. His sister had hoped that he would settle down, marry and bring another woman into the house. He did wait until after harvest before dashing her hopes and returning to the city.

Enough time had passed, he thought, for his face to have been forgotten. He set up his academy far from swordsmen's haunts, in a large attic above a dry goods shop. The ceiling sloped in, and it was stifling in summer, but it provided that rare city commodity, a stretch of unbroken space. After a few years there he could afford to move to a large hall built over a stable at the far eastern edge of town. It had been designed as an indoor riding ring, but the flooring was too weak to bear the weight of many horses. He soon hired a couple of assistants, young men he had trained himself who would never be swordsmen, but knew enough to teach. They could supervise the drills that went on the length of the studio, and keep the straw targets with their red patches in repair. Applethorpe was still the Master. He demonstrated the moves for his students, describing what he could not perform. So, ten years after his accident, at a time when he would have had to begin to consider abandoning the active swordsman's life, he was still in command of his career. And in his demonstrations he retained the fire, the precision of motion, the grace that made every move an explication of the swordsman's art, at once both effortless and imperative.

Michael Godwin admired him with a less than scholarly interest. He could not yet appreciate the technical clarity of Applethorpe's movements, but he was thrilled by the Master's vividness – it was almost a glow he projected when he demonstrated a move. Lord Michael wondered if this was what was meant by 'flair'. He'd always imagined flair to be tied up in dramatic movements of the arms, one of which the Master lacked. As with St Vier, there was a grace and dignity to his carriage that was neither the deliberate languor of the aristocrat nor the choppy energy of the city tradesman. Michael extended his right arm as instructed, trying for a fluidity that looked easy when Applethorpe did it.

'No,' the Master said to the line of beginners hopefully strung out before him like birds on a washline. 'You cannot hope to get anywhere near it while you stand like that.' His voice was remarkably calm, giving off neither impatience nor annoyance – nor any particular kindness. Seeing students doing something badly never upset Vincent Applethorpe. *He* knew the way it ought to be done. He kept explaining, and eventually they would get it, or they wouldn't. He surveyed the entire line and observed dispassionately but accurately, 'You look like you are all waiting to be beaten. Your shoulders are afraid to set upright, and your heads crane forward on your necks. So your whole stance is crooked, and your thrust will be crooked, too – Except you. You. What's your name?'

'Michael Godwin,' said Lord Michael. He hadn't bothered to change it; there were Godwins all over the country, and no one in this place was likely to know him by sight.

Applethorpe nodded. 'The Godwins of Amberleigh?' Michael nodded back, amused that the man had come so close in his lineage and region. Maybe it was the hair. 'A handsome family,' the Master said. 'You're lucky. Extend.' Michael did so, clumsily. 'No, never mind the wrist for now, just show us the arm. Look, all of you, look at that. The carriage of the shoulders, the lift of the head. It gives the whole extension a natural smoothness. Do it.'

He always came to this point in his instruction, when the explication of cause and effect came to an end and his instruction was, 'Do it.' They tried, fingering Michael with the edges of their eyes, trying to shake their shoulders into place without thrusting out their chests, to lift their heads without ruining their sight lines. Michael stopped worrying about his wrist, and fell into a trance of motion as his arm stretched itself out and pulled back in, over and over. He had never before considered his carriage as especially useful. It was an aid to an effect, handy to show off the line of a coat or the turn of a dance step. Now everything fell into place as the steady movement of his arm rolled through his shoulders.

Applethorpe paused in his round of surveillance and correction. 'Good,' he said. 'Godwin. You've got the wrist now.'

At home in his large, airy dressing room, with the fire lit against the cold, Michael took off his sweaty practice clothes. His manservant bore away the plain, unstylish garments without comment. Other servants brought up the hot water for his bath. He sank gratefully into the tub, whose steam rose up agreeably scented with clove and rose petals. He had time only for a short soak before he must dress for supper. It was the night of the duchess's party, and he had no desire to be late and miss his place on the barge. Even the prospect of Lord Horn's company was not enough to dampen his excitement. He could not imagine needing to converse with anyone else when Diane was present. He had forgotten how hard she was to talk to, and his estimate of his own powers was back to its accustomed level.

Michael rose naked from the bath, to be confronted with his own form, reflected down from the large mirror over the fireplace. He paused, staring, in the act of reaching for the bath towel. He was accustomed to thinking of his shoulders as frail; he had to pad them out sometimes to meet the demands of fashion. Now they seemed trim and competent. His collar bones followed their line, lithe as birds' wings. A gentleman did not uncover his neck in public, so their delights were reserved for his intimates. But in the room above the stable one grew hot, and adopted the open collar of the workman.

He followed the line they pointed to like an arrow, down his chest. All that the world had counted beautiful could be trained, turned on the lathe of practice to become a dangerous weapon. Looking up, he met his own eyes. The dark lashes that framed them made them seem deeper than they were, the pupil a stone dropped into ripples of colour blue-green as the sea. He had the sense of being closely examined by a stranger, of falling into his own beautiful eyes. He didn't know the man in the mirror, but he wanted to. The more he stared, the further from himself he went, asking, *Who are you? What do you want?*

His feet were very cold. The floor was like ice, and his stiff body had begun to shiver. Michael grabbed the towel and rubbed himself briskly. He would have to hurry to dress. The fireworks were due to begin at dark over the river, and the barge must not leave without him.

The day had been clear, almost mild; but with twilight a chill had struck that deepened as the dark winter sun began to fall, pulling the temperature with it. It hung low over the city's profile, as red as summer raspberries. The Riverside street was strangely empty, as silent as dawn. The slush of the ground had re-formed into frozen crusts, eerie landscapes-in-miniature of ice and mud. Alec's new boots demolished a fairy castle. He skidded on a patch of ice and righted himself, cursing.

'Are you sure you want to see these fireworks?' Richard asked him.

'I love fireworks,' Alec answered glibly. 'I value them more than life itself.'

'The west bank up by Waterbourne will be crowded', St Vier said, 'with carriages and upper city folks and vendors. Too many people live there. Half of Riverside will be over picking pockets. We'd better stay on the east side, it won't be so bad.'

'The pickpockets, or the crowds?' said Alec; but he went along with Richard.

They made for the lower bridge, which connected Riverside to the Old City. Some people still lived there, but mainly the east bank was given over to government buildings: the old palace, the castle/fort and barracks. . . . Richard marvelled at the foibles of the rich. He had nothing against fireworks. But to require your friends to sit in their barges in the middle of the river late in winter to enjoy them, that seemed eccentric. He felt the cold, the wind cutting across the river, even in his new clothes. He had bought himself a heavy cloak, jacket and fur-lined gloves. Alec, too, was warmly dressed, and had stopped complaining of the cold. He liked having money to spend, money to waste on food and gambling.

Across the dark breadth of the river the populated section of the city loomed, rising from its banks in steeper and steeper slopes until it became the Hill and blotted out the evening sky. St Vier and Alec had already passed the docks and warehouses, the fort guarding the old river-entrance to the city, and were coming on the Grand Plaza of Jurisdiction, Justice Place, where the Council of Lords had established its hall. Upriver the orange glow of torches from already assembled barges stained the growing darkness. Alec quickened his pace, anxious to catch the first fireworks. Richard had to break into a trot to match his long-legged stride.

Footsteps rang behind them on the frozen stone across the plaza. He heard young men's voices, raised in laughter. One of them called, thin and clear, 'Hey! Wait up!' Out of habit St Vier checked out the area. There was no one else they could be calling to. Alec did not look back, nor did he slow his steps.

'Hey!' The callers were insistent. 'Wait for us!' Alec kept on walking, but Richard stopped and turned. He saw a small group of boys, all dressed like Alec in black robes, long hair falling down their backs. When he'd chosen this route, he hadn't been thinking how close they'd pass to the University's domains.

Alec's hair streamed out behind him like a comet's tail. Richard ran to catch up. 'I can get us out of here if you'd like,' he said casually. For reply Alec only looked down at him, and slowed his pace to a deliberate snail's saunter. The swordsman had no trouble matching it; it reminded him of leg exercises.

The students' shoes whispered closer across the stone, until one of them drew abreast of Alec. 'Hey,' the student said friendlily, 'I thought you were locked up with your books.'

Alec stared straight ahead, and didn't stop. Richard's hand was on his sword-hilt. The students seemed unarmed, but Alec could be harmed by many things.

'Hey,' said the boy, 'aren't you – '

Alec looked down at him, and the student stammered in confusion, 'Oh – hey – I thought you were – '

'Think again,' said Alec harshly in an odd voice, a Riverside voice that troubled St Vier. It was effective, though; the students clustered together and hurried away, and Richard took his hand from the sword.

Chapter VII

The Tremontaine barge rocked when Lord Michael set his foot on its side; but he had been getting in and out of nobles' barges since he'd come to the city, and had grown proficient at not falling in. A torchman conducted him to the pavilion in the centre of the flat-bottomed boat. The hangings were green and gold, the duchess's colours. All of the sides were down while the barge waited at the dock; through the brocade he heard laughter, and the clink of metal. It was one of the most beautiful barges of any noble on the water. He had always wanted to ride in it. But now that he had the chance his mind was scarcely taking it in.

One corner of the brocade was pulled aside for him to enter the pavilion; the people seated at the table inside gasped and shivered at the blast of cold air that entered with him. Diane's guests were already dining off slices of smoked goose, washed down with a strong red wine that took the chill out of the night and the river. Michael slipped into the only empty seat; he had lingered too long choosing a jacket, and paid the price by being the last to arrive. And his clothes weren't even going to matter, he realised now: no one at the table would remove their outer layer of furs, despite the brazier under the table warming their feet. They looked like a country hunting party, swathed in thick greys and browns and blacks that glowed and rippled like living pelts in the candlelight.

The duchess raised her goblet to him. The curve of her wrist was achingly white even against the white fur of her cuff. Michael's throat tightened, but he replied with a courtesy. His cup was filled with wine the colour of rubies. The drink, though cool, was warmer than the air outside had been; he seemed to feel it flowing straight into his veins.

They were all there: young Chris Nevilleson and his sister, Lady Helena, whose ringlets Michael could remember pulling at childhood parties; Mary, Lady Halliday, without her lord, the Crescent Chancellor, who had been detained by city business; Anthony Deverin, Lord Ferris, the bright young hope of the Council of Lords, already Dragon Chancellor at the age of 32; and Lord Horn. Horn's fair skin was flushed with warmth. He wore splendid longhaired grey fox. The shadowlight was kind to him, rendering him with a lean, over-bred elegance. He wore silver rings, which called attention to his slender hands when he reached for things at table.

He looked at Michael with cool deliberation. It was a look that implied further intimacy, and it made Michael's skin creep. The smile at the edges of his mouth made Michael want to hit him.

The goose and red wine were whisked away, and small bowls of hot almond soup were set down, their contents rocking lightly with the tide. 'Oh, dear,' said the duchess. 'I was afraid of this. We're about to cast off. I hope the river isn't choppy.'

'It isn't,' said Michael. 'The sky is clear, it's perfect fireworks weather.'

'Except for the cold.' Helena Nevilleson shivered theatrically.

'Pooh,' said her brother, 'you used to climb out of the window in winter to check on your pony.' Lady Helena hit him with her pomander ball.

'My lord,' the duchess admonished, 'no woman likes to be reminded of her past. Not all of them come as well armed as Lady Helena, though.'

'If she's trying to prove what a lady she is now,' Horn said primly, 'she'd do better to put it away.'

'And who', Helena demanded, 'will protect me if I do?' The young woman's eyes sparkled with the delight of being the centre of attention.

'From what?' asked her brother innocently.

'Why, insult, of course,' the duchess defended her.

'With respect, madam Duchess,' Lord Christopher answered, 'the truth cannot be considered an insult.'

'Idealism,' murmured Lord Ferris, while Diane responded, 'Can it not? That depends on your timing, my lord.'

'I had a pony,' quiet Lady Halliday spoke up. 'It bit me.'

'Funny,' said Christopher Nevilleson; 'Helena's was always afraid *she* would bite *it*.'

'Timing?' asked Michael, emerging from a cold draught of stony white wine. He didn't care much about ponies and pomander balls. Diane had barely looked at him since her initial greeting. He was beginning to strain for the cryptic messages she had been sending him the other day. The party felt so normal that it was making him uncomfortable. To find her again he felt he would have to walk a labyrinth of hidden meanings.

Now, at last, her grey eyes were fixed on him. 'Is the wine to your taste?' she asked.

'The timing of truth,' said Lord Horn with heavy self-importance. 'That's a matter for politicians like Ferris, and not mere ornaments like you and me.'

The messages, god help him, were coming from Horn. Michael gritted his teeth against the archness of the man.

'The wine for the fish', the duchess continued with relentless, impersonal politeness, 'I think is even better.'

'Fish?!' Lady Halliday exclaimed. 'My dear, I thought you said this was just going to be a picnic.'

The duchess made a moue. 'It was. But my cook got carried away with the notion of what would be necessary to sustain seven people on the river in midwinter. I don't ever dare to argue with her, or I get creamed chicken for a week.'

'Poor Diane,' said Lord Ferris, smiling at her. 'You let everyone bully you.'

The sky over the river looked as though it were burning.

'Hurry!' Alec said. But as they rounded the corner to Water-bourne they saw that the light came from torches set in the nobles' barges in the middle of the river. Some ten or fifteen of them were clustered in the centre of the dark water. They looked like elaborate brooches pinned to black silk shot with ripples of gold.

Alec whistled softly through chapped lips. 'The rich', he said, 'are looking particularly rich tonight.'

'It's impressive,' said Richard.

'I hope they aren't too terribly cold,' Alec said, implying the opposite.

Richard didn't answer. He was absorbed in the sight of a new barge making its way upriver to join the others. Flames and black smoke spun back from the torches set in its prow, surrounding it with danger and glory. The green and gold pavilion was still closed. But it was the barge itself that intrigued him. He must have made some sound; Alec turned sharply to see what he was looking at.

'But of course,' sneered Alec; 'no party would be complete without one.'

The prow of the barge reared up in the graceful curve of a swan's neck. Its head was crowned with a ducal coronet. In perfect proportion were the wings, fanning back to protect the sides of the boat. Despite the hangings, despite the flat bottom and outsized stern, the barge managed to give the illusion of a giant swan on the river. Its oars dipped and rose, dripping jewels with each stroke, so smoothly that the barge seemed to glide across the surface of the water.

'Who is it?' St Vier asked.

'Tremontaine, of course,' Alec answered sharply. 'There's the ducal crown all over everything. I should think even you would recognise that get-up.'

He had thought they were ornamental. 'I don't know Tremontaine,' he said; 'I've never worked for him.'

'Her,' said Alec sourly. 'Can't you detect the woman's touch?'

Richard shrugged. 'I can't keep them all straight.'

'I'm surprised you've never done a job for her. Diane is such a lady of fashion, and you are fashion's darling – '

'Diane?' Richard groped for and found the connection. 'Oh, that one. She's the one who had her husband killed. I remember that. It was before I got fashionable.'

'Killed her husband?' Alec drawled. 'A nice lady with such a pretty boat? What a terrible thing to say, Richard.'

'Maybe she didn't like him.'

'It hardly matters. He was crazy anyway. She was made duchess in her own right, and they locked him up. Why kill him?'

'Maybe he ate too much.'

'He died of a stroke.'

St Vier smiled down at the ground. 'Of course he did.'

The barges were tilting and rocking as friends tried to get close enough to one another to exchange gossip and pieces of fruit. There were also several competing musical consorts. Their ears were assaulted by a dramatic volley of brass, uncomfortably tangled in the sinews of a harp and flute and the anaemic arms of a string quartet.

'Well,' said Alec, taking in the chaos down below, 'at least we can be fairly sure he didn't die of boredom.'

In the barges all around them people were hurling food and greetings at each other with impartial good cheer. They received a couple of oranges, but in Diane's calm presence the party on the swan boat forbore to join the mêlée, while the swan's wings shielded them from missiles.

Mary Halliday, who, unknown to many, had a good ear for music, winced at the mélange of instruments and tunes. Smiling sympathetically at her, Diane said, 'I wonder if we could get them to cooperate on "Our City of Light"?'

'Not if you love me,' said Ferris, the Dragon Chancellor. 'I don't know much about music, but I know what I'm sick of hearing. We open every Council season with it.'

'But', the duchess grinned at him, 'have you ever heard it as a trio for trumpet, harp and viola d'amore?'

'No; and with any luck I never will. What a pity you didn't bring your portative organ so we could drown them all out with "God Hath Warmed my Heart".'

'We would have to set the pipes at the rear, and the image would be unfortunate. If you're cold, my lord, just bite down on a peppercorn.'

Suspicion was creeping into Michael's heart. Diane and Lord Ferris seemed terribly familiar. Could they have an intimate connection? Michael tried to tell himself not to be an ass. Lord Horn was boring him and Helena with a complicated story about some state banquet he'd attended, for which it seemed necessary to keep touching Michael's knee for emphasis. If he were a woman, Michael reflected, Horn would never dare to touch his knee. If it were true about Diane and Ferris, perhaps he could contrive to have Ferris killed. Or even – of course, he was still a beginner, but Applethorpe seemed to think he had some promise as a swordsman – he could call the chancellor out himself, without any warning so that Ferris couldn't hire someone else to come up against him. But fighting one's own duels was unknown.

Might the duchess find it in poor taste? Or was it the sort of daring originality she looked for in him –

'As I'm sure Lord Michael would agree,' Horn finished complacently.

Lord Michael looked up at the sound of his name. 'What?' he said inelegantly.

Laughing, Lady Helena tapped his shoulder with her pomander, and Horn's clear grey eye fixed on him. It gave Michael a sudden distaste for the poached whiting he'd been eating.

'Helena,' Michael demanded testily of the young lady with the pomander ball, 'can't you learn to control your pet?'

The duchess's silvery laughter was all the reward he needed for what he considered a laudable, indeed a magnanimous, rein on his temper.

It vexed Alec not to be able to provoke St Vier into betting on which barge was going to overturn first. He had the odds all figured out, considering the way those people were carrying on. 'Look', he insisted patiently, over his own knowledge that St Vier never bet anyone on anything, 'I'll make it very simple for you. If you think of – '

But a sennet of trumpets, well coordinated by the master of the fireworks, drowned Alec out. Amongst the barges servants hastened to put out all their torches at once. The barges rocked wildly as they did so; the musicians, less well bred than their betters, swore. The backwash from the bobbing boats slapped at the shore. Laughter shivered up from the water. Then, abruptly, all was still as the first of the fireworks exploded against the sky.

It burst over them as a blue star, filling the sky with fiery petals for one awesome moment before beginning its lazy disintegration in point by point of blistering fire. On both sides of the river there was a hush as its sparks trickled down into the waiting blackness, leaving a ghostly trail of smoke that vanished even as they stared.

In the pause before the next one, Richard turned to his friend. But Alec's eyes hadn't moved from the empty sky. His face was a mask of blind desire.

Some local people had joined them on the rampart above the

river – tradespeople, not scholars. They came in couples, courting, maybe, leaning close together with their arms around each other's waists. Alec never noticed them. Gold and green washed across his face, as fiery garlands were hung across the sky.

Now a shrill whistle split the air; some people behind them jumped. Into the silent breach budded a knot of scarlet flame. Slowly it blossomed, and slowly dissolved into a host of tendrils, a flowering-tree of a flower, with a golden heart that emerged, pulsing, at its centre. For long slow seconds all the landscape was drenched in scarlet. In those red moments Richard heard Alec give one passionate sigh, and saw him raise both his hands to bathe them in the glow.

The boom and snap of the fireworks, echoing from bank to bank, made it hard to catch footsteps. Richard was only aware of the newcomer when he felt the subtle disturbance of cloth at his side. His hand snaked down and caught the intruder's wrist, poised where most gentlemen kept their purses. Without looking down he pinched it savagely between the bones. Then he turned slowly to find out who was making the controlled gurgle of pain.

'Oh,' said Nimble Willie, smiling up at him weakly but winningly, 'I didn't know it was you.'

Richard let go of his arm, and watched him massage the nerve. The little thief was as slight as a child, and his face, though peaky, was guileless. His speciality was housebreaking. Richard was sorry to have hurt his crucial hand, but Willie was philosophical. 'You fooled me, Master St Vier,' he said, 'in those naffy clothes. I thought you were a banker. Never mind, though; it's just as good I've found you. I've got some news you might want to have.'

'All right,' said Richard. 'You may as well get a look at the fireworks while you're here.'

Willie lifted his eyes, then shrugged. 'What's the point? It's just coloured lights.'

Richard waited for the thrill of the next to be over before answering, 'They're devilish expensive, Willie; they must be good for something.'

It was hopeless. The fireworks must be almost over, and Michael saw that he was to be nothing more on the swan boat than one of a party of friends. The duchess treated him no differently than any of the others; if possible, with more distance, since she knew him the least well. Moodily he slung back a draught of burgundy, and picked at his duck. At least she hadn't mocked him as she had Horn, when the fool went on and on about the fireworks he had seen in better days. Horn hadn't the wit to catch the two edges of her meaning. Michael had, but much good it was doing him. He had laughed at her sally, but she turned her eyes then to Lord Ferris.

Why Ferris? Was he better dressed than Michael? He was certainly more powerful; but the duchess wasn't interested in politics. Her money, wit and beauty were all the power she needed, Michael thought. Ferris was dark where he was fair. Ferris wasn't even whole. He'd lost one eye as a boy, and what was otherwise a handsome face was unbalanced by a stark black eyepatch. An affectation: he might at least have had a number of them made to match his clothing. Well, Ferris was not the only one with an attractive eccentricity. Michael himself was already deep enough in the adventures of the sword to cause a minor scandal. Just because he kept it hidden beneath a well-groomed exterior. . . . He must find some way to tell her what he had done at her prompting; some way to get her alone, away from these others. . . .

There was a sudden silence. The fireworks seemed to have ended. The others were exclaiming with disappointment, while servants cleared the fifth course away, and lowered the sides of the pavilion again. The duchess gestured to a footman, who nodded and headed for the stern.

'If no one minds,' she explained to her guests, 'I think we should make our way out of this press before everyone else starts trying to. I know Lord Ferris has somewhere else to go tonight, but the rest of you may want to come into the house to warm up after.'

'Oh?' Lord Horn leaned over to the chancellor. 'Are you by any chance attending Lord Ormsley's little card party?'

'No,' Ferris smiled. 'Business, I'm afraid.'

The duchess rose, gesturing to her guests not to. 'Please, stay comfortable. I'm only going forward for a little air.'

Michael's skin tingled. It was as though she had read his mind. He would give her a moment, and then follow.

The final volley of fireworks was a fugue of sound and light. Colours followed upon one another in ecstatic arcs, each higher and more brilliant, until the splendour was almost unbearable.

An awed but hopeful silence followed the last sparks down into the river. But the sky remained empty, a neatly folded blanket of stars on the bed of night. People shivered, then shrugged.

Alec finally turned to Richard. 'Do you think', he asked avidly, 'that an exploding firework could kill you?'

'It could,' Richard answered. 'You'd have to be sitting right on top of it, though.'

'It would be quick,' said Alec, 'and splendid, in its way. Unless you kept it from going off.' Nimble Willie shifted from foot to foot. 'Oh. Hello, Willie. Come to pick –' Richard shook his head, indicating the tradesmen behind them. ' – Come to see the fireworks?'

Once more the trumpets sounded, though less enthusiastically than they had at the start. Across the river the crowds were milling apart. The barge torches were being relit, and the string quartet had begun making a squeaky go at jollity. On the swan barge a woman emerged at the prow and stood facing into the wind that ruffled her cloak of fine white fur.

'There,' Alec told Richard drily. 'You may admire the owner of your favourite boat. That's the duchess.'

'She looks beautiful,' Richard said in surprise.

'Anyone would', said Alec tartly, 'in a great white boat in the middle of the river. You ought to see her up close.'

It was hard to tell what he meant when he talked like that, as though he were making fun of himself for speaking, and you for listening. Richard had heard other nobles use that tone, though not, in general, to him. Nimble Willie, who had never enjoyed any nobleman's conversation, cleared his throat. 'Master St Vier . . .'

He beckoned, like a small boy with a robin's nest to show. The two men followed him into a corner of the wall out of the wind and most people's sight.

The little thief brushed away the lock of hair that always seemed to be hanging over his nose. 'Ah, now. I just wanted to say, there's been someone asking for St Vier these past two nights at Rosalie's.'

'There,' Alec said to Richard. 'I knew we shouldn't have gone to Martha's' – although it was he himself who had insisted on it.

'And this man', Willie persisted, 'has gold, they say.'

'In Riverside?' Alec drawled. 'He must be mad.'

St Vier said, 'Why wasn't I told about this before?'

'Ah,' Willie nodded sagely. 'He's paying, see. Putting out a bit of silver for word to get passed on to you. Two nights running, that's not bad.'

'You want us to stay away another night?' the swordsman asked.

'Nah. My luck to find you, but there are probably others out looking, by now.'

'Right. Thanks for your trouble.' Richard gave the pickpocket some coins. Willie smiled, flexed his nimble fingers, and folded into the darkness.

'How the simple people do love you,' said Alec, looking after him. 'What happens when you don't have any money?'

'They trust me', said Richard, 'to remember when I do.'

A moment of silence fell when the duchess left the pavilion. All her guests were experienced socialisers, but the departure of their hostess demanded a hiatus of reorganisation.

In agony Michael listened to Chris and Lady Halliday talking about the weavers' revolt in Helmsleigh. Every second was precious; but he must not hurry out after her. At last he judged enough time to have passed. It being impossible to slip away unnoticed, he yawned extravagantly and stretched his arms as far as he was able in his fitted jacket.

'Not tired already, my dear?' said Horn.

'Tired?' Michael smiled his sweetest smile. Now that he was about to get what he wanted, he could afford to be tolerant. 'How could I be tired in such pleasant company?'

'Wine always makes me sleepy,' Lady Halliday said in a sombre attempt at graciousness. Lady Helena allowed that it did her, too, but she would never dare to admit it before gentlemen. Satisfied that attention was diverted from his movements, Michael began to rise.

Like a filigreed anvil, Lord Horn's hand descended on his

shoulder. 'Do you know,' Horn leaned over to confide in him, 'when I first knew Ormsley he barely knew ace from deuce? And now he's giving exclusive card parties in that great big monstrosity his mother left him.'

Michael murmured sympathetically, and kept his muscles tensed to rise. 'I gather', Horn said, 'that you are not engaged tonight?'

'I'm afraid I am.' Michael tried to smile, keeping one eye nervously on the doorway. He thought he could just see the white glow of the duchess's fur outside. At least Horn was no longer touching him; but he *was* looking slyly at Michael, as though they shared some understanding. It conveyed roguish charm with a confidence more appropriate to a younger man.

'You certainly are kept busy,' sighed Horn, lowering his eyelids alluringly.

'As busy as I can manage,' Michael said, with the arrogant glibness that is the opposite of flirtation. He saw Horn's face freeze, and added, 'I do try to keep my dignity.'

It was needlessly cruel – and hypocritical from a man met climbing out of a window. But Horn must learn sometime that ten years had passed since the days of his glory were even possible – and besides, the duchess had just appeared in the doorway, flushed and beautiful, like some river goddess, crowned with stars. Michael felt his heart knot in a little hard lump that slid down into his stomach.

'It's snowing,' the duchess said. 'So lovely, and so inconvenient. Fortunately there's plenty to eat if we're slowed by it.'

She seated herself in a flurry of fur. The diamonds of snow that spangled her hair and shoulders glittered for a moment in the candlelight before vanishing in the heat. 'Now, I am sure you were all too polite to talk about me, so what gems of conversation have I missed?'

Lady Helena tried to match her banter, but fell short at brittle affectation: 'Only the delight of Christopher telling us all what a hero he was at Helmsleigh.'

'Ah.' The duchess gave Lord Christopher a serious look. 'The weavers are of some importance.'

'To my tailor, anyway,' said Horn jovially. 'Local wool, he

62

claims, will soon become inordinately priced. He's trying to sell me all of last year's colours at a bargain.'

Across the table, Lord Ferris raised the eyebrow not covered by his patch. 'Hard to keep your dignity in last year's colours.'

Michael bit his lip. He hadn't meant his put-down of Horn to be public, much less to be taken up by others.

Horn inclined his head courteously. 'I believe my tailor and I will reach an accord. He has known me for many years, and knows I am not to be trifled with.'

The lump in Michael's stomach did a little somersault.

Ferris said to Diane, 'I suppose we must call Lord Christopher one of Lord Halliday's circle, if so great a chancellor may be said to have something so small as a circle. But on behalf of my own office I must commend his work at Helmsleigh.'

'You're kind,' Lord Christopher murmured, assuming the stoic look of those forced to witness their own praise publicly.

'He isn't, really,' the duchess told him. 'My lord Ferris is horribly ambitious, and the first rule of the ambitious is never to ignore anyone who's been of use.'

General laughter at the duchess's wit broke the tension.

There were four more courses in almost an hour of slow rowing before they found themselves once again at the Tremontaine landing. When they arrived they were all a little cold, a little tipsy, and very full.

All Michael wanted was to be off the barge and away from this disastrous group. The duchess had first led him on, and now she was making him feel like a fool – and, worse yet, act like one. But Ferris had no right to take a private comment and use it against Horn, in a way designed to stir up ill-feeling. Now Horn was sulking like a child over nothing at all. If Horn himself had been more subtle, Michael would not have been forced to be so overt in his rejection. Horn spent the rest of the trip directing his attention everywhere but to Michael. Michael preferred it to his flirtation. The man was carrying on as though he'd never been turned down before, a situation which Michael considered most unlikely.

Despite his later appointment, Lord Ferris was induced to join the party inside the duchess's mansion for a hot drink. And despite his desire to get away, Michael felt it went against his dignity to leave before Ferris did. He knocked back his punch, and found the warmth of it dissolved some of the lump in his stomach. When Ferris called for his cloak, though, Michael did also. Diane said all the right things about how he really should stay; but there was no special light in her eyes, and he didn't believe her. She did escort both him and Lord Ferris to the door, and there she let Michael kiss her hand again. It was probably the punch that made him tremble as he took it. He looked up into her face, and found a smile so sweet fixed on him that he blinked to clear his eyes.

She said, 'My dear young man, you must come again.' That was all. But he lingered outside under the portico while the groom patiently held his horse for him, wanting to turn back and ask her whether she meant it, or to hear it again. A pair of missing gloves occurred to him, and he started back to the door. Through it her voice came clear to him, addressing Ferris: 'Tony, whatever were you tormenting poor Horn about?'

Ferris chuckled. 'You noticed that, did you?'

It was a voice of extreme intimacy. Michael knew the tone well. The door opened, and he pressed back into the shadows, to see the duchess's white wrist pressed to Ferris's lips. Then she took a chain from around her neck and drew it across his mouth once before giving it to him.

Before his own reaction could betray him, Michael was out of the shadow of the house and up on horseback. And now he knew something about the duchess that no one else even suspected. And he wished, on the whole, that he were dead, or exceedingly drunk.

Bertram was able to oblige him in the latter. But even while dizzily wrestling in his friend's appreciative grasp, striving for oblivion, Michael was thinking of whether he could hurt her with it – just enough to give him what he wanted.

Chapter VIII

It had started to snow again by the time they got to Rosalie's. Soft flakes formed out of the darkness just before their eyes, falling like stars. Alec followed Richard down the steps and into the tavern, ducking under the low lintel. Rosalie's was in the cellar of an old townhouse. It was reliably cool in summer and warm in winter, always dark and smelling of earth.

The tavern's torchlight dazzled their eyes. Their clothes were steaming in the heat, their noses assaulted by the smells of beer and food and bodies, their ears by the shouts of gamblers and raconteurs.

As soon as Richard was spotted someone shouted, 'That's it, everybody! No more free drinks!'

'Aww,' they chorused. The serious dicers turned back to business, the serious drinkers reminded each other that life was like that. Certain of the Sisterhood came forward hoping to tease Alec, who would snap their heads off before he let them make him blush.

'Who told you about it this time, Master St Vier?' asked Half-Cocked Rodge, a local businessman. 'I've got my money on Willie.'

His partner, Lucie, leaned across the table. 'Well, you can lay odds it wasn't Ginnie Vandall!'

The laughter this provoked meant something. Richard waited patiently to find out what it was. He had a guess.

Rodge made a place for him at his table. Lucie explained, 'It's Hugo, my heart. Ginnie's bonny Hugo is after your job. Must have heard about the silver, and thought of gold. So Hugo walks in here last night, bold as you please, first time he's been here in months, he knows good and well this is your place for work. And he goes right up to this noble, tries to get his interest, but the man's no fool, he isn't having any.'

'I'd like to meet this Hugo,' said Alec doucely from where he stood behind Richard, leaning against a post.

Rosalie herself brought Richard some beer. 'On me, old love,' she told him; 'you wouldn't believe the business you've brought me the last two nights by not being here!'

'Don't I get any?' Alec enquired.

Rosalie looked him up and down. The tavern mistress was conservative: to her he was still a newcomer. But Richard stood close to him these days, and she'd already seen a few fights fought in his defence; so she called for another mug for him. Then she settled down to argue with Lucie. 'It's not a noble,' Rosalie said. 'I know nobles. They don't come to this place, they send someone else to do the arrangements for them.'

'It is so one,' Lucie insisted. 'He talks like one. You think I don't know nobles? I've had a dozen; ride you up in their carriages on the Hill, put you to bed in velvet sheets and serve you hot breakfast before you go.'

Richard, who really had had nobles, smiled; Alec sniggered.

''Course it's a noble.' Mallie Blackwell had joined the fray, leaning with both palms on the table so that her charms dangled in front of their faces. 'He's in disguise. That's how you can tell 'em. When they come down to the Brown Dog to gamble, the nobles always wear their masks. I can tell you, I've had a few.'

'It isn't a mask,' Rosalie said. 'It's an eyepatch.'

'Same thing.'

'Oh, really?' asked Alec with elaborate nonchalance. 'Which eye? Does it change from night to night?'

'It's his left,' Rosalie attested.

'Oh,' said Alec softly. 'And is he a dark-haired gentleman with – '

'Hugo!' a joyful roar greeted the newcomer for the benefit of all. 'Haven't seen *you* in a boa's age!'

Hugo Seville made a stunning picture standing in the doorway, and he knew it. Hair bright as new-minted gold curled across his manly brow. His chin was square, his teeth white and even, revealed in a smile of confident strength. When he saw who Rodge was sitting with, the smile faltered.

'Hello, Hugo,' Richard called, cutting off his retreat. 'Come and join us.'

To his credit, Hugo came. Richard read the wariness in his body, and was satisfied that he would make no more trouble. Hugo's smile was back in place. 'Richard! I see they've found you. Or haven't you heard yet?'

'Oh, I've got the whole story now. Sounds like it has possibilities. I haven't had a really challenging fight since Lynch last month.'

'Oh? What about de Maris?'

Richard shrugged. 'De Maris was a joke. He'd got fat, living on the Hill.' Hugo nodded gravely, keeping his thoughts to himself. De Maris had beaten him once. 'Oh, Hugo,' St Vier said, 'you won't know Alec.'

Hugo looked over and slightly up at the tall man standing behind St Vier. He was watching Hugo as if he were an unusual bug that had fallen into his soup.

'I'd heard,' Hugo said. 'Ginnie told me there was a fight at Old Market.'

'Oh, *that* Hugo!' Alec exclaimed, his face animated with innocent curiosity. 'The one who pimps for Ginnie Vandall!'

Hugo's hand leapt to his sword. Rodge let out a chuckle, and Lucie a gasp. The buzz of conversation at nearby tables trickled to nothing as all eyes focused on them.

'Hugo's a swordsman,' Richard told Alec, unruffled. 'Ginnie manages his business for him. Sit down, Hugo, and have a drink.'

Alec looked down at Richard, sitting calm and easy, one hand on his mug. Alec's lips parted to say something; then he only licked them and took a drink, his eyes fixed on Hugo over the rim of his mug.

They were green eyes, bright in the angular face, like a cat's. Hugo didn't like cats. He never had.

'I beg your pardon,' the young man said, smooth as a nobleman. 'I must have been thinking of some other people.'

'I can't stay,' Hugo said, sitting uncomfortably. 'I have to meet someone soon.'

'Well, that's all right,' Richard said. 'Tell me about this man. What did you think of him?'

Hugo could pay for his gaffe with information. It wasn't like him to try to steal Richard's jobs. Richard guessed that he had been unable to resist the money smell.

Hugo made much more money than Richard did. He was in great demand on the Hill for lovers' duels, and as a ceremonial wedding guard. He was dashing and gallant, well dressed, graceful and fairly well mannered. He had not taken a challenge to the death in years. Hugo was a coward. Richard knew it, and a few others guessed it, but they kept their mouths shut because of Ginnie and the money he was making. Hugo's nerve had broken years ago, at a time when he was still fighting dangerous fights. He could have turned to alcohol to see him through a few more duels before it betrayed him; but Ginnie Vandall had seen the possibilities in Hugo and turned him from that path to a more lucrative one.

Richard appreciated Hugo. Now that St Vier's reputation was flourishing, the nobles were always after him to take dull jobs that challenged nothing except his patience. Richard turned them over to Hugo, and Hugo was glad. Hugo's income was steadier; but when a man was marked for killing, or a point needed to be made in blood, it was St Vier they wanted, and they paid him what he asked.

'Everyone here', Richard prompted, 'seems to think he's a lord. Except Mistress Rosalie. What would you say?'

Hugo's flush was just discernible in the dim light. 'Hard to tell. He had the manner. But then, he might have been putting it on.' He glared in Alec's direction. 'Some do, you know.'

'Let's face it,' said Rodge; 'we wouldn't know him if it was Halliday himself. Who's ever seen any of 'em up close?'

'I have,' said Alec coolly. Richard held his breath, wondering if his proud companion were going to declare himself.

'Lucky you! Where? Was he handsome?'

'At University,' Alec said. 'He came and spoke after there'd been a riot over the city's tearing down some student lodgings. He promised to found a scholarship and some new whorehouses. He was very well received: we carried him on our shoulders, and he kicked me in the ear.' They laughed appreciatively at that, but Alec seemed unaffected by his new popularity. He said sourly, 'Of course you'll never see Halliday here. There are too many important people who want to kill him already; why should he come down here and let just anyone do it for free?' Alec slung his

68

cloak around his shoulders. 'Richard, I'm off. Let me know if the eyepatch changes eyes.'

'Don't you want to stay and see for yourself?'

'No. I do not.'

Alec made his way across the tavern with his usual posture: head thrust forward, shoulders slumped, as though he were expecting to run into something. Richard looked curiously after him. After the fight at the Old Market Alec was probably safe enough on the streets, but his mood seemed strange, and Richard wondered what had made him leave so suddenly. He thought he'd go after him, just to ask; just to see what he'd say and listen to him talk in that creamy voice . . . the one-eyed messenger could come again tomorrow night if he really wanted him. Richard excused himself and hurried after Alec, who had stopped in front of the door as it opened inward. A tall man in a black felt hat came in. Alec looked up sharply at him, then brushed past, almost elbowing him aside in his haste to get up the stairs. Richard was about to follow when the man removed his hat, brushing snow off the crown. His left eye was covered with a black patch. He had turned his whole head to look over his shoulder after Alec. Then he slammed the door shut behind him, and turned and saw Richard.

'Dear me,' he said wearily, 'I hope you're not another un-employed swordsman.'

'Well, I am, actually,' said Richard.

'I'm afraid my needs are quite specific.'

'Yes, I know,' he answered. 'You wanted St Vier.'

'That is correct.'

Richard indicated an empty table. 'Would you like to sit by the fire?'

The man's mouth froze in the act of opening; then it stretched into a smile, a speaking smile that conveyed understanding. 'No,' he said courteously, 'thank you. If you won't be too cold there, I would prefer a corner where we will not be disturbed.'

They found one, between a support-beam and the wall. Richard folded himself neatly into his seat, and the stranger followed, taking care with the placement of his clothes and the end of his sword. It was an old-fashioned, heavy sword with an ornate basket handle. Carrying it exposed him to the danger of a challenge, but not carrying it left him looking more vulnerable than he would wish.

The man's face was long and narrow, with a dark, definite jawline, heavily shadowed. Above it his skin was pale, even for winter. The cord of his eyepatch disappeared into hair as dark as a crow's plumage.

Unbidden, Rosalie brought two mugs to the table. The one-eyed gentleman waved them away. 'Let us have wine. Have you no sack? Canary?'

The tavern mistress nodded mutely, and snatched the beer-mugs back. Richard could have told him that Rosalie's wine was sour, her sherry watered; but no one had asked him.

'So you're St Vier,' the man said.

'Yes.' The stranger's face went opaque as he scrutinised the swordsman. None of them could ever resist doing it. Richard waited politely as the man took in his youth, his uneven good looks, the calm of his hands on the table before him. He was beginning to think this was going to be one of the ones who said, 'You're hardly what I expected,' and try to proposition him. But the stranger only nodded curtly. He looked down at his own gloved hands, and back at Richard.

'I can offer you 60,' he said softly.

It was a very nice sum. Richard shrugged. 'I'd have to know more about it first.'

'One challenge – to the death. Here in the city. I don't think you can quarrel with that.'

'I only quarrel on commission,' Richard said lightly.

The man's lips thinned out to a smile. 'You're an agreeable man. And an efficient one. I saw you fight off two men at Lord Horn's party.'

'You were there?' Richard hoped it might be a preface to his identity; but the man only answered, 'I had the fortune to witness the fight. It's a mystery to everyone still, what the whole thing was about.' His one eye glinted sharply; Richard took the hint, and returned it: 'I'm afraid I can't tell you that. Part of my work is to guard my employers' secrets.'

'And yet you let them employ you without any contract.'

Richard leaned back, entirely at ease. He had a fair idea of where this was going now. 'Oh, yes, I insist on that. I don't like having my business down on paper in someone's drawer.'

'But you open yourself up to a great deal of danger that way. Should any of your duels be investigated, there is no written proof that you are anything but a casual murderer.'

St Vier smiled, and shrugged. 'That's why I'm careful who I work for. I give my patrons my word to do the job and to keep quiet about it; they have to be trusted to know what they're doing, and back me up if need be. In the long run, most people find they prefer it that way.'

Rosalie returned with two dusty pewter goblets and a flagon of acidic wine. The man waited until she had gone before saying, 'I'm glad to hear you say so. I've heard your word is good. That arrangement is suitable.'

When he drew off one of his gloves, the expensive scent of ambergris drifted up. His large hand was as creamy and well tended as a woman's. And when he lifted the flagon to pour out the wine, Richard saw the marks of rings still pale on his bare fingers. 'I am prepared to pay you 30 in advance.'

Richard raised his eyebrows. No point in pretending that half in advance wasn't unusually generous. 'You're kind,' he said.

'Then you accept?'

'Not without more information.'

'Ah.' The man leaned back, and drained half his cup. Richard admired the self-control that let him lower it from his lips without an expression of disgust. 'Tell me,' he asked, 'who was that tall man I passed, coming in?'

'I've no idea,' Richard lied.

'Why do you refuse my offer?'

Richard said in the comradely tone that had so bemused Lord Montague over his daughter's wedding, 'I don't know who you are, and I don't know who the mark is. You can offer me all 60 in advance, I still can't give you my word on it.'

The gentleman's eye glared at him with the intensity of two. But he kept the rest of his face blandly civil, contriving even to look a bit bored. 'I understand your need for caution,' he said. 'I think I can set some of your fears to rest.' Slowly, almost provocatively, he removed his other glove.

Again the scent of ambergris assailed the air, rich and sensual. It made Richard think of Alec's hair. The man held up his hand.

71

Dangling from it was a long gold chain, with an eight-sided medallion spinning at the end of it so that Richard could not make out its design. The candle between them winked a gold sequin in his eyes. With one finger the man stopped the spinning, and Richard had one sight of the device engraved on the medallion before it disappeared again into the glove.

'Sixty royals,' the man said, 'half in advance.'

Richard took his time as he brought the goblet to his lips, took a sip of the dust-flecked wine, put the cup down and wiped his mouth. 'I don't take money on an unnamed man. – It is a man?' he added abruptly, somewhat spoiling the effect, but wanting to keep things clear. 'I don't do women.'

The man's lips quirked; he had heard the Montague story. 'Oh, yes, it is a man. It is a man of some importance, and I am not going to tell you any more without further indication of interest on your part. Are you at liberty tomorrow night?'

'I may be.'

'It would be advantageous. Do you know the Three Keys, on Lower Henley Street?' He did. 'Be there at 8. Take a table near the door, and wait.' The gentleman reached into his coat and withdrew a little silk purse that clinked when he set it on the table. 'This should cover expenses.' Richard didn't pick it up. It made a sound like silver.

The gentleman rose, spilling a little shower of copper on the table for the tally, and pulled on his scented glove. 'It took a long time to find you,' he said. 'Are you always so hard to get?'

'You can always leave a message for me here. Just don't make it worth people's while not to deliver it.'

'I see.' The man smiled wryly. 'Your friends are not to be bribed?'

The idea amused St Vier. 'Everyone can be bribed,' he said. 'You just have to know their price. And remember that they're all afraid of steel.'

'I will remember.' The man sketched him the slightest of bows. 'Good night, then.'

Richard did not bother to finish the wine. He considered taking it home for Alec, but it was bad enough to leave. Rosalie did keep a stock of decent vintage, but you had to know how to ask for it.

72

Ignoring the curious looks of his friends, he left the tavern and went home.

The eaves of the house were fanged with icicles. Marie's rooms were quiet, she must still be out. He looked up at his own rooms. The shutters were open, the windows dark. He let himself in by the courtyard stairs, mounting quietly to keep from disturbing Alec.

Despite his care, the floorboards creaked. It was an old house, built of heavy materials with a great care for solidness. At night they heard it settling on its foundations, like an old woman on her doorstep shifting into a comfortable position in the sun.

From the other room Alec called blearily, 'Richard?' The bedroom door was open; Alec usually left it that way when he went to bed alone. Richard could see him in the dark, a white figure propped against the heavily carven headboard. 'Are you going out again?'

'No.' Richard undressed quietly in the dark, laying out his clothes to air on the chest. Alec held the covers back for him – 'Hurry up, it's cold.' Between the linen sheets Alec's warmth had spread; Richard sank into it like a hot bath.

Alec lay on his back, his hands folded demurely behind his head. 'Well,' he said, 'that didn't take long. Don't tell me it was another wedding.'

'No, it's not. It's a real job, looks like it could be interesting. Move your elbow, you've got both pillows.'

'I know.' Richard could hear the satisfied smile in the dark. 'Don't go to sleep. Tell me about it.'

'There's not much to tell.' Abandoning the pillow, he moved his head into the crook of Alec's arm. 'They're playing hard-to-get. I have to show some more interest.'

'Who's *they*?

'You'll laugh.'

'Of course I'll laugh. I always do.' It was the voice, rich and arrogant and taut with breeding, that always undid him in the dark. He felt for Alec's lips with his fingers, and softly brushed over them.

'It's funny. I think he's a lord, all right, but he seems to be working for another house.'

'Working *with* them, more likely.' Alec's lips moved against his

73

fingers, the tip of his tongue touching them as he spoke. 'I bet you're right, it must be something big. The fate of the state is in your hands –' Alec seized the fingers that were touching him, and Richard's other hand as well, drawing them from what they were doing in a convulsive grip, feeling there for the old ragged scar on Richard's wrist. Richard guided his mouth to it. 'So how do you know', Alec murmured into his skin, 'that it's two houses?'

Gently Richard freed one hand, and began stroking the length of Alec's back. It pleased him to feel the taut body relax under his touch, straining langorously to be closer to his. 'He showed me a medallion with a device,' he said.

'Which you didn't recognise and were too embarrassed to ask about . . . ah, that feels nice.'

'As a matter of fact, I did recognise it. It was that swan woman's, the duchess.'

For all the tricks Alec played with his voice, he had never realised how easy it was for the swordsman to read his body. It stiffened suddenly, although Alec's voice rambled on, 'How delightful. Isn't it nice to know, Richard, that you're not the only one to have succumbed to the allure of the swan boat?'

'I haven't succumbed,' Richard said comfortably. Alec must have recognised the nobleman. 'Although I wouldn't mind a ride on that boat. But they have to name their mark first. If it's a good job, I'll succumb to the money.'

'You think so?'

'I think so.'

Alec breathed out in a feathery sigh as Richard sought out his pleasure, always careful not to startle him with anything sudden or unexpected. Sometimes finding it was like stalking prey, or coaxing a wild creature to his hand. Alec stopped speaking, let his eyelids fall thin over his bright eyes, and Richard felt his body coursing fluid like water, as though he held the power of a river in his arms.

When they kissed, Alec's arms tightened around his shoulders; then they began to move up and down Richard's body as if looking for something, trying to draw something out of the taut muscles of his back and thighs.

'Ah!' Alec said, contentment mingled with surprise; 'you're

so beautiful!'

Richard stroked him in answer; felt him shudder, felt the sharp fingers sink into his muscle. Richard teased himself, pulling Alec along with him deeper into no-return with the smoothness of skin against skin, the harshness of breath and bone. Alec was talking now, his voice rapid and full of air – not making any real sense, but a pleasure to have that light voice in his ear, gasped syllables stirring his hair, lips teasing his earlobe, breaking off occasionally to sink sharp teeth there....

'There is no one like you, they never told me there was anyone like you, I had no idea, it amazes me, Richard – Richard – if I had known – if I – '

Alec's hands struck against his throat, and for a moment Richard didn't realise that pain was pain. Then he pulled away, catching the fragile wrists before they could try again whatever mad notion Alec had of attacking him.

'What in hell do you think you're doing?' he demanded, harsher than he'd meant to because his breathing was not yet under control.

Alec's body was rigid, and his eyes were wide, glinting with their own unhealthy light. Richard ran one hand along his face to soothe his terror; but Alec wrenched his head away, gasping, 'No, don't!'

'Alec, am I hurting you? Has something happened? What is it?'

'Don't do that, Richard.' The long body was trembling with tension and desire. 'Don't ask me questions. It would be easy now, wouldn't it? You could ask me anything. And I'd tell you like this, I'd tell you ... now that you have me like this I'd tell you anything – anything – '

'No,' Richard said, gently gathering him into his arms. 'No you won't. You're not going to tell me anything. Because I'm not going to ask.' Alec shuddered; some of his hair worked loose across his face. 'There's nothing I want to know, Alec, I'm not going to ask you anything ...' He started to brush back the hair, soft and brown as an old forest stream; then he changed the gesture and lifted it to his lips. 'It's all right, Alec ... lovely Alec ...'

'But I'm not,' Alec said into his shoulder.

'I wish you wouldn't argue all the time.' Richard's fingers luxuriated in the high-bred bones. 'You are very lovely.'

'You are very . . . foolish. But then, so is Ferris.'

'Who's Ferris?'

'Your friend in the tavern. The Mysterious Mr One-Eye. Also the one and only Dragon Chancellor on the Council of Lords.' Alec carefully licked his eyelids, one at a time. 'He must be crazy to come down here. Or desperate.'

'Maybe he's just having fun.'

'Maybe.' Alec's long body twisted around him, adding weight to his statements. 'Somebody has to.'

'Aren't you?'

'Having fun? Is that the idea? I thought we were supposed to be providing material for poets and gossips.'

'I kicked them out.'

'You skewered them.'

'I skewered them. Roast Poet on a Spit.'

'Gossip Flambée . . . Richard . . . I think I can see what you mean about having fun.'

Richard intercepted the hand poised to tickle him, and turned the motion into quite another one.

'I'm glad. You are lovely.'

Chapter IX

There was, after all, no real reason for Richard not to go to the Three Keys the next night. If Ferris took it to mean that Richard accepted the job, that was his mistake. When he knew the name of the mark he would decide whether to take the job or not. He only hoped he would find out now, and not be offered more circumlocutions and little bags of silver.

Richard crossed the Bridge well armed. The poor who lived around the wharves tended to be desperate and unskilled, without pride or reputations to lose. They would jump a friend as readily as they would a stranger, and give no challenge first. The upper city people thought they were a spillover from Riverside. Riversiders sneered at them as graceless incompetents who knew enough not to cross the Bridge.

The Three Keys was admirably suited to mysterious rendez-vous. It was set in the middle of nowhere, between warehouses and countinghouses that were vacant at night, silent except for the occasional step of the Watch. People with nowhere else to go went there, seeking anonymity. Some sought oblivion: as Richard approached the tavern he saw the door open, a rectangle of dusky light, and a body come pitching out. The man lay snoring stertorously on the melted snow. St Vier stepped around him and went in.

He had no trouble finding a table near the door. It was a chilly night, with damp fog off the river, and the room's population was clustered at the other end, near the fire. They were mostly men, companionless, nameless. They noticed the newcomer; a few looked at him twice, trying to figure out where they'd seen him before, before going back to what they had been doing.

His contact aroused more interest. It was a woman who appeared poised in the doorway, cloaked and deeply hooded, her shadowed face turned toward the table. Richard wondered if it might not be the duchess herself this time, imitating Ferris's feat of bravado slumming. Whoever it was, she recognised him at once, crossing to his table with a firm stride. Before she could reach him, however, a large red-faced man sauntered up and barred her way, saying in a less than ingratiating growl, 'Hello, sweetheart.'

Richard started to come to her, then saw her flash of steel. 'Clear off.' She was holding a long knife to the drunken man's chest.

'Hey, sweetie,' the man coaxed, 'don't get upset.' And he wasn't as drunk as he looked, or else he'd once been a fighter, because suddenly the knife was on the floor. He had her wrist in his hand, and was pulling her in to him when she twisted away, shouting, 'Richard!'

St Vier came forward, his knife already out. The man saw and his grip slackened enough for the woman to pull away. 'Get out of here,' Richard told him, 'or find yourself a sword.'

A man in a leather apron came hurrying up from the back. 'Outside,' he said; 'you know the rules.'

The drunk rubbed his own arms, as though he had been hurt. 'Lenny', he said to the tapster, 'you know I don't mean anything. What the hell have I got to fight for?'

Richard gestured with his dagger: Back. The man backed off, and faded with Lenny into the rear of the tavern.

With Richard covering her, the woman picked up her own knife and replaced it in her sleeve. She sighed, and shook herself all over. 'I can't believe I did that,' she said.

'I can.' Richard returned to the table. 'You've got that hood in your eyes, how do you expect to see anything?'

She laughed and shook the hood away from her face. A mass of fox-coloured hair tumbled down with it. 'Buy me a drink?' she grinned.

'Just one?' he answered her smile. 'Not eight? Or have you lowered your limit these days?'

'I'm not testing it here: this place serves river water, mixed with raw spirits to cut the taste.'

'It seems' – he looked back at her assailant – 'to do the trick, whatever. Sit here, so I can keep an eye on him.'

'Yes.' She snuggled down, with her elbows on the table. 'They told me you'd look after me. I think you're *awfully* brave. Do you really *kill* people with that thing?'

'Oh, well, only for money.' He looked at her blandly. 'Is that modest enough for you?'

'It's an improvement. You're the best in the city now.'

'I was then, too.'

She laughed, exposing brown teeth in a strong pretty face. 'That's right. But word's trickled up to the ones who make the judgements. You know the channels as well as I do.'

Richard snorted. 'Channels! You kill enough people for them, they finally realise you know how to.'

Impatiently she said, 'Don't start up with that. You're important now, and you know it.' She looked stern, her grey eyes opaque and businesslike. 'How long do you think that you can keep on playing him out?'

'I don't mean to. I just need more information. Tell me about the other . . . lady.'

'What other lady – ' Her face began to flush and she dropped her eyes. 'I don't think that that has anything to do with this,' she said gruffly.

'I'm sorry.' Richard reverted to his polite, dealing-with-clients voice. 'I thought you were with another household.' He had learned a great deal from her discomfort – more than he'd really intended to.

'I'm his chambermaid.' She gave him a hard, defiant look across the table. 'One of them. We keep the place clean. It's a nice house.'

'You look well,' he said. Neither of them brought up the name of her master, she by instruction and Richard because he obviously was not supposed to know it. 'Life on the Hill agrees with you.'

She looked directly at him, cutting through the sociableness. 'It agrees with me better than jail. I thought it would be nothing, being whipped; it happened to everyone else, and they just laughed and went back to stealing.' She lowered her gaze to her hands, folded on the table. They were well shaped, the rounded fingers in pleasing proportion to the palm. Richard saw that their skin had coarsened from menial work. 'But that straw they give you *smells*, and they strip the dress off your back as though it

79

meant nothing, as though you're some actor putting on a good show for the crowd. I saw what it was like, and how it all came out – What happened to Annie?'

It took him a moment to remember who she meant. 'She got better. Then she lived like a queen for a while, before they caught her again.'

'And then?'

'She died that time.'

She nodded. 'I'd rather die in private. Or take a nice clean sword thrust, like you did to Jessa – '

'No,' Richard said. 'You wouldn't.'

But she'd left Riverside long ago, and she wasn't afraid any more. The past was a story told, a battle fought. 'I really thought you loved her, that one,' she said quietly.

'I don't know,' Richard said. 'It doesn't matter. Why did you get sent down here?'

She shrugged. 'He – I work for him. He had to send someone.'

'He knew you'd know me.'

She looked down at the table, deeply polished and carved from the flow of other people's hands. 'He just knows I'm from Riverside. You know the way they lump us all together up there.'

She had a right to her privacy. That her noble employer was also her lover seemed sure; how else would Ferris know that her past included St Vier? Nor would the lord be likely to entrust a common servant with such a delicate mission. For Katherine, it was a good thing: Ferris was not unattractive, and his favour could help her stay out of Riverside.

'And you,' she asked. 'Are you alone now?'

'No.' She let out a tiny sigh. He said suddenly, 'Katherine. Is he hurting you?'

She looked tired. She shook her head. 'No. I don't need anything. Just an answer to bring back.'

'You know I can't answer yet,' Richard said; 'you know the way I work.'

'You haven't heard all the question.' She was smiling strangely, looking at him out of the corners of her eyes. It was another woman's smile; he didn't know whose, but he knew what it meant.

Richard reached across the table, and covered her hand with his. 'It's an idea,' he said; 'but not yours or mine. Tell him you asked; tell him you plied me with drink, but I was more interested in money. It's actually true,' he added lightly. 'People get the strangest ideas about swordsmen.'

Calmly she repossessed her hand, saying dryly, 'I can't imagine where they got them.' Then, following his tone with its offer of safe trivialities, 'They miss you on the Hill, now you're not young and wild anymore. Who've you finally settled down with, Ginnie Vandall? No one seems to know.'

'It's a man,' he told her, 'a stranger called Alec.'

'What's he like?'

He seemed to consider the question carefully. 'Nothing else, really. He's not like anything I've ever seen.'

'What does he do?'

'He used to be a student, I'm pretty sure of that. Now he tries to get himself killed,' he told her with perfect seriousness.

'With what, falling rocks?'

'Falling rocks, knives, people . . . anything that's handy.'

She considered the prospect. 'A student. Can't fight.'

'Total incompetent. It keeps me busy.'

'Protecting him.'

She let the words hang in the air. She could hurt him now with a name – or try to. *Jessamyn.* A beautiful woman, an accomplished thief, rising con-artist . . . she and the young swordsman together had dazzled Riverside like twin stars. Jessamyn was not incompetent, she knew how to use a knife. Jessamyn had a temper, and one night she had made Richard lose his. There had been no protecting her.

Katherine could try to hurt him with it – but what if nothing happened? Richard had always been likeably sure of himself. But these last few years had cast a glamour over him. There were no more rough edges, no hesitations. He turned a smooth face to the world, making it see him as he saw himself. It pleased her to think that here was someone who didn't care what others thought of him, someone free from the daily struggle for dominance. And it chilled her to think that he believed it himself, that his heart was free of all that made human life impossibly painful. She found she did not want to try.

81

'Really,' Richard said, 'if you want another drink, you can have it.'

'I know,' she said. 'What's he trying to kill himself for?'

'I don't know. I haven't asked.'

'But you don't want him to do it.'

St Vier shrugged. 'It seems stupid.'

Slowly, not to alarm him, she took out her knife to look at it, and shook her head. 'When I came in here . . . I shouldn't have called for you. I should have stuck that idiot when I had the chance.'

'This isn't Riverside. You could have got into trouble.'

She kept shaking her bent head, hair dancing along her cheeks like snakes. 'No. I just couldn't do it. I missed my chance because I couldn't do it.'

'You were cumbered by the hood.' She looked up, smiling: 'cumbered' was a country word. But he met her eyes gravely: 'Anyway, it doesn't matter. You'll never have to go back to Riverside.'

She hoped it was true. 'Don't tell him I fumbled,' she said.

'I won't. I probably won't even see him again.'

'I don't know.' She pulled a flat, folded piece of paper out of her cloak. It was closed with blank gobs of sealing wax. 'It's what you think it is. Open it when you get home. He says he doesn't want to rush you: you've got a week to think about it. If you decide to go ahead with it, be at the Old Bell a week from tonight, same time. Someone will be there with the first half of your payment.'

'Half in advance . . . he really meant it. Generous. How will I know the messenger?'

'*He'll* know *you*. By the ring you're wearing.'

'What ring?'

This time she handed him a small doeskin pouch. Richard loosened the drawstrings, and glimpsed the heavy glow of an enormous ruby. Hastily he closed it, and tucked the pouch inside his shirt, along with the sealed paper.

'And if I don't go . . . ?'

She smiled at him, a ghost of her old street-smile. 'Wear it anyway. He didn't say anything about giving it back.'

The ring was worth almost as much as the job itself: double

payment, the gift that was a bribe. Lord Ferris was no idiot, nor was he heavy-handed.

Katherine stood up, wrapping herself in the cloak. She stood only shoulder-high to St Vier. He dropped one of Ferris's silver pieces on the table for the tally. When she queried with her eyebrows he explained, 'It's the smallest he gave me. Maybe he thinks I only drink rare wines.'

'Maybe he thought you'd get change for it,' she replied. 'Get the change, Richard, or there'll be talk.'

He got the change, in brass, and pocketed it. Then he stood very close to her and handed over the silver pouch. '"For expenses" was what he told me. I wouldn't want to be guilty of a cheap evening.' Mutely she took what he offered. She could buy a lot with that money; and if he didn't need it, so much the better for him.

As they walked out, the rows of men muttered flatly, 'Good night, sweetheart. Take care of yourself, darling.'

They left the tavern. Over their heads the three iron keys, with a few flecks of gold still clinging to them, jangled in the wind. They turned up Lower Henley Street, making for the Stooping Eagle Tavern, where one of Ferris's footmen, discreetly attired in buff, waited to escort her back to the Hill.

It was late when Richard came in, but Alec was still up, reading by the light of a candle. Alec looked up out of the circle of light at him, blinking at the darkness across the room.

'Hello, Richard.'

'Hello,' Richard said amiably. 'I'm back.'

Slowly St Vier unbuckled his sword. He removed his knives gingerly, as though they were infants, or creatures who might bite, and placed them on the mantel.

'I see you're back,' Alec said. 'You've missed all the excitement. Marie got into a fight with one of her clients. She chased him three times around the courtyard, throwing socks and using language. He tried to hide behind the well. I threw an onion down at him. I missed, of course, but it scared him. Maybe he thought it was you. Anyway, he finally went away, and then the cats started yowling up on the roof and I didn't have anything left to throw at *them*. Have you?'

'No. I don't think so. I think they've gone away,' said Richard, who hadn't heard anything.

'I think we should get a cat of our own. We could train it to fight. It could chase them away. After all, there's no point in sending *you* up on the roof.'

'Why not?' Richard asked, going over to the window. He looked up. 'I could get up there. Easy.' He hoisted himself onto the sill.

'It would be much easier', Alec said, 'to get a cat. We could save its life – pull a thorn out of its paw or something – and it would be forever grateful.'

Richard swung open the window and leaned out, holding on with one hand. 'You are making me giddy,' said Alec, 'and anyway, all the cats are gone. You said so yourself.'

'I'm not going to fall. But it isn't far. You could jump, and probably not break anything, if you had to. Right down to the courtyard.'

'Marie would have a fit. You look like an idiot standing in that window. You look like you're expecting to fly away.'

Richard laughed, and jumped back down into the room. He landed badly and staggered upright. 'There!' he exclaimed. 'That's what comes of listening to you.'

'I didn't tell you to jump out of the window.'

'You're always telling me to get drunk. Well, now I've done it, and I don't like it.' He sat down hard on their only chair, assuming the pose of one who didn't intend to get up for a long time.

'Drunk on what?' Alec asked; 'the usual blood?'

'No, brandywine. Really horrible brandy. I knew I didn't like getting drunk, and now I can remember why. I keep having to remember where my feet are. I really don't like it at all. I don't see how you can stand it so often.'

'Well, I never care where my feet are. Don't tell me you let Ferris feed you horrible brandy!'

'No, I did it myself. All by myself. I thought I might like it. You're always saying I'd like it. Well, I don't like it. You were wrong.'

'You've said that', Alec said, 'twice. If you think I'm going to apologise because you can't keep track of your own feet, you're mistaken. Let's go out. I'll teach you to dice.'

'I'm drunk, not insane. I'm going to bed.'

Alec stretched on his chaise longue like a cat, one thumb still in his book. 'Richard, *why* did you get drunk? Wasn't Ferris there?'

'Of course he wasn't there. Someone else was there.'

'Were they horrible to you? Are you going to kill them?'

'No, and no. God, you're bloodthirsty. I'm not going to kill anybody. I'm going to sleep. Get me anything you want for breakfast, just not fish.'

Somehow he must have got himself undressed and into bed, because suddenly there was a hand gripping his shoulder and Alec's voice saying over and over, 'Richard, Richard, wake up.' He noted crossly how slow his reaction was as he groaned and turned over, saying in a thick voice unlike his own, 'What is it?'

He hadn't closed the shutters; a dim bar of silvery moonlight fell across the bed, illuminating Alec's hand tense on the coverlet, crushing Lord Ferris's paper.

'You were snoring,' Alec drawled ingenuously; but the whiteness of his knuckles on the paper betrayed him.

'Well, I've stopped.' Richard didn't bother to argue. 'What do you think of Ferris's message?'

'I think his spelling stinks.' With the weight of the seals for ballast, Alec flipped the paper open.

There was no writing on it; only a drawing of a phoenix rising from the flames over a series of heraldic bends.

'It's a coat of arms,' Alec said grimly. 'Do you know whose?'

'Of course. I've seen it all over the city. On his banners, and carriages, and things.'

'It's Basil Halliday,' Alec said portentously, as though he hadn't answered.

'It's Basil Halliday,' Richard agreed. 'You're stealing all the blankets, and you haven't even got into bed yet.'

Somewhat frantically, Alec tucked the covers around him, and began to pace the room. 'This *is* the man Ferris wants you to kill?'

'Ferris or that duchess does. I haven't quite figured them out yet. He must be protecting her.'

'He can't be running errands for her. A man of his rank would no more do that than polish his own boots. Could the drawing mean that Halliday's another patron?'

'No. This is the usual way the smart ones announce a mark. I should burn that paper. Remind me in the morning.'

'Don't go to sleep,' Alec ordered.

'I don't think I . . .' His jaw cracked in a yawn. But he forced his eyes to stay open. 'What's the matter?' he asked. 'I've told you everything I know. Can you tell me any more? Is there something I should know?'

It was the wrong thing to say. Alec's face closed like a trap door. 'Know?' he repeated, honey and steel. 'I know enough to stay out of their way when they're playing these games. You think you're above it all, Richard – but they'll chew you up, and then you won't much care whether they swallow you or spit you out.'

Richard wanted to explain that that didn't happen to swordsmen: they took their pay for whatever the job was and went home, leaving the nobles to argue the results out amongst themselves. For the first time he seriously wondered whether Alec knew the Hill at all, not to know that. But all he said was, 'I'll be fine – if I take the job at all. I've got time to say no. But the duchess will pay for it, and Ferris will keep me out of trouble. You'll see. Maybe they'll send us up to Tremontaine until it blows over – live in a nice cottage by a stream, go fishing, keep bees . . . how'd you like to go to the country for a while?'

'I detest the country,' Alec said icily. 'Go back to sleep.'

St Vier closed his eyes, and finally it was dark enough. 'All right. But only because I'm feeling so agreeable. It's too bad. I'm going to feel awful in the morning.'

'Sleep in. You always feel splendid in the afternoon.'

And that is just what he did.

Chapter X

It was too soon, Lord Ferris was thinking as he mounted the street to the Halliday townhouse; too soon for Basil Halliday to know what the game was.

Katherine's errand was freshly executed. In a week, if all went well, Ferris would have the swordsman's answer, and plans for the Crescent Chancellor's mortal challenge could begin to go forward. Even if Katherine had contrived a look at the closely sealed paper she carried, Ferris was certain of her movements for the last day; and he thought she was not false to him. St Vier was no agent of Halliday's either; of that Ferris had made sure.

There was no telling what today's invitation from Lord Halliday to come and 'talk privately' meant. It was an informal note in Halliday's own hand; perhaps his secretary did not even know of it. It put Ferris on his guard, but the Dragon Chancellor of the Inner Council could not ignore a summons from its Crescent, however mysterious – and perhaps it was only a tricky piece of Council business that Halliday wanted to discuss with him before anyone else heard about it. The informal note might be just that: Halliday's secretaries had been heard to complain that their master's informalities drove them to distraction. Ferris might have to wait behind whoever else had the official appointment at this hour.

The Halliday townhouse stood alone at the top of a steep street; inconvenient, but possessed of a magnificent view. It was a house without a gate: all its gardens were at the back, overlooking the river. Ferris saw a couple of well-built men lingering about the edges of the property. It was not too soon, it seemed, for the Crescent Chancellor to have begun to worry about the danger the election put him in. He was going to be well guarded from now on. It eased Ferris's mind a little: the defence was sufficiently vague to imply that Halliday knew of no specific plan. He was well guarded. St Vier was going to have to be clever. But then, St Vier's reputation said he was. He had just better not be too clever to take the job.

Perhaps, Ferris thought, he should have timed things more tightly, given the swordsman less time to think the offer over. But Ferris had acted on an impression of St Vier at the Riverside Tavern: the swordsman had the self-respect of an artist, the vanity of a lover. Like a lover, he must be wooed; like an artist he must be flattered. Giving him time to think things over was an act of trust and respect that Ferris hoped would clinch the deal. It also wouldn't hurt for St Vier to have made up his mind long before the next set rendezvous, so that he came to it eager, straining at the bit.

Ferris found Basil Halliday in his study, surrounded by papers and half-empty cups of chocolate. Halliday's hair was mussed; he must have been running his fingers through it. There was an inkstain on his forehead to prove it. His smile on seeing Ferris was all the more charming for its preoccupation. Ferris relaxed a shade, and began to wonder what he was expected to be charmed into this time.

'What', Lord Halliday said to Ferris without preamble, 'do you think friend Karleigh is up to now?'

'The duke?' Ferris answered. 'Sulking out on his estates, I should imagine. Where he should be, after you had St Vier beat his swordsman at Horn's.'

'I? I didn't hire him. I know that's what they're saying, but that duel was the first I knew of any challenge.'

'It's what Horn's saying.' That answered that question. Ferris did not like the implications. Who else but Halliday had the power to frighten Karleigh through a purely formal duel into retreating into the country at this time of year? Someone strong and secret, who wanted no impediment to the Crescent Chancellor's re-election . . . or else Halliday was capable of a dirtier game than he pretended. 'I should know not to listen to Horn's opinions.'

'You're young,' Halliday said cheerily; 'it will pass.' And it was too bad if it hadn't been Halliday's swordsman: Ferris liked the ironic symmetry of Halliday's chasing Karleigh away, since it would make it easier to fix suspicion on Karleigh if he were out of town.

'So Karleigh is trying to unseat you in absentia, is he?' Ferris helped himself to some lukewarm chocolate.

'My lord duke has gone and put up the money for Blackwell's theatre to revive *The King's End* next month – assuming it's stopped snowing by then.'

'Oh, it will. It always does. They'll open right on time. You know, Basil, *The King's End* is a really awful play.'

'Yes.' Halliday grimaced. 'I remember it well. It's got a lot of stirring speeches against monarchic tyranny in it: "Rule by one man is not rule but rape," that sort of thing. Mary and I will have to sit somewhere obvious and applaud loudly.'

Ferris stroked the chair arm. 'You could close them down, you know. Blackwell's theatre is a thieves' den and a public health hazard.'

The older man's eyebrows lifted. 'Oh, Tony. And I thought you *liked* the theatre. You sound like Karleigh – that's just the tyrannic gesture he's trying to goad me into making. But he gauges everyone else's temper by his own. I won't close the theatre – especially because I hear they'll also be reviving one of the old blood-and-revenge tragedies, which I adore. They manage to be rigidly moral, without rubbing your nose in it – unlike *The King's End*, which grinds its point home three times in the first speech. I wonder which actor looks enough like me to play the deposed king?'

'None, I expect; they're all undernourished.' Ferris adjusted his eyepatch. He must remember not to be so surprised when Halliday showed himself able to see through the machinations of others. And he must resist pushing too hard right now: if it were possible to destroy the Crescent Chancellor through giving him bad advice, Ferris would have contrived to do so long before this, and the forthcoming scene with St Vier would be unnecessary. 'I must say you're taking it all pretty calmly. If the city riff-raff get turned against you by Karleigh's second-hand agitation, it won't help your re-election in Council any.'

'Oh, Mary gets all the temper,' her husband smiled; 'you get the carefully thought-out plan.'

'You have a plan.' Ferris walked to the other end of the room, letting amusement mask his relief. Far from uncovering the plot against him Halliday was about to take him further into his counsels. Well, why not? He had never given the Crescent cause to doubt him. Oh, he disagreed with him in Council from time to time, as a respected opponent. But their true policies lay so far apart that there was no point in even trying to diminish Halliday by orthodox means.

Halliday's policies were built on an uneasy fusion of city and country. He seemed to believe that the nobles no longer provided the link between the two that their control of the land had given them for so many years; that as the city grew more prosperous independent of them, they would lose their influence there, and meanwhile were also losing the land through inattention. Admittedly, the Crescent Chancellor's rapprochements with the Citizens' Council and his popularity with the general populace, were doing some good; but to Ferris it was a hazy plan for an even hazier future. If Halliday didn't love the city so much, he would have gone back to the country long ago and made a model of his own estates. He was not an inefficient administrator; and Ferris had to admire the way he achieved his ends by disguising them in concepts the Council could accept; but it was all too clear that he was, in the end, a dreamer – and that sooner or later his prized innovations would catch up with him and lose him the support of the nobility. Karleigh, the arch-conservative, had already sniffed out the tone, if not the content, of Halliday's programme. The Crescent was dangerously overreaching himself by pressing the election this spring; but then, circumstances left him small choice. And if he won, the support would cement his position, possibly for life. If he lost, his successors might make such an administrative muddle that he could still return in glory.

As for his plan . . . Ferris decided to assume the best. 'You honour me with your confidence, my lord.'

Halliday smiled. 'I have my reasons. *Despite* the fact that you do not make up one of my faction of vocal supporters.'

'But neither do I stand up for Karleigh. My reasons for that are evident to everyone with eyes to see it. My lord duke is nothing but a pompous meddler with a touching faith in his own rhetoric.'

'Oh, no,' Halliday said in smooth surprise. 'You mistake him.

The Duke of Karleigh is a hero, the last man of integrity with due regard for Council law. Many people have said so, not least himself. We have here a wealthy, and thus powerful man who now proposes to exercise that power. He gave some marvellous dinners before he found it necessary to leave for the country – at least, I hear they were excellent; I was not invited, though you may have been. Hospitality may obscure pomposity. And his rhetoric has already divided a formerly unified Council. We had an interest, a mutual purpose we had not known in years. Now he is planning to disband it, so that his fantasies of the golden days of Lordly Rule may be given full scope to take us all on the long run off a short dock!'

'You haven't considered', said Ferris gently, 'that, technically, he is in the right? The Crescent was a courtesy title; it was never meant to be what you've made of it.'

Halliday turned a bleak eye on him. 'Wasn't it? Then why do things work better when someone takes central authority, bearing the brunt of complaints by election, rather than by fashionable whimsey? When someone can formally represent us to the Citizens' Council? I have no more power than people and necessity give me. Even Karleigh cannot say I have broken a single procedural rule. Hear me out, Ferris – and then question me. It's not a question I want to see buried and disposed of. But behold Karleigh's vision: where is his candidate to replace me?' Halliday put his chocolate cup down with a little more force than he'd intended. 'He hasn't got one. He doesn't care what happens to the Council once he's pulled me down.'

'He wants the Crescent for himself, of course,' Ferris said. 'Several of his forebears held it, back when it meant giving good parties and making sure no one spoke out of turn in meetings. All the dukes are a little crazy about their hereditary rights.'

'Which is why, I suppose, he is working so hard to deny me my elective ones! Holding the Crescent will not suddenly bestow greatness on that idiot,' Basil Halliday said with rancour. 'I should think even *he* would know that by now. His ideas are popular, but *he* isn't. He's quarrelled with half the Council over their lands, and with the other half over their wives.'

'But not with me,' Ferris said quietly.

'Not with you. Not yet.' Halliday leaned back in his chair. 'Tell me, Tony; what would happen if I set up a puppet to hold the Crescent in my place until I became eligible for the position again?'

'Almost anything. Your man might become too impressed with his own power, and refuse to listen to you. He might try to follow your suggestions and simply be too weak to hold the Council together as you do.' And, Ferris was thinking, he would have to be a weakling in the first place even to consider the position.

'Exactly,' said Halliday. 'A weak man couldn't do it, and a strong man wouldn't want to.' Ferris smiled a sour smile at Halliday's insight. 'But if the measure to prolong my term is voted down,' the Crescent continued, 'I shall have to support someone after me. I've given it a lot of thought. I expect you have, too.'

Under Halliday's clear gaze, Ferris felt horribly exposed. He thought of the guards outside, and himself in Halliday's house, alone and vulnerable to mortal challenge. But that was not the drift of Halliday's message. Unlike Ferris and the Duchess Tremontaine, Basil Halliday was not given to hiding double meanings behind his words.

Ferris said, 'It's all very well for this once. But when I became eligible for re-election, you might not find me so easy to defeat.'

'But', Halliday grinned, 'it would put me on the same side as Karleigh in this one, if I'm voted down. He'll hate that.'

'What a motive!'

'Then you're willing?'

'For the Crescent? I'd be lying if I said I wasn't. To take what you've made of it, to guide a strong Council under the cloak of your support . . . ' He told Halliday what he wanted to hear. It wasn't hard to do. But even this surprising act of visionary generosity made him want to laugh. Halliday's eyes were so fixed on the future, he couldn't see what was right in front of him!

'But how is any of this going to solve your problems with Karleigh? I should think you'd want to put your energies into seeing that there's no *need* to support my election!'

Basil Halliday looked surprised. 'It's simple. Go and talk to Karleigh.'

For once, Ferris was utterly at a loss. 'My lord,' he said. 'That would be fatal. Karleigh can't keep his mouth shut, and I would lose all your supporters in a stroke.'

Halliday suppressed an impatient gesture. 'Ferris... I've watched your careful stratagems to remain neutral in Council. It drives people crazy – they come to me complaining that they can't tell which side you're on. Do you think I don't know how hard it is to build that base? I want to use it, not tear it down. Speak to Karleigh on your own behalf. Say what you need to say. You're not my man; I can't send you to plead my cause, especially not now that I've offered you such a plum if I lose. Just go and confuse him a little – make the issues less clear cut – I know you can do that, Tony.' His smiling face hardened. 'But mark this: if you play me false, I'll know it. And I'll see that there's no cloak for you to step into.'

Ferris said, 'You don't like duelling, do you?' Halliday shook his head. 'You don't approve of the use of swordsmen in general; perhaps because you've had to preside over the outcomes of too many Duels of Honour. It can make one jaded. But there is a duel on between you and Karleigh. You think adding me will make it a new form of sport?'

'Something like that.' The Crescent Chancellor gave an unwilling smile. 'Karleigh is so old-fashioned.'

'And I am, at heart, a sportsman. But a cautious one. When did you want me to see Karleigh?'

'As soon as you can conveniently make the trip.'

'Ah,' said Ferris; 'that won't be for another week. I have some affairs in hand here that need tying up. But then... then, we shall see. It may well be convenient then.'

Chapter XI

Both Michael Godwin and Lord Horn were to remember the duchess's barge party, but for different reasons. Michael had already put the Horn incident out of his mind as one more unpleasantness in a evening rife with them. To be perfectly correct, he should have sent Horn a formal apology; but he was young, and arrogant, and very much preoccupied with banishing Diane from his mind. It required him, in the days that followed, to plunge into a feverish round of purportedly pleasurable activities: running and riding races, exchanging large sums on their outcomes; going to parties with people one's mother wouldn't know about, and being fitted for clothes to wear to them. It was clear that the duchess didn't want him. She was merely an accomplished flirt. If she were carrying on with Ferris, that was her affair; on reflection Michael realised that to call her reputation to question publicly would only damage his own. There were plenty of other distinguished beauties to be had with far less trouble. He continued to see Bertram Rossillion, and took to flirting with Helena Nevilleson until her brother told him to stop. He had begun the flirtation to annoy the treacherous Olivia, Bertram's wife; by the time Chris caught up with him it had done its work: Lady Olivia was as formal and distant as if she had never stumbled against Michael's coat to whisper to him the time to come to her room. Michael was glad of her distance; when he remembered how he had first encountered Lord Horn, he blamed her for that, too.

It was surprising, with all his other activities, that Michael found time to continue with his sword-fighting lessons. But in fact he found that only in Applethorpe's studio was he entirely free of Diane's image. He was ripe to fall on the day when the Master pushed him.

Standing in front of a group of sweating men, all paired off and glaring at each other after a workout of stroke and counterstroke, Applethorpe had said mildly, 'You all want to be the best. Forget about it. The best already exist, and you'll never touch them. Just be good enough to do what you have to do.'

The young men had shaken their muscles out and laughed, some at the Master's tendency to lecture, others in shamefaced recognition of their own ambition. Lord Michael stared at him, still panting from the exercise. He felt the blood pounding in his head. Of course he was good enough to do what he had to do. He always had been. For the first time he realised that perhaps not everyone was; that some never would be.

After the lesson, his mouth dry, he went up to the Master and asked, 'What did you mean by that, *the best*?'

Applethorpe held out his arm, and one of his assistants removed his glove for him. He said to Michael, 'The true swordsmen, of course. Men who must earn their living fighting to the death – and who must win every time. There aren't very many of them, of course; most last only a season or two before they die, or retreat into a cosy guard post on the Hill, or take to easier jobs.'

'Where do they come from?'

The master shrugged both shoulders. 'You mean, where did they study? Who knows? I had a teacher; crazy old man, drunk half the time, brilliant when he could see straight. If you need to learn, you do it.' He waved his hand as though swatting away gnats. 'It's not the sort of thing you come *here* to do. It takes more than two hours a week.' The point struck home.

Soon Michael's friends were making up stories to account for his disappearances: he had a low-bred lover on the other side of town; he had discovered a genius tailor living in some garret. . . . someone who saw him near the stables said it was a horse he was training for the spring races. But nothing could be substantiated. Michael was careful. He went to Applethorpe's every day to drill, and took a private lesson weekly.

Lord Horn's reaction to the events of the fireworks night was to send a letter to Richard St Vier in Riverside. Alec brought it home from Rosalie's on the day after Richard's meeting with Katherine at the Three Keys. Richard had just got up. He didn't have a headache and he didn't feel sick, but he was moving cautiously in case something should begin. He was terribly thirsty, and was drinking well-water.

Alec waved a large parchment at him. 'Letter. For you. It's been at Rosalie's since yesterday. You get more letters than a first-year debutante.'

'Let me look at it.' Richard examined the large crest that sealed the paper. 'Oh, no!' He laughed, recognising it from the gates of the winter ball. 'It's from Lord Horn.'

'I know,' Alec said demurely. When Richard shook the paper it fell open, and he saw that Alec had already slit the wax away from the paper in one clean piece. 'Not bad,' he approved; 'but didn't they teach you how to seal it up again?'

'I generally don't bother,' he answered blithely.

'Well, what does it say?' Richard asked. 'Is he trying to hire me, or does he want to take me to court for messing up his shrubberies?'

'I haven't read it yet. I just wanted to know who it was from. The handwriting is really bad – I bet it's his own. No secretary writes like that.'

'Clever Horn,' Richard observed sarcastically. 'Doesn't want his secretary to know he's trying to hire me, but lets everybody in Riverside see his crest. What does it say?' he asked again; but Alec was laughing too hard to tell him.

'Take a deep breath,' Richard advised. 'I can't understand a word you're saying.'

'It's the spelling!' Alec chortled helplessly. 'Pompous idiot! He thinks – he wants – '

'I am going to put snow down your back,' Richard said. 'It's a sure cure for hysterics.'

Alec read aloud, '"As you may be no doubt aware, my servant Master de Maris encountered grave misfortune in his profession last month – " He means you killed him. *Grave misfortune* – I wonder if Horn knows about puns?'

'What is he after, an apology? If he wants a new house swordsman, tell him my rates are 20 – no, make it 30 a day. An hour.'

'No, wait, it's not that. "– Happily, this may be turned to your advantage, for I am prepared to offer you employment of the sort

96

which I believe you usually engage in, and will no doubt find acceptable."'

'No doubt.' Richard flipped a knife at the ceiling. 'You're right. He's an idiot. Tell him no.'

'Oh, come on, Richard,' Alec said cheerfully. 'Just because he's an idiot doesn't mean his money's no good.'

'You'd be surprised,' St Vier said, retrieving the knife in one high jump. 'I don't like working for stupid people. They can't be trusted. And he doesn't know much, or he'd never have hired de Maris.'

'They don't care who they hire. It's only fashion.'

'I know,' he answered imperturbably. 'Who does he want me to kill?'

'*Challenge*. Please. We are gentlemen here, even those who cannot spell. Or read.' Alec held the paper at arm's length, squinting at the writing. '"There is a matter of honour which has touched my honour – " No, that's crossed out – "which has touched my spirit, wounding it with a mighty g-gash that may only be . . . "'

'Steady, Alec.'

'" . . . only be healed by the sword! The matter of the injury need not concern you. I am prepared to pay you as much as 40 royals as a hiring fee. In return for which sum you will act as my surrogate by means lawful and honourable in the challenge to the death of Lord Michael Godwin of Amberleigh."'

'Who's that?'

'Who cares? You can off him and be home in time for supper with 40 lawful and honourable royals under your belt.'

'Can he fight?'

'"All they know how to do with their swords is poke lapdogs." I believe I quote you directly. I don't suppose this Godwin rises above the other doggie-prodders.'

'Then Hugo can kill him.'

'Ah.' Alec tapped the letter against his palm. 'Shall I tell Lord Horn that?'

'Don't tell Lord Horn anything,' Richard said bluntly. He picked up an iron shot and flexed his wrist against it. 'I don't do business by letter. If he had any brains he would have found that out first.'

'Richard . . .' Alec was swinging his heel over the arm of the chaise longue with an irresponsible air. 'How much do you suppose it would be worth to Lord Michael to find out that Horn is trying to kill him?'

Richard tried to see his face, but it was hidden by shadow. He asked, 'Why? Have you been losing at dice again?'

'No.'

The swordsman stood poised on the balls of his feet, the shot balanced between his two hands. 'You do understand', he said carefully, 'that my reputation rests on people knowing I will keep their secrets.'

'Oh, I understand,' Alec said blithely. 'But it was stupid of Horn to put it in writing, wasn't it?'

'Very. It's why I'm more interested in working with Ferris and his duchess' – he swung the weight in the air – 'than with Horn. Burn that letter now, will you?'

When Michael wasn't dreaming of the duchess's chilly eyes, he was thinking of ways to disengage a man coming at him in perfect form. They knew him at the school, now. A couple of the other serious students, servants training to be guards, wanted him to come drinking with them after, and he was running out of excuses. It wasn't that he disdained their company; in fact, he liked them for being serious about the same thing that he was; but while he was confident of being taken for a commoner through the rigour of lessons, he wasn't sure he could keep it up socially. He was learning to speak more quickly in their company – and had, in fact, recently alarmed his manservant by rapping out the demand that his boots be cleaned 'any which way'. Michael amused himself around the city by singling out shops he could pretend he worked in; by handling precious stones and imagining he spent his days selecting them for clients instead of for himself . . . but it never could feel real to him.

Michael was not entirely surprised when the Master drew him aside after his lesson to speak with him. He had been asking for an additional weekly lesson, but so far Applethorpe had only nodded absently and said that he would see. Now Michael offered to take him out and buy him some dinner so they could discuss it in comfort.

'No,' said the Master, looking off at a tall window at the end of the studio. 'I think we can talk in here.'

He led the way into a small room originally designed for the old stable's tack. Now it was cluttered with gloves, throwing-knives, pieces of canvas and other detritus of the academy. They sat down on a couple of targets that gently oozed stuffing.

Applethorpe rubbed his chin with his fist. Then he looked at Michael. 'You want to be a swordsman,' he said.

'Umm,' said Michael – a habit he was supposed to have had trained out of him at an early age. There was no question what the Master was talking about: men who earn their living fighting to the death – and who must win every time.

'You could do it,' said Vincent Applethorpe.

A series of inadequate responses flashed through Michael's head: *Oh, really? . . . What makes you say that? . . . May I ask if you're serious? . . .* He realised he was blinking like a fish. 'Oh,' he said. 'You think?'

Swordsmen were not expected to be masters of drawingroom conversation. Applethorpe answered as though he were making perfect sense, 'I think you're suited. And I know you're interested. You should begin at once.'

'I should . . . ' Michael repeated numbly.

The Master began speaking with the terse excitement he used in the thick of a good lesson: 'Of course it's a bit late for you – How old are you, 19? 20?' He was older than that, but the easy life of a city noble had spared his youth. 'You have the feel, though, the movement, that's what's important now,' Applethorpe rushed on without waiting for him to answer. 'If you're willing to work, you'll have the skills as well, and then you'll be a match for any of them!'

Michael managed, finally, to come up with a complete sentence. 'Does it work that way? I thought it took years.'

'Of course it does. But some of it you've already got. You had the stance on your first lesson, many of them take months just on that. Still, you'll have to work, every day, for hours on end if you want to be able to take on the others and stand a chance to live. But if you'll take it seriously, if you'll let me teach you, I can give that to you.'

Michael stared at him. The Master's one hand was clenched on

99

his knee. Michael was arrested by the sight of the swordsman's body, perfectly poised, tensed for an answer. He thought sadly, Now I have to tell him. I've come to the end of this particular game; I have to tell him who I am. I can't possibly be a swordsman.

Applethorpe studied his face. The tension left the Master, his enthusiasm snuffed out like a candlewick. 'Of course, this may not be important to you.'

It came to Michael then that he was a fool to think that Applethorpe hadn't known all along who he was.

'Master Applethorpe,' he said, 'I'm honoured. Stunned, but honoured.'

'Good,' said the Master with his customary mildness. 'Then let us begin.'

Chapter XII

St Vier's answer, when Lord Horn received it, was soon reduced to a crumpled rag on the floor. In an eccentric handwriting distinguished by strong vertical strokes, it read:

> Thank you for your kind offers. We have enjoyed reading them even more than you intended. Unfortunately, the job in question does not really suit our current needs. We wish you luck with it elsewhere. (Your future letters will be returned unopened.)

It was signed, 'The St Vier Duelling Corporation, serving Riverside and Gentry of Distinction.'

It was enough to make him stop thinking about Michael Godwin for a while. Wrapped in mute fury, Lord Horn went off to salve his pride with the prestigious company of the Lords Halliday, Montague, and other notable gentlemen at a dinner party given by the Dragon Chancellor.

Tomorrow night, Ferris would have his answer. He had given St Vier enough time to think the job through; enough time to become eager. Once the swordsman took the advance payment he was committed to the venture, and would wait until he was instructed to strike. Once St Vier was committed, Ferris was going to let him wait, as close as he could come to the Council election. It gave Ferris time to fan the Karleigh/Halliday feud. It gave St Vier time to learn Halliday's routines. There must be no obstacle to the formal challenge being met and Halliday heroically dispatched: Ferris planned to inherit a martyr's crown. By then some of Halliday's supporters might have learned of his favouring Ferris, so Ferris could take the Crescent before suspicion lit on him. Once he had it, suspicion would light where he willed it to.

Anticipation heightened Ferris's senses, sharpening his appetite for all activities the way that when he was a child the most mundane events of the days before New Year's and its presents had been inexplicably thrilling: the ice breaking on the surface of the washbasin was like a promised revelation; the untying of a shirt savoured of unwrapping packages; and every night's blowing out the candle brought the glad day one flame closer. Lord Ferris found some of the same savour in being Dragon Chancellor: something was always about to happen, and every action was invested with meaning. As he sat now at the head of his table, surrounded by wealthy and powerful men and the remains of the dinner they had shared, he cracked a nut between his strong white fingers and smiled to feel the thrill it undeniably gave him.

One by one they departed, for bed, for other engagements, until all that remained were the Lords Halliday and Horn. Ferris knew that Halliday was hoping to talk to him after the last of his guests had gone; what Horn wanted only Horn knew. Perhaps he simply had nowhere else to go, and didn't want to return to his empty house.

The ornate dining room seemed to swallow the three men; even rank cannot stand up to architecture. Lord Ferris suggested that they adjourn to a sitting room to drink hot punch. Ferris was a bachelor, at 32 considered one of the prize catches of the city. The sitting room of his townhouse remained as his mother had decorated it when she first came to the city as a bride, in the bulky, comfortable furniture and deep colours of the previous generation. Although he himself preferred it, Lord Horn had banished the best of his old pieces to his country house, where style mattered less.

A young woman came in to tend to the fire. Ferris smiled when he saw her, inclining his head so that he could encompass all her movements with his one eye. She was broad-hipped, big-breasted, and handled the iron tools deftly; but something about her suggested malnourishment – maybe only her small height, or the tight way she clutched her plain skirts back from the fire. As she curtsied to her master at the door Ferris said, in his lovely speaker's voice that swayed the Council of Lords, 'Katherine, stay. We are all a little drunk; we need someone sober to look after the fire.'

102

Her eyes darted nervously to the other two lords and back to him. 'I'll get my mending,' she said finally.

But Lord Ferris raised one elegant hand. 'Indeed you will not,' he drawled affably. 'You will sit there – there, under the mirror, where the light catches your hair, and I will send for John to bring you a glass of sherry. Unless you'd prefer something else?'

'Sherry will be nice,' she said, settling into the chair he had indicated, across the room from the gentlemen; 'thank you.'

Her voice was flat, the vowels clipped and curt. Lower city. But she moved with assurance, a certain flair to the wrist and the set of the head. It didn't occur to either of the visitors to identify Riverside haughtiness; but then, neither of them had ever been there. They were surprised to see Ferris behaving this way – he must be drunker than he appeared. Bringing a mistress into a bachelor gathering was not unheard-of; but it was unlike Ferris, and inappropriate for the company. If she were only a servant, it was unkind to impose their society on her.

Ferris smiled disarmingly at his guests, inviting them to excuse his whimsey. 'A touch of feminine beauty', he explained, 'is essential to the after-dinner drawing room.'

'If we speak of feminine beauty,' Lord Horn put in expertly, 'it is a shame that Lady Halliday is not with us.'

But Lord Halliday resisted being drawn into the conversation. He had had reports of the Helmsleigh weavers that disturbed him; nothing that wouldn't keep until morning, but he would sleep easier knowing that Ferris was worrying about it too. So he kept quiet, in the hope that Horn would be content with centre stage long enough to talk himself out and leave. The woman in the chair was now ignored: a momentary whim of Ferris's, that he seemed to have forgotten about.

Ferris was enjoying himself immensely. Everyone in the room was now confused except for him. He always took pleasure in Horn's company, for what he knew were ignoble reasons: Horn's dullness, his relentless second-rate innuendo reinforced Ferris's estimation of his own social cleverness and political subtlety. He could run conversational rings around Horn, make him jump through hoops, bat him across the floor like a cat with its food. It was a private pleasure: the trick was not to let Horn know he was doing it.

Katherine folded her hands in her lap. She knew that Ferris was not so drunk as he was pretending to be. It was nice to sit down and rest, but she was quietly bored, watching the nobles showing off for each other. Lord Horn and her master were avidly discussing swordsmen, although they didn't seem to know much about the subject.

'Bah,' Horn was saying. 'They have no power. They do what you pay them to, and that's all.'

'But,' said the younger man, 'should they choose not to accept your commission . . . ?'

'Mine?' Horn said sharply; but Ferris's one-eyed countenance was as benign as it could be. He was looking at the girl, smiling.

'Oh, anyone's,' Ferris answered. 'A figure of speech.'

'Starve 'em out,' Horn said. 'If one won't take your money, another will.'

'You don't think it's dangerous, then, to have someone knowing your plans not being in your employ?'

'Dangerous?' Horn repeated, his face flushing with the thought. 'Not unless he goes over to the other side. Which isn't likely, knowing the way they work. If he betrays you, he'll never get another job.'

Ferris twisted a gold ring on his hand. 'That is certainly true.'

'It's not so much dangerous – ' Horn warmed to the subject, assured now that Ferris knew nothing of his recent disappointment with St Vier, and happy to be able to complain about it all on a theoretical level – 'not so much dangerous as it is disgraceful. After all, no one's asking them to think. *They* don't have to rule in the city, they don't have the care of the land in their hands. They've no need to concern themselves with the judgements of their betters. They just take the money, and do the job. Look – my tailor doesn't refuse to make me a riding jacket because he doesn't like horses! It's like that. You let them start thinking they have the right of refusal – '

'But they do have the right.' Basil Halliday shifted in his soft chair, unable to keep still any longer. 'That at least you must grant them, Asper. They're risking their lives for us, poor fools;

104

it's up to us to make it worth their while, so that they won't refuse the work.'

Ferris looked sympathetically at Lord Horn. 'Yes, but rejection is never pleasant,' he said softly. 'No matter who it's from. Asper is right, really: it all comes down to a question of power. Do we have the power, or do they?'

'They have the swords.' Lord Halliday smiled down at his hands; 'We have everything else. It comes out fairly even, though, with the tip of one pointed at your throat.'

'Every man lives at swordspoint,' Ferris intoned.

Horn laughed by reflex, scenting an epigram.

'I mean,' Lord Ferris elaborated, 'the things he cares for. Get them in your grasp, and you have the man – or woman – in your power. Threaten what they love, and they are absolutely at your mercy: you have a very sharp blade pressed to their throat.'

'And so,' Lord Halliday picked it up, 'you can disarm someone emptyhanded. Take honour, for example: if you held mine in your power, I would have to think twice about refusing you anything.'

'But honour', Horn broke in, 'is a property of nobles, not of common swordsmen – at least, as we understand it. For them, it's a commodity they market along with their swords, and hang on the chimney with them when they go home to their trulls and their drink and their petty quarrels. They live like dogs in Riverside, caring for nothing: they change their women as we change our coats, and waste our money as fast as we can give it to them.'

'But you're wrong,' Ferris said softly. 'There is no man living who cares for nothing.' His head was turned to face Horn, but his good eye was on the girl. 'All you have to do is to find it.'

She downed the last of her sherry in one swift gulp.

'He may not want to admit it – who does? – but even in Riverside human vices bespeak human passions.'

'No one's denying that.' Basil Halliday spoke calmly. From the tension of the girl across the room, he saw that the exercise in philosophy had ceased to be a game – maybe had never been one. He recognised the impulse in Ferris to play with the power he had been given; it was something one went through at a certain stage. Ferris's end seemed to be domestic. It was not for Halliday to judge another's personal relationships: everyone in the city was strange, if you looked deeply enough. But he saw no need to be a silent accessory.

So Halliday continued, 'But Horn is right. Ours is a different kind of honour, because we hold a different power. No lord acts as one man only: he has the power of the state behind him, the power of his birth and wealth. I should say it was beneath our honour to use them in a personal quarrel.'

Ferris turned his head to look at him. 'That is why swordsmen are so useful, my lord: they represent private enterprise. Indeed, as Horn was saying before, a swordsman's honour extends only so far as he may be trusted.'

'And no further?' Halliday asked. 'What about what it means to the man himself?'

Ferris smiled his thin-lipped smile. 'There's some disagreement on that point. But why not ask Katherine? She's our local expert on swordsmen's honour.'

The small woman got up, making for the hearth. But Ferris stopped her. 'Sit down, Katherine. The fire is going fine by itself. Tell us about the home life of swordsmen.'

She sat stiffly, her spread fingers clenched on her knees. Her eyes on the floor, she said, 'It's like what the other gentleman said. Drinking and dicing and fighting.'

Ferris sat back, enjoying himself. 'I hear they do us a service, pruning out the undesirables of Riverside.'

'There's a lot of killing that goes on,' she said. 'That's why you don't want to go there.'

'But their women are safe, surely? There must be something they cherish.'

A grim smile spread across her face, as though she'd just got the point of a joke. 'I knew a man once who killed his ... mistress.'

'Out of jealousy?'

'No, in a fight.'

'A swordsman with a temper.'

'Hers was worse, much worse. Nobody blamed him, really; or if they did, there wasn't much they could do about it. We all knew her.'

Even Halliday sat transfixed. Riversiders were seldom found

as house servants; under her humility a wildness burned, the fear of a trapped animal.

'What about the man,' Ferris asked. 'Is he dead too?'

'Hardly. He killed two swordsmen in a garden last month.'

Horn's breath caught. 'Despicable!' he muttered. 'First he killed my house swordsman, now he's murdering defenceless women.'

'Not the sort of man', Ferris said, 'who seems to care for anything. Probably wise of him, considering the position it would put him in otherwise.'

'He was well enough cared for himself a few years back, before he got so fussy about commissions,' Horn said with sudden rancour. 'Of course, I couldn't say whether he took money for it ... you know how they are when they're fresh from the country: young, and easily impressed.'

'Asper,' Basil Halliday said quietly. 'The woman's a friend of his.'

But Katherine was smiling at Lord Horn. 'Yes,' she said, 'those were wonderful times. He used to bring flowers back from the Hill with him. Kind of a shame he ever took up with ... that woman as he did. But he's turned his back on Riverside *and* the Hill now: got himself a student with no money, and he kills for him for free.'

Ferris too turned to smile at Horn. 'I suppose vices learned in youth stay with you. He was not in your set, I take it?'

Horn allowed his lip to curl slightly. 'I have never approved of chasing after swordsmen. There's no ... dignity in it.'

'You're right,' said Ferris.

Katherine got up hastily, bunching her skirts in her fists, and bobbed a curtsy to Lord Ferris. 'Will that be all, sir?'

'Yes, thank you.' Ferris smiled the melancholy smile his lean face was suited for. 'You look tired. Forgive me for keeping you. Yes, that's enough. Good night.'

Lord Halliday felt strangely tired himself. The evening had not been pleasant: something was going on between Ferris and Horn, something petty concerning swordsmen – and sex, probably knowing Horn's proclivities. He had a distaste of staying further in the other men's company. Confessing to himself that Horn had outlasted him, he rose to go. Horn, naturally, followed him. As they waited for their coats, they heard a commotion at the door. The messenger was looking for him, for Lord Halliday, had been to his house already and could brook no delay –

Halliday's guts twisted at the thought of danger in his house; it was almost with relief that he saw the state seal on the paper, and knew that whatever had happened had not happened to his family.

He scanned the letter and looked down at the waiting faces. 'It's the Helmsleigh weavers, I'm afraid. They've taken their grievances south into Ferlie, and amassed quite a crowd. They're holding council there, Tony, hard by your estates.' Ferris swore. 'And they're burning looms and houses.'

'Well,' said Ferris, his face grim. 'Then all those negotiations were for nothing. I'll go at once. Give me a cordon of City Guard, and I can raise my own men on the way to Ferlie. Just give me an hour to settle my affairs – '

'You can't travel tonight. The local bailiffs have already called up some help. If you sleep and start in the morning you'll get there more safely, and far better rested.'

There was more clatter in the yard: the arrival of an eyewitness, one of Ferris's own men from Ferlie. He had come with an escort. The men must rest the night; the weavers knew the Lord Chancellor had been sent for, and were still for now.

Lord Ferris's guests left without further ceremony. After seeing to the arrangements of his messengers, the first thing Ferris did was to pen a note to St Vier. The matter could not go forward without his close supervision; he wanted no moves made while he was out of town. For the time being, Halliday was spared.

It was late when he finally sent for Katherine. Clad only in a shirt and dressing gown, he was lying on his bed, not in it, catching a few hours' rest before the dawn. He held the sealed note out to her: 'I want you to see that your friend gets this before tomorrow night.'

As her eyes widened in protest he said, 'Of course you needn't go to Riverside yourself. I've told you I wouldn't send you back there. You have contacts. Use them. I can't send one of my own people, someone might recognise them.' She took the letter, still staring at him. 'Kathy, you look frightened.' He drew her to the bed, and pulled a quilt over them both, undoing her clothes as he continued to speak: 'I promise you there won't be much more of this. You'll see him one more time, when I get back, and that will be all.' She gripped his shoulders, forcing him to hold her. 'I won't let him hurt you, as he did your friend.'

'It's not that,' she said; 'you never thought it was that.'

'Well, I'm sorry if I embarrassed you in front of company. There was a point I needed to make.'

'Well you made it. But he won't care what you do to me.'

'Ah,' he smiled dreamily, 'you can't believe that. But even if you do, it doesn't help him any. You see it works both ways. I can tell how you'd feel if St Vier came on any mischance.' He stilled her protests with his thin lips. 'Now don't worry. He isn't going to refuse me, and I'm not going to hurt him. But it's nice to know that I can trust you both.'

Pressed under him now, she began kissing his chest, his neck, his jaw, as though her fever of nerves could be mistaken for passion and silence his flow of words.

Ferris, breathing hard above her but refusing to be taken in, continued, 'Have you seen his scholar lover, by the way?'

'No.'

'I have; although it wouldn't have done to say so. I heard all about him in that Riverside place you sent me to. And then he nearly knocked me down coming in the door.'

She stopped still, and had to start again. 'Oh? What's he like?'

But his hands were on her shoulders now, it didn't matter what she did. 'Thin. Ragged. He's very tall.

He leaned his full weight into her.

He slept for awhile; when he woke up she was still there, limply curled around a pillow. He said to her, 'Incidentally,' interrupting her dreams, 'incidentally: Asper – that is, Lord Horn – will probably come around asking you for more information about St Vier and his friend. Tell him everything you can, and remember what he says for me. It will amuse me to hear what he's thinking.'

She said nothing.

'Horn's a fool,' he said; 'you can see it yourself. Don't worry so much. I want you to do this for me.'

She said, 'Yes, my lord.'

In the morning, Lord Horn found St Vier's note stuffed in the back of a drawer. He uncrumpled it and looked at the forceful handwriting, trying to spare his eyes its insulting message. What had Ferris said? *Every man lives at swordspoint*. It had been an epigram, after all – and a clever one, too.

Chapter XIII

The new note was sealed on the outside with a thumbprint, and on the inside with the swan signet. There was only one word: *Delay*.

'D.E.,' explained Alec, chalking it on the hearth with a burnt twig-end, 'that spells *de*. L.A.Y., *lay*. *Delay*.'

Richard eased the note into the fire, where it burned merrily for a few seconds.

'Waste of perfectly good paper,' Alec protested. 'It was hardly written on!'

'Never mind,' Richard said; 'when Tremontaine pays me the 30 advance, I can buy you a sheaf. Is that the same D that's in *Richard*?'

'Ver-ry good!' Alec drawled, diverted. 'And in *Diane*. And *duchess*. There is, of course,' he added daintily, 'no D in *Alec*.'

'Of course.' Richard picked up a practice sword, nimbly sidestepping the small grey kitten the neighbourhood cat-lady had foisted on them in return for a gift of wood ('Removing the poor thing from evil influences,' Alec had said, accepting). The kitten loved moving swordpoints.

'You'll have time for Michael Godwin now,' Alec said brightly.

'Horn's job? I thought you wrote him a letter.'

'I did. But you could change your mind.'

'I don't think so.' Richard stopped, the tip of his sword just out of kitten jumping range. 'Do you have something against Godwin too?'

'Not yet. But you're always complaining about being poor –'

'*You're* always complaining about being poor. I keep trying to tell you, it's a matter of challenge. You understand about boredom, don't you? Now, Halliday will be well guarded. I may have to fight several of his people before I can even reach him, unless I can plot a way to get him alone – maybe along the roofs and in through a window. . . .'

'You know,' Alec said, 'you're going to kill that cat one of these days.'

'No I'm not.' A barely perceptible turn of his wrist brought the blade out of its reach.

'Neat,' said his friend sourly. 'They should pay you to do that.' He sat silent for a while, watching Richard exercise. The cat stalked the swordsman's right heel in its rhythmic dance across the floor, neither making a sound. Only the wall sent up a steady thud and crack of steel; but either the neighbours were out, or they'd grown used to it. When the kitten came close, Alec darted his arm down and scooped it up. It snuggled under his chin; with one finger he absently stroked the length of its spine. He gazed between its ears at the moving swordsman, and said silkily over the exercise, 'You've never actually seen the duchess, have you?'

'On the barge,' Richard panted. 'The fireworks.'

'So did a thousand other people. You haven't spoken to her.'

The swordsman jumped back, spun on his toe and came in low. 'No.'

'Why should she want Halliday killed, do you think?'

Richard paused, wiping sweat out of his eyes. 'It's none of my business.'

'Then keep it that way.'

Richard was silent. He didn't mind Alec being there watching him: Alec never paid real attention to what he was doing. He still couldn't follow a fight intelligently. Richard changed his line of attack and winced as his arm protested: a mistake to let it stiffen in one line. His imaginary opponent parried, and he used all his reach in a complex defensive counter. His imaginary opponents were always so much better than his real ones.

'Richard.'

Alec had spoken his name quite softly, but the intensity of the syllables froze him like a scream. Carefully he put the sword down, hearing its clatter loud in the tense, vibrating silence. Alec was sitting very still, with his arms wrapped around himself, but that was good: Richard checked to see that there was no knife near him, no glass he could break. It had happened once before like this, in another time that should have been easy: the sudden change in the air, and then Alec snarling and cursing at him as Richard wrested the steel from his hand, spattered with blood

112

from Alec's ineptly sliced wrist; Alec shouting at him: 'Don't you understand? I can't do anything right!' But he hadn't really been trying.

The memory was with Richard clearly now. He stood still, outwardly patient, his senses alert for the sudden movement, the twist of revelation.

'Do you understand what they meant by *Delay*?' Alec's voice was as icy-clear as an actor's off the bare walls. 'They want you, Richard, and they think they're going to have you.' Winter light from the window turned one side of his face to silver. 'Are you going to let them?'

'Not let them have me, no.' He answered as he had before. 'I make bargains, not pacts. They know that.'

'Richard,' he said with the same intense calm, 'they are not pleasant people. I have never liked them.'

'Well I'll tell you something,' Richard moved closer to him; 'I don't like most of them myself. I don't like very many people, really.'

'They like you.'

'I'm nice to them, that's why. I have to be nice to them, or . . .'

'Or you'll kill them?'

'Or they'll get upset. I don't like it when they do that; it makes me uncomfortable.'

Alec smiled thinly, the first trace of expression on his face since the conversation had begun. 'And I make you comfortable?'

'It doesn't matter. You're not boring, like the rest of them.'

'I'm a challenge.'

'In a way, yes.' Richard smiled.

'Well, that's something.' Alec uncurled his arms from around his knees. 'Nice to know there's one thing I'm good at.'

The kitten came back to him then, looking for the warm spot he had made with his legs.

It was his house, but Michael didn't feel right practising there. The swordstudy had started out as a joke, an unorthodox skill he might in time present to society as a colourful eccentricity; but now that it was in earnest he felt the need for secrecy. He worked his practice and lesson times at Applethorpe's around his old schedule, being careful to appear when he was expected amongst his peers. He practised early afternoons with the academy's targets, then changed into fine clothes and made a round of visits, took his dance lessons or went riding with his friends in the hills above the city. Every other day he dined alone, early and sparsely, and walked to Applethorpe's in the twilight for lessons in the empty studio, before his round of evening entertainments began. As it grew dark they had to light candles; but both he and the Master tacitly preferred this time of day when no one else was there to observe them.

The Master was less patient with him now. The calm detachment he showed in his public lessons was no part of his personality, but a real unconcern for the achievements of his students. None of them were expected to be *swordsmen*: they learned what they could, what they wanted to, that was all. Michael was to master all that his teacher knew. It was a lot; and it was very precise. From his years of teaching, Applethorpe had learned to explain accurately the mechanics of any movement: what rhythms, stresses and balances were brought into play, and why. And always after these explanations came the bending of his body to specification, and the imprinting of the pattern on his muscles and nerves. Michael would be caught in a frenzy of drill-work, trying to perfect a twist of the wrist that deflected the blade without moving its tip; sweat pouring down his face and breathing a nuisance since it was more hard work; and in his ears, over the roaring of his lungs, a voice like a persistent insect would be shouting, 'Balance! Balance! That arm is for balance!' – one more thing to correct without losing what he'd gained. He turned once and shouted back, 'Will you leave it? I can only do so much!'

The Master regarded him with a calm, sardonic gaze. 'Then you are dead, and we may as well not be bothering.'

Flushing, Michael dropped his eyes, following the line of his blade to its tip on the floor. 'I'm sorry.'

The Master persisted unemotionally, 'You're not even facing an opponent yet. When you are, you have to think of where *his* arms are, as well as your own. In fact, you can't be thinking of your own at all: you have to know them. I'll show you.' He picked up another blunt sword, and faced off to Michael. 'Let's try it. I won't use anything you don't know.'

They had drilled together before, but always in predetermined sequences. Facing him, Michael felt a thrill of nerves, excitement – and suddenly wondered whether the Master's missing arm might not be used to throw him off balance if Michael were skilful. . . .

As instructed, he watched his opponent's eyes. Applethorpe's were like mirrors, signalling nothing, only reflecting. Michael thought suddenly of St Vier's at the bookshop, aloof and opaque. He knew that look now.

In that instant the Master struck. Michael's defence grazed the Master's sword on its return from his chest. 'You're wounded,' Applethorpe said. 'Let's go on.'

He tried to laugh, or feel admiration, but he was filled with rage. He forgot about eyes, about one-armed men; he silently ordered himself in the Master's voice: *'Feet straight – grip loose – head up. . . .'*

He was retreating, fighting only for defence, sick with the knowledge that Applethorpe wasn't even trying to touch him. He tried at least to anticipate the attack, to have the right move ready for it; he had the feeling he was forgetting something vital he'd learned. . . . Suddenly he found himself advancing, the Master falling back before his attack. He thought of his newest move, the little twist that could give him an opening. . . .

'You just fell on my blade,' Applethorpe said, his breathing only slightly ruffled. 'Balance.'

Michael dusted himself off. 'Very nice,' the Master said to his surprise, 'for starters. Did you enjoy that?'

Michael gasped, getting his breath back. 'Yes,' he said. He found he was grinning. 'Yes, I did.'

He met the duchess once, on an afternoon ride. She was dressed in grey velvet, and was sitting a nervous grey mare. Her face and hair gleamed above them like snow on a mountain. Her party reined in, and his followed suit. She leaned across to Lord Michael, offering him her hand to kiss, a perilous exercise that he was able to accomplish dextrously while their horses danced underneath them.

'I understand', he said over the general greetings, 'that Lord Ferris has gone south to quell the riots.'

'Indeed,' she said; 'the dictates of responsibility. And such dreadful weather for travelling, too.' His pulse was beating so hard he was afraid she might see it disturbing the ruffles over his throat. 'And how is your new horse?'

He didn't know what she was talking about.

'One hears you are off to the stables a good deal,' she elucidated.

Someone was spying on him. Or was it just a rumour to account for his absences? He may have started it himself. Did it mean he'd have to get a horse now? He smiled back at her. 'Your ladyship looks quite charming. I hope your lovely mount is not too tiring.'

'Not at all.'

Her eyes, her silvery eyes like mirrors . . . He knew that look now, and knew how to respond to it. There was her challenge to be met – met, not fled with backward glances over his shoulder to make sure she was pursuing him. It was she, in a way, who had set him on his current road with her taunting. Some day she might learn of it, and wonder. It did not occur to him yet that in attaching himself to the discipline of the sword he had already met the first part of her challenge.

He steeled his own eyes as well as he could, knowing that, with their sea-colour, they would never be as immutably hard as he would like. And he smiled at her. 'Madam, perhaps I might have the pleasure of calling on you soon.'

'Indeed, it may be soon.'

The wind blew her words away from him; but that was what he thought she said. Their parties were separating amid laughter and the jingling of harness. In a few days, a week . . . He rode on into the hills, without looking back.

Chapter XIV

Two more weeks passed in Riverside without word from the one-eyed nobleman. Richard and Alec amused themselves spending the last of the winter garden money. Minor swordsmen whose reputations needed improvement found that once again St Vier would fight them, if they offended his friend first. No one had done it so far and lived; it became the kind of wild sport that fashion imposes on the restlessness of winter's end. Alec seemed to sense them, before they'd even opened their mouths; it was he as often as they who led the attack. He said it amused him to give Richard something to do. But he provoked them even when Richard wasn't there, smelling out the bravos, the ones with violence in their blood, raising their flow of viciousness like the moon calling the tide. Sometimes it was only the reputation Richard had built for him that saved his life. It always made him savage.

Besides self-destruction, his newest obsession was the theatre. He had always loved it; for once he had the money, and someone controversial to be seen with at it. Richard had been to the theatre a few times when he first came to the city, but it was hard for him to understand the appeal: he found the plays contrived, and the spectacle unconvincing. Finally, though, to quiet Alec – and take his mind off Horn and Tremontaine – he agreed to go when the theatre opened soon.

'And I have just the play,' Alec said happily. 'It's called *The Swordsman's Tragedy*. You'll love it. It's all about people killing each other.'

'Does it have swordplay in it?'

'Actors.'

'They can't be very good.'

'That's not the point,' Alec informed him. 'They are excellent *actors*. Blackwell's troupe, who did *Her Other Gown* three years ago. They're better at tragedy, though. Oh, you will enjoy it! It will cause such a stir.'

'Why?' he asked, and Alec smiled mysteriously: 'Ask Hugo.'

He cornered Hugo Seville and Ginnie Vandall in the market that afternoon. 'Hugo,' he said, 'what do you know about *The Swordsman's Tragedy*?'

Lightning swift, Hugo drew his blade. Richard had time to admire Alec's viciousness and to reach for his own weapon when he realised that Hugo had taken out his sword only to spit on it, and was carefully rubbing the spit into the blade with his thumb. With a sigh he resheathed it, never having noticed what St Vier had been about to do.

'Don't', said Hugo, 'go messing with the Tragedy.'

'Why not?'

Ginnie looked at him closely. 'You've been here how long – six years, seven? And no one's told you about the Tragedy?'

'I don't pay much attention to the theatre. But it's playing now across the river. Alec wants to go.'

Ginnie's eyes narrowed. 'Let him go without you.'

'I don't think he wants to. Can you tell me about it?'

Ginnie raised her eyebrows in an expressive sigh. She leaned her head against her lover's shoulder and murmured, 'Walk off for a while, Hugo. See if Edith has some new rings.'

'I'm sorry,' said Richard. 'I didn't mean to make you uncomfortable.'

'Never mind.' Ginnie pulled her velvet cloak more tightly around her and walked close to St Vier. She was scented with musk, like a great lady. She spoke softly, as though passing him stolen goods: 'Here it is, then. The Tragedy was first played about twenty-five years back. The actor playing the – you know, the lead, was killed in a freak accident onstage. They kept playing it, though, because it was so popular. And everything seemed all right. Then people started to notice. . . . Every swordsman that's gone to see it has lost his next fight,' she hissed; then she shrugged, trying to make light of it: 'Some badly, some not. We don't go see it, that's all. It's a good thing I told you. If people see you there, they'll think you're unlucky. And *don't* say the name.'

Alec was right: it did make the prospect of going to the theatre more appealing.

Alec greeted Richard's decision jubilantly. 'We shall sit in the gallery where we can see everything,' he announced, 'and get a bag of raisins and almonds to throw at the actors.'

'Will people be able to see us, too?' He couldn't imagine that that wasn't the point in going.

"I expect . . . ' said Alec evasively. Suddenly he turned to Richard with a dangerous gleam in his eye. 'Clothes,' he stated. 'You must wear something . . . splendid.'

'I don't own anything splendid. Not what you're thinking of, anyway.'

'Then you must get something.'

He did not like the fashionable tailor's. It made him nervous to stand still while the man attacked him with chalk and tape and pins for his measurements, muttering strange formulae under his breath. Alec was perfectly composed; but then, Alec had nothing to do but finger bolts of cloth presented by the goggling staff.

'There,' Richard pointed with all he had free, his chin, 'that one's good.'

'It's brown,' Alec said acidly, 'just like everything else you own.'

'I like brown. What's it made of?'

'Silk velvet,' Alec said with satisfaction, 'that stuff you said you wouldn't have.'

'Well, I don't have any use for it,' he said reasonably. 'Where would I wear velvet?'

'The same place you wear brown wool.'

'All right,' he conceded the colour. 'What about black, then?'

'Black,' Alec said in tones of deep disgust. 'Black is for grandmothers. Black is for stage villains.'

'Oh, do what you like.' Richard's temper was considerably shortened by the tape and the hovering hands. 'So long as it's not gaudy.'

'Is burgundy gaudy?' Alec asked with aggressive meekness. 'Or blue, perhaps?'

'Not that *peacock* colour you liked just now.'

'That was an indigo,' the tailor observed. 'Very fine. Lord Ferris had a coat made in it at the start of the season, sir.'

Alec smiled wickedly. 'Then by all means, Richard, you must have one too. It matches both your eyes.'

St Vier's fingers drummed on his thigh. He pointed to a bolt draped over a chair. 'That?'

'A very fine wool, sir, not much like it left this year. It's a russet, known this season as Apples of Delight, or Autumn Glory.'

'I don't care what it's called,' Richard said over Alec's sniff, 'I'll have that.'

'It's brown,' Alec said. '"Apples of Delight",' he further scoffed as they left the establishment. 'Peaches of Misery: another brown, like bruised fruit. Pears of Pomposity. Woeful Walnut. Cat's Vomit Pink.'

Richard touched his arm. 'Wait. We didn't get you measured for anything. Didn't you want that blue?'

Alec continued down the street. Affluent shoppers moved aside from the tall shabby figure. He said to Richard, not lowering his voice, 'It's probably called Hypochondriac's Veins this season. Lady Dysentery ordered a coat for her dog in it.'

'Don't you want anything new for spring? I've still got the money.'

'There is no point', he said, 'in trying to better the bested. Nice clothes only point out my inadequacies. And I slouch: it pulls the shoulders out.'

'Green,' Richard insisted, having nothing against bright colours provided he didn't have to wear them, 'for your eyes. And gold brocade. With a high neck, and a ruffle. You'd look elegant, Alec.'

'I'd look like a painted pole at a fair,' Alec said, giving his robe a tug. 'One Autumn Glory is quite enough.'

But on the day of the performance, Richard had his doubts. His new clothes were much more comfortable than he'd expected them to be: the richly coloured wool was soft, and moved with him like something he'd had for years. Alec's scholar's robe looked even more frayed by contrast, and it covered most of his new shirt and boots. He hadn't even used the enamel clasp for his hair; it was caught back with an old ribbon.

Richard didn't bother to argue. 'Sit down,' he ordered. 'And stay there.' And he disappeared into the bedroom.

From the front room he could hear Alec saying, 'What are you doing, trying to change your socks? They're perfectly clean and no one can see them anyway. . . .'

He reappeared with a plain wooden box, the kind used for keeping letters or bills. He opened it so Alec couldn't see in, and brought out its first treasure.

'God,' Alec said, and that was all he could manage.

Richard slipped the ring over Alec's finger. It was a massive black pearl, set in heavy silver scrollwork.

Alec stared at his own hand. 'That's beautiful,' he breathed. 'I didn't know you had taste like that.'

'It was given to me. A long time ago.'

He took out the brooch next, and laid it in Alec's palm: a gold dragon clutching a sapphire. Alec's hand closed on it, hard enough to feel the edges; then he pinned the collar of his shirt closed with it.

'That's very, very old,' he said at last.

'It was my mother's. She stole it from her family.'

'The banking St Viers?'

'That's right. She didn't like them very much.'

He found a small diamond ring that fitted Alec's little finger, and a gold band inlaid with a red-gold rose.

'Clients', he said, smiling down at the rose, 'who liked my work. The diamond was a woman's, a nobleman's wife who gave it to me privately because she said I saved her reputation. I've always liked it, it's so fine.' He reached into the box again. 'This next one I got early on, as partial payment from a man with more jewels than money. I've never known what to do with it; I should have known it was for you.' He brought out a square-cut emerald as big as his thumbnail, flanked by citrons and set in gold.

Alec made a peculiar noise in his throat. 'Do you know what that's worth?'

'Half a job.'

'*You* wear it. What are you giving me these for, anyway?'

'I like the way they look on you. They don't look right on me, and they don't feel right, either.'

Entranced despite himself, Alec lifted his hands, now heavy with gold and silver and precious stones.

'That', said Richard, 'is the way to dress you.'

'You've missed a finger,' Alec said, and Richard answered, 'So

121

I have,' and drew out his newest acquisition, still in its pouch. 'Here,' he said, 'you open this one.'

Even in the room's dull light the ruby glowed with liquid colour. It was a long red bar that spanned two knuckles, flanked on either side with diamonds set in white gold.

'Where did you get this?' Alec asked, his voice dangerously shaky.

'From another nobleman. It's my latest bribe.'

'I think you're lying,' Alec said tightly. 'I think you got it from a thief.'

'No, really,' Richard said patiently. 'It's from Lord Ferris. He wanted me to wear it to our next meeting.'

'Well, wear it, then!' Alec shouted, thrusting the ring at him.

'I'm not comfortable in rings,' Richard said quietly, and didn't take it.

'This one in particular,' Alec growled. 'He had no right to give it to you.'

'No problem, then,' Richard said, trying to turn things light again: 'I give it to you, my lord.'

Alec's face, if possible, grew paler and stiffer, his eyes wider. Despite the danger, Richard lifted one jewelled hand and kissed it. 'Alec,' he said against the cold, heavy fingers, 'they are for you. Do what you want with them.'

Alec's fingers slowly tightened on his own. When he looked up, Alec was smiling, his eyes sharp and green with wicked pleasure. 'All right,' Alec drawled, 'I will.' And he slid the ruby onto his forefinger. It glowed there like a live thing, an icon for the hand that bore it.

They were a noble's hands, now, a foreign prince's, rich and strange. Against the transparent skin, the high-bred bones, Alec's coarse clothing and scuffed boots faded to nothing.

'That's good,' Richard said, pleased with the effect. 'It's a shame to keep them all in a box. I never wear them; this way I get to look at them.'

'They like to be looked at,' Alec said. 'I can feel them purring with delight, showy little bastards.'

'Well, let's take them for a walk – not that anyone will notice them, next to my new clothes.'

The two men were noticed all the way through Riverside. The afternoon was golden from the ground up; the snow being gone, their path was covered with mud and winter deposits. Word of what they were planning had got around; people lined up to see them pass like a parade. Richard felt like some hero, going off to war.

He caught sight of Ginnie as they were crossing the Bridge. He called to her before Alec could say something rude, '*Hey*, Ginnie! What do you think?'

She eyed him up and down, and nodded. 'You look good. They'll be impressed.' Alec's hand flashed in the sun; she saw the jewels, and her face froze. Without a word she turned and walked past them.

'She doesn't approve,' Alec said cheerfully.

'Hugo wouldn't go see this play.'

'I imagine Hugo only likes the funny ones.'

Even in the city people watched as they went by. Richard kept wanting badly to giggle: all this fuss about two people going to see a play that probably wasn't even going to be very good. 'We should have hired horses,' he said, 'like the Council Lords, so people could see us ride by. My boots are muddy already.'

'Look!' Alec cried. 'The banners! We're almost there.'

'Banners?' But there they were, just like a story-castle's: made of bright cloth, painted with devices that appeared and vanished in the crackling wind: a winged horse, roses, dragons, a crown. . . .

Outside the theatre it was like a fair. Grooms were walking horses and clearing the way for carriages while girls walked amongst them, selling bouquets of flowers and herbs, cups of wine and packets of fruit and nuts. There were printed copies of the play, and scarves, and ribbons the same colours as the banners. Alec looked for Nimble Willie in the crowd but couldn't find him, although one or two of the other melting faces looked familiar. Two unknown swordsmen staged a quarrel and then a swordfight over and over in different corners of the yard. Against the wall someone was declaiming a speech from another tragedy and being drowned out by a blind fiddler with a dancing dog, which some young noblemen were distracting by throwing nuts for it to fetch. The nobles' costumes did indeed make Richard's look sombre. Even the middle city people, shopkeepers and craftsmen, were dressed extravagantly, trimmed up with bits of lacé and ribbon. They were coming early, to ensure themselves good seats.

'Come on,' said Alec, elbowing his way through the crowd, 'or we'll find ourselves sitting in some dowager's lap.'

The nobles stopped throwing nuts to look at them. A snatch of their conversation carried over: '. . . can't afford him anyway. . . .' A pair of serving-girls, arm in arm, simpered and turned away.

Richard was beginning to be sorry he'd come. The crowd grew tighter as they reached the entryway. Other peoples' toes and elbows and very breath intruded on him. He kept his hand on the pommel of his sword.

This fascinated a group of small boys, one of whom finally grew bold enough to approach. 'Hey, swordsman!' he shouted hoarsely. 'Could you kill my brother?'

Richard didn't answer; they always asked that. 'Shut up, Harry,' another said. 'Can't you even see that's St Vier?'

'Hey, are you St Vier? Hey, St Vier, could I see your sword?'

'You can see it up your backside,' said Alec, hitting one of them at point-blank range with an almond. Pleased with his aim, he led the way in, and tipped a boy to find them seats.

They got a private box in the upper gallery, directly opposite the stage. Alec was elated. 'I've always wanted one of these. It's pure hell on the benches, with every idiot and his wife trying to sit on your lap.' Richard winced at the thought. They were high above everything here, with a good view of the stage now bathed in sunlight. People were craning up to look at them from all corners of the house.

Alec put his feet up on the barrier and ate some of his raisins. There was a sennet of trumpets from above. 'Now you'll see the nobles' boxes fill,' Alec said. 'They always come in now.'

Set close to the stage, the nobles' boxes, hung with their occupants' arms, were visible from almost all the rest of the audience.

It was the first time in many years that Richard was able to observe them all at leisure. He recognised more than he expected to: handsome men who had stalked him at the parties he used to

124

attend; distinguished noblemen and -women whose money and patronage he'd refused, and others who had reason to be grateful.

He saw Lord Bertram Rossillion with a beautiful dark-haired woman on his arm, remembered him complaining about pressure to marry . . . poor lady. Alintyre was there, now Lord Hemmyng. He wondered if Hemmyng would recognise the emerald on Alec's hand and smiled, remembering that mad ride through the hills with the coach just ahead of them, Alintyre's lady love being trundled off to her aunt's; and her shrieks of laughter as they'd ridden back with her the way they'd come. He looked harder at the stately lady smiling up at Hemmyng, and recognised with a start the tilt of the nose. . . .

The man responsible for Alec's rose gold ring was also there, looking young and serene as ever. Of course, it hadn't been so many years ago. He was talking to an elegant redhead.

'Godwin,' said Alec. 'One of those delectable confections you're staring at is a Godwin of Amberleigh, there's the crest.'

'The redhead,' Richard said. 'I've seen him somewhere else before, I can't think where. . . . '

'How do you know it isn't the other one?'

Richard smiled. 'I've seen him before, too; but I remember where.'

Lord Thomas Berowne turned back to his companion. 'And there it is,' he said; 'he did come after all.'

'Why shouldn't he?' Lord Michael answered. 'He's not a coward.'

'No, but he's not flashy either. It's a flashy thing to do.'

'For a swordsman. Is he superstitious?'

'Doesn't matter. Alban was sure he wouldn't come; he owes Lucius 20 royals now.'

'He can afford it,' Michael said absently. His mind wasn't on St Vier: he was wondering what Vincent Applethorpe would say if he knew Michael was attending *The Swordsman's Tragedy*. 'It's just a fairy tale,' he said aloud. 'No one really believes it.'

'Maybe not,' said Tom; 'but wait for the betting when St Vier's next fight comes up.'

'He's stolen Halliday's fire, at any rate,' Michael changed the subject. 'They were saying that the Crescent was planning to cancel the performance, close down the theatre.'

'Where have you *been*, Michael?' Berowne asked in mock surprise. 'They were talking about *The King's End*, which is a piece of garbage saved only by the presence of one Miss Viola Festin as the king's page. I have already seen it twice, and I can assure you that Lord Halliday was at the last performance. All of it. I came in partway through, when the gentle page –'

'Oh, no,' Michael said. 'It's Horn. In the box across from us.'

'He's probably bet on St Vier. What's the matter?'

'Tell me if he's looking at me.'

'He isn't. Poor child, has he been pestering you with his attentions? Or do you owe him money?'

'He makes my skin creep,' Michael explained.

'Oh, yes,' Berowne said; 'I know about that.'

'They're all betting on you,' Alec said cheerfully, passing him the raisins. 'I wish we could get a percentage.'

'It comes out of my fees,' Richard answered. 'When does the play start?'

'Soon, soon; when the music stops.'

'What music?'

'There – on stage. You can't hear it, everyone's talking.'

'And looking at us,' Richard said. It was beginning to seem like a bad idea again.

'They're protecting their investments,' Alec said blithely. 'I wonder if they'll send you flowers.'

Richard groaned. 'Flowers. Is Ferris here? What does his crest look like?'

'He's not here. Lord Horn is. No Halliday. No Tremontaine. Nobody serious comes to see us.'

'Look away,' said Lord Thomas, 'he's looking at you.'

'Horn?'

'No, St Vier.'

'He's probably looking at *you*,' Michael said.

'I'm not blushing, he can't be.' Berowne looked pointedly away. 'Now Horn's looking . . . not at you, at him.'

'Who's that with him?'

'With Horn?'

'With St Vier. Thomas, turn around and *look*.'

'I can't. I'm blushing. It's the curse of my complexion.'

'At least you don't freckle. Send him a note – the swordsman, I mean. Ask him to join us.'

'Michael.' Lord Thomas looked at his friend. 'You offend my pride. Everyone is dying to ask him to join them. I refuse to herd with the common throng. I refuse to be the first to capitulate. And what if he refused?'

'I think', Richard said crossly, 'that I am not going to like this play. I think it's going to be a silly play. I think we should mess everyone's bets up by leaving now.'

'We could do that', Alec said. 'But those people who have begun walking around onstage are in fact the actors. Soon they will begin to speak. If you go now you will be walking out in the middle of the first scene, and everyone will stare at you even more. Sit down, Richard. Here comes the Duke.'

The Duke crossed the stage in great panoply, leaving behind some courtiers who wanted to talk about him. It sounded very much like an actual conversation except that all the words were ordered to fit a spoken rhythm. Like music, fragments were passed from speaker to speaker, while the rhythm stayed the same. Sometimes you lost the feel of the beat, but then a strange twist of words brought it back again. The courtiers liked the Duke. He was a wise man,

> . . . more fit to act the part of grace
> Than counterfeit a prince's righteous scorn.

His son and heir, however, had never been known to show any sign of grace. No one liked him much; he threw gloomy parties, and wore black in mourning for his mother, who had died giving birth to his only sister, Gratiana.

The courtiers left the stage. Some curtains at the back opened, and there was a girl with long golden hair talking to a parrot in a cage. She called herself

> . . . unhappy Gratiana – and yet most happy
> In having that which, lacking, many maids

> Must lie in torment on their narrow cots
> Or venture rites under full-moonèd skies.

Richard thought it might be a real parrot. She told it:

> You and I, bright captives both
> Of place and person, circumstance and birth
> Must share our burden, you with patient ear
> And I with tongue to tell the cause for tears!

But before she could explain herself, her brother Filio came in, made snide remarks about her maiden virtue and the parrot, and turned to the audience to remark:

> For none dares share my sorrow or my joy
> When I myself can neither either prove.

Richard had been looking forward to seeing the old, virtuous Duke; since he was the person everyone was talking about at the beginning, he'd thought the play would be about him. Instead he died suddenly, offstage, and Filio was named Duke. A stately minister with a long white beard came to tell Gratiana. His name was Yadso, and he suspected foul play. Later he was warned by his barber, who also shaved a close friend of Filio's, that his life was in danger of mortal challenge if he did not flee the country at once. Yadso took his leave of the girl:

> Not all that is, is as it seems. In knots
> Truth ties up silence; speech undoes us here.
> The game's afoot: Now foot we while we may!

Gratiana cried,

> Flee! Flee! you just and true
> And for your coin take Gratiana's love!

Then, alone, she lamented her treachery to all mankind. Perhaps she was the villain? But no; it turned out she only meant that she had fallen in love with an unsuitable man. The parrot suddenly chose to echo her words: 'Love!' it croaked. 'Flee love!' Everyone took it in their stride, so it must have been part of the play. Maybe it wasn't a real parrot after all; or maybe it was, but someone was behind the scenes doing its voice.

The new Duke kept pestering his sister. Finally he dragged out of her the fact that she was in love with a swordsman. He turned again to the audience and vented his rage in terms uncomplimentary to the profession. Richard caught Alec sneaking looks at him, and grinned. But to his sister, Filio was all sugary sympathy. Virtue, he said, like wine, was no less potent for being poured into unlikely vessels; wine could be drunk as easily from a skull as from a cup of gold. 'Oh, dear,' Richard muttered. He could see it coming already. Alec shushed him. But Gratiana was comforted, and promised to send her lover to meet her brother. As soon as she left, Filio stomped and shouted and wrung the parrot's neck. So it was either well trained, or a fake one after all. The Duke left the stage to try and find a cat to blame it on.

Richard didn't even bother to criticise the swordsman. Maybe, when the play had been written, swordsmen were like that. Of course, in a world where everyone talked in what Alec said was poetry, why should he expect a swordsman to be any different? Duke Filio greeted his prospective brother-in-law warmly. They drank wine out of twin skulls. The swordsman made a weak joke about it, and then toasted the downfall of all the Duke's house's enemies. It turned out Filio had a job for the swordsman to do: an enemy had besmirched the honour of the house, and only blood would wash it clean. Obviously flattered at the Duke's attentions, the swordsman agreed.

There followed a scene in a madhouse, with much singing and dancing. What it was doing there Richard never did find out; but when it was over the inner curtain was pulled back to reveal an enormous staircase that cleft the centre of the stage from top to bottom. The swordsman appeared at the bottom, announced to everyone that it was midnight, and that, after he'd got the Duke's little commission out of the way, he trusted to lie in his lover's arms as promised. Richard enjoyed his description of love; it was the most accurate part of the play so far, with its images of hot and cold, pleasure and pain. But at the same time, it made him uncomfortable to hear someone talking about it in front of a great crowd of strangers – even though it was only a play.

At the top of the stairs, a cloaked figure appeared. As the bells began to toll 12, the figure started down the stairs in a pretty flourish of yards of cloak. The swordsman drew his steel, and ran his victim through, crying, 'So perish all Filio's enemies!'

'For shame,' said Gratiana, falling forward into his arms; 'to love my brother more than you love me!'

She was a long time dying, while each of the lovers explained the Duke's trick to the other, and promised eternal fidelity. Richard endured it with patience. Finally, the swordsman carried his dead love off the stage, her cloak trailing behind them.

The stage was bare. Then people started clapping. Alec was still staring at the empty stage. His eyes were bright with the same elation he'd had the night of the fireworks.

'That was excellent!' he said. 'That was perfect.'

Richard decided not to argue; but Alec correctly interpreted the look on his face, and made a face of his own. 'Let me guess. The technique was bad. *You* would have killed her so she didn't have time for that speech at the end.'

Richard scowled a smile. 'It wasn't realistic,' he said at last. 'No, not the speech, the way it happened. First of all, he was an idiot to take a contract on an unknown mark, especially from that brother, who he didn't trust in the first place.'

'But he *needed* the Duke's support, that's the point!'

'Yes, but remember when Filio says. . . .' To Alec's surprise, his illiterate friend quoted the passage back to him accurately. '*That's* when he should have realised that he had no intention of letting them get away with it.'

'Well . . .' said Alec, at a loss. 'Well, *we* see that, but he isn't supposed to.'

'Then he's supposed to be a stupid man, and I don't see why we should care what happens to him. The brother's the smart one, really.'

'Then you can cheer for the brother,' Alec said sourly. 'But I warn you, he gets killed in the end. Everyone does, in fact.'

Richard looked down at the audience, who were milling around buying food, drink and trying to look into their box. 'If they want to see people killed, why don't they go to a swordfight?'

'Because your speeches are too short,' Alec snapped. 'Also,' he reflected more leniently, 'you're always doing it for money. In the play it's for love, or treachery. Makes it more interesting.'

'He should never have bargained with the brother. He lost the moment he let him see his weakness.'

'And we could all have gone home early.'

There was a scratch at the door of their box. Richard whirled, hand on his hilt. Alec unlocked the door, and accepted the first messenger's offering.

'It's just a rose. No note.'

Richard looked across the theatre to the nobleman who loved roses; but he was deep in conversation, and didn't look up.

There was plenty of time between the acts for the nobles to socialise in each other's boxes. Michael relinquished the pleasures of his friend for a talk that Bertram Rossillion seemed bent on having.

'Your friend,' Bertram said, 'Berowne . . .'

'He's a relation,' Michael answered the question. 'By marriage. On my mother's side. We've known each other forever.'

Bertram's soulful brown gaze slopped itself all over his face, with particular emphasis on the eyes. Michael stepped back, but Bertram came on. Michael said in an undertone, 'Tonight is bad for me, my dear. I'll be out late, and too tired when I come in.' He was going to Applethorpe's. Tiny creases appeared around Bertram's eyes, and his mouth pinched in the corners. 'I've missed you terribly,' Michael said, gazing back. 'You don't know how. . . .'

'Look!' said Bertram, 'the duchess.'

She was entering one of the boxes across the way. Already her footmen were unfurling the Tremontaine banner. Her dark skirts billowed around her, and under a tiny hat crowned with ostrich plumes her fair curls tumbled, each in careful disorder.

'She's late if she's come to see the play,' Richard observed. All eyes were off them for the moment.

'She hasn't,' Alex answered gruffly. 'She's come to make trouble.' He stood at the back of the box, huddled into the corner by the door. His hands were tucked in his sleeves, making him look more than ever like a sulky black bird.

Richard looked at the tiny, elegant woman surrounded by her well-built edifice of clothes and manners. 'I wonder', he said, 'if I should go and see her?'

'You can see her perfectly well from here, she's taken care of that.'

'I mean to talk to. Ferris is gone, he doesn't have to know I've done it. You're right, you know; I should find out what she thinks herself.'

He'd expected Alec to be pleased; after all, it was his misgivings Richard was trying to allay. But the tall man only shrugged. 'She hasn't invited you, Richard. And she's not going to admit to anything.'

'If I made it a condition of the job . . . ?'

'Oh, of course,' the light voice mocked angrily. 'If *you* make conditions. . . . Why don't you ask her to do your laundry, as well? I'm telling you, stay away – '

A knock interrupted him. He flung open the door, so that it crashed against the wall. A footman in the Tremontaine swan livery filled the doorway. Alec dropped the doorlatch as though it had burnt him.

'The duchess's compliments,' the servant said to St Vier, 'and will you join her to take chocolate.'

Alec groaned. Richard had to bite his lip to keep from laughing. He glanced at Alec, but the scholar was once again trying to hunch himself into nonentity. 'I'll be delighted.' He looked around at the accumulated greenery. 'Should I take her some flowers?'

'It's an insult', Alec said hollowly, 'to the senders. Save them to throw at the actors.'

'All right. Are you coming?'

'No. Stay there for the last act, if she'll let you; you'll be close enough to tell if Jasperino really is wearing a wig.'

Richard began to follow the footman. 'Wait,' said Alec. He was twisting the ring on his forefinger.

'Should I wear the ruby?' St Vier asked.

'No.' Alec shook his head fiercely.

For a moment Richard broke away from the footman's presence. 'What's the matter?' Alec's nervousness was physically palpable to him. Something had undermined Alec's arrogance; he didn't even deny the charge. He retained just enough of his usual air to press his fingers to his brow in mockery of the acting. 'I have a headache. I'm going home.'

'I'll come with you.'

'And leave the duchess waiting? She probably wants to find out who your tailor is. Hurry up, or you'll miss the chocolate. Oh, and if there are any little iced cakes, get me one. Say it's for your parakeet or something. I am uncommonly fond of little iced cakes.'

Not long after he left the theatre Alec realised that he was probably being followed. At least, the same two men seemed to have been behind him for several turnings now. They were the demonstration swordsmen from outside the theatre. They weren't Riversiders, they couldn't be going his way to the Bridge. His heart was clanging like a blacksmith's anvil, but Alec refused to alter his pace. If they wanted the rings, he supposed they could have them. Richard or his friends could probably get them back.

He might still return to the theatre; lead them there by another route, and find Richard. He discarded the idea as soon as he'd had it. He wasn't going back. The shops and houses went by like images from another life. Inns and taverns passed, while his mouth grew steadily drier. It was not unlike the effects of poppy juice.

If he got as far as the Bridge, he might see other Riversiders who could help him, or at least tell Richard what had become of him. What *was* going to happen to him? They were letting him get far from the centre of the city, into the lonely area you had to cross to reach the Bridge. It would be violent, and extremely painful; all he'd ever imagined, and probably something he'd managed to leave out. He'd been waiting a long time for it, and now it was going to happen.

Now, the ground said, each time his boot-sole struck it. *Now*. He tried to vary the rhythm of his walk, to get it to stop. He managed to slow it down to a whisper, and in the shadow of a gateway they caught him.

He had time to say, 'You know, your swordplay would make a cat laugh'; and then he found that it was impossible not to struggle.

'They are all jealous,' the duchess said, nodding graciously at her peers across the theatre, 'because they are all cowards.'

133

Richard St Vier and the duchess were alone in the box, with the chaperonage of about five hundred spectators. It didn't bother him; he was intrigued with her portable silver chocolate set. A blue flame heated the water under a little steel-bottomed pot suspended over it on a chain. There was a silver whisk, and china cups with her arms on them.

'They're not as well equipped,' he answered her.

'They could have been. Not only cowards, but stupid.' It was all said in a pleasant, intimate manner that took the sting out of her words, as though they were not meant so much to denigrate the others as to establish the boundaries of a charmed circle that included only the duchess and himself. Alec did the same thing; much more abrasively, of course, and more sincerely; but the sense it gave Richard of belonging to an elite was the same.

'You might have brought your servant, he would have been welcome. Perhaps I failed to make that clear to Grayson.'

He smiled, realising she meant Alec. 'He's not my servant,' he said. 'I don't have one.'

'No?' She frowned delicately. With her postures and careful expressions, she was like a series of china figurines displayed along a chronological shelf. 'Then however do you manage those great townhouses down there?'

She might be teasing; but he told her anyway about the manors that had been turned into rooming houses, or brothels, or taverns, or those warrens for extended families whose generations moved slowly down floors, with the youngest always at the top.

She was enchanted with it. 'That would put you where, now...' looking at him critically '...in the upstairs ballroom perhaps, with room to practise – or have they turned that into the nursery?'

He smiled. 'I don't have family. Just rooms: an old bedroom and I think a music room, above a... laundress.'

'She must be very pleased to have such a lodger. I have wanted to tell you for some time now how much I admired your fight with Lynch – and poor de Maris, of course. Although I suppose he deserved what he got, jumping in to challenge you when it was already Lynch's fight. I imagine Master de Maris had tired of

134

Lord Horn's service, and wanted the chance to prove to his party guests how employable he was.'

Richard considered the pretty lady with renewed respect. This was exactly his own estimation of de Maris's peculiar behaviour in the winter garden. Horn's house swordsman probably thought his lord didn't give him enough chance to show off, and he wasn't really needed as a guard; who would want to kill Horn? By killing St Vier he would have won himself an instant place back at the top of the swordsmen's roster. He should never have tried it.

'My lord Karleigh will be out of the picture for some time, I think.'

On the surface, it was a continuation of her compliment, assuming that Karleigh had fled because St Vier killed his champion. It was what everyone thought. But she seemed to be waiting for an answer – something in the posing of her hands, the cup held not-quite-touching the saucer . . . as though she knew that he could tell her more about the duke. He couldn't, really: he'd taken his payment and that was the end of it for him; but it meant she knew who his patron had been.

'I've never asked', he said evasively, 'why the duke and his opponent insisted on such secrecy for themselves, but still chose to have their fight in public. Of course I've honoured my patron's wishes.'

'It was an important fight,' she said; 'such are best well witnessed. And the duke is a vain man, as well as a quarrelsome one. He never told you what the fight was about, then?'

She left him little space for an ambiguous answer. 'He never told me anything,' he said truthfully.

'But now it may be coming clear. A political issue, worth a couple of swordsmen but not their patrons' lives. It put a healthy fear into Karleigh, but that may be wearing off. Lord Ferris will know when he returns from his trip south whether the duke stands in need of another sovereign dose.'

Did she want Halliday killed *and* Karleigh out of the way? It meant destroying two opponents, and leaving the field open for a third man . . . Ferris? The duchess hadn't named Halliday; if anything, she seemed to be defending him. Richard gave up: he didn't know enough about the nobles and their schemes this year to figure it out. But one thing still troubled him.

He looked at the duchess directly. 'I am already at your service.'

'Gallant,' the duchess chuckled. 'Are you really, now?'

She made him feel young – young, but very secure in the hands of someone who knew what she was about. He said broadly, to be sure, 'You know how to find me.'

'Do I?' she said with the same amusement.

'Well, your friends do,' he amended.

'Ah.' She seemed satisfied; and so, for the moment, was he. He hoped Alec would be too. Trumpets sounded for the play to begin again. 'Do stay,' said the duchess; 'you can get such a good view of the costumes from here. Some of the wigs are beyond belief.'

The swordsman whose tragedy it was lasted until the end. His revenge against the evil Duke consisted of a series of love letters from an unknown lady with the same initials as Filio's mother, whom the Duke fell in love with. The letters demand that the Duke do increasingly odious things to prove his devotion. After a colourful series of rapes, beheadings and one disinterment, even the most loyal of Duke Filio's courtiers had amassed several reasons to kill him. The only nice person left onstage, a doctor from the singing madhouse, stated the opinion that the prognosis for the Duke's mental health was not good.

In the final act, the giant staircase again dominated the stage. The Duke, labouring under the promise that the lady of his affections would at last reveal herself to him at midnight, came to the bottommost step. As the bell once again tolled the hour, the figure of his sister, wrapped in her bloody cloak, appeared above him. Too unhinged to be adequately frightened, he muttered,

> Nay, I'll not flee, but mount the tow'r of heaven
> And from your chaste and softly smiling lips
> Suck forth the secret of eternal life!

The Duke ran up the staircase, but suddenly the figure flung back its hood. To no one's surprise except the Duke's, it was the swordsman:

> Not life, but death's cold secrets will you kiss –
> Now please your mistress, let her give you joy

136

Of her. Come, come, and bid farewell to all
Earth's pleasures in one last ecstatic howl.

His gleaming sword plunged down from above into Filio's heart
(leaving his own front completely unguarded, but affording a fine
view of his gory clothes), and the Duke screamed, 'At last! It is
the end!'

It wasn't, of course. The Duke had no final speech, but a
crowd of courtiers came running on. Finding the Duke in the
arms of a cloaked figure, presumably his mysterious lover, they
shouted, 'Vengeance! Vengeance!' and fell upon the pair,
hacking to bits the already dead Duke, and delivering to the
swordsman his mortal wound. It left him strength for one last
declamation:

> Now is the trapper trapped, and in my blood
> Steel strikes on steel, and kindles a great flame.
> I burn, I rage, and shortly welcome death
> That long has been my handmaid, now my spouse.
> Are there no tears to put this fire out?
> Only my own, and those I will not shed
> So long as *he* regards me with his sanguine orbs.
> We'll too soon be two skulls, and jest at grinning then,
> But all our plays produce no single laugh
> From lungs no sighs will ever fill again.
> I hadn't planned on this – but hadn't planned
> Beyond it, either. Things were clear enough:
> I loved your sister, and I hated you,
> Pursued you both and killed you. Now all's one.
> Write Nothing on my tomb, that's all . . . I've done.

The swordsman was by then halfway up the staircase, where
he died. While everyone was reacting to this, a nobleman rushed
in to announce that a chimney sweep had discovered the Duke's
secret diary, in which were lovingly detailed all his heinous
crimes, beginning with his treatment of his sister. The people
agreed that the swordsman was, in fact, a hero, and will be given
a hero's funeral, interred next to Gratiana, while the Duke will be
cast into a bottomless pit. The virtuous and amiable old coun-
sellor, Yadso, will be called back from exile to become the next
Duke of wherever it was. And that was the end.

The audience's applause seemed as much for the happy resolution as for the actors. As they took their bows the duchess observed to St Vier, 'In the end, you see, it all comes down to good government. There can be no state funeral for the hero without a state; and true lovers cannot meet on a staircase that hasn't been properly maintained. I'm sure Yadso will make an excellent duke.'

Richard enjoyed the clear path the duchess's footman commanded for them out of the theatre. It would be pleasant to live in a world without crowds. At the door of her carriage she stopped and took a basket from her maid, rummaged in it and handed him a packet wrapped in a linen napkin. Bowing, he heard the swish of her skirts as she was handed up into the carriage. Then he left quickly, before any other of the departing nobles might claim his company. He did note that the Hallidays' phoenix-crested carriage had a door that locked from the inside.

The packet contained the little iced cakes he had forgotten to ask for. He wondered if they meant something; but determined to save them intact for Alec.

There was no sign of his friend's having been home to their lodgings. Probably off losing his last brass minnow at Rosalie's. Richard hoped he wasn't staking his rings. He decided to go down there and get some dinner.

The cooking fire was high; it was hot as the inferno in the little tavern, though fortunately not so dry. Rosalie wanted to hear all about the play; and because she was an old friend he told her. Lucie wanted to know about the heroine's costume; but he never could remember clothes. News of his visit with the duchess didn't seem to have leaked down yet.

Some men came in and looked at him curiously, as though afraid his bad luck might be fresh enough to rub off on them. They settled down in a corner to eat and play cards. Eventually another man joined them, sporting a kerchief full of stolen goods he was attempting to sell quickly.

'Here,' called Rosalie, 'let's see those things.'

She was admiring an enamel comb, letting Lucie twine it in her hair, when Richard saw the gold ring among the tangle of chains and gew-gaws. Yellow gold, with a red rose.

'Where did you get this?' he asked the man calmly.

'Trade secret.' The man laid a finger along the side of his nose. 'Do you want it?'

'It's mine.'

'Not any more, boy.'

'Tell me where you got it,' St Vier said, a weary edge to his voice. 'It isn't worth fighting over.'

The man swore. 'Swordsmen.' But he gave in. 'Some guy passed it on to me, down at the docks. Another swordsman, not Riverside though. Still a sight more civil than you, honey. He just wanted the money for it; I didn't ask any questions. What's the matter, you get robbed when you went out without your sword?'

'I don't get robbed.'

Taking a cautious step back, the man mocked, 'You're plenty sure of yourself. I bet you're St Vier or something, right?'

'I am St Vier,' Richard said quietly. At his side, Rosalie nodded. 'When did you get the ring?'

'Not long – hey, look, I'm sorry. I didn't mean – '

'Just tell me when you got it.'

'Not long ago. I came straight here. You'll never find him, though, not now.'

'I'll find him,' Richard said.

Chapter XV

During the long carriage ride Lord Horn had the leisure to examine his feelings minutely. They were, on the whole, pleasant feelings. Throughout the play he had barely paid heed to the stage, so pleased was he with the events unfolding from his own private gallery. He felt like a playwright, only he had not had to go to the trouble of inventing his characters: Lord Michael Godwin, blissfully young and arrogant, all the more lovely because his days under the sun were now numbered . . . Horn had thought of sending him a trenchant note; but a distinguished silence had seemed the most dignified . . . the swordsman St Vier, that fashionable paragon . . . in the sunlight, in the great public space, he too had looked young, his detachment a mere defence. Horn had enjoyed looking at the dangerous man and thinking how helpless he was about to feel.

The coach pulled up at last at the door of the empty hunting lodge. There were still some people left who owed him favours. St Vier's young man should have arrived here over an hour ago. Horn had stayed for the end of the play. He should find the boy chained in the empty buttery. Ferris's woman had said he couldn't fight, but these Riversiders knew all kinds of tricks, and how could you be sure that St Vier hadn't passed some on to him?

Up here in the hills, the spring was still chilly. Horn kept his cloak on and went straight to the buttery. A small sliding panel in the door, some watchman's convenience, had been left open. He could look through it without being seen, and he did.

The young man was lounging upright in his chains, making them look faintly ridiculous as he leaned against the wall. His hands were lax, long and useless-looking. They were covered with rings, and there was gold at his throat. His dress was strangely at odds: the jewels, good boots and shirt, under a jacket with narrow shoulders and too-short sleeves whose cut was a good five seasons old. His breeches, which no longer matched his jacket, had a piece of braid coming off them. And then there was his cascade of hair. In the candlelight he had been left with, it glowed chestnut and sable, heavy and thick as poured cream.

Some black cloth was folded behind his head to keep it from the wall. He was looking abstractedly across at the candle, head slightly tilted, his eyes veiled.

Lord Horn examined the face of St Vier's lover. His nose was long, flat-planed like a ritual painting's. High cheekbones, wide-set so that the eyes above them looked slanted from this angle. The hair pulled back from his high forehead made his face look even longer. Horn's eyes rested on the mouth, almost too wide for the narrow face. Even in repose, the flat lips looked mocking and sensual.

He unlocked the door and stepped inside. At the sound the young man raised his head like a deer scenting the wind. His eyes were vivid green, and open preternaturally wide; they held Lord Horn in frozen fascination, so that his first words were not at all what he'd planned.

'Who are you?'

'Your prisoner, I am told.' The wide gaze did not falter, but Horn saw that the skin around his eyes was drawn tight with tension. 'Are you going to kill me?'

Horn ignored the question, and noted how the face went paler. 'Your name?' he demanded.

'It's Alec.' The boy wet his lips. 'May I have some water?'

'Later. And your surname?'

He shook his head. 'I don't have any.'

'Your father's name, then.'

'Nobody wants me. . . . ' The mobile lips turned down mournfully, while above them the wild eyes glittered. 'And who are *you*?'

'I am Lord Horn.' He forgave the impertinence because it had put him back on the track of his planned opening.

'Oh,' said his prisoner. '*You're* Horn, are you?'

'Yes,' said Horn. 'I am indeed. My – friends tell me you're a scholar. Is that so?'

'No!' The syllable exploded with sudden vehemence.

'But you can write?'

141

'Of course I can write.'

'Fine. I have paper and pen outside. You will write a letter to St Vier telling him that you are in my hands, and that when he has performed the job I have asked him to, you will be sent back to him. Unharmed.'

You would expect the fellow to relax. If he'd thought he had been abducted by a mere thug, he knew better now. But his voice was still thin, high and breathy with fear. 'Of course. What a tidy plan. And who will you have read it to him?'

'He can read it himself,' Horn snapped. He found his hostage's responses unnerving: they walked the knife's edge between frivolity and terror.

'He can't read. I read them for him.'

Lord Horn bit his cheek to keep from swearing. The situation seemed to be eluding him. He grasped at his proper authority. 'Write it anyway.'

'But don't you see,' the boy said impatiently, 'I *can't*!'

'Are you ill? Have you lost the faculty of your eyes and hands? Or are you just too stupid to realise what predicament you are in?'

The boy went even paler. 'What are you going to do to me?'

'Nothing,' Horn exploded, 'if you'll just stop arguing and do as I tell you!'

St Vier's lover licked his lips. 'I don't want to be hurt,' he said with soft desperation. 'But you have to see how stupid it is to write him a letter.'

Horn stepped back, as though his prisoner's insolence were a fire too hot to bear. 'Do you hear what you are *saying*?' he demanded. 'Are you making *me* conditions?'

'No – no – ' the boy said desperately. 'I'm just trying to *explain*. Can't you understand anything I'm telling you? Richard St Vier,' he continued hurriedly, before Horn could object, 'he isn't going to want to let anyone else see a letter with – a letter like that. He doesn't like other people knowing his business. Anyone who reads it to him would know what your demands are, and then if he meets them, they'll know that he gave in to you. He can't have that. It's – it's his honour. So even if I write you the stupid letter, it's no good. You may,' here the pale lips flattened in the ghost of a smile, 'be stuck with me.'

'Oh, I doubt that,' the nobleman answered, smiling creamily.

The boy must be bluffing, playing for time. Perhaps he expected St Vier to come riding up at the head of a band of cutthroats, storm the house, lift him to the saddlebow and ride off into the night. . . . 'He seems to be very fond of you. I'm sure he is eager to get you back.'

The green eyes were staring frankly at him, at his leg. Before he could stop himself, Horn glanced down. His own fingers were curling and uncurling against the fabric. 'It must be done quickly,' he said, clenching his hand into a fist at his side, and thrusting his face almost into his prisoner's. 'I cannot waste time while he looks for you. I want the job done. Then he can have you back, for whatever he wants you for.'

'What do you think he wants me for?' The thin voice was taut with desperation. 'He can get others for that – whoever he wants. You've made a mistake.'

'No mistake,' Horn said, certain at last.

'Do you want money?' the boy said breathlessly. 'I can get some, if that's what you want.'

Lord Horn stepped back, awash in the fumes of power, poignant as pleasure. He would have what he wanted of the swordsman, and the swordsman's lover would provide him with another feast entire. His fear was strong wine, a sop to Horn's pride.

'No money,' Horn snarled. 'I'll have what St Vier has.'

The young man flinched, his hand raised in an oddly virginal gesture of defence. Horn's teeth showed in response. He knew that game from his own pretty-boy days, the titillation and the fear combined. . . .

For a moment, a trick of the light, he saw Lord Michael's features in the young man's face. He wouldn't dare set Godwin of Amberleigh's son in chains . . . but if he could! Michael Godwin would not have the chance to refuse Lord Horn again. Godwin and St Vier, with their blithe rejections! He, himself, Lindley, Lord Horn, had money; he had position; he knew what it was to have the town at his feet, men and women begging for a letter, for a ribbon, for the touch of his mouth. . . .

It occurred to him that if St Vier hadn't written him that letter, that short, insulting note of refusal, then someone else must have. That dark, eccentric hand might belong to the man before him. He would find out shortly.

'Why should I not want what St Vier wants?' he continued. 'He will not accept money when it runs counter to his desires. Such is his honour,' Horn said drily. 'Why should you expect less of me?'

'I can't help it,' Alec said pathetically.

'Write the letter,' snapped Horn.

'It won't do any good,' Alec answered. His eyes were staring wide as though they would speak for him. His hands strained against their bonds.

Horn saw them, and saw something else. 'That ring.' It was a ruby, tremendously long and thin, square-cut, set in white gold, flanked at the band with little diamonds. It rode the long hand like a familiar, a fire-beast, large and cold and alive. 'Give it to me.'

Alec clenched his fist on it, helpless and stubborn. 'No.'

Horn lifted his bleached and manicured hand, and slammed it hard across the bound man's face.

Alec screamed. The shrill echoes rang in the stone room, hurting Horn's ears. He dropped his hand and jumped back.

The red marks of Horn's hand, rough as a child's tracing, were rising to the surface of the bound man's skin. He stared owlishly at Horn, not blinking away the water in his eyes.

'I'm a coward,' Alec said. Horn lifted his hand again, to see the young man flinch. 'I'm afraid of being hurt, I told you so. If you hurt me, I'll only scream again.'

'Give me the ring.'

'You're a thief,' Alec said haughtily, his fear pushing him into fury, 'as well as a whore. What do you want with it?'

Horn managed to restrain himself from battering the flat mobile mouth into shapelessness.

'You will do as I say, or you and your Richard are going to be very sorry.'

At the swordsman's name, the strange young man stiffened. 'If you harm me, my lord,' he said, 'it is you who will be sorry.' His chin was up, his long eyes veiled, and his voice dripped breeding and contempt.

'Oho,' said Horn. 'Trying that trick, are you? And whose little bastard are *you* supposed to be . . . *my lord*?'

The boy flinched again, although Horn hadn't raised a finger. 'No one,' he mumbled, hanging his head. 'I'm no one, I'm nothing at all. And I'm glad of it.' He looked suddenly as if he wanted to spit. 'I am very, very glad of it, if you are the example I'm meant to follow.'

'Insolence!' Horn hissed. Clenching his fist behind his back he said, 'And I suggest you learn to control it, my young nobody. Or I will hurt you very much indeed, and no one will hear you scream.'

'*You'll* hear,' he said, again unable to stop himself.

'I will stuff your mouth with silk,' Horn answered smoothly. 'I happen to know it's very effective.'

'May I have a drink first?' he asked with proper humility.

'Of course you may,' said Horn. 'I'm not a monster. Behave yourself, do as I say, and we'll see about making you more comfortable.'

Horn pulled the ring off the long finger himself, since the chains didn't allow the boy's hands to meet. Horn wasn't stupid. The boy hadn't wanted to give it up: the ruby must mean something to St Vier.

'I shall write the note myself,' he said, 'and send it with the ring to St Vier at the usual tavern. As soon as the job is done, we'll consider the matter settled.'

'Perhaps,' Alec enquired, 'you will send one of your own rings in earnest?'

Horn looked with pity at the shoddy boy. 'I am a gentleman,' he explained. 'He knows my word is good.'

They let the messenger go, and St Vier was furious.

Rosalie realised that, for all the fights settled under her roof, she had never seen him angry before. His voice wasn't raised, nor his motions unusually abrupt. Those who didn't know him well might not even notice the pallor of his face, or the quiet that hung about him like the silences between thunder. But the pleasant ring of his voice was gone; his speech was flat, without inflection:

'I said anyone. Anyone who came asking for me.'

'It was only a messenger,' said Sam Bonner again, at his sweetest. He was getting more conciliatory with each repetition; but he was the only one there with the grape-sodden nerve to say anything at all. There was no knowing with men like St Vier

145

when they would decide to put a stop to all explanation. However, the swordsman remained quiet and still – if you liked that sort of stillness. Rodge and Nimble Willie glanced at each other. The little thief stepped forward. He looked up at St Vier with earnest gravity lining his childish face, and tried again.

'We did stop him, see. He was trying just to drop the packet on the table and run, but Rodge here stopped him. But he didn't know anything, see, not a thing – rabbit-scared he was, and ticklish with his steel; so we just lifted his purse and let him go. Not much in it.'

'You can bet we asked first,' Sam asserted; 'now you know we would.' ('Sam . . .' Rodge cautioned.) 'But he didn't know a thing. Got that packet third-hand; third-hand, and didn't know a thing.'

Anxiously they watched St Vier break open the wax seal. He flung the paper onto the floor. In his hand was a ruby ring. He stared at it, and they stared too. It was worth a fortune. But it didn't seem to cheer him up. Someone pressed a mug of beer into his free hand; he took it but paid no other notice.

'There's writing on that paper.'

It was Ginnie Vandall, who had gone out looking for him in the other direction. 'I can read,' she said huskily.

Richard picked up the paper, took her elbow and steered her out into the empty yard.

She peered at the note in the morning light. Fortunately it was full of short words. She read, slowly and carefully:

Do the Job for me at once and he will be
returned to you right away unharmed.

There was no signature.

The seal on the outside had been blank; inside, handsomely stamped in crimson wax, was the crest he'd seen on the other notes, the ones Alec had laughed at.

'Ah,' said Ginnie. 'That's not so good.' He would have to refuse. She knew that. No swordsman could afford to be blackmailed. He had lost his Alec – not that he wouldn't be better off without the unpleasant scholar in the long run. He'd see it himself in a few days, when it had all blown over. She didn't ask whose crest it was. Someone powerful, who had wanted the best swordsman in the city very badly.

She said, 'You'll want to lay quiet for a couple days. I'll tell Willie to bring the news round to you at Marie's. If you've got any appointments Hugo can – '

He looked at her as though she weren't there. 'What are you talking about?' His eyes were the mute colour of drowned hyacinths.

'His lordship won't like it,' she explained. 'The city's not a good place for you to be.'

'Why not? I'm taking the job.'

He handed her the full mug and walked away. At the doorway he turned, remembering to say, 'Thank you, Ginnie,' before he left.

For a moment she stood looking after him; then she spun on her heel and walked slowly back into the tavern.

It was true; he could not afford to be blackmailed. But neither would he let someone under his protection be taken away from him. And that was the more immediate problem, to which Richard St Vier addressed himself.

He had nothing against Lord Michael Godwin, and what he knew of Lord Horn he didn't like: the man was stupid, graceless and impatient. It meant there was little chance of Richard's finding Alec before Horn gave up on him.

Unfortunately, he couldn't count on Horn being quite stupid enough to have Alec in his townhouse. It was a shame: Richard was good at breaking into houses. A set of plans like crystalline maps unrolled before him; but they all took time, and the note had said *at once*. There was no one on the Hill who owed him favours: Richard took care to keep himself debt-free both ways. There were people up there who might help him, if he asked, for his own sake; but it was bad enough that most of Riverside now knew about Alec's disappearance – he didn't want the whole city talking about it.

He crumpled the note in his fist. He must remember to burn it. Tonight he would challenge Godwin, take care of him, and hope that the duchess or someone would want St Vier badly enough to protect him from the Godwin family lawyers, should the need arise. He had no faith in Horn's protection. What happened after that, St Vier would have to take care of himself.

Chapter XVI

He left Riverside well before the sun set, wearing his comfortable brown clothes. He knew that most nobles were at home at that hour, getting dressed up for the evening's activities.

There were very few pedestrians on the Hill; he passed only random servants on last-minute errands. The meat and produce delivery wagons had departed with the last of their charges hours ago, leaving the cooks to their own devices; the visiting-carriages were being burnished in the yards. The gates and walls of the riverward estates cast long purple shadows across the wide streets. In the shadows, night's chill had already set in. He was glad of his long cloak, chosen to hide the sword he wore. Because of the spring damp, the ruddy clay in the street was not yet dusty. In the squares of sunlight between houses it glowed golden, blocked out by shadows in geometric patterns arbitrary and beautiful.

The Godwin townhouse was not large, but it was set back from the street, with a conveniently corniced gate. If the lord drove or rode out, he would certainly come through it. Richard positioned himself in a shadow against the wall, and waited.

The wait gave him time, unfortunately, to think about Alec and Lord Horn. He doubted the scholar was curbing his tongue any, and hoped, despite the note's assurance, that Alec would not be too badly damaged. These nobles were not like Riversiders: they were used to acting on their wills, they didn't understand about signs that something wasn't safe to handle, or instinct that said to let it go for now. That was what had first preserved Alec when he'd entered Riverside alone. People had sensed something not right about him, and had not exacted retribution for his offences. But Lord Horn wouldn't be thinking that way. And Richard already knew Alec's opinion of Horn. He felt himself smile with the memory.

St Vier shrugged and shivered at the chill that had settled in the folds of his cloak. There was nothing he could do about it now: only wait, and hope Lord Michael was not too heavily attended. So far as he knew he did not have his own bodyguard; if Richard issued the formal challenge to Lord Michael on the street he would have no choice but to fight St Vier then and there. But he was a long time coming out. Richard looked at the sky. He'd give it until sundown before going up to the door to call the noble out. That was a risk, because Godwin might have some servant inside who could take the challenge for him, fight in his stead and give Lord Michael time to flee the city before Horn could find another challenger. They were a silly bunch of rules, but they made death by duel with a professional seem less like assassination. It was all correct within the boundaries of formal challenge; but Richard doubted that Horn would be pleased, and he needed to keep him happy.

He'd challenged other young lords in his time, and was not looking forward to this. Often they made a great deal of fuss over their clothes, taking off and folding their coats as though they were going to be putting them on again. Even the ones with enough presence to strike a proper stance had hands that shook holding the sword. The only such challenge he'd ever enjoyed was one in which the lady hired him only to scar his mark distinctively.

He heard footsteps suddenly, and looked up. On the other side of the gate a small postern opened, and a man stepped out. When he turned to shut the door Richard recognised him as the red-haired nobleman who'd run after him that winter day at the bookshop, whom he'd pointed out to Alec at the theatre. Lord Michael was wearing a sword. He set off down the street, without looking behind him, whistling.

He could easily catch up to him. The space in the street was good, the light not yet failed. And, wonder of wonders, it was an excellent sword from what Richard could see of it: not the nobleman's toy they usually carried. He readied himself to move, and then paused. Where was this noble sauntering off to so purposefully, on foot and without attendance, carrying a real duelling sword? He wanted to know; and he did not really relish butchering the man in front of all his neighbours. Richard decided it would do no harm to stalk Lord Michael to his destination and satisfy his curiosity. Without undue hurry, he detached himself from the shadows and set off down the Hill after his guide.

'You're late,' observed Vincent Applethorpe, looking up from the sword he was polishing one-handed, the hilt wedged between his knees.

'Sorry,' Michael panted, having run up the stairs. He knew he was being accused, however mildly; and he had learned not to try to bluster his way out. He only explained, 'I had some people over, and they wouldn't go away.'

Applethorpe smiled slowly, secretly, into the polished blade. 'You may find that stops being a problem soon. In a year or so, after you've won your first duel. People become very eager to pick up the slightest of hints from you then.'

Michael grinned in return, more broadly than he'd meant to, at the thought of Lord Bertram and Lord Thomas flinching, putting down their chocolate cups and slinking away at the sign of a yawn. He found it hard to imagine really killing anyone; and if he did some day he certainly hoped none of his friends would find out about it.

Michael stripped down to his shirt and began limbering up. The master commented, 'The Tragedy's in town. Do you know about it?'

'I . . . it's at Blackwell's,' he answered noncommittally.

'It's not a good idea to go,' the Master said, putting the sword back on the rack. It hadn't really needed polishing, but he liked to keep up contact with his blades, and he didn't like sitting idle waiting for Godwin to come. Now he could pace, watching the young man from every angle, alert to any flaw. 'You want to avoid things like that.'

'Is there really a curse?'

'I don't know. But it's never done anyone any good.'

It satisfied him: practical, like all of Applethorpe's advice. 'Ready?'

Michael caught the practice-sword that was tossed to him – possibly Master Applethorpe's only theatrical tendency, but also good for his eye. It meant the Master would be calling out orders,

151

and his student must follow the shifting commands with precision. He hoped tonight Applethorpe would duel with him again. He was getting better at it, learning how to integrate the moves and defences he'd been taught. It excited him – but not, any more, past skill and reason. He was learning to think and act at the same time.

'Garde!' the Master snapped, and Lord Michael sprang to the first defensive position, already tensed for the rapid command to follow. He waited a beat, two beats, but there was nothing.

'That's strange,' the Master said; 'there's someone coming up the stairs.'

Richard couldn't think why the lord should be walking to a common hiring-stable, when he had plenty of horses at home. He watched him go in a side door, and heard the swift tread of feet on wooden stairs. In a judicious few minutes, he followed.

He took it all in at a glance: the clear space, the targets, and the two men, one without an arm, the other still at garde, both staring at him in surprise.

'Excuse me for interrupting,' he said. 'My name is Richard St Vier. I bear a challenge to Lord Michael Godwin, to fight past first blood, until a conclusion is reached.'

'Michael,' said Vincent Applethorpe calmly, 'light the candles; there won't be enough daylight soon.'

Carefully Michael replaced his sword in the rack. He could hear the sound of his own breathing in his ears, but he tried to get it to sound like Applethorpe's voice, steady and even. He was surprised at how well he could control his muscles, despite the racing of his blood: the tinder struck on the first try. He walked around the room, lighting the fat drippy candles, their flames pale and indefinite in the twilight, almost transparent. This was St Vier, the strange man who had bought the book of philosophy from Felman that winter's day. He remembered rather liking him; and his friend Thomas, at the theatre, had betrayed a definite interest. *He's watching you* . . . God, Michael thought, of course he was! He wished he had had the chance to watch St Vier fight, just once. Accidents did happen, and strokes of luck.

While Michael was making his rounds, Applethorpe came forward to greet the swordsman. 'I've heard of you,' he said, 'of course. I'm very glad to meet you.' They did not touch hands. St Vier's were inside his cloak, one resting on the pommel of his sword. They faced each other in the dim studio, two men of nearly identical height and build, but for the older man's missing arm. 'My name is Vincent Applethorpe,' the Master said. It was clear from St Vier's face that he'd never heard the name. 'I claim the challenge.'

'No!' said Michael without meaning to. He cursed as candle-wax dripped onto his hand.

'I wish you wouldn't,' Richard answered the Master. 'It will make things harder.'

'I was told you liked a challenge,' Applethorpe said.

Richard compressed his lips in mild annoyance. 'Of course it would be a pleasure. But I have obligations. . . .'

'I have the right.'

The wax was cooling on Michael's hand. 'Master, please – it isn't your fight.'

'It will be a very short fight if it is yours,' Applethorpe said to him. 'You won't learn a thing. It is very much my fight.'

'You do have the right,' St Vier admitted. 'Let's begin.'

'Thank you. Michael, get your sword. Now kiss the blade and promise not to interfere.'

'I promise not to interfere.' The steel was very cold against Michael's lips. At this angle the blade felt heavy; it seemed to pull his hand down. He made his wrist sustain the weight for an extra moment, and then saluted his teacher with it.

'Your honour's good,' the Master was saying to St Vier.

'Inconveniently good,' Richard sighed. 'I won't touch him if you lose. If I lose, please see that word gets back to Riverside; they'll know what to do.'

'Then let's begin.'

And the master swordsmen began. It was all there as Michael had studied it. But now he saw the strength and grace of Applethorpe's demonstrations compacted into the little space of precious time.

Michael watched with luxurious pleasure the rise and fall of their arms, the turn of their wrists, now that he could follow what was happening. Master Applethorpe was demonstrating again, as fine and precise as at the lessons; but now there was a mirror to him, the polished, focused motions of St Vier. Michael forgot that death was at hand as, indeed, the two swordsmen seemed to have done, leisurely stroking and countering their way across the scrubbed white floor, with the high ceiling catching and returning the ring of their steel.

As the swordplay grew fiercer the sound of their breath became audible, and the nearer candleflames shuddered in their passing. It was almost too fast for Michael to follow now, moves followed up and elaborated on before he could discern them; like trying to follow an argument between two scholars fluent in a foreign language, rich with obscure textual references.

St Vier, who never spoke when fighting, gasped, 'Applethorpe – why have I never heard of you?'

Vincent Applethorpe took the occasion to come in high in a corkscrew movement that turned the other swordsman in a half-circle defending himself. St Vier stumbled backward, but turned it to his advantage by crouching into a sideways dodge that Applethorpe had to swerve to avoid.

Subtly, something changed. At first Michael couldn't figure out what it was. Both men were smiling twin wolfish grins, their lips parted as much for air as for delight. Their moves were a little slower, more deliberate, but not the careful demonstration of earlier. They didn't flow into each other. There were pauses between each flurry of strokes and returns, pauses heavy with tension. The air grew thick with it; it seemed to weight their movement. The time of testing, and of playing, was over. This was the final duel for one of them. Now they were fighting for their lives – for the one life that would emerge from this elegant battle. For a moment Michael let himself think of it: that whatever happened here, he would emerge unscathed. Of course there would be things to do, people to notify. . . . He caught his breath as St Vier was forced to lunge back into the wall, between two candles. He could see a crazy grin on the man's face as he held Applethorpe off with elaborate wristwork. For the moment the two were evenly matched, arm against arm. Michael prayed that it would never stop, that there would always be this moment of utter mastery, beautiful and rare, and no conclusion ever be reached. St Vier knocked over a candle; it put itself out rolling on the floor. He kicked aside the table it had been on, extricating himself from the corner, and the action resumed.

Richard knew he was fighting for his life, and he was terribly happy. In most of his fights, even the good ones, he made all the decisions: when to turn serious, whether to fight high or low . . . but already Applethorpe had taken that away from him. He wasn't afraid, but the edge of challenge was sharp under him, and the drop from it irrevocable. The world had narrowed to the strength of his body, the trained agility of his mind in response to his opponent. The universe began and ended within the reach of his senses, the stretch of his four limbs and the gleaming steel. It was too good to lose now, the bright point coming at him always from another angle, the clarity of his mind anticipating and returning it, creating new patterns to play. . . .

He saw the opening and went for it, but Applethorpe countered at the last instant, pivoting clumsily so that what would have been a clean death stroke caught him raggedly across the chest.

The Master stood upright, gripping his rapier too tightly, staring straight ahead. 'Michael,' he said clearly, 'that arm is for balance.'

Blood was soaking through the sweat in his shirt, the smell of it like decaying iron overlaying the tang of exertion that still hung thick in the air. Quickly Richard caught him and eased him to the floor, supporting him on his own heaving chest. Applethorpe's breath made a liquid, tearing sound. Michael found his cloak, and spread it over his teacher's legs.

'Step back,' St Vier ordered him. He leaned his head down next to Applethorpe's and murmured, 'Shall I finish it?'

'No,' Applethorpe rasped. 'Not yet. Godwin – '

'Don't talk,' Michael said.

'Let him,' said Richard.

The Master's teeth were gritted, but he tried to untwist his lips to smile. 'If you're good enough, this is how it ends.'

Michael said, 'Are you telling me to give it up?'

'No,' St Vier answered over Vincent Applethorpe's hissing breath. 'He's talking about the challenge. I'm sorry – you either know it or you don't.'

'Shall I get a surgeon?' Michael asked, clutching at the world he was master of.

'He doesn't need one,' St Vier said. Again he bent his dark head. 'Master – thank you. I do enjoy a challenge.'

Vincent Applethorpe laughed in triumph, and the blood spattered everything. The marks of his fingers were still white on St Vier's wrists when he lowered the corpse to the floor.

Richard wiped his hands on the young lord's cloak, and covered the dead man with it. Without quite understanding how they had got there, Michael found himself standing across the room, facing the swordsman's commanding presence.

'You have the right to know,' Richard said, 'it was Lord Horn set me on. He won't be glad you're still alive, but I've fought your champion and I consider my obligation discharged. He may try again with someone else; I suggest you leave the city for a while.' He caught the expected clenching of Michael's fists. 'Don't try to kill Horn,' he said. 'I'm sure you're good enough to do it, but his life is about to become complicated; it would be better if you left.' The young man only stared at him, blue-green eyes hot and bright in his white face. 'Don't try to kill me either; you're surely not good enough for that.'

'I wasn't going to,' Michael said.

Calmly, St Vier was collecting his own belongings. 'I'll report the death,' he said, 'and send someone to look after it. Was he married?'

'I . . . don't know.'

'Go on.' The swordsman put Michael's sword and jacket in his hands. 'You shouldn't stay.'

The door closed behind him, and there was nowhere to go but down the dark stairs.

Outside it was still early, a warm spring night. The sky was that perfect turquoise that sets off the first scattering of stars. Michael shivered. He had left his cloak upstairs, he was going to be cold without it – but it was no use, was it – he passed his hand over his face in an attempt to clear his thoughts, and felt a hand close around his wrist.

All the violence of the past hour exploded in his body like fireworks. He couldn't really see what he was doing through the red-gold flare, but he felt his fist connect with flesh, his body

156

twisting like a whirlwind, heard a long drawn-out howl like the centre of a storm – and then a sharp thumping noise that heralded the most glorious set of fireworks yet, before night fell without stars.

Chapter XVII

When his vision cleared he was in a coach. His hands and feet were tied, and the curtains were drawn. His head ached, and he was thirsty. Considering how soon he would likely be dead it shoudn't matter, but he badly wanted a drink. The jouncing of the carriage over cobblestones was intolerable. Cobblestones – that meant they were somewhere on Hertimer Street, going up towards the Hill.

'Hey!' he shouted. The reverberations in his skull made him wish he hadn't; but at least he could make some trouble for someone. Something terrible had just happened, which was in some way his fault, and shouting might stave it off. 'Hey, stop this thing at once!'

The only answer he got – or was like to get – was savage pounding on the roof of the carriage. He felt like a handsomely trussed-up pea rolling around in the centre of a drum. He'd meant to eat when he got back from Applethorpe's –

Something in his brain tried to warn his thoughts away, but there was no stopping the flood that broke through. The image struck in his stomach first, so that he thought he was going to spew – but then the pain rose and took over his breathing, knotting the muscles of his throat and face.... He would not come before Horn weeping. That at least he could withhold. He had been disarmed by his captors; but there were other ways to kill a man. He'd wrestled, and learned some of them. Never mind what St Vier had said; St Vier hadn't known how soon he would be facing his enemy. Or had he? Michael was amazed at Horn's effrontery: presumably the carriage had been left as a backup in case St Vier failed. Perhaps Horn meant to bed him before setting him up for another challenge.... Erotic, violent visions wound through the labyrinth of pain and all the emotions he'd never had to feel before, the pain and grief and fury weaving themselves into a strangely seductively soothing trance. Rapt in it, he only noticed the carriage had stopped when he heard the squeak of the opening gate.

As it clattered into the yard he came fully alert. His breathing was quick, his awareness of his body seemed supernaturally heightened. The pain was there, but also the strength and coordination. When they opened the door he would be ready for them.

But they didn't open the door. The carriage pulled up to what he supposed was the house's main entrance. He could hear his captors getting down, the muffled growl of voices issuing orders. Then there was silence. They weren't going to leave him here all night, were they?

When the carriage door opened it heralded a light so bright that his eyes blinked and watered.

'Dear me,' said a woman's voice out of the dazzling nimbus. 'Was it necessary to be quite so thorough?'

'Well, your ladyship, he did try to kill me.'

'All the same . . . Untie his feet, please, Grayson.'

He didn't even look down at the man kneeling over his ankles. The Duchess Tremontaine stood framed by the little doorway, in full evening dress, holding up an inelegant iron lantern.

Finally, he was too bruised to care what she thought of him and his sense of style. 'What are you doing here?' he asked hoarsely.

She smiled, her voice like long, cool slopes of snow. 'This is my house. My people brought you here. Do you think you can stand up?'

He stood up, and sat down again swiftly.

'Well, I am not a nurse,' she said with the same cool sweetness. 'Grayson, will you see that Lord Michael is made comfortable indoors? My lord, I will attend you when you are rested.'

Then the colour, the sweetness, the perfume were gone, and he was left to the unpleasant task of imposing his will on his own unruly person.

Several ages seemed to pass as Lord Michael worked his way up through strata of dirt, fatigue, hunger and thirst. Diane's servants had put him in a handsome room with a hot bathtub and a set table. The room was lit by fire and candlelight. Curtains of

159

heavy red velvet were drawn, so that he could not see which way the room faced. The red hangings, the mellow light, the sense of enclosure, all made him feel unreasonably safe and cared-for, like a child wrapped up in a blanket in someone's arms.

The terrible pain of what had happened lay hard and bright at the centre of his physical contentment. The memory came and went, like the ebb and flow of waves, but with no predictable pattern. When Michael was a little boy, there was a painting on the wall of his home that he was terrified of: it showed the spirit of a dead woman rising from the tomb, her baby in her arms. He had been afraid even to pass the room where it was. Whether he wanted to or not, he would think of it at the worst moments: in the dark, going up the stairs; so he started making himself think of it all the time, until it became so familiar that he could contemplate it without a tremor. He wasn't quite ready for that yet, not while the confusions and strangeness still enfolded him. Before he went bathing in the events of Applethorpe's death he had to know where the dry land was.

He was sunk in an easy chair before the fire; but at the click of the doorlatch he jumped like a cat. It was not the door he had come in by. This was a smaller one cut in the red wall.

Diane said, 'Please, sit down. May I join you?'

Mutely he indicated a chair. She helped herself to some cherry cordial from the array of decanters, and seated herself across from him. She had changed her clothes: as if to prove that this was indeed her home, she wore a flowing house-dress of soft blue silk. Her loose curls tumbled over her shoulders like the crests of waves.

'Please don't be too angry with Asper,' she said. 'You upset him rather badly the night of my little party. He is a vain man, and proud, and lecherous – you shouldn't find him so hard to understand.'

For a moment he made the duchess fear for her personal possessions. But his fingers only left a dent in the pewter flagon at his side. She continued, 'You should have come to me, as soon as you suspected he was up to something.' Michael still cared enough for her esteem not to want to tell her that he hadn't known. The duchess sighed. 'Poor Asper! He isn't very subtle, and he isn't very clever. He was pestering some young woman of Tony's. . . . By the way, Lord Michael, did you kill St Vier?'

'No. He killed my fighting-master.'

'I see.'

'I am not the swordsman you would have me, madam.'

She smiled a bewitching, knowing smile. 'Now, why should you say that?'

'I'll never stand a chance against him,' he said bitterly, staring not at the beautiful woman, but into the dregs of the fire. 'Everyone knew that. Applethorpe was humouring me.' Another pain, a little sharp sliver that he'd borne since the challenge and almost forgotten in the weight of the other. 'He knew I'd never make a swordsman.'

'Once in a generation there comes a swordsman like St Vier. Your teacher never said you were that one.' Sunk in his feelings, he did not respond. But her voice was no longer light. 'But, for St Vier, there is nothing more. It is all he wants out of life, and probably all he'll ever get. That's not what you want; not all. It just comes closer than most things.'

He looked at her, not really seeing her. He felt as though his skin had been peeled back with a scalpel. 'What I want . . .'

' . . . I can give you,' she said softly.

'Fine – if I'm to be Horn!'

He heard the harsh clang of metal, and realised that he was standing up, and that he had thrown the tankard across the room. The duchess hadn't stirred. 'Madam,' he said stiffly. 'You chose to embroil yourself in my affairs. I hope it has given you pleasure. I believe all my desires ceased to be a matter for discussion between us some time ago.'

She chuckled richly. He was appalled to find himself thinking of strawberries and cream. 'There you are,' she said. 'I wonder if you men have any idea of how insulting it is to women when you assume that all we can offer is our bodies?'

'I am sorry.' He looked up and met her eyes. 'It is as insulting as to have it thought that's all we want.'

'Don't apologise. I made you think it.'

'You made me think a great many things this winter.'

'Yes,' she said. 'Shall I apologise?'

'No.'

'Good,' she said. 'Then I shall go on making you think. I know what you want. You want to be a man of power. I'm going to give you that.'

His face unfroze; he was able to smile his charming smile. 'Will it take long?'

'Yes,' she said. 'But it won't seem long.'

'I want to be your lover,' Michael said.

'Yes,' said the duchess, and opened the red silk door to her chamber.

Inside it he paused. 'Lord Ferris,' he said.

'Ah, Ferris.' Her voice was low; it made him shiver to hear it. 'Well; Ferris should have told me he knew Lord Horn was planning to kill you.'

He seemed to float – as though he never touched her body, but was held suspended in some directionless space whose charts only she held. All pride, all fear were gone from him. Even the desire for it not to end was swallowed by the overwhelming present. His vaunted sophistication gave way to something new; and in that infinite space he rose and fell in the same moment into a world's end of fireworks reflected in a bottomless river.

'Michael.'

The tip of her finger touched his ear, but all he did was sigh. 'Michael, you're going to have to leave the city now. For two weeks, maybe three.' He turned over and kissed her mouth, and felt a roaring in his ears. But her lips, while still soft, were not pliant, and he drew back to let her speak. 'I would like to send you out of the country. There are some things I would like you to see. The people of Chartil respect a man who can use a sword, especially a nobleman. Will you go?'

His hands refused to leave her flesh, but he said over them, 'I will.'

'It must be now,' she said. 'The ship sails in three hours' time with the dawn tide.'

It was a shock to him, but he mastered it, stroking her skin for the deliciousness of it, for the memory, without arousing the honeyed longing that would not let him go.

162

His clothes were set out in the red room. She followed him there, trailing silk and instructions. He should be tired, but his body tingled. It was the feeling he got after lessons – Like a club, the memory struck him hard. Bent over, strapping on his useless sword, he said nothing.

The duchess sat, smiling, swinging one white foot, watching him cover his collar bones. 'I have something to give you,' she said. He thought of roses, gloves and handkerchiefs. 'You will keep it for me, and no one can take it from you unless you offer it. I am convinced you will not offer it. It is a secret. My secret.'

Fully dressed, he kissed her hand formally, the way he had that first afternoon at Lady Halliday's. 'Ah', she said; 'I was right about you then; and you were right about me. You see, it's true, Michael. Those men who died, Lynch and de Maris, they were not hired by the Duke of Karleigh. *I* hired Lynch – and de Maris got in the way. I needed to teach Karleigh a lesson, to tell him I was serious about a matter he thought I was joking about. He never took me seriously enough. Karleigh hired St Vier. His man won . . . but Karleigh – Karleigh knows he is going to lose in this matter, because I stand against him. If the duke is wise, he will stay in the country this spring.'

That was all she was going to tell him, and then trust him to figure the rest out for himself. He didn't feel clever or triumphant, after all. Excited, maybe, and a little frightened.

The duchess reached up and touched his rough cheek. 'Good bye, Michael,' she said. 'If all goes well, you will come back soon.'

There was a private side door, this time, for him to leave Tremontaine House by; and a chilly walk before the dawn, home to give his orders and depart. His sword hung at his side again, a heavy weight, but good protection in the dark.

Chapter XVIII

When the door opened Richard stayed where he was, sitting in the chair opposite. The cat had tolerated his steady stroking of her for almost an hour; but when his lap tensed she jumped off it, and darted over to the man coming in.

'Hello, Richard,' said Alec. 'What a surprise: you're awake, and it isn't even noon yet.'

He looked terrible: clothes wrinkled, face unshaven; eyes within their dark circles a particularly malevolent shade of green. He stood in the middle of the room, refusing to sit down, trying hard not to sway. The door swung shut behind him.

Richard said, 'Well, I went to bed early.' If Alec didn't want to be touched, he wasn't going to force it. It was enough for him to see that Alec was on his feet, and whole. Alec's face was unmarked, and his tone as light as ever, though his voice was thick with sleeplessness.

Alec said, 'I hear you bungled Horn's job.'

'Where did you hear that?'

'Straight from the horse's . . . mouth. Godwin's not dead.'

'I'm a swordsman, not an assassin. He didn't say to kill Godwin, he said to challenge him. I did. Someone else took the challenge; I killed *him*.'

'Naturally.'

'I don't see what you're fussing about it for; Horn must have been satisfied, or he wouldn't have – Alec!' Richard stared harder, trying to see beneath the shakily composed exterior. 'Did you *escape*?'

But Alec only smiled scornfully. 'Escape? Me? I couldn't escape from a haystack. I leave that kind of thing to you. No, he let me go when he found you'd fought the challenge. In the name of honour or something. You understand these people so much better than I do. I think' – Alec yawned – 'he didn't like me.' He

164

stretched his arms up over his head; high in the air the jewels flashed rainbows over his hands.

Richard's breath caught with a tearing sound.

'Oh.' Alec pulled his cuffs back into place. 'I'm afraid I've lost one of your rings. The rose. His so-called swordsmen took it. Maybe you can bill him for it. God, these clothes stink! I haven't changed them for three days. I'm going to roll them into a ball and drop them out of the window for Marie. Then I'm going to bed. I kept trying to sleep in the carriage, but it didn't have any springs, and then every time I was about to drop off I thought I smelt civet. I spent most of the trip with my head out of the window. And then they made me *walk* from the bridge! The near bridge, not the far one, at least, but even so. . . . '

Everyone in Riverside knew what shackle marks looked like. Richard followed him to bed, and later on he tried to kiss them. But Alec wrenched his wrists away.

'What else did he do?' Richard demanded harshly.

'Nothing! What more do you want?'

'Did he – '

'He didn't do *anything*, Richard, just leave me alone!'

But late that night, when Alec was drunk and excited and no longer cared, Richard kissed the marks again, and thought of Lord Horn.

The swordsman's business kept him out late the next day. When he came back he expected to find Alec asleep: Alec had been out of bed that morning at dawn, despite his late ordeal. But to his surprise a fire was blazing in the hearth, and Alec was kneeling in front of it. His loose hair, unbraided and unclasped, curtained his face like a temple mystery. With his black robe and long limbs he looked like a child's image of a wizard, peering into the mysteries of the fire. But he was busy doing something: with a shock Richard realised that Alec was tearing pages out of a book, carefully and methodically feeding them to the flames. He did not look up when St Vier shut the door, or when he took a few steps into the room.

Afraid to startle him, Richard said, 'Alec. I'm back.'

'Are you?' said Alec dreamily. The page he was holding burst into flame; his eyes were fixed on the blaze. His face was lit to flatness like an idol's mask, his eyes two dark slits. 'Did you have a nice time?'

'It was all right. What are you burning?'

Alec turned the book's spine around, as though he needed to be reminded of the title. '*On the Causes of Nature,*' he said. 'I don't need it anymore.'

It had been his gift; but Richard didn't give gifts to hold onto them. He stretched out before the fire, glad to be home. 'I thought it would take you longer to memorise this one. You haven't even worn the words off the binding yet.'

'I don't need it anymore,' Alec repeated. 'I know everything now.'

Something in the careful way Alec was taking hold of each page should have alerted him already. St Vier sprang out of his chair and spun Alec around by the shoulder.

'Stop that,' Alec said with mild annoyance. 'You're hurting me.' He didn't resist the fingers prying wide his eyelids. He looked calmly at Richard with eyes that were like two matched emeralds, with only a speck of black to mar each one.

'God!' Richard's grip tightened. 'You're sotted on Delight!'

The figured lips curved. 'Of course. Am I supposed to be surprised? It's excellent stuff, Richard; you should have some.'

St Vier recoiled involuntarily, although his grip held. 'No I shouldn't. I hate what the stuff does. It makes you stupid, and clumsy.'

'You're just being stuffy. I have some right here –'

'*No.* Alec, how – when did you start doing this?'

'At University.' The drug intensified the languor of his aristocratic drawl. 'Harry and I, doing experiments. Taking notes. You could take notes for me.'

'I can't,' Richard said.

'No, it's easy. Just write down what I say. . . . We're going to do a book. It will influence generations to come.'

Richard held tight to his shoulder. 'Tell me where you got it. How much did you take?'

Alec waved his hand vaguely. 'Why, would you like some?'

'No, I would not like some. How often do you do this?' It was stupid of him never to have considered it before. He'd thought he knew Alec, knew his habits and his ways, even when he wasn't there. . . .

Alec looked at him complacently. 'Not often. Not for a long time. I'm occupied with . . . other things. You look so worried, Richard. I saved you some.'

'That's very kind of you,' Richard said dryly. 'We'll just have to wait it out, then. With other things.' He carefully placed his arm around his lover's neck, tasted the sweetness of the drug on his tongue. With his other hand he slipped the book from Alec's fingers, laying it down away from the hearth. Then he led him into the bedroom.

He wasn't much good to talk to, but his body was pliant and sensitive as Richard undressed him.

'Why are you doing that?' Alec asked, more than once, as Richard undid another button, another lace.

'So you won't be cold,' Richard answered; and later, 'So I can kiss it. There. Like that.'

Alec chuckled happily. 'I appreciate that. I appreciate *you*.'

'Thanks.' Richard tickled him gently. 'I appreciate you. . . .'

Then Alec stiffened and drew back. 'What's that?' he cried.

'Probably me. My heartbeat. Nothing, don't worry. . . .'

'They're watching me, Richard, they're watching me!'

The period of serenity had passed, and the nervousness Richard had hoped to circumvent was upon him. 'No one's watching.'

But Alec pulled out of his arms and spread himself before the window, his clothes half-off him, hanging by ribbons and half-sleeves. He was pressing his palms to the glass, trying to cover it with his spread fingers, while his eyes fixed on the sky above them.

'The stars are watching me,' he declared in a voice of terrible pain. 'Make them stop!'

'They're not watching. Why should they?'

'God, make them stop. They're watching me!'

Richard interposed himself between Alec and the window, and pulled the shutters closed. 'It's all right now. They can't see you.'

Alec clung to him, burying his face in Richard's shoulder. 'I tried to get away. . . . Stone and Griffin and I, we were so sure . . . we had the calculations, Richard, they were right, I

167

know they were . . . it didn't matter about me, but they needed that stupid degree . . . what's going to happen to Harry's sister?' he cried wildly.

'It's all right . . .'

'No, you don't understand – the chancellors tore it up! I wouldn't believe them, I didn't think they'd do that. . . .'

'The University chancellors?'

'Doctor Pig-Nose.'

'And that's why they kicked you out?' He'd always suspected something like this.

'No. Not me. I'm all right. It's *you* I'm worried for. . . .'

'Not me, Alec.'

'. . . Richard? You have to protect me. I was safe in Rhetoric – do you know what that is? – in History, Geometry, but consider the angle of the sun: the stars describe an arc without a tangent – but they're watching, all the time they're watching me – '

He started violently at the sound of knocking in the hall. Richard held him tighter. Was he trying to destroy himself for that, because the University had rejected his work? He must have put a lot of faith in the place to begin with. If it had been his escape from his nobility, it was understandable. And if he were not noble, the school must have been his last chance. . . .

'You're all right now,' Richard repeated mechanically. 'That's all over. No one can hurt you now.'

'Don't let them find me. You don't know what it's like, knowing they won't touch you, just your friends, and everybody thinking I'm some kind of spy for the nobles – all I wanted was to – '

The knocking was fierce, and it was at their door. A thought came to Richard, and he tucked Alec in the blankets. 'Alec,' he said carefully, 'stay here, don't move. It's all right, there's just someone at the door. I'll be back soon.'

He waited until he'd left the bedroom to take up his sword.

Richard flung the door back in one sharp motion, blade already poised. It was a woman standing there, in a velvet cloak.

'Well,' said Ginnie Vandall, observing the sword, 'you're a little on edge.'

'Just being careful.'

'You should be. Are you alone?'

'In fact, I'm not. Can it wait 'til morning?'

She took the lowered blade as an invitation to enter, sweeping past him into the middle of the room. 'That's up to you, my dear. I'll make it short.'

'It can wait, then.'

'Look,' she said; 'I haven't come here alone at this hour to get turned away because you didn't want to put your clothes back on.'

He put the sword down. 'All right. What is it?'

'It's two men found dead at the bottom of Ganser Steps not an hour ago. The Watch found them, and the stupid bastards can't figure out why they were killed expertly with a sword. Neither can I. It was that neat upper stroke through the heart, and sooner or later someone's going to point out that you're the only one who can do that more than once.'

'They're supposed to.'

She stared at him angrily. 'Those men weren't Riverside. You're not a nobleman, you can't run around the city picking off whoever you want without a contract and expect no one to care. If you're going to commit your little murders, be careful how close to the Bridge you leave the corpses. We don't want the Watch coming in here looking for trouble.'

'They won't. And I had to make sure there was no mistake. Are you pretending, or don't you know who those men were?'

Her stare lost some of its hardness. 'Oh, Richard,' she sighed. 'I was hoping you weren't going to say that.'

'It's all right,' he said. 'The lord who set them after Alec isn't going to come forward and demand justice for them. He isn't the type. I really don't see what you're worried about. No one's going to harrow Riverside over a couple of bravos. And I've just made sure that that kind of thing doesn't happen again. Hugo should be glad.' He went to the door and held it open for her. 'Good night, Ginnie.'

'Wait,' she said, her hand raised to her throat. 'It doesn't have anything to do with Riverside, or with Hugo or any of the others. You've got to be more careful. They can't *let* you go around like that, not outside this district.' The hand lowered from her throat, glided down over the velvet. 'If it comes to an Inquiry, my dear, you'll hang, no matter what this lord's done to you.'

'Thank you. Good night.'

She moved closer, not to the door but to him, looking into his face. The shadows picked out the lines etched by her mouth and the corners of her eyes. 'I know what I'm doing,' she said, her voice as hard as her face. 'I've taken care of Hugo, and Hal Lynch, and Tom Cook before him. You don't want to die rich, that's fine with me. You want to take up with people who hate you, that's fine too. Just don't ignore what I say.'

'I understand,' he said to get rid of her. She wasn't a nervous talker; she had kept her eyes on him, and hadn't noticed the ruined book on the floor, or the mess in the fireplace.

'Richard,' said Ginnie, 'you don't.'

Her arms lifted slowly, and he let her fingers twine through his hair, pressing the back of his skull until his lips were bent to hers.

Richard had never actually kissed Ginnie Vandall before. Even in the heat of her moment she was expert and careful. The softness of her lips and the sharpness of her teeth fluttered down to the base of his spine. He shifted closer to her, catching the heat of her hipbone jutting into his thigh, her breasts flattening against his chest. He pressed his palm into the small of her back, parting his lips to reach her, when she pulled violently away.

The recoil jolted him backwards. He stared at her, still breathing deeply. Ginnie wiped her mouth with the back of her hand. 'Fool's Delight,' she said in disgust. 'That's something new for you. Is that what it takes these days?'

He shook his head. 'I don't do that.'

She glanced toward the back room, but didn't say Alec's name. Ginnie pulled her cloak around her and shrugged. 'Good luck.'

He stook for a moment listening to her feet going down the stairs. He heard the sound of another woman's voice: Marie, who must have let her in.

Then a floorboard creaked close behind him. Alec had drifted into the room, unnaturally soft-footed. His shirt still hung loose around his waist.

'I thought I heard something,' he explained. He seemed to have forgotten about the stars.

'Someone came to see me,' Richard said; but Alec wasn't

listening. He stalked the leather-bound book where it lay, just within range of the fire's dying glow, its gold tooling coursing with reflected light.

Alec crouched down. His clever fingers lifted the book from the floor, smoothing the crumpled pages, stroking the grime from its cover. He put the decorated leather to his cheek. The book rested against his face like a beautiful ornament, his eyes large and dark above it. His bare collarbones and shoulders framed its bottom edge.

'You see,' he said, 'you mustn't give me things.'

'Stop it,' Richard said, frightened and angry. The pale face looked otherworldly, but he knew it was just the drugs.

'Richard.' Alec stared at him without blinking. 'Don't tell me what to do. No one tells me what to do.' He turned to the fire with the book in his left hand held out behind him like a balance. Alec stretched his right hand toward the embers glowing red in the hearth. It was like watching a magic trick that might succeed . . . . Before his hand could close over the hot coals Richard sprang, pulling him roughly back into his arms, half-sprawling on the floor.

'Ah,' Alec sighed, going limp with dead weight on him. 'You're such a coward.'

'I'm not going to let anything happen to you,' Richard said doggedly, as though he were losing an argument.

'It isn't worth it,' said Alec dreamily; 'you won't always be there. They've got it all worked out now, haven't they? What do you suppose they'll want from you next?'

So he'd figured it out. For once, it had cost Richard something to protect him. But drugs couldn't keep that away forever.

'Don't worry,' said Richard. 'I'm taking care of that. It won't happen again.'

It was hard not to be angry with Ginnie's meddling. Richard owed her too much from the past to lose his temper with her because this once she was wrong. Even Alec knew that she was wrong. The men who had done Lord Horn's work must be found dead at the hands of St Vier.

Chapter XIX

It was too early in the year for an outdoor party, but one didn't refuse an invitation from the Duchess Tremontaine. Actually, the whole thing was impromptu and very delightful, as the ladies assured each other, bending over their flamingo mallets to give their wooden urchins a dainty tap: the weather unseasonably warm, the food fresh, the company delightful. Trust Diane to be so whimsically original! The gentlemen, their escorts, were quietly bored. One could flirt, but one couldn't bet – not on other people's wives and sisters, it wasn't decent.

Lord Ferris wondered whether his mistress kept inviting Horn because she thought it would amuse him. Usually it did; but this week he was not eager to be entertained by Horn. His equable settling of the weavers' rebellion had returned Ferris to the city a hero to his peers, and it was important that he circulate amongst them now, visible and accepting praise. The little man and his troubles were of no consequence now. But Horn kept edging up to Ferris, knocking his ball over to where he was standing, even when it was patently obvious that it was doing his game no good.

Diane was, as always, careful not to show any interest in Ferris, although it was the first time she'd seen her lover in weeks. Ferris, too, was careful. He remembered the first time he had been long out of town, near the beginning of their association. On his return he had gone straight to her house, to report to her on his mission, and to peel the silks from her body, inflamed with the memory of her. But he was more experienced now, and more cautious. He had not wanted to provoke comment by coming to see her immediately. He had a dinner engagement later tonight; but perhaps after her party there might be time for them to go to bed.

The glitter of sunlight on water, the merry music, the sparkling laughter and radiant colours of spring wardrobes set free from the confines of winter were giving Lord Ferris a headache. Horn's blue suit was a prime offender. Here it came again. Enthusiastically Ferris turned his back on the approaching nobleman to immerse himself in the nearest pool of gossip.

'We seem to be losing people at a stupendous pace this winter,' a sharp-faced noble called Galeno was expounding to a knot of men. 'At this rate the town will be empty before the season's officially ended, and there'll be no one left at all to vote in Spring Council.'

'Oh?' said Lord Ferris, ignoring Horn's peripheral gesticulations. 'Who's missing now?'

'First the Filisands left before New Year because of illness,' Galeno elaborated comprehensively, not to be balked of his list; 'then Raymond had that falling out with his wife's father; then there was the business with Karleigh and the swords; and now young Godwin's house is shut up, with no word of explanation. No one's seen him for days.'

That explained Horn's perturbation. 'I hope nothing's happened to him,' Ferris said politely.

'Oh, no; the servants said they'd received his personal orders to close up. But no one knows where he's gone, not even young Berowne, who usually can be counted on.'

Something must have gone wrong. Too bad for Asper. But Lord Michael had clearly left town, maybe even left the country, and that suited Ferris's purposes. Suddenly he thought, What if Godwin hadn't left at all, what if Diane were hiding him here in her house? But he dismissed the idea as abruptly as it had come. She wouldn't like the bother, or the risk. Her interest in the young man couldn't extend that far already. Godwin had been warned off, and that was all that was necessary.

'Karleigh,' said someone with insight. 'You didn't see him, Lord Ferris, when you went south? His hospitality's always good, and he must be bored to death out there. Glad of a little company, even from the opposition.'

'No, I didn't see him.' Let them believe that or not, as they liked. The truth was that he had not gone. He saw no need to let Karleigh feel important, and he'd been in a hurry to get back and settle with St Vier. He would tell Lord Halliday that Karleigh had seemed docile. It didn't much matter what he told Halliday now. 'Karleigh's old news,' Lord Ferris told his peers; 'midwinter madness. No one with any sense will want to unseat the Crescent next month.'

'But the rule – '

'We'll call an emergency and vote it down. There's always an emergency somewhere.' Appreciative laughter in reference to the weavers.

'Oh,' said old Tielman crustily. 'So that's the plan, is it? A sudden emergency that never quite lets up?'

The temperature around the little group dropped suddenly. Tielman was of Karleigh's generation; had been raised, perhaps, on the same stories of evil kings and the sovereign rights of the nobility. Ferris felt attention on him, like a single ray of heat. All across the lawn heads were turning to the knot of men, although no one knew exactly what they were looking for. Ferris had no desire to get himself into a challenge in Halliday's defence; at the same time, it would not hurt for the Crescent's supporters to see him as a benevolent force.

'My lord,' he fixed his good eye on the old man. 'Your words do no one credit.'

The Dragon Chancellor had weight and power. He had presence. Tielman backed off. 'I pray', he said with dignity, 'that my lord will not take offence. But we do not speak of a joking matter.'

'Then indeed you must!' a woman's voice chimed. It was the duchess, who, attentive as always to the mood of her company, had attached herself to the fringes of the circle. Now she took Ferris's arm. The wind fluttered the green and silver ribbons that streamed from her hat and dress. 'I smell a political discussion: no jokes allowed! But at my party we will be merry, and tell jokes that everyone can laugh at. Such a lovely day, on loan from summer. I don't know why you gentlemen must always be looking out for a chance to quarrel.' Her voice rippled on over the last of the dissolving tension. 'And if you must quarrel, let it be over women, or something else worthwhile. . . . '

Still talking, she led Ferris across the grass. Those nearest saw her lean her head into him, and caught snatches of her chiding, 'Really, my lord, you are just like all the rest of them. . . . '

Not lowering her voice she said, 'Now come, sit where I can keep an eye on you and you won't get into mischief, and tell me all about your trip. I don't suppose you were able to pick up some wool at a reasonable price . . . ?'

He allowed himself to be led to a wide seat under a linden tree. With the spread of her skirts and flounces there was barely room for him to sit down beside her; but he expertly flipped back the hang of his sleeves and poised himself on the edge of the seat.

He was, unfortunately, a sitting target for Lord Horn. To desert one's hostess would be rude; so when the fair nobleman came strolling up to them Ferris determined to stick it out with reinforcement from Diane.

To his dismay, the duchess showed no inclination to assist him in his evasion. 'Asper! How splendid you look. You should always wear blue, it is your best colour; don't you think so, Tony?'

'Unquestionably.' His head was beginning to ache again. 'Although I find green always gives him a certain . . . wicked air.'

'Indeed?' Horn preened. 'And is wickedness something to be cultivated, my lord?'

Oh, God, Ferris groaned inwardly. Desperate, he let his eye stray to the flamingo game. 'Madam Duchess! You have no champion. Allow me to take up your cause.'

She turned her mouth down mockingly. 'Flamingo, my lord? Isn't that a bit tame for you?'

He shrugged. 'It's the game of choice. Anyway, I play a poisonous game. I learnt it from my sisters. Even with one eye, I'll bet I can see your ball through to the stake ahead of those field-mice.'

'How ungallant – for the field-mice. I, of course, am flattered. But I'm afraid you can't have my ball, Tony, it's cracked. You'll have to champion someone else.'

'Never mind the flamingo,' Horn said affably; 'come and walk with me, my dear.'

'Oh, yes, Tony! You can show Asper the sculpture garden – I don't believe he's seen my additions to my lord the late duke's collection, although I know he saw the originals when dear Charles was alive. Of course I can't leave everyone now, so it will have to be you. I hope you don't mind. . . .'

Defeated and fuming, he bowed. 'It will give me the greatest pleasure.'

175

Lord Ferris maintained a frosty silence as he led the other noble across the lawns toward the statuary garden.

'What a wonderful woman,' said Horn, complacent now that he'd achieved his desire. Lord Ferris did not answer him, and the two men stepped onto the gravel path bordered by privet. The bushes were just beginning to come into leaf, creating a green-grey screen between them and the party across the lawn.

The first of the sculptures jutted a toe into their line of vision. It belonged to a nymph, innocently bathing her foot in a presumed stream that ran at about the level of their noses. On the pedestal behind her a leering satyr lurked, preparing to pounce, balked of his desire by an eternity of marble.

They passed it without comment. Horn's light satin shoes crunched rhythmically on the gravel path, leading deeper into the maze. The smell of sap and damp earth drifted past the barriers of their perfume. Under the next statue Horn paused. It was a classic piece depicting a now-defunct god in his avatar as a ram begetting a future hero on a virgin priestess who, according to this particular sculptor, was enraptured with her good fortune. For a moment Horn looked vaguely at it, and then took his carved ivory wand and began tapping the crucial juncture absently, with the nervous rhythm of someone drumming his fingernails.

'It didn't work,' he said at last.

'Obviously,' said Ferris, at no pains to hide his boredom.

'That little bastard Godwin's run off somewhere. God knows what he told St Vier first. I'll be a laughingstock!'

'You'd better ask the swordsman. Pay him something extra.'

Horn swore. 'How the devil am I to ask him anything? Getting this job out of him was bad enough.'

'Well, you've still got his friend, haven't you? Just send him —'

Horn's pale eyes protruded further. 'Of course not! I sent the fellow back! It was in the agreement. I couldn't go back on my word. Anyhow, he was a damned bother.'

Ferris lowered his hands and walked away.

When Horn caught up with him he stopped. 'You realise', Ferris said, 'that now St Vier is going to try to kill you?'

Horn lifted his chin, an arrogant and somehow tantalising gesture left over from his days of beauty. 'He wouldn't dare. Not on his own. Not without a contract.'

'St Vier doesn't work on contract. You should know that.'

'But I sent the fellow back!'

'Well, get him again.'

'I can't. The men I used – they're dead. Two days ago. My agent told me this morning.'

Ferris laughed. Birdlike, his one eye glinted at Horn. 'Can you imagine who killed them? Poor clever St Vier; I'm sure he was hoping you'd have figured it out by now. He doesn't know you; or his faith in humanity is high.'

Lord Horn's face had turned the colour of old cheese. His age showed on it suddenly, lined and hollowed. 'Your woman – Katherine – tell her to call him off!'

'I won't have you bothering Katherine; you've been too much with her already.'

'I can't leave the city – there'd be talk – '

'Stay, then, and guard yourself.'

'He wouldn't dare,' Horn hissed. 'If he touches me, he'll hang!'

'Yes, if he's caught,' Ferris said, and added reasonably, 'He's a madman, Asper; all great swordsmen are. It's the devil of a job. But they have their rules, just as we have ours. If you hadn't chosen to act outside them, you wouldn't be having these problems.'

He turned to go, eager to rejoin the party; but Horn caught the end of his sleeve, and he was forced to stop lest the fabric be torn.

'You!' Horn spat. 'Dragon Chancellor! You're a fine one to talk of rules. Shall I tell them how you encouraged this? You knew all about it from that girl of yours – you sent her to meet me, she told me you wouldn't mind. . . .'

'If by *them* you mean the Council . . .' Ferris tried to repress a slight smile. 'All right, I was careless.' He had been nothing of the kind. Horn knew only as much as was good for him. But it wouldn't do to have Horn completely against him, in case he got out of this alive. He began to play him out, the catspaw. 'But Asper, I beg you to reconsider. To denounce me before them means exposing your own part in this. I would not have you ruin my career at the expense of your own reputation.'

Horn's face was still belligerent, but faintly puzzled. He'd missed the irony, but some of the logic was getting through to him. 'There's no crime in setting a swordsman on some young puppy. . . .'

'But they'll want to know why,' Ferris said gently. 'As you say, there'll be talk. And it *is* a crime to abduct someone, although of course when you've explained your reasons. . . .'

Horn swallowed convulsively, the carefully hidden webbing of his throat moving against the cloth. 'I can't. . . .'

'No, of course not,' the orator's voice soothed. A sudden provocative image of the duchess touched Ferris's mind. He never wanted to go to bed with men, although many people said the excitement and sense of mastery were greater. Ferris liked women, and intelligent ones. For men, he liked the exercise of manoeuvring them, not just stupid ones like Horn, but clever ones like Halliday, feeling them hurtle down the slope with him on a sled of his own devising, turning the corners at his chosen rate of speed . . . it was a pleasure as dense and complex as lovemaking, with effects far more lasting and rewarding.

'Go on,' he said kindly to the now humble nobleman. 'Increase your guard, get a couple of swordsmen. . . .'

Horn passed a hand over his face. 'You don't suppose he would swear out a complaint against me . . . ?' It would be humiliating, but safer.

'And let people know what you did to him? No, I don't think so, Asper. He wants you to sweat; that's why he killed your other men first. I suppose the best thing you can do is to be as carefree as possible. Maybe find someone to challenge him first. It's a bit irregular, but better than being set on yourself some night, don't you think?' They came to another statue, of the ram god enjoying the eternal gratitude of his armourer. 'Ah,' said Ferris with ruthless good humour; 'Now this is new. It's by the same sculptor as the nymph; the duke commissioned it just before his death, so of course it's taken the fellow years to deliver. . . .'

But Horn barely had a glance to spare for it. Nervously twisting the ivory wand in his palm, he seemed to be looking about the garden for a means of escape; or perhaps he saw swordsmen lurking in the shrubbery.

Ferris released him, saying, 'Go on. Make a few enquiries. Perhaps he's just trying to scare you.'

'He killed de Maris. . . . '

'And Lynch. You'd better get three. Good thing you can afford it. Good luck, my dear!'

When Horn had vanished down the path Ferris swore, and kicked the statue's base. He felt silly immediately, but better. Did Diane know about this? St Vier was about to become a difficult man to do business with. If the swordsman was to kill Halliday, he must do it before he murdered Horn and became a wanted man. To his regret, Ferris decided it would be best to leave the party at once, to return home and begin setting things in motion.

Chapter XX

'I hear', Alec said, 'that you've been conducting a few small murders.'

It was two days since his bout with Delight. Neither he nor Richard had spoken of it since. Today was an unusually warm spring afternoon. On the Hill, the Duchess Tremontaine was giving a garden party.

Richard said, 'A few.'

'Those two were rotten fighters, even I could see that. Everyone's very excited about it.'

'They should be.'

'You're a hero. Small children will press bunches of flowers into your hands as you pass by. Old women will fling themselves weeping into your arms. Don't stand too still; pigeons will think you're a commemorative statue and crap on you.'

'Ginnie thinks I'm buying trouble.'

Alec shrugged. 'She just doesn't want you to have a good time. She doesn't understand the fighting spirit. When there's no one left to kill in Riverside, you have to expand.'

Richard wanted to touch the hard edges of his lips. But outside of bed, they didn't do that. The swordsman said, 'There's always someone to kill in Riverside. That reminds me: I'm going out tonight, as soon as it gets dark.'

'Again? Are you going to kill someone?'

'I'm going to the city.'

'Not to see Ferris – ' Alec demanded.

'No; I still haven't heard from him. Don't worry about that. You'll read me the letter when it comes.'

'Who read you the last one, the one from our friend?'

'Ginnie did.'

Alec hissed.

'You can go where you like, now,' Richard said; 'no one's going

180

to give you any trouble. Where will I find you tonight?'

'That depends on how long you're out. Home; Rosalie's; maybe Martha's if there's a game going there. . . .'

'I'll try home first. Don't wait up for me; I'll wake you when I come in.'

The woman twisted in the nobleman's grasp, making him hurt her with his refusal to let go of her arms. Her hair was in his mouth, and across her eyes; but there was a purpose to her twisting, as he found when her heel hit the back of his knee and he stumbled against the bed.

'Y' little street-fighter!' Lord Ferris grunted, hauling her in half by her hair. 'Y've nothing to fear down there!'

'You promised!' she cried, a vanquished wail despite the ferocity of her fighting. 'You said I'd never have to go down there again!'

He turned her, so that her naked breasts were crushed against his throat. 'Don't be a fool, Katherine. What's the harm in it? I'll buy you a lovely dress, I'm sorry for this one. . . .' The top of it straggled in pieces over her thighs. 'Just this once . . .'

She was crying. 'Why can't you send a note?'

'You know why. I need someone I can trust, to find him tonight.' He eased her onto his lap, nuzzling her throat. 'Little whore,' he said fondly; 'I'll send you down to the kitchens again . . . I'll have you turned out for stealing. . . .'

'I never –'

'Shh!' Gently, Lord Ferris kissed his mistress. 'I don't want your temper now, Kathy. Just do as you're told. . . .'

In the darkest corner of Rosalie's she waited, a shawl covering her head, a dagger naked on the table in front of her to discourage conversation. She had slipped past Marie, but there was no one at home in St Vier's rooms. On the stairs, her heart had thundered like a drum in a too-small space, in the terrible closeness of the limitless dark. She'd listened outside the door, trying to silence her body's noisy breath and pulse of panic. Riverside was a sector of ghosts for her now; everywhere she looked she saw the past. If she opened his door there might be dawn light and a dead woman on the floor, with Richard St Vier looking at her in perplexity saying, 'She was screaming at me.'

But no one answered her knock. With relief she gave up and went to the tavern, remembering how to hide in a crowd. She didn't want to draw attention to herself by asking if Richard had been there. There were people who would recognise her if she spoke, or if she uncovered her hair. Rosalie's had the same wet smell as ever; it was one of her earliest memories, her mother taking her down there, giving her to some old woman to hold who'd give her a bite of cake if she was good and sometimes braid her hair to make it pretty, while her mother talked with her friends and argued with dealers.

She'd met Richard there, when he was not much more than a new boy come from the country who'd found his way to Riverside because he'd heard the rents were cheap. She'd liked him because of the way he laughed, softly and privately, even then. She watched him fight his early duels, become a fad on the Hill, and finally take up with Jessamyn, a woman who had always scared her a little. But the three of them had sat at one of these tables, laughing together one night until their eyes ran; now she couldn't even remember what it had been about.

She heard echoing laughter across the tavern and lifted her head. The crowded knot of interest looked almost like a fight, but only one man seemed angry; everyone else was laughing. A tall man in black blocked her view. A couple of women were high-talking the tall man, flirting, teasing; and the angry man was turning away from the group in disgust, trying to ignore their mockery. Katherine realised who the tall one must be.

'Alec,' she said, when she got close enough for him to hear her. He turned sharply; she guessed people didn't use his name much. 'I'll buy you a drink,' she said.

He asked, 'Do you gamble? Max has given up on me – I can think faster than he can cheat.'

She drew her breath in softly. She knew the voice. She couldn't place it, but somewhere on the Hill she'd heard it before. She couldn't picture him well dressed, though, hair cut and ruffles ironed. And with his height she'd remember having met him. Still, she knew it, somehow: lazy, cool and self-assured. Richard said he tried to kill himself. He must be crazy. He couldn't be stupid: Richard wouldn't like that.

'I'll dice,' she said, 'if you want.'

They had to wait for a table to come free again. 'Who sent you?' Alec asked.

'What do you mean, who sent me?'

'Oh', he said after a moment. 'You want Richard. Have you got a bribe?'

'I don't need one. He's already doing business with us.'

'Oh.' He looked her up and down. 'I hope you're armed. It's nasty down here.'

'I know.'

It went beyond aristocracy, his arrogance. Now she wasn't sure she had heard him before. She didn't remember anyone who spoke without care for effect, without courtesy or irony, as though his words were dropping into darkness and it didn't matter who heard them. No wonder Richard wanted him. He wasn't safe.

They found a seat against the wall.

'Are you the one who gave him the ruby?' Alec asked.

'Yes, the ring.'

He put his hand flat on the table. The token glittered there on his finger. 'Can you accept for him,' she asked tartly, 'or does he just like to decorate you?'

'Very good,' said Alec with lazy amusement. 'He just likes to decorate me. Who are you, anyway?'

'My name is Katherine Blount. I work on the Hill.'

'For Lord Ferris?'

Nervously she looked around for listeners, then bypassed the question. 'If Richard accepts the job, I can give him the money.'

'Where is it, sewn into your petticoats? he enquired politely. 'Interesting to watch him get it out.'

Despite her annoyance, she laughed. 'Tell me where I can find him, and I'll let you watch.'

A look of distaste crossed his face. No wonder the whores liked to tease him. It was a striking face, too bony for handsomeness, but beautiful in its way, sharp and fine as the quills of a feather.

He fished in his purse, picking out a few coins of silver that he shifted from hand to hand. 'Do you know Tremontaine?' he asked.

He wanted to bribe her for information. She kept her face

straight. She wasn't going to refuse the money; not straight off, anyway. 'The duchess, you mean?'

'Tremontaine.'

'She's a lady.'

'God, you *can't* be that stupid!' he said irritatedly.

He had the money; she kept her temper in check. It wasn't his fault he didn't know what he was doing. She imagined Richard liked him that way. 'What do you want to know?'

'What does Tremontaine have to do with all this?'

She shrugged. 'I couldn't say.'

'She didn't give you the ring?'

'No, sir.'

He didn't even notice the sudden servility. 'Then who did?'

'My master, sir.'

He let one coin fall to the table. 'Where the hell did *he* get it?'

'I didn't ask,' she said tartly, dropping the demureness. 'If it's hers, then she gave it to him.'

Another coin fell. 'Is that likely?'

'Very likely.'

He spilled the rest of the coins in front of her, and pressed a fist into his palm; but not before she saw how his hands were shaking. His voice, though, was careless: 'Now give me a chance to win them back from you.'

'Unless I cheat faster than you can think? You don't know how to cheat, do you, Alec?'

'I don't need to.'

'Where can I find Richard?'

'Nowhere. You can't. He doesn't want the job.'

'Why don't you want him to take it?'

He looked down at her. 'Whatever makes you think I have anything to say about it?'

There it was again, the evasion cloaked in rudeness. She put her chin in her hands, and looked into his haughty, stubborn face. 'You know, he's told me about you,' she said, putting into her voice all she knew of them both. 'He's not going to kill you, don't pin your hopes on that. He tried it once before, and he didn't like it.'

'That's odd,' he mused; 'he didn't tell me about *you*. I expect he thought I wouldn't be interested.'

She stood up. 'Tell him I was here,' she rapped out, the flat rapid patter of Riverside back in her voice. 'Tell him I need to see him.'

'Oh?' he said. 'Is it a personal matter, then? Or is it just that your master will beat you?'

He would say anything to get a reaction, she told herself; all the same, she found herself leaning over him, saying into his face, 'You don't belong here. Richard knows that. You can't keep this up forever.'

'You belong here,' he answered coolly, real pleasure in his voice because at last he had pierced her. 'Stay with us. Don't go back to the Hill. They don't let you have any fun there.'

She looked at him, and saw in the disdainful face just how badly he wanted to be attacked. And she straightened up, picked up her cloak. 'I'll be at the Old Bell tomorrow night with the advance money. Tell him.'

Alec sat where he was, watching her leave. Then, since he'd given her all the money he had, he went home.

She thought about checking a couple of other haunts. The streets were so terribly dark, outside the circle of torchlight that marked the tavern's door. She'd grown unused to not being able to see at night, not knowing what her hand would next encounter, what her feet would find beneath them, what sounds would come lurching out of the hollow silence. Her own fear made her afraid. People could tell from how you walked how well you could handle it. Here there was no attempt made to light the entries of houses, no Watch treading the mud and cobbles on their regular route. She stood outside Rosalie's in the circle of torchlight. Richard could be anywhere. She wasn't going to search all of Riverside for him, she'd done what she could. For all she knew, he could be on the Hill. She'd delivered her message to his usual place, and that was that.

A child came by, carrying a bundle of torches. Only children and cripples were torchbearers here; no strong man wanted to earn his money guarding those who couldn't take care of themselves.

'Lightcha, lady?'

'Yes. To the Bridge.'

'That's extra, to cross it.'

'I know that. Hurry up,' she said, and drew her cloak around her like a blanket.

Chapter XXI

It was Richard's second night of watching Horn's house, and already it was paying off. The guards seemed to be concentrated at the front: apparently Horn was expecting a formal challenge, and wanted to be sure of not meeting it himself.

Richard was standing outside the back garden wall, among the leafless branches of an old lilac bush. He would never understand why these people left such good camouflage so near the entrances to their houses, when the whole purpose of walls was to keep people out. Braced halfway up it, between the bush and wall, he'd been able to see all he needed to of the back of the house. When he heard the approach of the guard who occasionally patrolled the back garden, he'd dropped back to the ground. Now he listened to the receding footsteps rounding the far corner of the house. He waited in the darkness listening, for one minute, two, timing by his own breathing to make sure that excitement didn't betray him into moving too soon. A carriage clattered by in the street, the torches of its outriders throwing a streak of shadow against the wall, himself entangled in the lilac branches.

The back of the house was silent. He knew Horn was at home this night, and alone, without visitors. He even had a fair idea now of where to find him: the pattern of lights passing behind the windows had indicated hallways and occupied rooms. Richard took off his heavy cloak, which was fine for waiting out of doors but no good for climbing trees; he wrapped it around the light duelling sword he carried – his pride, a new blade of folded steel, light as a kiss and sharp as a surgeon's tool – and tucked the bundle under his arm. With the help of the bush, climbing the outside wall was no great feat. He remembered the drop on the other side as not too far, and made it. Without the snow, the garden looked a little different; but he had in his head the map the Duke of Karleigh had provided of the formal gardens the night he fought Lynch and de Maris here.

Richard stood still, accustoming his feet to the new ground. The air was very chill; without his cloak he felt it, even through the layers of clothing he wore. He heard the Watch pass on the other side of the wall, making their usual racket. He felt his cold lips curve in a smile. There was almost an acre of ground between him and the house, heavily decorated with topiary. By the faint and steady light of stars he picked his way among the carved bushes, stopping to shelter under a yew shaped like a castle, skirting the outside of the boxwood maze whose paths could be glimpsed through gaps in the hedge.

At last the house loomed above him; just another wall to climb to reach the first-storey window he had targeted: a tall window, with a convenient wrought-iron balcony that should hold a man's weight. An immense rose trellis climbed up to it. Very pretty, no doubt, in summer.

He buckled the sword on close to his body, and pinned his cloak at his neck, knotting it into a heavy ball behind him. The rustling of dry branches, the scrape of his toe against stone, sounded loud in his ears; but his world was shrunk to a tiny point where the least sound and movement were mammoth.

The climb warmed him. He tried to make it quickly, since too much deliberation might expose him like a fly on the wall if anyone looked up; but the strong rose stem was obscured by a tangle of creepers and branches, and he had to feel his way. He found toeholds in the joined stone blocks, and was able to rest his hand against the top of the groundfloor window cornice. His own breath rose in front of his face in puffs of vapour. Leather gloves protected his hands, but now and then he felt the piercing of a heavy thorn, and the warm blood flowing down the inside of them.

Finally his hand closed around the metal underside of the balcony. He pulled hard on it. It was firmly bolted to the stone, so he swung himself up onto its ledge.

Richard crouched on the balcony, resting, breathing softly. He took an old knifeblade and a bent piece of wire out of his jacket and unhooked the latch; then he slipped inside, closing the window after him.

He had hoped the window led onto a hallway, but from the sound he seemed to be in a small chamber. He pulled back an edge of curtain to let some of the night's silver glow in. He felt his way carefully around the furniture. The carpet was as thick and soft as a pelt.

A sudden flash of movement in the corner of his eye froze him. Across the room from the window, a streak of black had shot across the grey surface. Now it was still. He stared across the room into the darkness at it, looked sideways to catch it again. It resolved itself into a small square of light; another window, maybe guarded. He raised his arm silently to shield his eyes, and a slash of black ran across it again.

It was a mirror. He wasn't used to them. Alec was always complaining that their palm-sized disk of polished steel was not big enough to shave by. Richard supposed he could afford to buy a mirror the size of a window; but he didn't like the idea of it hanging on his wall.

He was glad to find that the bedroom door wasn't locked from the outside. The hallway was lit with tapers, a forest of them in the dark. He ducked back behind the door to give his eyes time to adjust to the light. Then he followed the hall to the room he'd marked.

Lord Horn sat in a heavy chair, reading in a circle of light. He didn't hear the door open, but when a floorboard creaked he snapped, 'I said *knock* first, you damned fool.' The lord leaned around the side of the chair to look at the intruder. 'And why have you left your post on the stairs?'

St Vier unsheathed his sword.

Horn started convulsively, like a man touched by lightning. He knocked the chair back, and his mouth flapped with a frozen scream.

'It's no good calling your guards,' Richard lied, 'I've already taken care of them.'

It was the first time he had come face to face with the man. Horn was younger than he'd expected, although his face was now hagged with shock. There was nothing to admire in him: he had bungled everything, and finally knew it; he had misused his power and now he would pay. It was quite clear that he knew what was happening. Richard was glad of that; he didn't like making speeches.

'Please – ' said Horn.

'Please what?' Richard demanded icily. 'Please, you'll never meddle with my affairs again? But you already have.'

'Money – ' the noble gasped.

'I'm not a thief,' said Richard. 'I leave it all for your heirs.'

Lord Horn walked shakily to his desk and picked up a crystal bird. His hand cupped around it protectively, stroking the smooth glass with longing. 'You like a challenge,' he murmured, almost seductive.

'I've got one,' Richard answered softly. 'I want to see how long I can make this last.'

First he silenced him, and then he took, very slowly, the life from the four corners of his body, being careful not to render him unrecognisable. Richard never spoke, although the man's wild eyes begged him for it while they could.

He had planned it carefully, and he stuck to what he planned, except that, in the end, he didn't deliver his characteristic blow to the heart. It was unnecessary: the precision would label his work, and he didn't want it to look as though he had mutilated an already dead body.

He unlocked the study window and left again through the garden. No swordsman could afford to be blackmailed.

Alec was sleeping, diagonal across the whole bed as usual, one arm flung out with fingers loosely curled over his empty palm. The mark the shackles had left on his wrist was a dark streak in the pale light.

Richard meant to go and wash first; but Alec stirred and said sleepily, 'What is it?'

'I'm back.'

Alec rolled over to look at him. The hollows under his cheeks went taut. 'You've killed someone,' he said. 'You should have told me.'

'I had to make sure he was at home first.'

Alec's long white arms reached out to him. 'Tell me now.'

Richard fell onto the bed, letting the tall man gather him in.

He wasn't tired at all. 'You smell strange,' Alec said. 'Is that blood?'

'Probably.'

Alec's tongue touched his ear, like a hunting cat getting the first taste of its prey. 'Who have you gone and killed this time?'

'Lord Horn.'

He hadn't been sure how Alec would take it. With wonder he felt Alec's body arc sharply against his, Alec's breath let out in an intense, vicious sigh.

'Then no one knows,' he said dreamily in his lovely accent. 'Tell me about it. Did he scream?' The pulse was beating hard in the hollow of his throat.

'He wanted to, but he couldn't.'

'*Ahhh.*' Alec pulled the swordsman's head to him until Richard's mouth lay close by his ear. His hair was warm across Richard's face.

'He begged,' Richard said, to please him. 'He offered me money.'

Alec laughed. 'He hit me,' Alec said; 'and you killed him.'

'I hurt him first.' Alec's head tipped back. The cords of his neck stood out like vaulting. 'I took his hands, then his arms, and his knees. . . . ' The breath hissed through Alec's teeth. 'He won't touch you again.'

'You hurt him. . . . '

Richard kissed the parted lips. Alec's arms bound him like supple iron.

'Tell me,' Alec whispered, mouth touching his face; 'tell me about it.'

They slept together until past noon. Then Alec put on some clothes and went downstairs to borrow bread from Marie. In one hand he held a heap of bloody clothes. It was a sunny day, almost as warm as the last one. He found her in the courtyard, skirts hiked up, already begun on the laundry, and held out the clothes to her.

'Burn those,' their landlady said.

'Are you out of your mind?' Alec asked. 'It'll make a horrible smell.'

'It's up to you.' She made no move to take the clothes.

'You look awful,' Alec said cheerfully. 'What's the matter, someone keep you up all night?'

She began a smile, and dropped it. 'This morning. You must have been dead not to hear the racket. I tried to keep 'em quiet, not to let 'em upstairs. . . .'

'You should choose your friends more carefully. What's for breakfast?' He sniffed at her pot of boiling laundry.

'*Don't* you go putting your stuff in there,' she said automatically; 'that blood'll never come out in hot water.'

'I know, I know.'

'You know . . .' Marie grumbled. She liked Alec; he teased her and made her laugh. But it wasn't any good now. 'You know what he's done, then?'

Alec shrugged: *So what?* 'Got blood all over his clothes. Don't worry, we'll pay you for it.'

'With what?' she said darkly. 'You going to turn him in for the price on his head?'

For a moment the long face was still. Then he tilted his chin up, eyebrows cocked audaciously. '*Is* there a price on his head? How much?'

'I don't know. They say there might be.'

'How do they know he wasn't working under contract?'

She looked scornful. 'Down here, they know. Up there, it may take them a little longer to figure it out. But that wasn't any duel. They say that noble was marked up like a shopkeeper's tally, and not with any dagger.'

'Oh, well!' Alec sighed blithely. 'I guess we'll have to leave town for a while until it's blown over. Too bad: the country's such a bore, but what can you do? Keep bees, or something.'

'I suppose . . .' Marie sounded dubious, but brightened. 'After all, everyone else leaves when things get hot. He might as well too. I'll save your rooms, don't you fear.'

Richard had long ago given up arguing with Alec over the use of his left-hand dagger for cutting bread. Alec claimed it was the only knife they had that cut the pieces fine enough for toasting, and that was that.

'I wish you'd told me', Alec said, slicing Marie's loaf, 'that we were going to be leaving town. I would have had my boots re-heeled.'

'If you're going to toast cheese, look out for the point on that thing.'

'It's not your best knife, what do you care? You haven't answered my question.'

'I didn't know you'd asked one.'

Alec drew a patient breath. 'My dear soul, they're already lining up with banners to see you off, and you're not even packed yet.'

'I'm not going anywhere.'

Alec fumbled with the toasting-knife, and swore when he burnt himself. 'I see. They've found Horn, you know.'

'Have they? Good. Let me have the cheese.'

'It's rotten cheese. It tastes like shoeleather. Cheese is much fresher in the country.'

'I don't want to leave. I've got another job coming up.'

'You could become a highway robber. It'd be fun.'

'It's not fun. You lie in the grass and get wet.'

'They've found Horn,' Alec tried again, 'and they're not happy.'

Richard smiled. 'I didn't expect them to be. I'll have to stay here for a while.'

'In the house?'

'In Riverside. They don't trust us down here, so they aren't going to risk sending the Watch, and spies I can handle myself.' It wasn't like Alec to worry about his safety. It made Richard feel warm and content. He was going to curl up in the sun today and let other people worry if they wanted to. After last night he felt secure, better than he had in days. The theatre, Alec's abduction, the unpleasant notes, the strange young nobleman and the killing of the sword-master all faded into a past resolved and dispatched. No one was going to try Horn's little trick again or try to force his hand; and no Riversider who'd heard about it would touch Alec now. And from what Marie was saying, they'd all heard about it. Richard laid precisely the right pattern of pieces of cheese on his bread, and set it on the hearth near enough to the fire so that it would melt without getting brown.

In the long shadows of late afternoon they wandered down to

Rosalie's for food and drink. Some little girls were skipping rope in the front yard of the old house. They were dressed, like most Riverside children whose parents acknowledged them, in bright eclectic splendour: scraps of velvet and brocade pieced onto old gowns cut down to size, trimmed with ruffles of varying-coloured lace culled from a multitude of stolen handkerchiefs. The jumper's plaits bounced as she chanted:

> Mummy told me to have some fun:
> Kick the boys and make them run,

'Charming,' said Alec.

> Kick them 'til they run for cover;
> Don't forget my baby brother!
> *How* many *of* them *did* you *get*?
> One – Two – Three – Four –

One of the twirlers suddenly missed her beat. The jumper caught her feet in the rope and stumbled. 'Sylvie, you goon!' But Sylvie ignored her.

'Hullo, old love!' she called to Richard, just like her grandmother, Rosalie.

'Hullo, Sylvie.'

'Got any candy?'

'Not on me, stinker.'

She stamped her foot. '*Don't* call me stinker! That's for babies.'

'Sorry, brat.' He tried to walk past her, but she blocked the way to the stairs.

'Gramma says you can't come in.'

'Why not?'

'There's people looking for you. Have been all day.'

'Are they in there now?'

She nodded. 'Sure are.'

'Armed?'

'I guess so. You gonna kill 'em?'

'Probably. Don't worry, I'll tell your gramma you told me.'

'No.' Alec caught his sleeve. 'Don't. For god's sake, Richard, let's go home.'

'Alec . . . ' They couldn't argue out here. Richard nodded at the children. 'Do you want to give them a little brass?'

Alec fished in his purse and came up with some coins, which he handed gingerly to Sylvie as though she might bite him.

'Thanks, Richard! Thank you, o my prince!'

A flurry of giggles covered their retreat, mixed with cries of 'Sylvie, you goon! I can't believe you did that!'

'What', said Alec, 'was *that* all about?'

Richard shrugged. 'They've probably made up some story about you. They always do.'

'Nasty little objects. I wonder which one made up that rhyme?'

'All little girls say it,' said Richard, surprised. 'They did it where I grew up.'

'Hmph. I don't think *my* sister did. But then, Mother frowned on poetry.'

It was perhaps the first time he had mentioned his family. He was tense; the business at Rosalie's had shaken him. Of course, Richard thought: Alec wasn't used to being hunted. And there was no way to reassure him: it could be an unpleasant business, if you let it. It placed constraints on your life that Alec wasn't at all accustomed to. In fact, Alec probably had been right to insist on avoiding Rosalie's once they'd been warned. There was no sense in walking into trouble. But Richard didn't like having to put up with it. Alec, less patient than the swordsman, was going to like the new restrictions even less.

They stopped at Martha's for beer. Unless the informers were working double-time, no one would be looking for him there yet. When they came in there was a stir of movement that subsided into tight-knit groups doing their best to ignore them. It didn't particularly bother St Vier; it was almost welcome relief from the usual fuss they made over him. The two men drank quickly, and left.

'It'll get better come nightfall,' Richard told him, walking home. 'Everyone's easier then, there's fewer strangers around.'

'That's a life for you,' said Alec; 'just coming out at night, like a mooncrawler.'

Richard looked curiously at him. 'I don't think it'll come to that.'

195

The rapid patter of footsteps behind them put an end to the discussion.

'Move,' said Richard, hand on his sword. 'Into that doorway.'

For once, Alec did as he was told. Already it was dusk under the lowering eaves of the close-set houses. Their pursuer rounded the corner at too fast a clip to have a prayer of holding ground against the swordsman standing ready.

The small white figure skidded to a halt. 'Holy *Lucy*!' Nimble Willie swore. 'Master St Vier, for godsakes put that thing away, and come into that doorway.'

'Alec's already in there.'

'That's all right,' the doorway interjected, 'we'll have a lovely time. What the hell's the matter with you, Willie,' Alec demanded, emerging from it, 'coursing like a stoat after rabbits?'

'Sorry,' Willie panted. He motioned them off to one side; what he had to say wasn't fit for the middle of the street. 'Don't go home that way. Cut through Blind Max's Alley; they're watching Dolphin's Cross.'

'How many?'

'Three. City toughs, with swords, out for the reward.'

'There's a reward?'

'Not for you yet. It's just the usual; for suspects to be brought in. But these boys think it's you – they might be friends of those other two you killed last week.'

Richard sighed wearily. 'I'd better kill them.'

'No, wait!' cried Willie. 'Don't do that.'

'Why not?'

'They've already paid me. I figured it'd be easy to give them the slip. But if one gets away, I'll be in for it. . . .'

St Vier sighed, running a hand through his hair. 'Willie. . . . all right. Only for you. I'll just keep away from Dolphin's Cross.'

Alec paid him without having to be reminded.

The house seemed quiet. It was set in a cul-de-sac where no one in his right mind would want to take on St Vier. Nevertheless, he went first up the stairs, scanning for reckless intruders. There was nobody, not even a neighbour.

'God,' Alec huffed, throwing himself down on their old chaise longue. 'Hadn't we better check under the beds?'

Richard answered his real question. 'I don't think they'll come in here. Even if they can get someone to show them the way, people don't like to attack a swordsman on his own ground.'

'I see.' Alec sat thoughtfully, turning the rings on his fingers. After a while he got up and found the Nature treatise with the burgundy leather binding and half its pages missing. He flipped through it while Richard limbered up and began practising. The grey cat came and sat on Alec's lap, trying to interpose her head between his eyes and the page. He scratched her chin, and finally snapped the book shut irritably and replaced it on the mantel, taking instead his worn philosophy text. Finally he gave up all pretence of reading, and watched the swordsman steadily working his body through parrys and extensions and recoils so quick and intricate Alec's eye couldn't make out the discrete elements. All he could do was sense their perfection, a dance made of deadly movements whose goal was not to entertain.

For a while Alec seemed to be drowsing, like the cat on his lap, eyes half-shut watching the swordsman. Only his hand moved, idling along the cat's spine, deep in the lush fur finding the ridges of its bones. The cat was purring; Alec put his fingers on its throat, and left them there.

The frenzy of Richard's movements had slowed to a deliberate pace. It was the cat's favourite stalking-game, but Alec's fingers left her too sedated to care. Richard's body obeyed him in his tortuous demands, and Alec watched.

'You know,' Alec said conversationally, 'they would be so pleased if anything were to happen to you.'

'Hh?' It came out a grunt.

'Your friends. They'd finally get their chance at me.'

'You'd have to leave.' Richard put up his sword and began slowly stretching his muscles out. 'They wouldn't follow you out of Riverside.'

'If you were dead.' Alec finished the thought bluntly.

The anger surprised Richard. 'Well, yes.'

Alec's voice was low, almost harsh with repressed fury. 'It doesn't particularly bother you.'

'Well, I'm a swordsman.' He shrugged, no easy feat with his head touching the floor. 'If I stay active, I can't last much past 30. There'll be someone better some day.'

'You don't care.' Alec was still lounging picturesquely, long limbs on display; but the rigidness of his hands clenched on the frayed upholstery betrayed him.

'It's all right,' Richard said; 'it's what happens.'

'Then what,' Alec articulated with crystalline clarity, 'in hell are you doing all that practising for?'

Richard picked up his sword. 'Because I want to be good.' He lifted it over his head and dived at the wall the way he would at an opponent who'd uncovered his front guard.

'So you can give them a really good fight before they kill you?'

Richard twisted and came in high again, his wrist arced like a falcon stooping. 'Mm-hm.'

'Stop it,' Alec said very quietly. 'Stop it.'

'Not now, Alec, I'm – '

'*I said, stop it!*' Alec rose to his full height, towering and angular in his wrath. His eyes were green as emeralds uncovered in a casket. Richard put the sword down and kicked it into a corner. When he looked up he saw the raised hand, knew Alec was going to hit him, and stayed still as the palm crashed across his face.

'You coward,' Alec said coldly. He was breathing heavily and his cheeks were bright. 'What are you waiting for?'

'Alec,' Richard said. His face stung. 'Do you want me to hit you?'

'You don't dare.' Alec raised his hand again, but this time Richard caught it, gripping the bony wrist that was so much frailer than his own. Alec twisted the wrong way, making Richard hurt him. 'I'm not enough of a challenge,' he hissed through gritted teeth, 'that's it, isn't it? It would make you *look* bad. You wouldn't enjoy it.'

'Enough,' Richard said; 'it's enough.' He knew he was holding Alec too hard; he was afraid to let go.

'No, it isn't enough,' the man in his hands was saying. 'It's enough for you – it's always enough for you, but not for me. Talk to me, Richard – if you're afraid to use your hands, then talk to me.'

'I can't,' Richard said. 'Not the way you do. Alec, please – you know you don't want this. Stop it.'

'*Please*,' Alec said, still pulling against his arm as though he were ready to start hitting him again; 'that's a new one from you. I think I like it. Say it again.'

Richard's own hands sprang open; he flung himself away from the other man. 'Look,' he shouted, 'what do you want from me?'

Alec smiled his feral smile. 'You're upset,' he said.

Richard could feel himself shaking. Tears of rage were still burning behind his eyes, but at least he could see again, the room was losing its red tinge. 'Yes,' he managed to say.

'Come here,' Alec said. His voice was long and cool like slopes of snow. 'Come to me.'

He walked across the room. Alec lifted his chin and kissed him. 'You're crying, Richard,' Alec said. 'You're crying.'

The tears burned his eyes like acid. They made his face feel raw. Alec lowered him to the floor. At first he was rough, and then he was gentle.

In the end, it was Alec who couldn't cry. 'I want to,' he said, curled on Richard's chest, fingers digging into him as though he were slipping down a rock face. 'I want to, but I can't.'

'You don't really want to,' Richard said, his hand cupped around Alec's head. 'It makes your nose run. It makes your eyes red.'

Alec gave a strangled laugh and clutched him tighter. He tried an experimental sniff, and gasped with a sudden convulsion of some emotion: misery, or frustration. 'It's no good,' he said. 'I can't.'

'It doesn't matter,' Richard said, stroking him. 'You'll learn.'

'If I'd known you were such an expert I would have made you teach me long ago.'

'I offered to teach you the sword. It seemed more useful.'

'Not to me,' Alec said automatically. 'Did you know you were talking just now, too? It sounded like you were reciting poetry.'

Richard smiled. 'I didn't notice. It might have been.'

'I didn't know you knew any poetry.'

Richard knew that he ought to be upset. He had just been thoroughly overturned by Alec: had lost his temper, lost his control, behaved in ways he didn't even know he could. But Alec had caught him as he fell, had taken pleasure in it. And now he felt wonderful, as long as he didn't think hard about it. There was no need to think. He never wanted to move again; he never wanted Alec's head to shift from the crook of his shoulder, or the warmth of their legs entwined to dissolve. 'I know a lot of poetry,' he answered. 'My mother used to say it to me. Old things, mainly.'

'Something about the wind, and someone's face.'

> *After awhile, he began to grow younger.*
> *The years were torn from his face*
> *Like leaves scattered before the wind....*
> *In the end, she made all others seem impossible.*

'That's an old one', he explained, 'about a man who was taken by the Faery Queen.'

'I've never heard it.' Alec nestled under his chin, lulled by the words. 'Tell it to me.'

Richard thought for a minute, reaching back for the beginning, absently stroking Alec's hair:

> *It was never cold under the hill, and never dark.*
> *But the light was not a light for seeing. It deceived.*
> *He tried to remember the sun,*
> *To remember remembering the moon.*
> *He thought –*

Alec's hand was at his lips.

'You've *got* to go!' His voice cracked. 'They won't let you walk out of this, they don't dare! I *know them*, Richard!'

Richard tightened his arm around Alec's shoulders, wordlessly trying to comfort, to drain the tension from the anguished spirit.

But the touch was not enough. 'Richard, I *know* them – they won't let you live!' He turned his face in to Richard's chest, his body clenched again in a frozen spasm not of weeping but of fury.

At a loss, Richard turned again to the words that still flowed through his mind like water:

> *Day followed day, with never night between:*
> *Feasting and all manner of delight*
> *Hedged him 'round like hounds their quarry's heart –*

200

'I'm cold,' Alec said suddenly.

He knew that arbitrary voice: it was as warm and familiar to him as bread. 'Well, we are on the floor,' he answered.

'We should get into bed.' Alec propped himself on one elbow to observe, 'Your clothes are all a mess.'

'That can be fixed.' Richard stripped his shirt off in an easy motion, and helped Alec to his feet.

'You look as though you've been in a fight,' Alec said complacently.

'A lot you know about that. I look', he said, 'as though someone's tried to tear my clothes off.'

'Someone has.'

They were warm that night, never apart long enough to be cold. They talked for hours in the dark; and when words were not enough they were silent. At last they slept, twined helplessly in each other's arms.

Some time in the morning, when the light was still grey, Richard felt Alec slip out of bed beside him. He didn't even open his eyes; just sighed and rolled over, spreading into the spot where Alec's warmth had been.

When Richard came fully awake, it was full daylight. He got up and opened the shutters. Sun streaked the floor in long buttery bars. Richard stretched, feeling the glories of the night in his whole body. Nothing hurt: even the memory of tears and pain produced only a warm glow, the distillation of raw spirits into liquor.

Alec was up and dressed already, his clothes gone from the top of the chest. Richard didn't smell cooking; maybe he was out getting food. Or he might be sitting in the front room, reading. Richard thought, all in all, that it might be a good thing for them to eat and go back to bed.

He heard a noise in the other room, body on upholstery, and pictured Alec sprawled on the chaise longue with a book in his hands, waiting for him to get up. He knew he was smiling senselessly, and didn't care.

He stared at the empty chaise for a moment longer than necessary. The cat leapt down across it, wanting to be petted.

He felt something wrong in the room. There was no presence of intruders. Something was out of place, a space rearranged. . . .

201

He looked again and saw it at once: Alec's books were missing from their corner. Not, he hoped, another bout of self-righteous poverty! Alec was always trying to pawn things, but who would want his books? At least he'd taken his own stuff this time –

But he hadn't. The richest things he owned, the most worth pawning, those he had left behind, in plain sight on the mantelpiece. The rings that Richard had given him, that he'd had so much trouble accepting, lay in a heap together, regardless of their beauty. Richard looked, unwilling to touch them: the pearl, the diamond, the rose, the emerald, the dragon brooch . . . all but the ruby; that he had taken with him.

There was no note. Richard couldn't have read it, and Alec knew this time he would not ask someone else to read it for him. The meaning of the things he'd left behind was clear: he'd taken only what he thought of as his. He wasn't coming back.

It was plain enough what had happened. Alec was fed up with life in Riverside. He'd never really been suited to it. And Horn's killing would make it harder. Alec had been badly shaken yesterday by the first signs of the caution they would have to use for awhile. He might be afraid of a manhunt. Maybe he meant to wait it out, come back when the danger was past. . . . Richard closed his mind to the thought, like a key turning a lock. He would not wait for Alec. If Alec chose to return, Richard would be here. If not, life would go on as it had before him.

He couldn't blame Alec, really. Leaving was the sensible thing to do. Most people thought so. Alec had a right to decide for himself. Everyone has their limits, the border between what they can and cannot tolerate. Alec had tried to tell him; but Richard had been too confident, too sure of himself – and, frankly, too used to ignoring Alec's complaints to give any heed to this one. Not that it would have changed anything. Richard had no intention of skulking out of the city just when it needed his presence to remind them all of how dangerous it was to cross him. And he could hardly run from Riverside as though he were afraid of his own peers.

He found himself back in the bedroom, looking in the clothes press. Alec's fur-lined winter cloak was still there, along with two shirts, his old jacket with the braid, odds and ends. He'd left wearing only his scholar's robe over the clothes he'd had on yesterday. Only what he could walk in. It angered Richard: the fool was going to be cold, summer was still a good way off. . . . But of course, he thought, Alec had gone where he didn't need old clothes. He wouldn't just have walked aimlessly out into the street, he was too proud for that. And he wouldn't have gone back to the University, not after what he'd said against it. But he never did speak of his family. That meant something. Of course they must be rich. Of course he was a lord, or a lord's son. They would be furious with him, but they'd have to take him in. His future was secure.

It made Richard feel vastly relieved. Alec was, in essence, back where he belonged. He would never again be cold in winter, or drink inferior wines. He'd marry well, but know where his other desires lay. Last night, in his farewell, he'd proved that.

Richard shut the chest. Mingled with the smell of wool and cedar was the faint aroma of meadowgrass. He'd have to see to giving away the clothes. But not now. A long fine hair was caught on one of his fingers. He untwisted it; it glowed chestnut in the sunlight as it drifted to the floor.

Chapter XXII

Lord Basil Halliday put his face in his hands and tried to massage some of the heat out of his eyeballs. When the door opened he sat perfectly still, recognising the sound and scent of his wife's presence.

Lady Mary looked at the undisturbed bedding still spread invitingly on the couch, pressed her lips together and said nothing to the man sitting bent over the table littered with crumbs and empty glasses. She drew back the curtains to let in daylight, and snuffed what was left of the candles.

'You just missed Chris Nevilleson.' Her husband roused himself to converse. 'He ate the last of the seedcakes. We'll have to remember he likes them.'

'I'll remember.' She stood behind him, her cool hands on his brow. He leaned his head back into the soft satin of her morning-robe.

'I *did* sleep,' he said defensively; 'I just didn't lie down.'

'There are no more seedcakes,' she told him, 'but there are fresh rolls and eggs. I'll have them brought in, with dark chocolate.'

He pulled her head down to kiss. 'There are no more like you,' he said. 'If it's a daughter, we'll name her Mary.'

'We will not. It's too confusing, Basil. And we should name her something pretty . . . Belinda?' He laughed, and smoothed her hair. 'What did Chris have to say?'

With regret he returned to the night's activities. 'What I've been sure of all along. It was a swordsman, not a ruffian's murder. Nothing was stolen. And Horn had lately increased his guard. Someone broke into the house expressly to kill him. That looks like a duel, simple enough. But none of our people has been able to ferret out any rumour of a challenge called out against Horn, or any reason for one. He had no debts, his reputation for once was clear. . . . No one much liked Asper, really, but he was harmless. His political importance was over the day his friend the old Crescent died. . . . ' He stopped himself and shook his head. 'Sorry. Of course you already know that. Well, Chris was there tonight at the examination. There was no question but that it was the work of one skilled sword. A virtuoso job, in fact. As if someone had left a calling card. But who? Chris said Horn's hired swordsmen looked positively green. We're holding them for questioning, but I think it's pointless. They didn't do it. Someone flashy and brilliant and crazy did it, and he's out there walking free in my city right now.'

'It might be private justice,' Mary said, 'such as swordsmen practise amongst themselves.'

'Against a Council Lord? Utter madness. It *must* have been another noble's challenge, it's the only way anyone would dare. . . . Maybe something new will come to light, maybe someone will declare himself. A swordsman with a grievance against Horn could have sought redress from the civil court, or even from the Council of Lords.'

'But with what hope of gaining it?' his wife asked gently. 'The nobles have too much power in the city, you say so yourself.' He opened his mouth to defend himself, but she silenced him with the pressure of her hand, which said she knew already and agreed. 'But even if it was a swordsman working under contract, one doesn't like to think of a man using his skill for such an unclean death.'

'St Vier,' Halliday said, 'always strikes one blow straight to the heart. I have always thought, if I were challenged to the death, I would prefer it be by him.'

'Seville, then, perhaps, or Torrion. . . . '

'Yes, you're right.' Halliday passed a hand over his unshaven face. 'The first thing is to identify the swordsman himself. There are far fewer good ones around than there are men with money who carry grudges. All the major ones will have to make depositions, and lay bond not to leave the city until this matter is settled. The murder of a Council Lord strikes too near the centre of our peace. I'm having the roads watched, offering rewards for information. . . .

'Meanwhile, Mary, I've called up some of our own people to

strengthen the house guard. And you – please don't go out alone. Not now.'

She pressed his hand to tell him she'd look after her safety as carefully as he would.

He knew he should sleep, or go and tend to business; but even more than he needed rest he needed to offer his thoughts to her. 'It's the problem of a system that incorporates swordsmen. They say without them we'd be doing all the work of killing each other ourselves; like the olden days, the streets full of miniature wars, and every house a fortress. . . . But swordsmen are a wild card. They're only useful under the strictest codes. . . .'

Still talking, he let her lead him to the couch. They sat side by side, leaning only slightly against each other, alert for the first sounds of intrusion, the demands of government and house-keeping.

'Basil,' she asked when he finally paused, 'do you have to do it all yourself? If it's a murder, the city can investigate. Chris can act as liaison.'

'I know. . . . but it's the slaying of a Council Lord, and with a sword. Which means it still might turn out to be a matter of honour – or something else we don't want to make common knowledge. I'm the head of the Council. I want to go on being the head of the Council – or so everyone keeps telling me. Silly or not, Horn was a member of government. And I have to look after my own. Whoever killed him was a poacher on a very private estate.' Despite himself, his eyes kept dropping shut. 'Horn . . . I'll have to stop calling him that. There'll be a new Lord Horn now. His grandson, I think. . . .'

She waited until she was sure he was asleep before getting up. One poor dead man, she was thinking, and the whole city threatens to crumble. Mary Halliday pulled the curtains in the study closed again, and let herself quietly out of the door.

A fine fall of rain hung like a curtain of mist over the city, veiling one section from another across the long stretches of sky dividing them. The various greys of the city's stone glittered and glowed with the sheen of the water on them; but that was an effect best admired from indoors, preferably through a pane of window-glass. The Daw's Nest in Riverside didn't have one. It didn't have much, except an interesting clientele and enough for them to drink. There was always something going on there. One section of the earthen floor had been a mumblety-peg arena for as long as anyone could remember.

What really made it attractive was its location: on the south bank of Riverside, far from the Bridge and any encroaching of upper city life. No one who didn't belong in Riverside got this far in. When he didn't have to make himself available for job contracts, Hugo Seville found it a good place to relax.

'Your star is on the rise,' a fortune-teller was informing him. 'Terrible things are happening in the upper houses. . . . '

'You wouldn't know an upper house from the back of your neck,' a failed physician growled at her. 'You can't even chart your way home from this place.'

She hissed at him.

'Never mind,' Ginnie Vandall consoled her; 'Ven can't even *see* his way home. Go on, Julia.' Ginnie didn't believe in fortune-telling per se, but she understood the techniques involved: a judicious blend of gossip and personal assessment. She did have faith in gossip, and in Hugo's susceptibility to flattery. Ginnie's hair was a new bright red, her bodice purple. She sat on the arm of Hugo's chair enjoying herself.

'The Sword of Justice is lifted high in the northern quadrant, ready to strike. The Sword. . . . Do you want to see the cards?'

'No', said the swordsman.

'Hugo,' his mistress caressed his golden curls, 'why not?'

'They're creepy.'

'They're powerful,' said Julia, unwrapping them. She handed the deck to Hugo. 'Cut them.'

'Oh, never mind,' said Ginnie Vandall. 'I'll do it.' The rings on her fingers glowed against the dull backs of the cards. She gave them a professional shuffle and handed them back to Julia, who laid them out in an incomprehensible pattern.

'Money.'

One of Ginnie's crew of friends looked on, hanging over her shoulder. 'Lucky lady. You know who's worth a lot these days?'

Ginnie said, 'He's always been worth a lot. Only this time he hasn't got any choice about it.' It was hard to tell whether she was pleased.

'I'm talking about St Vier.'

'I know,' said Ginnie Vandall.

'He doesn't dare to leave Riverside now. Someone's going to turn him in: what they're paying out for information alone's enough to. . . .'

'No swordsman's going to turn him in,' Hugo rumbled. He could be forbidding when he wanted to.

'Well, no,' Ginnie's friend simpered; 'you've just gone up on the Hill and made your depositories, haven't you?'

'Depositions,' Ginnie corrected sharply. 'Well, of course. It's crazy not to clear yourself when you can. Sign a piece of paper, give them some money and promise not to leave town. Let them think we want to cooperate – keep them from coming down here and snooping around. . . .'

'Well that's just what I'm saying,' her friend insisted: 'When all the swordsmen have gone up to say they didn't do it, it's going to look funny if he's missing, isn't it?'

'That's not proof, though,' Ginnie said; 'not enough to hang him.'

Hugo pulled his pretty Ginnie over to him. 'The whole thing's a pain. Nothing funny about it.'

'They don't need enough information to hang him yet, they just want something they can arrest him on, or try to. The reward'll be astronomical.'

Solemnly, Hugo lifted his cup. 'To information.'

'Think they'll catch him?'

'Not if he hides.'

Hugo said, 'His boyfriend's probably turning him in right now. Shifty bastard. Just like in the play.'

Ginnie sneered. 'Alec? He's not that shifty. He's got butterflies for brains.'

'Think it was the Tragedy that did it for him?'

'Did what?' said Ginnie languidly. 'Wait and see if the fight kills him first.'

Hugo laughed. It caught in his throat when he saw St Vier come through the doorway. He nudged Ginnie but she paid no mind, so he let his laughter continue to its natural end.

Richard ignored the little group in the corner. Ginnie Vandall was draped over Hugo like a carpet claiming its owner. They were laughing over some fortune cards. Ven, the drunken old bonesetter, got up and shuffled over to St Vier.

'You're young,' Ven said thickly; 'you should live! Don't fart around with these types. Get out of here while you can.'

'I like it here,' said Richard, and turned away. Ven stumbled forward and clutched at the swordsman's arm. The next second the old man was rolling on the floor. 'Don't do that,' Richard said, straightening his sleeve. 'Next time it'll be steel.'

'Hey!' an old woman protested. 'He don't mean no harm. What're you pushing people around for?'

The barmaid cautioned her, 'Leave him alone, Marty. He's a swordsman, you know how they can get. What's your drink, master?'

The beer was not as good as Rosalie's, but it was better than Martha's. Alec would have something to say about it. Alec would start a fight. He always seemed to like fights on rainy days.

Richard wandered over to watch the mumblety-peg tournament for a while. He'd been addicted to the game when he first came to Riverside, having finally found some people who were as good with a knife as he was. He was better than any of the ones playing now, though. The players' bodies were close together, not letting anyone in.

He wouldn't come here again; it was not a good idea to establish a recognisable pattern of habits now. Soon the price would be fixed on his head – funny expression, like a hat.

He wasn't interested in Julia's cards. Hugo and Ginnie were laughing again as he went out of the door.

Although it was only a short walk to the Hallidays', Lord Christopher ordered up his carriage because of his companion. He was proud of himself; he felt as if he were bringing home a trophy. A liveried footman brought them into the Crescent Chancellor's presence.

'Tell him,' Lord Christopher prompted the nervous, overdressed woman. She was small, pretty in a garish way, with painted eyes. 'He's the second noble witness we need to make your testimony official, and you can't do much better. We'll record it; then you can go.'

'I'll want my mm-money,' she said, her clipped Riverside speech marred by a stammer.

'Of course you'll have it,' said Basil Halliday. He nodded to his secretary to begin the transcription. 'Go ahead.'

'Well the man you want's St Vier. Everyone knows it.'

'How do they know it?'

She shrugged. 'How do you know anything? People don't mm-make mm-mistakes like that. He mm-must have told someone. But you can ss-see it. Nnn-nobody else that fast, or d-does that good a j-j-job.' Chris winced.

'Do you know why he did it?'

'He's a bb-bastard. Probably that scholar told him to.'

'What scholar?'

'Some bb-boy he had with him. Who knows? Swordsmen are all crazy. You just pay me, and I'm getting out of this city and hope I never see another one.'

She left, and the two noblemen signed the transcript. Halliday swore bitterly. 'The one man I was sure of!'

'It's no good,' Christopher said sensibly, disturbed to see his mentor so distressed. 'They all tell the same story. Unless it's a conspiracy. . . .'

'Among thieves?'

'It isn't very likely,' Chris continued earnestly. 'That leaves us with a handful of consistent testimonies, and the depositions of every other notable sword in town. St Vier must be arrested on suspicion of Horn's death.'

'So he must,' said Halliday heavily. 'Now how do you propose we get him out of Riverside?'

Lord Christopher picked up a pen, opened his mouth, put it down, and shut it.

'Never mind,' said Halliday a bit more gently. 'I won't have to call in my own landguard. It's very simple, really: we cry the arrest, post the reward, and wait for someone to turn him in.'

A fire was burning brightly in the Duchess Tremontaine's little parlour. The curtains were pulled back the better for their owner to savour the contrast with the rain outside. She sat curled up in a round chair of velvet, her feet tucked under her, enjoying the comfort and surveying a delightful incongruity.

He stood dripping in her doorway, a lanky figure in tattered black flanked by the gilded cherubs guarding the entrance.

'You're very wet,' she observed. 'You shouldn't have stayed out in the rain so long.'

'I didn't think you'd admit me.'

'I have left standing orders to admit you.' She lifted her cordial glass; the crystal chimed melodiously off the gold tray. 'I suppose you're out of money again?'

'You suppose right.' His tone mirrored hers. 'But that's not why I came.' He released from the folds of his robe the one rich thing about him, glowing on his finger like a heart of fire. 'Look what I've brought.'

'Goodness!' The duchess raised her fine eyebrows. 'Now how did that manage to find its way back to you?'

'It doesn't matter,' he scowled. 'You really shouldn't let it out of the house.'

'You said you didn't want it any more. The scene is clearly imprinted on my memory: I can see it when I close my eyes.' She did so. 'I can see it when I open my eyes, too: you were just as badly dressed, although of course you were drier.'

'I don't think I have ever been wetter. You should get someone to do something about all that rain.'

'Sit down,' she said in a friendly tone that did not conceive of disobedience. She patted a cushion at her side. 'If you're going to trust me, you'll have to tell me everything.'

'I'm not going to trust you.'

'Then why did you come, my dear?'

The knuckles of his hand whitened, his fingers storming around the ring. She'd never managed to teach him to hide his thoughts, which had a marked predilection for denying reality — when he was aware of its existence.

At last he sat, arms tightly clasped around his knees, staring rigidly at the fire. 'All right,' he said. 'I'll tell you what I know if you'll do the same.'

'I already know what I know,' the duchess said sweetly. 'Why don't you dry yourself off while I send for some little iced cakes?'

Chapter XXIII

It was getting harder and harder for Willie to find St Vier these days. Which was good, in a way: Master St Vier had always been fair to him, and was a great sword; Willie wished him well in this adventure. But he resented having to consider leaving messages for him with Marie: there was nothing and no one Nimble Willie couldn't find; that was known, and was going to stay known. Still, as the shadows of the afternoon got longer, it began to look as though he'd miss his mark entirely, which was bad for his reputation and his purse – plus it would annoy St Vier to miss a message. Disconsolately, Willie turned his feet toward Marie's; after all, there was still the chance St Vier might be home, although it was less likely these days. His route brought him past Rosalie's tavern. He decided to stop in for a consoling drink.

He couldn't believe his eyes, so he rubbed them, but there was still the dark head of the swordsman. No one was sitting near him, but he seemed unperturbed. He was eating stew.

Willie sidled up to Lucas Tanner. 'What's *he* doing here?'

'I don't know,' Tanner rumbled, 'but I wish to hell he'd leave.'

'Trouble?' Willie looked ready to sprint.

Tanner shrugged. 'There's a price on him, you know that. I'm not interested myself, but you never know who is. Makes people edgy; hard to have a good time.'

Willie scanned the room for unreliable strangers. There was a man he didn't know talking to one of the women, but he looked pretty drunk, and harmless.

'I had a price on my head once,' Willie said wistfully. 'I was pretty young, see, and nervous. It was some old guy with a really nice cane, not much bigger than me. I felt pretty bad after.'

'How did they find out it was you?'

'Somebody saw me. It was up on Gatling Street, in the city. They just about got me, too, but I slipped away and got over the

Bridge, and didn't I just keep close for a while after that!' Tanner nodded. 'I just about starved; no way of getting money for a bit. But nobody turned me in; we don't do things like that down here.'

'Maybe. Maybe not. Hard to catch him, anyway, without a troop. But it may come to that.'

Willie laughed. 'A troop? You're crazy. They'd be ankle-deep in dead cats and rotten eggs before they were halfway down the Loop. Not to mention thrown stones,' he added reflectively, his innocent face lit with soft pleasure.

'You want a riot, you can have one. Not but I wouldn't fight if it came to that; but why won't he just leave town! Make everything easier.'

Willie nodded over at the man peacefully eating his supper. '*You* tell him.'

'I'm no friend of his . . .' Tanner muttered.

'Wouldn't matter,' said Willie with cheerful wickedness; 'he'd kill you anyway!'

Nevertheless he approached the swordsman carefully. It was the opposite of stalking prey: you definitely wanted him to know you were coming.

Richard saw him, and saw that Willie actually wanted to speak to him, unlike most people these days. 'Hello, Willie,' he said, and swung a stool out for him. Richard didn't waste time with preliminaries: idle conversation in public places was not what anyone wanted him for. 'What's the word?'

'You won't believe who I saw,' Willie said chattily, 'uptown and dressed like nothing going!'

Richard's heart chose that moment to become athletic; but he managed to match Willie's tone: 'Oh? Who?'

'Kathy Blount! Hermia's girl, that was. You remember her.'

'Yes, I do.' His pulse settled back to its plodding motion.

'She says she'd like to see you again sometime. You've got the luck, haven't you?'

He had put the Tremontaine job out of his mind, being more concerned with the business at hand, and not having heard from them in weeks, not since their 'Delay'. It might not be a bad idea now: give him something to do, and enough money to see out the summer. He'd have to be more cautious slipping out of River-side, but he could manage.

'Says she'll be at the Dog tomorrow night, say, if you're free.'

'Thanks, Willie.'

The swordsman's lack of surprise at his news had not escaped Nimble Willie. Still, he leaned over to Richard, lowering his voice: 'Look, I think it's a trap. Sure, the Dog's in Riverside, but only just barely. You don't want to meet anyone anywhere for a while, Master St Vier, not when they know you're coming.'

'Maybe.' It was true, after all; the Brown Dog tavern stood closest to the Bridge. Its clientele consisted almost solely of city people looking for thrills, and Riversiders eager to fleece them. It was within shouting distance of the Watch. But where else could Katherine meet him safely? He had said he would help her if she were in trouble; it might not even be the job at all. 'Was that all the message?' he asked.

'Not quite. She said something funny about a ring.'

The ruby was gone, gone with Alec. If they needed it now they'd have to ask him for it. 'What about it?'

'She said, she knows where it is now. That's all.'

Willie saw with nervousness how St Vier's fist clenched on the table. But the swordsman's face remained calm. Willie was glad he only carried the messages.

In the end, Richard chose to go. He said to Marie on his way out, 'Look, there's a chance I won't be coming back tonight. If you hear anything certain, take what I owe you out of the rosewood chest, and do what you want with the rest of the stuff.'

She didn't ask where he was going. These days she liked to be able to tell people who came asking that she didn't know.

He hadn't eaten any supper yet; the best thing about the Dog was its food. When he was new to the city he'd gone there a lot; it was a good place for young people of all professions to pick up work. He and Alec had taken to dropping in every few weeks: Alec liked the food, and liked dicing with the city people because they bet high and they were even clumsier cheaters than he was. But drunken young men were always challenging Richard there to impress their friends; one night one of them had annoyed

Alec, and Richard had ended up killing him, putting a strain on St Vier's relationship with the tavern keeper.

No one seemed to be following him as he took the long way round. The tavern shone like sunrise at the end of the street, its doorway alight with beacons like any uptown establishment. The light showed no one waiting for him by the entrance. Over it hung the brown dog, a large painted wood carving that bore no resemblance to any living breed.

Inside was just as well lit. The place had a carnival atmosphere, fevered and bright. Richard felt as though he'd stepped outside Riverside into another world. Whores were talking animatedly with well-dressed men, completely ignoring the gaudy ones whose hands shuffled and reshuffled decks of cards, who might be their neighbours or brothers. A couple of nobles in half-masks leaned against the wall, trying to look detached and amused, their eyes darting here and there about the room, glittering in the mask-slits, their naked hands playing on the pommels of the swords they wore for security. Richard thought he would pass unnoticed amongst them, but he saw how the card-players deliberately flattened their eyes against seeing him, how the whores turned their backs and raised their volume. Riversiders didn't turn each other in; they just stopped knowing you. That way was easier. It told him he was recognised, though, and warned him that not everyone might be so considerate.

He didn't see Katherine, which further roused his suspicion. His sword hung, a solid weight, at his side. He touched it under his cloak. and found the tavern keeper edging up to him.

Harris had his perpetual harried, unctuous expression. 'Now, sir, if you will recall an adventure I would not like repeated. . . .' He rarely spoke in sentences, but in insinuation; people said he had started as a pimp.

'I'll be careful,' Richard promised. 'Who's here tonight?'

Harris shrugged. 'The usual . . .' he said vaguely. 'You understand, I don't want trouble. . . .'

Something made Richard turn around. He was not entirely surprised to see Katherine coming through the doorway. He waited until she saw him, then moved to a table with a good command of the room, brushing past a pretty-boy lolling in the lap of a heavily powdered man who was feeding him whisky in small glasses.

Katherine followed, ridiculously relieved that Richard was here already. He moved through the room with careful assurance, betraying no sign of nervousness, although watchfulness glowed off him like magic. It almost surprised her that the entire room didn't rise up and follow him: Richard at work was more than impressive, he was magnetic. He wanted to be sought after for his skill; but the nobles desired him for his performance.

She couldn't keep her hands from twisting together, so she hid them under the table. Absurdly, Richard said, 'Thank you for coming.'

She said, 'You weren't at the Old Bell last week.'

'Was I supposed to be?'

'Not if you didn't know. Of course he didn't tell you.'

'Who? Willie?' Her silence made it plain. 'Alec.'

A young woman cruised by their table, and smiled into Katherine's eyes like an old friend. Richard's hand moved a fraction on the table, ready to take action if she needed it. But Katherine shook her head. 'I can't stand it in here,' she said fretfully. 'Can we go out?'

'Where?' Richard asked. 'Shall we go deeper into Riverside? You don't mind?'

'It doesn't matter.' There was a dull edge of hysteria to her voice that made his taut nerves quiver.

'Katherine.' He would have taken her hand if he could. 'Were you sent here, or did you come yourself? If it's business, we'll get it over quickly and you can go.'

She glanced quickly behind her. 'I came,' she said. 'On my own.'

Anger surged and hardened in him. With a cause to form around, his nerves twisted together into a strong cord of purpose. It was too long since he had had a real fight, too long that he had been sitting, waiting.

'It's bad, then,' he said quietly, without any gentleness. 'Ferris has done you no good. Never mind. You don't have to tell me about it. I said I would help you and I will.'

He couldn't see his own face, set and white with a rage whose coolness his eyes betrayed by being too wide, too blue, too fixed.

It was a look she had seen only once before in him, and it froze the life in her bones. 'Richard,' she whispered, *please –*'

'It's all right,' he said calmly. 'We'll leave here, go somewhere else where we can talk. Do you need a place to stay? Don't worry. You should have known I'd come.'

'Come, then,' she echoed, rising from the table. She was shaking with chill. She wanted to run, to push her way out of the tavern, to flinch from the cold swordsman walking beside her. She took his arm, and together they made a way past the card-players and revellers, out of the doorway into the orange light burning a hole in the dark street.

'There,' he said; 'better?'

She held him tighter as a shadow fell across them. Behind them the door had opened, blocked by dark figures. To the right, and to the left, and in front of them the shadows had become men, ringing the aura of light with solid darkness.

'Richard St Vier?'

'Yes?'

'In the name of the Council I charge you to stand –'

He flung her reeling into the darkness, but her weight had held his arm too long, and he drew his sword only as the first of the wooden staves crashed into him.

The impact staggered him back, but he did not fall. The next one drove the breath from his side. He turned blindly in a new direction, where he thought the attack might come. His eyes cleared and he saw the staff descending, glowing like a comet with pain. His cut went wild but so did the staff. The man's guard was down; Richard followed his torch-gold blade true to its mark, and heard the man cry out a moment before the thwack of another blow caught St Vier across the shoulders. His knees hit the ground, but he kept hold of his sword and was on his feet again, just like practice, only he would pay for this later. This time he saw the staff come swinging out of the darkness toward his face. He almost raised his sword to break the blow; but steel would not stand up to oak, so he ducked instead, and missed the one that caught him in the back of his legs.

There certainly were a lot of them. He fell sprawling, scraping his hands along the stone. His sword was gone – he felt for the hilt, somewhere nearby, but the cobbles seemed to be coursing with light. Not light but pain. He was seeing pain flowing like gold, like a basket full of jewels and summer fruit.

He heard roaring in his ears, and a voice he agreed with shrieking, 'Stop it! Please stop it, that's enough!'

But they weren't ready to stop until the swordsman had ceased rolling and dodging and lay perfectly still. Then the Watch picked up their prize and carried him over the north Bridge. The prison where he would eventually rest lay on the south side of the river. They'd bring him there by boat, in the daylight.

Nimble Willie waited silent in the shadows of a bridge parapet for the knot of men to pass him. Except for their staves, nothing to attract attention. But he guessed before chance showed him the face of the man they carried.

'Oh, Master St Vier,' he murmured to himself in the shadows; 'this is a terrible thing.'

And Katherine Blount returned to the one who had sent her. She managed to make a clear report; then she asked for brandy, and was given a large decanter without question.

Chapter XXIV

Lord Michael Godwin lay back on the embroidered cushions of his couch, loosened his shirt collar and tried to encourage himself to be hungry. He thought about early winter mornings after hunting, and about interminable music recitals before dinner. But the expanse of dishes set before him grew no more alluring. He wondered how the small, agile men around him managed. They were cheerfully digging into piles of dyed eggs with unfeigned vigour, cracking the shells in interesting patterns and rolling the eggs in spices; deflowering piles of fruit, cut and arranged like blossoms; spearing little deep-fried objects with the ends of carved picks. He took a grape, for form's sake; it had come from a hothouse, and must be worth its weight in eggshells.

Across the table his compatriot caught his eye and smiled. In the few weeks Michael had been in Chartil, Devin had lost no opportunity to point out to him his deficiencies in local custom. Devin was the second son of a second son; an aristocrat by courtesy, whose lineage came nowhere near Michael's. In the city of his birth Devin felt it sharply; in Chartil he was exalted to the rank of ambassador, and his hospitality was legendary. His saving grace was a sense of humour, which took the sting out of his self-defensive manoeuvres. Michael liked Devin; and he thought Devin had decided to like him, in spite of his background.

Above the racket of conversation, the ambassador said to him in their own tongue, 'Packet came in today. Lots of gossip from town.'

A servant was trying to refill one of Michael's three wine glasses. Michael gave up and let her. Her thigh rubbed against his shoulder. Automatically he turned his chin to nuzzle her waist, but his eye fell on the bangles around her ankles, and his head jerked back. She was a bonded slave. Devin's sardonic eyes glinted at him, reading his thoughts: of course no free woman here, not even a servant, would seek to entice him; that lot fell to those whose bodies and their issue were pledged to an owner. For women, it was a step up from prostitution. He wondered if he had been selected by his host to breed, or to be flattered. Either idea repelled him.

'She likes you,' said the ambassador.

Michael hid the colour of his face in his widest-brimmed wine cup.

'It's no worse', Devin persisted, 'than one who takes your money and wishes you in hell. She'll get paid at the end of her term. More gracious this way.'

'Nevertheless . . .' Lord Michael took refuge in an aristocrat's shrug. 'What's the gossip?'

'Seems Lord Horn's been killed.'

Michael forgot that he was holding a wine cup when his hand opened. He caught it on its way down before it hit the table, but not before its contents had liberally bestowed themselves on their surroundings. The slave mopped at it all with a napkin.

'Friend of yours?' Devin was enjoying himself mightily.

'Hardly. I just didn't think he was ready for death.'

'Probably wasn't. They're saying a swordsman did it.'

'Oh? Any idea which one?'

'*Swordsman*?' A Chartil noble on his left caught the word, and continued in his own tongue, 'That's one of your labourers, isn't it, who dishonours his sword in the service of other men?'

Devin translated the comment for Michael, and chided the speaker, 'Now, Eoni, if that were so, it would be dishonour to be a soldier.'

'*Ffft.*' Eoni made the usual Chartil comment of disdain. 'You know very well what I mean. For the killing of noble enemies, only two things will serve: either the challenge direct, or, saving your courtesy and that of the table, the certain use of poison. None of this pussy-footing around with surrogates. And I've served my time as a soldier and I'm proud of it, so don't think to gall me that way, you small-minded, round-faced foreign excuse for a gentleman!'

'"Insult, the last refuge of blighted affection. . . ."' Devin quoted sweetly.

Barred by language from the conversation, Michael rolled a grape between his fingers and thought about Horn. Murdered, and he knew by whom. *His life is about to become complicated....* Yes, what was left of it. The clear eyes of the swordsman looked out from his memory, blue as spring hyacinths.... self-serving little murderer, using his skill with a sword to destroy better men than he'd ever be....

'Excuse me.' Michael nodded to his host, and set off in the direction of the urinals. But he didn't stop there; his will took him out onto the street, walking swiftly through the sun-baked alleys of the town. He passed enclosed gardens whose feather-topped trees showed over the walls.

It wasn't that he had any love for Horn. He would have killed Horn himself, if he could. But St Vier couldn't have any quarrel with Horn; no one forced a swordsman to take a job he didn't want. No one had forced him to kill Vincent Applethorpe.... Michael stopped for a moment, involuntarily pressing his hand to his mouth. He still dreamed about it, when he wasn't dreaming of wool.

That was what the duchess had wanted – not a swordsman, not a courtier, but someone to look into the direct shipping of wool from her estates to Chartil. She was eliminating the middle-man by having the raw wool dyed and woven here into the popular shawls, then shipped back to sell out of her own warehouses.... At first he'd thought this tradesman's assignment an elaborate and degrading joke. But on the ship, studying the records and notes she had given him, he came to see how much politics was bound up in business, and how much of his skill the task would require, especially in a place where no one knew him. There were laws, and import taxes to consider.... It was the stuff of the Council meetings he always made sure to avoid, the hidden agenda of the grain reports from his father's land, which he glanced over grudgingly each month, whose revenues supported his life in the city.

The wool business had caught Michael up, intrigued him, even made him feel a certain power; but it had not made him forget Applethorpe. He would bear the death to the end of his days. And St Vier, whose skill had lured his Master into the endless night; St Vier who at the end had seemed to share with

221

his Master a spirit and understanding that Michael could not approach. . . . St Vier had walked away and gone to wield his power elsewhere.

Michael looked down. A little man in a dirty headcloth was jabbering at him, asking him something. He shook his head helplessly: I don't know. Doggedly, the man repeated the question. Michael caught the words for 'lord', and 'buy'. He shook his head again; but the man blocked his path, not letting him move on. Michael pulled back a fold of his robe, showing the sword he wore to threaten him. The little man grinned excitedly, nodding with great vigour and enthusiasm. He reached inside his own robe and pulled out a little vial; one, two, three of them, all different shapes, thrusting them under Michael's nose, gesticulating with his other hand:

'Four bits! Four times four – ' or maybe it was four *and* four – 'bits for one! All three, even less!'

Michael had spent time in the market. Still not sure what the product was, but amused despite himself, he employed the bulk of his vocabulary: 'Too much.'

The man expressed shock. The man expressed dismay. Perhaps the lord did not fully understand the exceptional quality of his stock. He pointed to the vials, pantomimed drinking one, and clutched his throat, emitting realistic choking noises, reeling backwards as though looking for a resting place. He sat down hard on the ground, rolling up his eyes, then grinning happily at Michael.

They were poisons. Poisons for his enemy.

'Five!' the man said. 'All three, five each!'

A death no one could stand against, swift and sure. It would not be impossible to arrange it for St Vier. Michael Godwin had friends in the city, and money.

Michael shuddered in the sunlight, remembering the swordsman's animal grace. It was a foul death to offer such a man; a worse death than he had given Applethorpe or Horn. However the Chartils might romanticise expedience, it remained a death without honour, unheralded and unchallenged. *The challenge . . . you either know it or you don't.*

Michael touched the sword he wore. He knew it; and for him it did not lie in feats of arms. He was a nobleman, and nobles did not seek revenge against swordsmen on commission. If anything, he should be plotting against Horn; but the nobleman had gone beyond Michael's revenge. He had no reason to want to avenge Horn, and for Applethorpe no vengeance would ever be enough. It was natural for him to want to hurt the man who had been the instrument of his first adult grief; natural, but not right. He was glad he had not even held one of the vials in his hand.

Michael's face told the little man that the bargaining was over. He drifted back around the corner, and Michael turned back toward Devin and the feast.

It was true, as the duchess had told him, that the Chartils respected a man who could use a sword. The friends he made who practised with him were intrigued by some of his straight-point technique, and amused at his lack of experience; but one of them said seriously to him, 'At least you are a man. Your countryman the feastmaster is a good sort, but. . . .'

When he came back in the hall the eating was still going on, and there was a fourth winecup at everyone's place. He found he was ready for it, and even managed some enthusiasm over almond tarts.

Devin looked at him as he sat down. The ambassador's face was grave, but his eyes glinted with dry mirth: 'Get lost?' he said.

'Only temporarily.' Michael bit into a cake.

Chapter XXV

The Old Fort guarded the mouth of the channel to the old city, on the east bank. It was still used as a watch tower, but now its honeycomb passages housed important state prisoners. St Vier had been brought there early this morning, and Lord Ferris had come as soon as the news reached him.

Half an hour in the Fort found Ferris trying hard not to lose his temper. Finally, he sat in the chair he had first been offered, spreading his cloak out not to wrinkle it. It was as comfortable a room as could be made of the heavy stone cells of the old fort. It was the deputy's sitting room, where visitors waited to be escorted to the prisoner of their choice. But it seemed that, in the case of Richard St Vier, they were reticent with the privilege.

When Lord Ferris sat, the deputy sat too, across the table from the nobleman. The deputy was a steady man, but having to match wills with a Council Lord made him uncomfortable and turned his virtues to stubbornness. Doggedly he repeated his information: 'You will forgive me, my lord, but the orders I have come from the Crescent himself. St Vier is to be kept closely guarded, and no one is to see him without Lord Halliday's own express permission.'

'I understand,' Lord Ferris said for perhaps the third time, trying to make it sound freshly compassionate. 'But you must realise that, as a member of the Inner Council, I comprise a portion of the Justiciary. All of us will be questioning St Vier as soon as my lord duke of Karleigh arrives in the city.'

'In the court you will, yes, my lord. But I have no instructions as to private interviews beforehand.'

'Oh, come.' Ferris essayed a smile, wilfully misreading him. 'Surely the serpent is defanged, and I cannot be harmed now.'

'Surely, my lord,' the deputy agreed, with the formal tolerance reserved for aggravating superiors. 'But *he* might be. We are guarding Master St Vier for his own protection as well as others'. In affairs of this sort, it is not always the swordsman who is the guilty party.'

'What?' Ferris exclaimed. 'Has he said anything?'

'Not one word, my lord. The gentleman – that is, the young man is most quiet and well behaved. He has not asked to see anyone.'

'Interesting,' said Ferris, in his role of chancellor, 'and possibly indicative of something. But there, I mustn't ask questions of you before the actual Inquiry.' He stood up briskly, shaking out the heavy folds of his cloak. 'I expect you have also been required to inform Lord Halliday of any who come asking to see St Vier?' The man nodded. 'Well, you needn't bother in my case,' Ferris said heartily; 'I'll go and call on him now myself, inform him of my breach of etiquette, and see if I can't procure that necessary bit of paper for you.'

'Very good, my lord,' the deputy said – or one of those non-committal phrases implying measured credulity and the desire to be left in peace by the mighty.

Ferris hurried out of the chill of the fort and into his waiting carriage, where he put his feet on a hot brick that could have been hotter. He did not drive to Lord Halliday's. He went home. He had no intention of letting Halliday know that he was interested in seeing St Vier. But he very much wanted to see the swordsman before he could tell Basil Halliday about the plan to have him killed.

There was no certainty that St Vier would tell about him, of course. It would not absolve the swordsman of Horn's murder. And, of course, there was not even the certainty that St Vier had ever known the identity of his one-eyed contact. Nothing was certain; but Ferris wanted to control all the odds that he could. He had the best, the surest plan, if only he could implement it: to offer St Vier his protection in the matter of Horn's death, if St Vier would agree to carry through on the Halliday challenge as soon as he was freed. Taking the charge as patron of Horn's disgusting murder would not be good for Ferris, but he could think of some story to explain it, to subtly blacken St Vier's character and add yet another taint to Horn's; and it was convenient that St Vier kill Halliday. The debt would bind the swordsman to Ferris for life, and when he had been elected to the Crescent Ferris would have much use for him.

As soon as Karleigh came up from his estates to sit on the Justiciary, they would try the swordsman. St Vier would see Ferris on the panel of justiciars, and could recognise him. Ferris didn't dare risk what the swordsman might try to do then to save his life. It was remotely possible that St Vier might think of the double blackmail on his own, but Ferris must find a way to let him know that he would cooperate in it.

But he could not get in to see him now without creating suspicion. He needed a proxy. Katherine had failed him once, when he sent her to Riverside. Now she must serve him again – for the last time, if all went well. Surely they would not deny St Vier's own *wife* permission to see him? It might work – nobody knew what sort of arcane pairings there were in Riverside, and she was a fetching piece.

A servant took Ferris's cloak; another was sent to bring him something hot to drink, and another to summon Katherine Blount.

The hot drink came, but Katherine did not. The footman said, 'I sent one of the maids up to her room, my lord. It seems it is empty.'

'Empty . . . ? Of what? Of her person, or . . . ?'

'Of her, ah, belongings, my lord. The girl appears to have fled. She was paid two weeks ago for the month. But she seems to be missing since night before last.'

'Fled!' Ferris tapped his fingers on the cup rapidly, thinking. 'Send Master Johns to me, I shall require some letters sent.'

He had not meant to keep her much longer: she was the link that tied him to St Vier, should the matter be investigated. Perhaps he had been too hard on her, and she had simply run away, in which case he didn't care what happened to her. But if she had gone, say, to Halliday. . . .

His letters dictated and secretary dismissed, Ferris realised, ruefully, that he must turn to Diane. The duchess's connections were better than his; she might even be able to get him access to St Vier. He would not tell her everything; that would be a great mistake. And a mistake to think that he could simply bend Diane to his will; that had once been tried, and quickly discarded. But

226

he might be persuasive, if she were in the right mood for it . . . even now it was not good to lie to her, but she could be charmed. Once again Ferris called for his carriage to be sent round, and ordered the familiar route to the Duchess Tremontaine's.

He stood in the duchess's front hall, trying to hand his gloves to the footman, but the footman wouldn't take them.

'My lady is not in, my lord.'

From upstairs Ferris heard her laughter, and a snatch of song.

'Grayson,' he said slowly, 'do you know me?'

'Of course he knows you,' a new voice drawled from the shadows. 'You're a very recognisable figure.'

A young man of no more than 20 years was lounging against the side of the staircase, surveying Ferris with an expression that contrived to be both bored and amused at once. He was very beautifully dressed in deep red, and wore a collar of rubies. He held a book in one hand.

'If the duchess told Grayson to tell you she is not in,' the young man continued, 'it actually means that she doesn't want to see you. Is there a message?' he asked helpfully. 'Perhaps I could take it.'

He was tall, and fine-boned, theatrically languid in his motions. He turned and drifted partway up the stairs, stopping to look down at the Dragon Chancellor, the hand with the book resting on the rail. Ferris stared up at him, still saying nothing. Was this his replacement? Some young nobody — oh, very young — someone's son fresh from the country? A consolation after her loss of Michael Godwin, an insult to Ferris, a replacement. . . . It was not possible that she was throwing him over. She had no cause. Her refusal to see him was some new game, or a trick of this smug young man's who might, after all, be some distant relation of Diane's. . . .

'Is there any message, my lord?' Grayson asked, professionally deaf to the antics around him.

'Yes. Tell my lady I will call again.'

'Who knows,' the mocking voice drifted after Ferris as he left, his stride so swift that his cloak billowed out, brushing the man who held the door open for him, 'she may be in.'

And as the door closed behind him Ferris heard the duchess's laughter echoing in the marble hall.

Answers to the letters he had sent were waiting for him when he got home. No one had seen any sign of Katherine; or at least, no one was admitting to it. Perhaps she had gone back to Riverside where, in truth, she belonged.

He stood with his hands on his desk, leaning his weight on his arms. In another minute he would straighten, raise his head and find another order to give. Before Diane, it had been like this, too often: a sense of his own power blocked; of not being taken seriously; of not being able to choose for himself the strongest course. He was Dragon Chancellor now. People knew him, admired him, looked to him for guidance, for advancement. Basil Halliday confided in him, and would help him if he could. . . . Ferris started, hearing his own sharp laugh. Go to Halliday with his problems, like all the rest of them – tangle himself in that net of compassionate charm, and exchange Diane's dominion for Halliday's . . . that was not the way to the power he sought, cold and uncompromising, the terms his own and his alone. Most people were like Horn: they could be manipulated, rendered agreeable or untroublesome in their actions. Blocks like Halliday could be duped and got rid of. Ferris sighed, shaking his head. If only they all could be ignored. But of course that was unrealistic.

Ferris thought of the day that stretched ahead of him, and decided to emulate the duchess. Turning his back on his study, he ascended to his bedroom where he wrapped himself in a heavy robe, had a large fire made up, settled next to it with a book and a bowl of nuts, and gave instructions that, to anyone who called, he was not in.

For Richard St Vier, imprisoned, that day passed very slowly. He had a headache, and there was no one to talk to, and nothing very interesting to think about. Shrugging the day off as a loss, he made himself as comfortable as he could, and retired early to bed with the sun. The next morning brought news of his trial.

The pleasant young nobleman had already explained to Richard all that he needed to know about his coming questioning. The pleasant young nobleman, whose name was Christopher Nevilleson, had been sent expressly from Basil Halliday to do so the day he arrived in the Fort. Richard disliked the young man intensely. He knew there was no good reason for it, but he did. Lord Christopher had had the shackles struck from Richard's wrists and legs, and had expressed official dismay, tinged with personal horror, at the condition the Watch had left him in. But the bruises would heal in time, if there was time left to him. He was horribly stiff, but nothing was cracked or broken.

Halliday's aide was serious and fresh-faced. In him the Hill drawl sounded like a speech defect he had never grown out of. He told Richard that he would be questioned first in private by a collection of important lords, to determine how culpable he was in the killing of Lord Horn. They had to know whether he was working for any patron so they could then decide whether to try him in a Court of Honour or turn him over to the civil authorities as a murderer.

'There are so few laws that really cover the use of swordsmen,' he explained. 'If you have anything in writing it would be very useful.'

Richard stared at him out of one swollen eye. 'I don't work on contract,' he said frostily. 'They should know that by now.'

'I . . . yes,' Lord Christopher said. He told Richard that he would be required to answer questions under oath, and that depositions had already been sworn against him by witnesses. Richard asked, 'Will I see any of these people at the trial?'

Lord Christopher answered, 'No, that isn't necessary. They've already signed statements witnessed by two nobles.' He kept saying, 'You do understand, don't you?' Richard said that he did. Finally, the pleasant young nobleman went away.

Early this morning they had sent someone in to shave and barber him, because the Duke of Karleigh had driven in last night and now the Justiciary was complete. Richard had submitted to the combing fingers and the scissors, but when it came to the sharp-edged razor he asked if he might use it himself, and offered to go unshaven otherwise. In the end they let him shave himself, and stood solemnly around watching to make sure he didn't cut his throat.

It would be interesting to find out what the trial was like. In the past, when he had been hired to kill a lord the noble who hired him had always stood up in the Court of Honour for himself, so that St Vier need not appear at all. Part of his care in choosing his patrons had involved their ability to do so. The Court of Honour was a secret thing, presided over by the Inner Council. Swordsmen who had been called to it were never very clear in their descriptions after: either they had been confused, or they wanted to impress by being mysterious, or both. Richard suspected that the truth was seldom told in the Court of Honour: a noble's ability to manipulate it and his peers seemed to be the key to success there. That was why St Vier took only patrons who seemed to have that knack over men who offered him contracts where his 'innocence' would be cast in writing – that, and his own desire for privacy.

He wished now that he had been a little more pleasant with Lord Christopher, and asked a few more questions. But it didn't matter: soon he would find all about the court for himself. He could think about that; could think about the future but not the past. He'd already gone over everything he'd done wrong; once was enough for that sort of thing, to satisfy his mind; any more was useless and unpleasant. If he lived, he could find out who in Riverside had sworn against him. The reason for Katherine's nervousness was clear now. But she wouldn't have done it on her own – somehow, they had made her afraid. He couldn't help her now.

Doggedly he stretched and paced in the small stone room. Whatever happened, there was no point in letting himself get stiffer. His bruised body protested, but he was used to ignoring it. The room was not terrible; there was light, and a bed bolted to the wall. His injuries and the inactivity made him feel tired; but the temptation of the hard bed was resistible.

He paused by the window, leaning on the stone embrasure. It was a privilege, of sorts, not to be thrown in the Chop with the common city criminals. Richard was in one of the upper rooms of the Old Fort, looking out over the mouth of the channel guarding the oldest section of the city.

Far below, the river glittered, grey and bright as the surface of a mirror. His window was an arrow-slit, tapering to an opening in the outer wall. The cold stone felt good against his forehead. The tide was running; he watched trade boats passing down to the channel.

Habit made him clap his hand to his side when he heard the door opening behind him. He did not bother trying to convert the gesture when his fingers closed on nothing.

'Master St Vier.' The deputy of the Fort stood just within the doorway, backed by a phalanx of guards. 'Your escort is here to conduct you to the Council Hall.'

He was surprised at the respect they accorded him. He didn't know if it was just the formal good manners extended to all Fort prisoners, or if his being a well-known swordsman outweighed his living in Riverside.

'Is there a crowd?' he asked the deputy.

'A crowd? Where?'

'Outside, in Justice Place,' Richard said, 'waiting to see us go by.' He had assumed that the guards were to keep the curious from pressing in on them on their walk across the plaza. There would be friends there, and enemies; hordes of curious gogglers with nothing better to do than shove and stare.

'Oh, no,' the deputy smiled. 'We don't go that way.' He read St Vier's look. 'The guards are for you. My lord would not have you chained, so we need a convoy to prevent your escaping.'

Richard laughed. He supposed he could injure the deputy, and maybe capture one of the guards' weapons. He could turn their orderly walk into a slaughter. But the chances were bad, and he had an appointment with the Council.

They came to a stair, and picked up more torches. Their way led downward, underground smelling of stony water and iron earth. It was a passage system under the plaza, connecting the fort with the hall.

'I never heard of this!' Richard said to the deputy. 'How long has it been here?'

'Well before my time,' the deputy answered. 'I've memorised the passage. It's part of my duties. There are a lot of dead ends and unexplored turns.'

'I'll try not to wander off,' Richard said.

'Do that.' The deputy chuckled. 'You're sure of yourself, aren't you?'

Richard shrugged. 'Isn't everyone?'

The stairs leading up weren't as long as the ones they had taken down. The guards had to pass single file through the door at the

231

top, with Richard between them. They came into a hall filled with sunlight. Richard's eyes burned, and he felt himself drenched in the fire of day, saturated with the colours of the wood-panelled walls, the marble floors and painted ceiling. The sun-baked warmth of the hall, with its high windows, was welcome to them all after the chill of the passage. But the disciplined guards were silent as they marched their prisoner down the corridor.

They came at last to large oak double-doors, guarded by liveried men who opened them portentously. Richard was expecting something splendid; instead there was another antechamber, more doors. These, too, were opened, and he and his escort paraded into the Court of Honour.

The room was dim, as though drenched in perpetual afternoon. He had an impression of maybe a dozen men in splendid robes like theatre costumes, seated behind a long table facing him. He was given a chair in the middle of the floor, facing Basil Halliday and some others. Halliday wore blue velvet, with a huge ring stitched in gold on the chest: emblem of the Crescent whose chancellorship he held. Richard thought wryly what a wonderful target the circle made. But that job was off for now.

'Master St Vier.' The irritatingly nice young man who had briefed him now came forward. 'These are the lords justiciar, fully assembled in Inquiry before us. They have already heard all the signed depositions; now they will ask you some questions.'

'I do understand,' said Richard. 'But isn't one missing?'

'I beg your pardon?'

'You said, *fully assembled*. But there are two empty seats: yours and one next to that red-face– next to that man in green.'

'Oh.' For a moment, Lord Christopher looked flummoxed. He hadn't prepared to answer questions from the accused in front of everyone. But Basil Halliday smiled and nodded to him; so, taking heart, he said, 'That is the seat for Tremontaine. Next to my lord duke of Karleigh. Every ducal house has the right to sit on the Court of Honour – '

'But the damned woman won't take her duties seriously!' roared the red-faced man who had been pointed out as the Duke of Karleigh. Although he'd taken the duke's job and his money, Richard had never seen him in person before. Karleigh seemed

232

like the type to require swordsmen frequently: proud and quarrelsome, as well as powerful. 'Didn't take long to get *her* the message, I'll warrant! *She* didn't have to come tearing up from the hinterlands on a day's notice for this. . . .'

'Now, my lord.' A man with a bird emblem stitched on his chest tried to calm the duke. 'That is between the duchess and her honour, not ours.' Richard recognised Lord Montague, a man he'd worked for and liked. Montague was Raven Chancellor now, and less given to fights; Richard had been wounded once in his service, and taken into Montague's own house to recover.

When the Duke of Karleigh had been settled, Lord Halliday began the questions. 'Master St Vier, we have heard many people swear that you killed Lord Horn. But no one witnessed the event. References are all to your style, your skill, to rumour. If you can summon proof positive that you were elsewhere on the night of his death, we would like to hear of it.'

'No,' said Richard, 'I can't. It *is* my style.'

'And is there someone you think might copy that style to get you into trouble?'

'No one I can think of.'

' – my lord,' Karleigh injected. 'Damned insolence. *No one I can think of, my lord* – mind how you speak to your betters!'

'And you mind', a quiet voice said lazily, 'how you make a shambles of these proceedings, Karleigh.' The florid duke fell silent, and Richard could guess why: the speaker was a man of average build, perhaps as old as Karleigh, but with flexible hands that were younger, more capable, and eyes that were much older. ('Lord Arlen,' Chris Nevilleson mouthed at him.)

'I'm sorry,' Richard said to the Crescent. 'I haven't meant to be rude.'

He'd noticed that Halliday had been ignoring Karleigh's outbursts; of course, there was trouble between them. Halliday shrugged and said to the Raven Chancellor, 'See that that exchange is struck from the notes, my lord?'

Montague jotted something down and motioned to the scribe behind him. 'Of course.'

'You understand, then,' Halliday said to Richard, 'that all evidence points to you?'

'I meant it to,' Richard said. 'That was its purpose.'

'You do not deny that you killed Horn?'

'I do not.'

Even in the small group, the noise of reaction was loud. Finally, Lord Halliday had to call for silence. 'Now,' Halliday said to Richard, 'we come to the particular business of this court. Can you name a patron in Horn's death?'

'No, I can't. I'm sorry.'

'Can you give us any *reason*?' Montague leaned forward to ask.

Richard thought, framing his answer in words they might understand. 'It was a matter of honour.'

'Well, yes, but *whose*?'

'Mine', Richard said.

Halliday sighed loudly and wiped his forehead. 'Master St Vier: your firmness to stand by your word is known and respected in this court. Any patron you select must have complete faith in you, and I'm sure this one does. But if he is too cowardly to reveal himself and stand the judgement of his peers, I want to make it clear to you that your life is at peril here. Without a noble patron, we will have to give you over to a civil authority to try you as a murderer.'

'I understand,' said Richard. A thought with the voice of Alec whispered silently: My honour isn't worth your attention. But secretly he was relieved. They honestly didn't seem to know why he had had to kill Horn. Since Godwin had escaped his challenge, Horn had not been eager to boast about the blackmailing of St Vier. So far, only Riverside knew anything about that. And Richard would do what he could to see that it stayed that way. He didn't think it would even matter if he did tell them the reason; it probably wouldn't stand up under their contorted rules. The court was turning out to be interesting only in an eerily nasty way: like their rationales for killing each other, there was a separate set of rules that seemed to double back on itself, whose origins they'd long ago forgotten the purpose of.

'Might I ask a question?' said a new voice, faintly familiar. Richard looked at the speaker, and found why: a man with coal-black hair and an eyepatch had risen. He, too, was in blue velvet, and there was a nice-looking dragon on his chest. It was Ferris, who'd come from the duchess to ask him to kill Halliday.

'Master St Vier.' Lord Ferris courteously introduced himself:

'I am the Dragon Chancellor of the Council of Lords. I, too, have heard in many places just how well you may be trusted . . . in many places, sir.' He had his head turned so that his good eye was fixed on Richard; his speaking eye. Richard nodded, to show he understood the reference to their meeting.

'Speechmaking, my lord Dragon?' asked the Duke of Karleigh in a low but carrying voice.

Ferris smiled warmly at him. 'If you like. It's what comes of being a good boy and waiting my turn.' The other nobles laughed, breaking the tension and letting him continue: 'And I think, Master St Vier, that in view of your reputation we are perhaps doing you a disservice. For your style bespeaks not only a man of honour, but a man of sense. If you did kill Lord Horn, you did so for a reason. It may be a reason we all wish to hear. The death of a noble concerns all of our honours, whether in formal challenge or no.' Down the table, Halliday nodded. 'Now, the civil court has been known to use methods less gentle than our own. . . .'

The old–young nobleman asked dryly, 'Are you proposing that we torture St Vier, Ferris?'

Lord Ferris turned his head to look at him. 'My lord of Arlen,' he said pleasantly, 'I am not. But, in fact, it's not a bad idea. Something formal, and harmless, to keep his honour intact.'

Richard felt as though he were fencing blindfold. Words were deceiving; one had to move by tone and inference, and by sheer sense of purpose. Remembering Ferris's style in the tavern, Richard thought the lord was saying that he knew what had happened with Horn. If so, he was threatening to reveal it . . . unless what? Unless Richard assured him that he would not reveal the plot against Halliday? But how could he assure him in front of them all?

'Ferris,' Halliday interrupted, 'Arlen; I must ask you to be serious. Do you really want that proposal put on record?'

'I beg your pardon,' Ferris said a little haughtily. 'I think it should be considered before we give St Vier over to death at the hands of the civil court. I realise that such a proposal would draw this Inquiry out – longer, perhaps, than some would care to spend on it. But I would like it noted that my own hand is held out to the swordsman as willing to entertain any answer he gives

235

us here. In the privacy of this court, any nobleman's honour is secure, and his reasons may remain his own. I cannot give St Vier that assurance. But I will answer whatever else he asks.'

There was the message, as clear as it could be: Whatever they can do to me is nothing compared to what they'll do to you. Use me. But Ferris would not come forward and claim Horn's death himself. He wanted Richard to name him before them all, and destroy the swordsman's own credit with the nobles of the land. If he did it, Richard would be forced to turn to Ferris for patronage. The Halliday job, it seemed, was still on.

Richard sat and thought, and for once no one got up to make a speech. He could hear the scribes' rough scratching. Ferris was promising him immunity, protection, and privacy in the matter of Horn. It was as much as he could hope for. But it was only Horn's game all over again: save Alec's life or save his own; show he couldn't protect what was his or show that he could be bought with the right coin. Still, Ferris had made the offer; his hand was 'held out to the swordsman'. If Richard refused to take it Ferris might see that the law descended heavily on him, if only to secure his silence. The idea of honourable torture was ingenious – though too sweet and rich, like one of their banquet prodigies, the spun-sugar cage with the marzipan bird inside. Whatever he chose, they had him: there was no more to hope for.

Richard stood up. 'The swordsman thanks you,' he said. 'May I ask the noble court one question?'

'Certainly.'

'My noble lords; I would – '

But his words were lost in the sudden commotion from the antechamber. Shouts, the clang of metal and the scuffle of feet echoed between the two oaken doors. All attention left Richard, as startled birds leave a washline. Halliday nodded to Chris Nevilleson, who unlatched the door to the room.

The guards were holding onto a richly dressed man, trying to keep him from entering. He appeared to want to enter on all fours, since he seemed to be not so much trying to escape them as trying to hit the floor. When the door opened his captors jerked him upright. Green eyes stared across the room at the Crescent Chancellor.

'I've dropped it,' the intruder said.

236

Richard kicked over his heavy chair for a diversion. Sure enough, someone shouted, and in the ruckus he could reach Alec, disarm one of the guards and get them both out of there. . . . Then he realised that Alec hadn't even looked at him. Alec was still talking to Lord Halliday.

'I don't know what you feed them, but they're awfully nervous, aren't they? An excitable job, I suppose.'

Two more guards had appeared to right Richard's chair and sit him in it. He craned his neck, enraptured, staring at the young nobleman in the doorway. Alec's hair was cut and washed so that it fell in a soft cap around his head. He wore green brocade and gold, and it looked just as splendid on him as Richard had always known it would. He was even contriving not to slouch, probably because he was so angry that he had gone all stiff and straight and precise.

'If they weren't so eager to turn everyone they meet into rice pudding, I wouldn't have dropped it, and then perhaps we could have avoided all this.'

Lord Christopher darted forward and picked up the object in question, a gold medallion on a chain.

'Oh, hello,' said Alec. 'Nevilleson. I pushed your sister in the fishpond once. How is she?'

Lord Christopher looked up into his face and gasped. 'Campion! They – I thought you were dead!'

'Well, I'm not,' said Alec. 'Not yet, anyway. May I have that, please?'

Halliday nodded, and the guards released him.

'See?' Alec came forward, holding out the medallion. 'Tremontaine. It's my signet. And my pass. The duchess sent me. May I sit down?'

The entire room was staring at him as he walked to the empty seat between Lord Arlen and the Duke of Karleigh. He nodded courteously to the scribes, and introduced himself, 'Lord David Alexander Tielman (I, E, one L) Campion, of Campion and Tremontaine.' He waved one hand airily. 'It's all in the heralds' books, you can look it up later.'

Even Richard could see the fierce look Lord Ferris was giving the newcomer. He thought, if Ferris recognises Alec from Riverside, there could be trouble. But Alec only caught the look and smiled at Ferris with a private, malicious joy. Then he addressed the assembled nobles. 'I am so sorry to be late. It was very exasperating: no one seemed to be willing to tell me where you were meeting. You really should leave instructions about these things. I've seen more of the Hall of Justice than anyone should have to. It's quite tired me out. I hope it will be lunchtime soon. And now, shall we get down to business, my lords?'

They were all staring at him now, even Basil Halliday. Only Lord Arlen seemed to be amused. Arlen said, 'You will want to read the notes first, Lord David. I'm afraid we have started without you.'

Alec looked at him with the wind, as they say, momentarily knocked out of his sails. Richard's opinion of the unknown nobleman went up several more notches. He was still too stunned to do much more than take in Alec's performance. So Alec was a relative of the pretty woman with the swan boat after all. The admirable duchess with the wonderful chocolate set had sent her young kinsman to his trial. Maybe *Alec* – or, as it seemed, *Lord David* – was going to claim to be the patron in Horn's death? It wasn't completely wrong. The thought of the elegant young noble with the blistering tongue and terrible manners acting as his patron made Richard feel slightly cold. A lot of Alec's outrageous behaviour was due to simple fear and some embarrassment. Whatever he was planning to do here, Richard hoped he could pull it off. He had silenced Ferris for now, anyway.

Alec finished reading the notes, and put them down with a brisk nod. The reading seemed to have given him the time he needed to regain his nerves. 'I have several things to add,' he said, 'and not all of them are suitable to this Inquiry. Tremontaine has been dealt several offences in this case, and would like to see them brought before the entire Council of Lords. I can't be more specific now without prejudicing the case. Also, as some of you know' – here he looked mildly at Lord Christopher – 'I'm interested in old books. Some of them actually contain some useful facts. In one I've found an old legal custom called the threefold challenge. It has never been officially rescinded, although it has fallen out of use. I know observance of the old ways is very much respected by some gentlemen' – and the look he gave Lord Karleigh was less mild – 'and hope that by bringing

St Vier into the hall before all the assembled lords of the state, we could require his patron to come forward by crying it three times.'

'It sounds very dramatic,' said Halliday. 'Are you sure it will really be effective?'

Alec shrugged. 'It will, as you say, be good theatre. And you wouldn't want to punish the wrong man.'

'But,' said Lord Montague gently, 'can we summon the entire lordship of the city to a piece of good theatre?'

Alec's chin lifted dangerously. 'You must be joking. They'd *pay* to see this. Two royals a head, and standing room only. Make 'em vote up the land tax while they're all in there. All card parties will be cancelled.'

Basil Halliday nearly disgraced his position by chuckling helplessly. 'He's right.'

'And that', said Karleigh, glad to have something to disagree with at last, 'is what you think of the dignity of the Council, my lord?'

But in the end, the vote was passed.

Chapter XXVI

Two days later, the deputy of the Fort was getting tired of being beaten at chequers.

'Beginner's luck,' said Richard St Vier. 'And anyway, we're not playing for real stakes. Come on, just one more game.'

'No', the deputy sighed, 'I'd better go and find out who wants to see you this time. Don't these people understand, orders are orders, they don't change from hour to hour. But I'll tell you, I could retire to the country with the bribes I'm offered.'

'I'm fashionable,' Richard said; 'it happens.'

The cell was full of flowers, like their box at the theatre. The gifts of food and wine had to be refused as possibly poisoned, but the clean shirts, bouquets and handkerchiefs were checked for secret messages and then gratefully accepted. It might be in poor taste to make a hero of St Vier with Lord Horn barely cold in his grave; but the nobles of the city had always been intrigued by the swordsman. Now popular feeling was that Horn's real killer, Richard's patron, would soon be uncovered at the impending Council. Even Horn's empty house was fashionable; people drove past it several times, looking for the wall St Vier had climbed over and the room where It had happened. And young David Campion, the instigator of the exciting proceedings, was very much sought after at the Duchess Tremontaine's – but he was never in.

Alec spent much of his days lying on his back in a darkened room, sleeping. The duchess sent up trays of exquisite food at regular hours, which he roused himself to eat. She would not allow him nearly enough wine. At night he prowled the house, haunting the library and reading things at random, scribbling notes and throwing them away. He came across an early copy of the banned *On the Causes of Nature*, and read it through twice without taking in a word it said. The only thing that kept him from dashing back to Riverside was the fact that Richard was not there.

Nor was the duchess at home to Lord Ferris. His letters to her were received, but not answered. Once, he met her in a public place where he knew she would be. She was charming but not flirtatious. Her eyes and words contained none of her usual doubles entendres, and she answered his own blandly. He wanted to scream at her, to beat her, to close his fingers on her flowerstalk neck; but there were people present, he dared not begin a quarrel for no apparent reason. Her delicate features and clear skin drove him to a frenzy he had not known in many months with her. He wanted to stroke the tight satin over her ribcage, to rest his hands in the curve of her waist and pull her featherlight body to him. He felt like a poor man looking through a park gate, helpless and unrelievedly unhappy. *He* knew what he had done to offend her; but he did not see how *she* could possibly have learned of it. Even if she had, he could not continue to live with her begrudging him his independence. He had been her willing apprentice for three years now. She had taught him love, and politics. Through her he had become what he was. And he had served her well, advancing her views in Council while she sat at the centre of the city, a delicate hostess everyone adored who everyone knew had no interest in politics. . . .

He couldn't remember how she had cast off the one before him. Her love affairs were discreet. The city was full of her friends; some of them, perhaps, old pupils who had left her more gracefully. He had been so sure that Godwin was targeted to be the next one. It had suited Ferris to assist Horn's little folly, to chase him away. If he had been right about her interest in Godwin, then she might well be angry now – although a lesser woman would be flattered at his jealousy. But how did she *know*? She was playing with him. Should he have come to her with an accusation? Waited to be given his marching orders? It occurred to him now that perhaps he had just been given them: not because of Godwin, but because of this young kinsman of hers, the brash young man with the high cheekbones. He looked Lord David up in the Heralds' List and his eyes widened. The bonds of blood were too close, surely. But nothing was sure with the duchess.

Lord Ferris tried through intermediaries to get word to St Vier; but his agents were all turned away, and finally he had to give up lest his interest become known. For some purpose of her own, Diane was sending in her young kinsman to champion St Vier's cause. He had been sure, at the Inquiry, that St Vier had grasped his meaning, and had been about to answer him affirmatively – but then Tremontaine had interfered. He wished he knew what Diane's game was. The simplest explanation was that she wanted St Vier for herself. But Ferris was not ready to abandon his own purpose. Without Diane's support, his bid for the Crescent would be more difficult, but still not impossible. If St Vier had truly understood him, he would have his chance again in open Council to acquire the swordsman's full cooperation. Why, after all, should St Vier listen to Tremontaine's young emissary, who was obviously using St Vier for his house's own ends? Ferris could promise him freedom, patronage and work. David Alexander Campion was offering St Vier nothing that Ferris could see.

In the Council Chamber, which had once been the Hall of Princes, a festive chaos reigned. Every noble in the city who had the right to sit in Council was sitting today – or standing, or milling, leaning on benches to talk to friends two rows over, or calling their servants to fetch another bag of oranges. The mingled scents of oranges and chocolate overlaid the hall's usual ones of waxed woodwork, ceiling dust and human vanity. The Council was beginning early this morning, and men unused to going without their breakfast were not about to give it up.

The Lords Halliday, Ferris, Montague, Arlen and the other members of the Justiciary panel were not partaking of the general merriment, or its sustenance. They sat at a table on a dais at the head of the hall with the panelled wall behind them. The Inner Council chancellors wore their blue robes, and Arlen and the Duke of Karleigh were richly dressed for public viewing. Of Lord David Campion there was as yet no sign.

Halliday looked out over the milling throng. 'Do you suppose', he murmured to Ferris, 'that we could get them to pass an act or two while they're all here?'

'No,' Ferris answered flatly. 'But you're welcome to try.'

'Where's Tremontaine got to?'

'You don't imagine', Montague said, 'that he's got lost again?'

'Probably.' Halliday glanced out at the crowd of nobles. 'Better get started anyway, before they begin having orange fights.' He leaned across to his aide. 'Chris, tell the heralds to call for silence, and then go and tell the deputy we're ready for St Vier.'

Richard and the deputy of the Fort were waiting patiently in an overcrowded antechamber stuffed with guards.

'I'm telling you,' the deputy was saying to his charge, 'you never saw a set of knives like that foreigner had, each one long as your forearm, and balanced like God's judgement – '

Then the huge double-doors swung open like shutters on the confining chamber, revealing a world of immense magnificence: a hall whose ceiling reached up to four times a man's height, studded with tall windows letting in sunlight that gilded the expanse of carved wood above and tilework below. The deputy dusted off his knees, and Richard straightened his jacket before they passed through those portals.

Closer up, Richard had a dazzling impression of ancient oak and freshly gilded scrollwork; and of a vertical sea of faces, bobbing and roaring just like real waves, but multi-coloured, as though struck to rainbows by the sunlight. He sorted it out into three banks of seats, filled with nobles, and on the fourth side a raised table behind which were seated the men from the Inquiry. Alec was missing. But Alec would be there; must be there. Richard wondered if he would be wearing the green and gold again. Now that he was allied with the Duchess Tremontaine, it was fitting that he look the part. Richard pictured the clever duchess giving Alec the kind of look she had given *him* at the theatre, long and appraising and amused, perhaps saying in her aristocratic purr, 'So, you're seeing sense and giving up on poverty at last. How convenient. I have a use for you. . . . ' But just what that use was, Richard couldn't begin to fathom. Perhaps she was simply confirming Alec's return to the fold in sending him to Council. Obviously, there'd been some rift with Ferris; maybe she'd decided not to kill Basil Halliday after all, and sent Alec to stop it. Richard assumed that, with the duchess behind him, Alec could save his life as efficiently as Ferris could, and at less cost to himself. He didn't think that Alec would want to hurt him.

They gave Richard a chair facing the panel of justiciars. Their interest was all on him: Halliday's look gravely considering; Ferris's cool; the Duke of Karleigh frankly staring. Lord Montague raised his eyebrows at Richard, grinned and mouthed the words, 'Nice shirt.' Behind Richard the stands were noisy with comment. He really didn't like having his back to so many strangers. But he watched the faces of his judges like mirrors for what was going on behind him. Halliday's betrayed irritation; he gestured, and heralds began pounding for silence.

Slowly the ruckus died, with a hissing of 'Shhh!' and one clear, 'They're getting started!' At last the room was as quiet as one so full of living souls could be. Feet shifted, benches creaked, cloth rustled, but human voices were stilled to a soothing murmur. And in that silence one pair of footsteps rang on the tiles.

From the far end of the hall a tall figure in black made its way across the expanse of floor. As it drew nearer, Richard's breath caught in his throat. Alec's customary black was all of velvet this time. His buttons glittered jet. The snowy edges of his shirt were trimmed with silver lace. And, to Richard's utter amazement, a diamond glittered in one ear.

Alec's face was pale, as though he hadn't slept. As he passed Richard's chair he did not look at hm. He went up to the dais, and took his seat among the justiciars.

The duchess had advised her kinsman of the precise time to arrive. He had badly wanted not to be approached before the Council began, and not to have to talk to any of the other justiciars when he sat at the table. His seat was between Lord Arlen and the Duke of Karleigh, on the other side of the Crescent Chancellor from Lord Ferris.

The muttering in the stands was rumbling its way to thunder again. Quickly the heralds called for silence, and the questioning began.

Reading from notes, Lord Halliday repeated his questions from the other day, and Richard repeated his answers. At one point someone from the stands called out, 'Louder! We can't all hear!'

'I'm not an actor,' Richard said. He was snappish because they were making him feel like one. He almost expected Alec to make a crack about throwing flowers; but it was Halliday who told him,

'Move your chair back a few paces; the sound will spread.'

He did it, and felt the high ceiling somehow picking up and projecting his words through the chamber. These people thought of everything.

Finally, Lord Halliday addressed the Council: 'My noble lords: you have heard the Justiciary question the swordsman Richard, called St Vier, in the matter of the death of Asper Lindley, late Lord Horn. That he did conspire in that death and succeed in it is now beyond question. But the honour of a noble house is a fine matter, and not touched on lightly. We thank you all for your attendance in this hall today, and charge you silence in the attendant threefold question.'

He looked over to Lord Arlen, who leaned back in his high-backed chair. Through the relaxation of Arlen's gesture a terrible focus burned; and the hall, feeling it, was still. Arlen lifted his head, and the deep gaze of his old–young eyes seemed to touch all the sides of the chamber, from the solemn men in front to the young men wrangling excitedly in a corner where they thought they would not be noticed.

Arlen's voice was dry and clear. It carried to the ears of everyone. 'By the authority of this Council, and of the Justiciary that presides for it, and by the honour of every man here, I charge any man bearing title of the land, whose father bore it and who wishes his sons to bear it, to stand forth now and proclaim himself if his honour or the honour of his house was touched to the death by Asper Lindley, late Lord Horn.'

The first time he heard the question Richard felt a chill down his spine. There was not a sound to be heard in the hall, and the world on the other side of the windows had ceased to exist. When Arlen repeated the question, Richard heard shuffling, as though people were preparing to rise, though no one did. Arlen waited for silence before repeating it a third time. Richard closed his eyes, and his hands closed on the arms of his chair to keep himself from answering the challenge. It was not his honour these people were concerned about. And in the doom-filled silence, no one stood forth.

'Master St Vier.' Richard opened his eyes. Basil Halliday was speaking to him in a quiet, orator's voice that everyone could hear. 'Let me ask you one last time. Do you lay claim to any patron in the death of Lord Horn?'

Richard looked over at Lord Ferris. Ferris was looking at him in mute urgency, the lines of his face rigid with veiled frustration. It was a stifled command, and Richard didn't like it. He turned his eyes to Alec. Alec was gazing out over his head with an expression of abstract boredom.

'I do not,' Richard answered.

'Very well.' Halliday's voice broke Arlen's spell, decisive and normal. 'Has anyone anything further to add?'

As if on cue, Alec stood up. 'I do, of course.'

A long sigh seemed to issue from the corporate mouth. Alec raised his hand. 'With your permission,' he said to the others; and when they nodded, he went down the steps to Richard.

As the figure in black approached, Richard saw Alec's hand reach into the breast of his jacket. He saw the flash of metal, and saw his own death at the end of the fine blade wielded by the man in black velvet. His hand shot up to turn the knife.

'Jumpy,' said Alec, 'aren't we?' He held out the gold Tremontaine medallion, and, still a few feet away, tossed it to Richard. 'Tell me,' Alec drawled; 'and while you're at it, say it loud enough for everyone to hear, have you seen this *particular* object before?'

Richard turned it over. It had been in Ferris's hand, in Riverside, the night they'd spoken at Rosalie's. Ferris had shown it to him to dispel his doubts about going along with the unnamed job. The job which had proved to be the killing of Halliday. The job Alec hadn't wanted him to take. To identify the medallion and its purpose now meant pointing the finger at Tremontaine, in front of Halliday himself.

'Are you sure – ' he began; but Alec's voice overrode his: 'My dear soul; I've heard a lot of scandalous things about you, but no one ever told me you were deaf.'

Or it meant pointing the finger at Ferris. Tremontaine and Ferris had fallen out. Tremontaine would deny all complicity in the Halliday job. Or perhaps . . . perhaps there had never been any in the first place.

'Yes', Richard said. 'I've seen it.'

'You amaze me. Where?'

The tone of Alec's voice, the showiness of his antagonism, were hopelessly reminiscent of the first time they'd met. Then, his foolish daring and bitter wit had attracted Richard. He knew Alec better now, well enough to recognise his fear and desperation. Alec had come close enough for Richard to smell the steely smell of freshly ironed linen, the citron he'd been barbered with, and, under them, the sharpness of his sweat. Its familiarity made him feel suddenly dizzy; and to his dismay it streaked his senses with desire for the nobleman in black. He dared to look up into Alec's eyes; but, as ever, Alec looked past him.

'I was shown this – the Tremontaine medallion – a few months ago, in Riverside. By someone . . . by an agent of Tremontaine.' Richard did not look at Ferris.

'An agent of Tremontaine?' Alec repeated. 'Re-ally? Are you sure it wasn't just someone trying to sell you stolen goods?'

He thought, Re-ally, Alec! But that was probably what the nobles believed Riverside was like. 'He came about a job for me,' Richard answered.

'Was he a regular agent, one you recognised?'

'No. I'd never seen him before.'

'Would you know him if you saw him again?'

'Not necessarily,' Richard said blandly. 'I only saw him the once. And he seemed to be in disguise.'

'Oh, did he? A disguise?' He could hear the pleasure in Alec's voice. It felt as if they were fighting a demonstration match, the kind the crowds liked, with lots of feint and flash. 'What kind of disguise? A mask?' They both knew what was coming, and it forged the first bond of complicity between them that day.

'An eyepatch,' Richard said. 'Over his left eye.'

'An eyepatch,' Alec repeated loudly. 'Tremontaine's agent had an eyepatch.'

'But then', Richard added sweetly, 'so many people do.'

'Yes,' Alec agreed, 'they do. It's hardly enough to convict anyone of falsely claiming to represent Tremontaine in a matter of honour, is it, my lords?' He turned to the Justiciary. 'Nevertheless, let's try. May I have the Justiciary's permission to call as witness Anthony Deverin, Lord Ferris and Dragon Chancellor of the realm?'

No one had any trouble hearing Alec. But the hall remained desperately quiet this time.

Ferris rose smoothly and slowly, like oiled machinery. He came down the stairs and stood next to Alec, in front of Richard. 'Well, Master St Vier,' he said; just that. 'Well?'

He was trying to make Richard afraid. Richard felt something mad about the chancellor, even more intense and furious than Alec at his worst. It was as though Lord Ferris did not yet believe he had been beaten, and at the same time believed it so much that he was willing to do anything to deny it.

'My lord,' Richard said gently to Alec – and this time Alec could not make him take back the title – 'you must ask me what you want to ask me.'

Alec said, 'Is this the man you spoke to in Riverside?'

'Yes,' Richard answered.

Alec turned to Ferris. Alec's body was so stiff with tension that he couldn't tremble. His voice had changed: formal, dreamy, as though he were caught himself in the ritual of accusation and justice. 'My lord Ferris, Tremontaine charges you with falseness. Do you deny it?'

Ferris's good eye was turned to look at the young man. 'False to Tremontaine?' His mouth thinned in a sour smile. 'I do not deny it. I do not deny meeting the honourable St Vier in Riverside. I do not deny showing him the Tremontaine signet. But surely, my lords,' he said, his voice growing stronger with assurance as he faced the line of his peers, 'any of you can think of another reason for me to have done so.'

Richard's mouth opened, and then closed. Ferris meant that he had come to him to have Diane killed.

Alec said it for him: 'St Vier doesn't *do* weddings.'

The familiar phrase broke some of the tension in the room: 'No weddings, no women, no demonstration fights. . . . ' Montague rehearsed ruefully.

'Very well,' Alec said directly to Ferris, his voice ringing with restrained excitement. 'And if he refused the job, which he surely did, why then did you twice send your servant, Katherine Blount, to negotiate with him?'

Ferris's breath hissed sharply through his nose. So that was where she's gone – to Diane, her rival in his bed. The slut had no pride. But that must be it – how else would Tremontaine know about her meetings with St Vier? Knew it, then; but couldn't prove that *he* knew it.

'My servant.' Ferris forced himself to sound surprised. 'I see. Then I fear Tremontaine has been misled. Mistress Katherine is herself Riverside-born. I took her into my service to keep her out of prison. I had no idea she was holding to her old ways, her old friends. . . . '

'Just a minute,' said Richard St Vier. 'If you mean she is my lover, she is not. You should know that very well, my lord.'

'Whatever she is', Ferris said coldly, 'does not concern me. Unless you intend to produce my servant here before this Council to testify that she was running messages from me, I'm afraid we'll have to let the matter rest.'

'*What about the ruby?*' Alec spoke to Ferris so quietly that even Richard could barely hear him. But the old note of mockery was back in his voice.

'Ah,' Ferris began, in stentorian tones for the public. 'Yes. The stolen – '

'It's mine,' Alec murmured. With an actor's grace and timing he opened his hand, holding it low between his body and Ferris's. The ruby ring blazed on his finger. 'Always has been, always will be. I recognised it at once when Richard brought it home.' Ferris was staring into his face. 'Yes,' Alec continued in an insinuating purr, 'you're awfully dim, aren't you? I even wore black especially so you'd make the connection. But I suppose you can't really be expected to see things as clearly as the rest of us. . . . '

The insult struck home; Ferris clenched his fist. Richard wondered how he was supposed to keep Ferris from killing Alec here in Council.

'My lord . . . ?' Basil Halliday's voice tried to recall the drama to the public sphere; but Ferris stood frozen by the sudden double vision of the young man before him as he had been the night of the fireworks, dashing up the Riverside tavern stairs.

They say he's got a tongue on him to peel the paint off a wall. Richard says he used to be a scholar.

Thank you, Katherine. *I've seen him. He's very tall.*

Tall, and much more handsome than he'd been with hair straggling in his face – dressed in black, to be sure: the black rags of a student, then. Ferris remembered asking about the swordsman and being told by a chortling taverner, 'Oh, it's St Vier's scholar you'll want to apply to, sir. He's the one knows where he is these days.' And Ferris had watched Alec go past him out of the door, noted the bones . . . but he never would have connected that ragged man with the honey-and-acid creature who'd insulted him at Diane's house.

It was not Katherine who had informed the duchess, then, but her own kinsman. With his information Diane would have pieced together everything Ferris had done, and intended to do. Ferris wanted to laugh at his own stupidity. He had been watching her right hand these last few days, the hand that held his affections, wondering like a jealous husband why she was casting him off; while all the time it was her left hand that held the key to his future, his plots and his mind.

Diane had discovered his treachery, and from her lover and student it was unacceptable. Basil Halliday was her darling, the cherished heart of her political hopes for the city. She had already hired the swordsman Lynch to fight one of Karleigh's in Halliday's defence, and succeeded in scaring Karleigh off. She would not forgive Ferris for trying to dispose of his political rival. For Ferris to have pretended that the orders were coming from her was doubly damnable.

He hadn't meant to do it. He'd thought he could convince St Vier to work for him on his own merits. But when the swordsman had proved recalcitrant, Ferris had remembered the Tremontaine signet resting in his pocket, lent by the duchess that night for an entirely different purpose. It had seemed the height of cleverness to show it to St Vier. He remembered thinking that if, some day, St Vier were called to trial for the killing of Halliday, the evidence would point back to Tremontaine, and the duchess, finally, would be forced to set foot in the Council Hall herself to defend her house before Ferris, the new Crescent Chancellor. . . .

Once he'd begun the charade with the signet, giving St Vier the Tremontaine ruby as well had seemed too good an opportunity to miss. Diane had tossed it to him one day with a joke about pawning it; she didn't seem to expect it back. It was Ferris's passion for detail, his love of dupes and of complexity, and his belief in his own power to control everyone, that had tripped him up.

Now he was caught on the gilded curlicues of his own plots. If he had left Godwin alone, if he had left Horn alone, St Vier might never have come before the Council; and Alec might never have returned to the Hill for help for his lover. . . .

Well, he could still take the blame for Horn's death – it was just that he do so, after all. That would be what they wanted, the duchess and her boy. Lord David wanted to save his lover's life. And Diane wanted her lover ruined. She possessed the means to do it. The duchess had seen to it that a considerable crowd was assembled to watch: every lord in the city was there today. If Ferris refused to act to save St Vier, Tremontaine would reveal the Halliday plot before them all.

'Well, my lord?' Tremontaine's voice spoke clearly for all to hear. 'And shall we have to let the matter rest? For you are quite right; I am not holding your servant up my sleeve, waiting to testify against you.'

There came to Ferris then one of the moments he treasured. He felt himself standing at the pinnacle of the past and future, knowing his actions would rule them both. And it seemed quite clear to him then that he must take control, and how. He would ruin himself by his own will, his own power, in front of the eyes all perfectly focused on him.

Lord Ferris turned, so that his back was neither to the Justiciary, nor to the mass of men who waited on his words. He addressed Tremontaine, but his words were for all of them, delivered in that carrying orator's voice which had so often swayed the Council. 'My lord, you need pull nothing from your sleeve. You shame me, sir, as I hoped never to be shamed in my life; and yet, for the sake of justice I must speak. You may say that I am willing to sell my honour to keep my honour; but to trade honour for justice, that I can never do.'

'Interesting,' said Alec conversationally, 'though it follows no rules of rhetoric known to man. Do go on.'

Correctly assuming that no one else had heard that little

251

commentary, Ferris proceeded. 'My lords; let the justice be yours, and let the honour be Master St Vier's.' Richard felt himself redden with embarrassment. For Lord Ferris to make a show of himself was his business; but Richard had no taste for theatrics. 'Before you all, I here freely confess that I did falsely represent myself to St Vier in Tremontaine's name, and it was through my agency that Horn met his death.'

And that, Ferris thought complacently, was not even a lie.

Basil Halliday was staring at him in disbelief. All of the justiciars were frozen, silent, calculating, looking at the one from their midst who had stepped onto the floor and broken himself. But the stands were another matter. The nobles of the land were shouting, arguing, comparing notes and comments.

Over the cover of their noise, Halliday said to him, 'Tony, what are you doing!'

And, riding the crest of his pure manipulation, Ferris found the delicious nerve to look him gravely in the eye and say, 'I wish it weren't true; I wish it with all my heart.' He meant it.

'Call for silence, Basil,' said Lord Arlen, 'or there'll be no stopping them.' The heralds pounded and shouted, and eventually some order was attained.

'My lord Ferris,' said Halliday heavily. 'You take responsibility for the challenge of Lord Horn. It is a matter for the Court of Honour, and may be dealt with there.'

But that would not serve Ferris, although the duchess might be pleased to have him swept away under the rug. For his purposes his downfall must be spectacular; something to be remembered with awe ... something to be returned from in glory. So Ferris held up his hand, a deprecating gesture that made his palm burn as though he held their living spirits in it. Of course they would all listen to him. He had been their prodigy, the bright young man of courage and charm. He had seen to it that they were ready to follow him: he could have had the Crescent for the asking. It would take longer now; but by his very act of abnegation he was already working his way back into their hearts.

'My lords,' he addressed the hall. 'The council of my peers, the noble lords of this land, is court of honour enough to me. I freely grant that I deserve chastisement at your hands, and do not shrink from the weight of their justice. But I believe that which fated my ill deeds to be revealed before you all has also fated me with the small gift of letting you hear my reasons, the "cause of honour" that impelled me to the deed, here, from my own lips.' The gallery stirred with interest. This was what they had come for, after all: the drama, the passion, the violence; the making and unmaking of reputations in one morning. Almost as an aside, but pitched for all to hear, Ferris pointed out, 'In matters of honour, the wise man fears his friends' censure far less than he does their conjecture.' There was a ripple of approving laughter at the epigram.

The justiciars muttered amongst themselves, deciding whether to concede the unusual request. Only Alec was worried: Richard knew that look of utter disdain and what it signified. Apparently a speech by Ferris was not on Tremontaine's agenda. But there was not much Alec could do about it, only stand there letting haughtiness mask his nerves. Richard couldn't take his eyes from him, slender and brittle and poised. All that which, in Riverside, coming from a shabby, long-haired academic reject, had inspired men to homicidal rage, was fit and meet in this elegant creature's world – refined almost to a parody, but still within the range of normal. The nobles wouldn't love him for it, but they would accept him in their midst. It was where he belonged, after all. Richard tried to picture Alec as he was now, back in their rooms in Riverside – and felt his stomach clench with an emotion he thought best to disregard. He pulled his eyes away from the secrets of Alec's comportment and back to Lord Ferris.

The chancellor had bowed his sleek head; but his squared shoulders spoke gallantry and a noble determination. Whether from his posture or the pure curiosity his plea invoked, Ferris got what he wanted. In the pause in proceedings while the Justiciary made its decision to let him speak, Ferris had been working out the details of his story; now he launched into it in a new key, not humble but fierce with the desperation of a man given one last chance to clear his name of calumny; yet tinged with the resignation of one who knows he's done wrong.

'My lords,' he began again, striding into the centre of the floor. 'As you know, in matters of honour some explanation is owed amongst ourselves. I give it to you all now, tardily and with some shame. The clear-eyed among you will already have guessed the reason: I called for the death of Asper Lindley, and then hid that fact, to prevent a surge of rumour in which the innocent might suffer. I pray that you will regard it now as I did then – as rumour only; as the malice, maybe, of an aging – ' His voice rising, Ferris stopped and passed a hand over his face. 'Forgive me. This is not the place to re-fight the challenge. Suffice it to say that I had come to believe that Lord Horn attempted to dishonour a kinsman of my mother's. In his cups, Asper spoke disrespectfully of my kinsman's wife, and even began to claim that the man's son resembled him more than he did his own father. The boy – the young man, I should say, since he was almost 25 – was in the city at the time, and I feared . . . what every man fears in such a case. The truth is, he *did* resemble Asper, in looks and . . . other ways.'

Ferris paused, as though collecting himself. The hall was stone silent. But he knew each man was going over the roster of slender, fair young men recently in the city. He might have been too obvious already; surely he had provided enough detail to label Michael Godwin as Horn's bastard, forever, in some people's minds. For all he knew, it might even be true. And there it was, his parting gift to Diane; a taint set deep on the man she had dared consider to replace him. Let her work her delicate strategems on that!

Lord David, oddly enough, was smiling as though amused. Ferris looked at him out of the corner of his eye, and was suddenly pierced with the awful thought that he'd got it wrong – that Tremontaine was not really who he said he was; she had deceived him one last time and was taking this awkward beauty to her bed – but it was too late to change his story now. He reined his fancy in sharply. It was his misfortune to be a jealous man. He must not let it get in the way of his next step, the performance he still had to give.

He turned to face the Justiciary, giving his left shoulder to the young man, not to see his face. 'My lords,' he said in a low but carrying voice, one of his specialities, 'I hope that the honour of the court will be satisfied with this. If – '

'Honour may be satisfied,' Lord David drawled in interruption, 'but Tremontaine is not. If we could dispense with honeyed rhetoric for a moment, I would like to point out that you lied to St Vier, and have tried to defame your servant's name in court to hide it.'

Ferris smiled to himself. A young egalitarian. This court didn't care how he used his servants; the boy had been in Riverside too long. If he was Diane's latest choice, she would have a job teaching him patience in statecraft; anyone could see that he *cared* about things too much. St Vier, on the other hand, sat like calm itself, betraying only an intelligent interest. Ferris was sorry to lose him. He had such perfect balance.

'I beg Tremontaine's pardon,' Ferris said gravely. 'I am not unaware that I have acted shamefully. Other restitution is for the Justiciary to require. As for the rest . . .' A gasp went round when they saw what he was doing. The blue velvet robe, richly embroidered with the chancellor's dragon of the Inner Council, hung loose now on his shoulders. With careful formality he undid the last buttons, and slid the robe of office from his body. Lord Ferris folded it carefully, keeping it from the floor. He stood before them all dressed in stockings, breeches and a white shirt whose full sleeves and high neck covered as much as the robe had, but to much less effect. Alec had the effrontery to stare.

In a cold and terrible way, Ferris was enjoying himself. It was all politics, after all. With every act of poignant humility, he drew his public closer to him. When he was down so low that he had nowhere else to go, they would be merciful. And of their mercy he would build his fortune.

Deeply he thanked them for permission to resign his office. Courteously he signed the depositions of his testimony. And humbly he stood in the shadow of the Justiciary dais from which he had fallen, while his recent colleagues recessed to decide his fate.

The nobles in the stands were all moving amongst themselves. They were sending out for oranges again. No one came near Ferris and St Vier, marooned in the centre of the floor. At last Ferris motioned to a clerk to fetch him a chair. St Vier was paying no attention. His friend had departed with the other justiciars.

It hardly mattered whether they believed Ferris's story or not. They were none of them anxious to punish St Vier, only to fix the blame for Horn's death. With a noble patron standing up in

255

court, all blame shifted from St Vier's shoulders – he emerged a hero, true to his patron's faith even unto death. Of course all swordsmen were crazy. People liked them that way. It had been risky for Ferris to insist on being heard in open Council: someone might easily have brought up the mauling of Horn. But they had respected his humility, or been distracted by it, and no one did.

Expectant murmurs in the stands told Ferris that the Justiciary was returning through the double-doors. He waited a long moment before turning his head to look at them. One by one the men took their seats again, their solemn faces telling him nothing. Would they still make an example of him? Had they somehow seen through his pretence? Or were they only suffering from the trauma of his divestiture? Ferris's fingers dug into his palm; he concentrated on keeping them still. His last image must be of meeting his fate with grace.

It was Arlen who spoke, not Halliday. Ferris kept his gaze averted from the still pool of the other man's eyes: he had known them to make men blush before. Arlen spoke of financial restitution to Horn's estate, published apology to Tremontaine. . . . Ferris tried to fight the growing lightness of his heart. Could it be all? Could he still hold Halliday's love and trust? The fool, he thought, the fool. . . . and set his face in lines of deep concern. It was a physical effort to keep it so when Arlen finished; as hard, in its way, as lifting rocks or climbing stairs not to break out in a grin of relief.

Before the silence attending Arlen's sentence could be broken, Lord Halliday said, 'This is the restitution the Council of Honour sees fit to demand. Let it be so noted. I speak now for the Council of Lords, of whose Inner Council you are late a member. We do not forget the services you have rendered there, or your skill in despatching them. Although your current position now makes it impossible for you to continue to serve there, it would please the Council to accept your service to the realm in another sphere. To that end we propose your appointment as Ambassador Plenipotentiary to the free nation of Arkenvelt.'

Ferris had to bite his lip to keep from laughing aloud – not, this time, in relief. But hysterical laughter was not the correct public response to crushing defeat. Arkenvelt! The journey was six weeks by sea, or three months overland; he would be far from the borders of his realm. The news would be two months' stale, his work useless and dull.

It was banishment, then, and they knew him at last. Banishment to a frozen desert of tribal anarchists who happened to control half the world's wealth in silver and fur. The port city, seat of all major commerce, was a giant international fishing village whose houses were carved into the very earth. He would sleep on a pile of priceless furs, and wake to chip a hunk of frozen bear meat from the carcass by the door. His work would be interceding between commercial interests, helping lost captains find their way home. . . . counselling the policies of merchants and of miners. The most he could hope for was to line his pockets with local riches, while he waited to be recalled. He could not know when that would be.

'My lord of Ferris, do you accept the position?'

What more could they do to him? What more could *she* do to him? He knew the law; he had Diane to thank for that. But then, he had Diane to thank for everything.

He heard his own voice, as if at the end of a tunnel, rattling off the right phrases of gratitude. It was not an ungenerous offer: the chance to redeem himself in a position of responsibility which would, in time, lead to others. If he behaved himself, it would not be long. And they would forget, in time. . . . So Ferris told himself. But it was hard not to give way to laughter, or shouting, to tell them what he thought of them all as they watched his dignified bow and straight back, all those eyes following his slow walk across the echoing floor and out of the door of the chamber of the Council of Lords.

Chapter XXVII

It seemed that the nobles of the city wanted to congratulate Richard St Vier. They wanted to apologise to him. They wanted him to admire their clothes, they wanted to take him to lunch. He was going to hit someone, he knew he was going to hit someone if they didn't back off, stop clustering so close around him trying to touch him, get his attention.

The deputy of the Fort appeared at his elbow. Richard followed the path his men cleared out of the chamber, into the little waiting room. There a voice he knew said, 'Surely you didn't think they'd just let you walk away?'

He was thirsty, and every bruise in his body ached. He said, 'Why not?'

'They adore you,' said Alec, sounding horribly like himself. 'They want you to have sex with their daughters. But you have a previous engagement with Tremontaine.'

'I want to go home.'

'Tremontaine wishes to express its gratitude. There's a carriage waiting outside. I've just spent a fortune in bribes to secure the path. Come on.'

It was the same painted carriage he remembered handing the duchess into, that day at the theatre. The inside was cushioned in cream-coloured velvet that felt like it had a layer of goose down under it. Richard leaned back and shut his eyes. There was a gentle jolt as the carriage began to move. It was going to be a long trip; the Council buildings were far south and across the river from the Hill. They couldn't be planning to drop him off in Riverside, the streets wouldn't accommodate a carriage this size.

He heard a rustle of paper. Alec was offering him his pick of a squashed parcel of sticky buns. 'They're all I could get.' Richard ate one, and then he ate another. And another somehow disappeared, although he didn't remember taking it, but he did feel less hungry. Alec was still poking around in the creases of the paper looking for dropped bits of icing. Despite the splendour of his black velvet he didn't seem to have a handkerchief, and Richard had lost his somewhere in prison.

'There'll be champagne up at the house,' Alec said. 'But I'm not sure I dare. I haven't been drunk in days; I think I've lost my head for it.'

Richard leaned his head back and shut his eyes again, hoping to go to sleep. He must have dozed, because he didn't have any coherent thoughts, and sooner than he expected they had stopped and a footman was opening the door.

'Tremontaine House,' said Alec, stepping down after him. 'Excuse me, please, I – ' he glanced warily at an upper window – 'I have a pressing engagement.'

It had, apparently, all been foreseen and arranged. Richard was led, alone, to the kind of room he remembered from his own days of playing on the Hill. There was a very hot bath, which he stayed in for less time than he'd have wished, because he didn't like the servants hovering around him. They left him to dress himself. He put on a heavy white shirt, and fell asleep across the dream-soft covers of the bed.

The door opening woke him. It was a tray of cold supper, which he was privileged to eat alone. He set the tray on a little table by the window, overlooking the landscaped grounds and lawns rolling down to the water's edge. The sun struck the river to burnished brass; it was late afternoon. He was almost free to go.

Servants always made him uncomfortable, especially the well-trained ones. They seemed to be trying to act not like people but like self-effacing automatons that just happened to breathe and have speech. Everyone was always very polite to them, but the nobles were adept at ignoring their presence, and he never could do that. He was always aware of the other person there, the unpredictable body and the curious mind.

The Duchess Tremontaine's people were among the best. They treated him with courteous deference, as though they'd been told that he was someone powerful and important. Keeping just far enough in front of him, they escorted him down halls and staircases to his interview with his benefactor.

259

He didn't know what he should expect, so he tried very hard to expect nothing. He couldn't help wondering if Alec would be there. He thought he would like to see Alec again, one last time, now that his head was clearer. He wanted to tell him that he liked the new clothes. In the duchess's house it seemed less surprising that Alec was a Tremontaine, as he walked through the ornate corridors whose overcareful display seemed to mock their own opulence.

The duchess's sitting room was so ornate that it confused the eye. It was cluttered with intriguing possessions of diverse shapes and colours, all caught up and reflected in the enormous convex mirror hung over the fireplace. On a chair in front of the fire, a woman sat sewing.

Richard saw the fox-coloured hair, and turned to leave. But the door had been shut behind him. Katherine Blount stumbled to her feet, dropping her sewing. 'My lady –' she said softly, her throat constricted with fear, 'my lady should be here –'

'Never mind,' Richard said, still standing by the door. 'I expect I was brought to the wrong room.'

'Richard,' she said, nervously rushing her words, 'you must understand – I was told you wouldn't be hurt.'

'You can't disarm a swordsman without hurting him,' he said calmly. 'But I'm fine now. Can I open the door myself, or am I supposed to knock and let a servant do it?'

'You're supposed to sit down,' she snapped; 'sit down and *look* at me!'

'Why?' he asked politely.

She gripped the back of the chair for strength. 'Don't you even care?' she demanded. 'Don't you even want to know how it happened?'

'Not any more,' he said. 'I don't think it matters.'

'It matters," she said fiercely. 'It matters that Lord Ferris pushed me too far – that I came here to my lady – that *she* sent me down after you. I didn't want to, but I trust my lady. She's been better to me than Lord Ferris ever was. She didn't want to hurt me, and she didn't want to hurt you. But Ferris wanted you to kill Lord Halliday. If you'd done it it would have bound you to him. We *had* to get you out of Riverside, to stand trial before the Council so that my lady could clear you and set Ferris up to be punished in your stead.'

'What did she have against Ferris? And does she expect me to work for her now?'

Katherine stared at the overly self-possessed man standing across the room. 'Don't you know? Alec is here.'

'Oh, I know he's here. He was at the trial.' He looked at her. 'You should be careful of how you let yourself be used, Kath. Once you let them start, they'll go on doing it.'

'It's not like that – '

'Why not? Because she's nice to you, makes it worth your while? Look, I'm all right – but I wish you hadn't done it.'

'Oh, shut up, Richard!' He realised with dismay that she was crying. 'I thought I'd never have to see you again!'

'Kathy . . .' he said helplessly, but made no move to comfort her. Her nose was red, and she was dabbing her eyes with the backs of her wrists. 'I don't owe you anything,' she sniffled. 'Except an apology – well, you have that. I'm sorry I can't be a tough little Riversider. I'm sorry I let people use me. I'm sorry you got beaten up and it was my fault – now will you please go away and leave me alone!'

He did turn to the door, but it opened and a woman in grey silk came in.

'Katherine, dearest!' said the Duchess Tremontaine. 'You made my dear Kathy cry,' she scolded Richard, sweeping past him to take the woman in her arms and let her tears stain the silk. The duchess offered her a snow-white square of lawn to use. 'Never mind it,' the lady said soothingly to them both. 'It's all right now.'

He realised that the duchess had meant for them to meet this way. Richard stared at the elegant lady busily comforting his friend, and kept his frank gaze on her even when she looked up at him.

'Master St Vier,' she said, as though nothing had happened, while Katherine continued to sob on her breast; 'welcome. And thank you. I know what you had to do to save – Alec's – life from Horn, and what it must have cost you. And I know you cannot be altogether pleased with my letting Lord Ferris take the credit. You have compromised your position twice to my benefit. I

261

cannot think of any repayment for all this that would be less than ingratitude.'

If she was expecting him to thank her in return, she would have to wait for it. Katherine blew her nose on the pristine handkerchief.

'But,' the duchess said, 'I would like you to have something. A memento only.' From between her breasts she drew a chain. On it hung a ruby ring.

'That's Alec's,' he said aloud.

She smiled. 'No. This one is set in yellow gold, you see? His is white. They are a matched set of twelve, culled from the disbanded ducal coronet. Valuable, and highly recognisable. It would be hard to sell; but it makes a pretty toy, don't you think?' She dangled the chain, setting the jewel spinning.

'You're very generous.' He made no move to take it. 'Would you be good enough to give it to Lord David as a' – what was the word she'd used? – 'memento from me? I think he'll have more use for it.'

The duchess nodded, and slipped the chain back into her bodice. 'Gallant,' she smiled. 'What a noble you would make. It's a pity your father was . . . but no one knows who your father was, do they?'

'My mother always claimed not to remember what she called insignificant details.' It was an old story; it had made the rounds on the Hill once already.

'Well, then, Master St Vier, I will not keep you any more. I wish you godspeed', she said with quaint, old-fashioned grace, 'in all your endeavours.'

Richard bowed to both ladies. He followed the servants out of the room and down the corridors he had already memorised coming in.

It was blue dusk in the city. He had his sword back, and a bundle of his old clothes, washed and pressed for him by Diane's staff. The new suit he was wearing, he realised now, was peacock blue – Hypochondriac's Veins, Alec had called it. It fitted Richard perfectly; but then, Alec knew the tailor who had his measurements. The cloth didn't look so gaudy out of doors. Now that he was popular with the lords again, he could wear it to their parties. He quickened his step, breathing in deep draughts of freedom in the evening air.

Alec found the two women still sitting together in the duchess's parlour. He burst in without knocking, announcing, 'He's not in his room. The servants said he might be with you.'

'Oh,' said the duchess sweetly, her calm only mildly disturbed. 'I'm so sorry. I didn't know you wanted me to keep him particularly for you to see, so I let him leave.'

'Leave?' The young man stared at her as though she were speaking gibberish. 'How could he have left?'

'I believe he wanted to go home, dear. It is getting dark, and it's a long walk down.'

For the first time, Katherine felt sorry for Alec. She'd never seen his face with that raw and defenceless look, and hoped she never would again. 'Oh,' he said finally. His face closed like a cabinet drawer. 'Is that it. I see.'

'It's for the best,' Diane said. 'Your father's getting old. He'll need help with the estate soon.'

'He wouldn't notice if the sows started farrowing two-headed calfs,' Alec said conversationally. 'And don't say my mother needs someone to wind yarn for her, either. She is in the prime of domination.' Katherine hiccuped a helpless giggle. Alec's eye fixed on her. 'What's the matter with her?' he demanded. 'Why are her eyes red? She's been crying – You let her see Richard, didn't you? You promised she wouldn't have to, and then you –'

'David, please,' the duchess said wearily. 'I was delayed upstairs, and he came too early.'

Alec stared at her, his face white with anger. 'There was no point to that,' he said to her. 'None. You did it to amuse yourself.'

Katherine's flesh prickled. In Riverside, there would have been a fight. But the duchess turned, still smiling. 'You're a fine one to talk, my dear. Don't you do most things to amuse yourself?'

Alec flinched. 'It amused you to go to University', she went on pleasantly, 'because it gave your parents hysterics. You liked that, you told me so.'

'But that's not why –'

'Oh, you could have thought of something else well enough. But that served.'

'You sent me the money. I wasn't of age; I hadn't any of my own.' Alec's flat voice tried vainly to match her insouciance. 'I didn't know which you wanted more – for me to spy on the University people for you, or just to upset my mother.'

'Well, you refused to spy for me, so I suppose it must have been to upset your mother. I don't like her very much. I told her she was throwing herself away on Raymond Campion, but she wouldn't listen to me. She thought she was getting a hero, but she ended up with an ageing cartographer with no dinner conversation. It has made her very unpleasant. I always could get a rise out of her through you. It's not as if I couldn't *afford* to support you. And there wasn't much she could do if I wanted to let her eldest study and drug himself with a lot of cowherds.'

'They weren't – ' Alec carefully unclenched his hands.

The duchess made a dismissive gesture. 'There's no need to justify any of it: they amused you, and that's quite enough. You see, already you know more about the perquisites of power than most who have it; and when the time comes you'll be able to use your knowledge. They amused you: and when they ceased to do so you abandoned them for other . . . pleasures.'

He must have done the same thing to other people hundreds of times: but here he was walking right into her trap, his emotions utterly engaged; reacting with the pain and fury of a man who's been kicked in his soft spot, no longer aiming his blows or planning his strategy.

'You're wrong,' Alec said, his voice gruffly musical like an angry cat's. 'They were kicked out – for having ideas no one else had, no one else could even understand – all stripped of their robes but me. The school didn't ask me to leave. I suppose no one wanted to *offend* you. I suppose it *amused* you to keep me there.'

'You amuse yourself, my dear. It wouldn't have been much fun for you to go home to mother, and you wouldn't come up here to me. So you chose to stay; because there were still the drugs, and the people who didn't know who you really were to argue with.'

'Can't you shut up about the drugs? They're on the Hill too, you know. But we *did* something with them, we made notes – '

'Was that your dangerous research?' she laughed. 'The revelations of drugged 16-year-olds? No wonder no one took you seriously!'

'The stars!' he shouted. 'Light! Did you know light moves? The stars, the planets are a measurable distance away. They're fixed, they don't move; *we* move. It's provable mathematically –'

'David,' she said softly, 'you're shouting. Lord,' she sighed, 'I really don't see what the fuss is all about. It makes no difference to me what the stars do with themselves.'

'Politics', he said flatly. 'Just like here. It went contrary to the ranking professors' findings, and they couldn't have that.'

The duchess nodded approval. 'Politics. You should have stayed there. You would have learned a lot.'

'I didn't *want* to learn that!'

His voice rang in the gilded reaches of the cornices. The duchess shrugged her shoulders as though shaking off a gossamer scarf. 'Oh, David, David . . . use some sense. You already have. What do you think you've been playing at in Riverside? Politics of the crudest nature: the politics of force. And you enjoy it, my dear. But you're capable of more. What about Lord Ferris? You convicted him admirably.'

'It wasn't . . . fun.'

'Mmm,' she nodded. 'More amusing when you get to watch them die when you're through with them.'

He picked up a green glass paperweight, tossed it from palm to palm. 'That disgusts you, does it?'

'Not at all. It's just the kind of charming eccentricity society looks for in a duke. Put down that paperweight, David, I don't want you breaking it.'

'You're mad,' he said. The edges of his lips were white. 'I'm not even your heir.'

'I'm about to name my heir,' the duchess replied with a hint of steel; 'and I'm not mad. I know you, and what you're capable of. I know it to a hair's fineness. I must parcel out the power that will succeed me; no one person can hold it all. You should be pleased; your part is one of the easiest, and you'll get all the money.'

'I am not going to be duke,' he said stiffly. 'Even if you died tomorrow. Or right now,' he added; 'that would be fine with me.'

'Don't be so quick to reject the dukedom, Davey. Wouldn't you like some real power, for once? You could build a library, even found your own University, independent of the city's. You could hire Richard St Vier to protect you.'

He turned as though he would have hit her if he'd ever learned how to. His eyes were hot, like molten emeralds, in his white face. 'Halliday,' he managed to say; 'your hope for the city. Make *him* your heir.'

'No, no. He has his place already.' She rose on a burst of angry energy, strode across the room in a hissing of skirts. 'Oh, David, *look* at yourself! You were born to be a prince – you were a prince in Riverside, you shall be so again! I've seen you do it. Just look at the men who love and follow Halliday – and look at the one who loved and followed you.'

'And then there's Ferris,' Alec said acidly, 'who loved you and followed Halliday, with a detour to Arkenvelt.'

'Very clever,' she answered. 'Very nicely reasoned. You should be this clever all the time. It would have spared your Richard a good deal of trouble if you'd been clever enough to tell Horn who you really were when he was stupid enough to abduct you.'

'Maybe,' said Alec. 'But I was hoping to avoid something like this.'

'Avoid it?' she said, scorn showing on her face. 'Is that all you want – to avoid things? Do you think the world exists to provide a playground for your whimsies?'

He looked blandly at her. 'Well doesn't it? I thought you'd just been telling me to amuse myself.'

The duchess's knowing smile was strained. 'Ah, so that's what you want to hear, my young idealist. Power for the good of the people; power to affect change; great responsibility and great burdens, which must be shouldered by those with the brains and the skill to use them. I thought you knew all that, and didn't want to hear it.'

'I don't,' said Alec. 'I've told you what I think. I don't want any part in it. I dont know why you think I'm a liar. Even Richard doesn't think I'm a liar. Richard doesn't like to be used, and neither do I.'

'And I, too,' the duchess said icily, all warmth gone from her, 'do not like to be used. You came to me because I could be helpful. You never could have saved him on your own. But my dear child, you can't just turn around and go back now. Surely you knew the risk when you took it. You've lost him. You let Tremontaine use him for its purposes today. He's a proud man, and a clever one. He knows what you did.'

He was trying to see past the net she was folding him in, and failing, by the pallor of his face and the dullness of his eyes. But even in his weakness, he had managed to anger her past the point where she should be. And because she was a mistress of men's weakness, of frailty, of uncertainty, she twisted truth around him like a decoy.

'I was going to spare you this,' she said stiffly. 'I don't want to hurt you – I thought you'd see reason on your own. But come here.'

Drawn by compulsion to the scent of danger, he came. She drew out the second ruby from her bodice. 'Do you see this? I offered it to him with my thanks. But he threw it back in my face. He knows exactly how we used him, you and I. He didn't want it. He told me to give it to you – as a parting gift. He's through with you, David – *Alec*. So you see, there's no way out.'

'Oh, don't be silly,' said Alec. 'There's always a way out.'

He turned from her and walked to the full-length window; and when his hand shattered the glass he kept on walking a few steps more, then stopped. He stood at the centre of a storm of broken glass. Shivers of it lay across his shoulders, rising and falling and winking in the light of his slow, ragged breath. His outstretched arm was flowing with blood. He was looking clinically at it.

The Duchess Tremontaine stood, too, watching the wreck of a man through the wreck of her picture window. Then she said, 'Katherine. Please see that Lord David does not die before he leaves here.'

She turned, and the grey silk whispered that the duchess was leaving, leaving to tend to some other piece of business that required her attention in the house, the city, the world.

She left Lord David Alexander Tielman Campion alone with his bleeding arm and a servingwoman who was ferociously and methodically tearing her petticoat to strips for him.

Finally the blood's flow abated. The cuts had been many, but not deep. 'The funny thing is,' Alec told Katherine conversationally, 'I can't feel anything.'

'You will later,' she said to him. 'When you get home, soak all the glass out. He did give the ring back, but he still wants you. I'm sorry I waited so long to tell you. It's going to hurt plenty, believe me.'

'You're upset,' he said. 'It's a good thing you left Riverside. Don't ever go back.'

'I won't,' she said.

'And *do* remember to let grandmama bully you. She's perfectly charming as long as you let her.'

'Yes – Alec, leave now, before she comes back.'

'I will,' he said, and pocketed some silver ornaments.

Chapter XXVIII

By the time Richard got back to Riverside, word of his release had spread through the district. Already a few of his possessions had been returned; he found them lying piled like offerings in front of his door: a small rug, the dragon candlesticks, and the rosewood box with a few coins in it. He stuck his candlestub in one of the sticks and went inside. The rooms were not much disturbed: some furniture had been shoved around, and a cushion he'd never liked was gone. He wandered the rooms, bathing in the familiarity of shape and shadow. He lifted clothes out of the chest, folded and put them back; puffed up pillows and rearranged his knives. There was very little of Alec left in the house, and he was glad. His circuit ended on the chaise longue. It had been almost a year since he'd sat on it regularly. He stretched out, with his ankles over the edge, and fell asleep.

When he awoke, Richard thought he was dreaming. A tall man in elegant clothes was shutting the door behind him.

'Hello,' said Alec. 'I've brought us some fish.'

The warm spring night curls itself silently around Riverside like a sleepy cat. One by one the stars come out in the clear sky, twinkling cheerily over whatever mischief is brewing below them in the twists of streets and houses there tonight. Under their gaze the chimneys rise up in jagged argument, cold and still and picturesque.

From the celestial heights the arbitrary acts of life seem patterned like a fairy-tale landscape, populated by charming and eccentric figures. The glittering observers require vital doses of joy and pain, sudden reversals of fortune, dire portents and untimely deaths. Life itself proceeds in its unpredictable infinite patterns – so unlike the measured dance of stars – until, for the satisfaction of their entertainment, the watchers choose a point at which to stop.

ACKNOWLEDGMENTS

This novel would not exist in its present form without the help of more people than I can name on one page. However, I would like particularly to thank

Isabel Davidson Swift for listening and ironing;

Linda Post, Caroline Stevermer, and the rest of You Guys for believing I could do it before I did (or putting on a convincing act);

The Kushner "Medici" Foundation for Assistance to Struggling Artists;

David G. Hartwell for waiting till I came 'round again;

Tom Canty for the jewelled box

... and Mimi Panitch for unplugging the telephone and inventing Writer's Stew.

Ellen Kushner
New York City
1989

ABOUT THE AUTHOR

Ellen Kushner grew up in Cleveland, Ohio, and attended Bryn Mawr College, graduating from Barnard College at Columbia University. She has worked in New York City as an editor, reviewer, and artists' representative, and now lives in Boston, where she is a producer and music announcer for WGBH-FM radio. She also teaches literature at Northeastern University College. Her short fiction has appeared in several anthologies, including *Borderland* and *After Midnight*, and she is responsible for five children's books in the Choose Your Own Adventure® series. *Swordspoint* is her first novel.

THE DRAGON REBORN

Sequel to *The Great Hunt*

Book Three ~of~ **The Wheel of Time**

by

Robert Jordan

Praise for *Eye of the World*

"A powerful vision of good and evil...fascinating people moving through a rich and interesting world." —Orson Scott Card

"Richly detailed...fully realized, complex adventure."
—*Library Journal*

"A combination of Robin Hood and Stephen King that is hard to resist...Jordan makes the reader care about these characters as though they were old friends." —*Milwaukee Sentinel*

Praise for *The Great Hunt*

"Jordan can spin as rich a world and as event-filled a tale as [Tolkien]...will not be easy to put down." —*ALA Booklist*

"Worth re-reading a time or two." —*Locus*

"This is good stuff...Splendidly characterized and cleverly plotted...The Great Hunt is a good book which will always be a good book. I shall certainly [line up] for the third volume."
—*Interzone*

The Dragon Reborn

coming in hardcover in August, 1991.

Robert Jordan's
THE EYE OF THE WORLD

The acclaimed first volume of
The Wheel of Time

"This one is as solid as a steel blade, and glowing with the true magic. Robert Jordan deserves congratulations."　　　　　—Fred Saberhagen

"The next major fantasy epic!"　　　　—Piers Anthony

"A splendid epic of heroic fantasy, vast in scope, colorful in detail, and convincing in its presentation of human character and personality."

　　　　　　　　—L. Sprague de Camp

☐　51181-6　　　　　　　　　　　$5.95
☐　　　　　　　　　　　　　Canada $6.95

THE DRAGON REBORN

Sequel to The Great Hunt

Book Three
of
**The Wheel
of Time**

by
Robert Jordan

Praise for *Eye of the World*

"A powerful vision of good and evil...fascinating people moving through a rich and interesting world." —Orson Scott Card

"Richly detailed...fully realized, complex adventure."
—*Library Journal*

"A combination of Robin Hood and Stephen King that is hard to resist...Jordan makes the reader care about these characters as though they were old friends." —*Milwaukee Sentinel*

Praise for *The Great Hunt*

"Jordan can spin as rich a world and as event-filled a tale as [Tolkien]...will not be easy to put down." —*ALA Booklist*

"Worth re-reading a time or two." —*Locus*

"This is good stuff...Splendidly characterized and cleverly plotted...The Great Hunt is a good book which will always be a good book. I shall certainly [line up] for the third volume."
—*Interzone*

The Dragon Reborn
coming in hardcover in August, 1991.

Robert Jordan's
THE EYE OF THE WORLD

The acclaimed first volume of
The Wheel of Time

"This one is as solid as a steel blade, and glowing with the true magic. Robert Jordan deserves congratulations." —Fred Saberhagen

"The next major fantasy epic!" —Piers Anthony

"A splendid epic of heroic fantasy, vast in scope, colorful in detail, and convincing in its presentation of human character and personality."

—L. Sprague de Camp

☐ 51181-6 $5.95
☐   Canada $6.95

ANDRE NORTON
THE GRANDE DAME OF SF

☐ ☐	54138-1	THE CRYSTAL GRYPHON	$2.95 Canada $3.50
☐ ☐	54712-8	DARE TO GO A-HUNTING	$3.95 Canada $4.95
☐ ☐	51008-9	FLIGHT IN YIKTOR	$3.95 Canada $4.95
☐ ☐	54717-9	FORERUNNER	$2.95 Canada $3.95
☐ ☐	50360-0	GRYPHON'S EYRIE *with A.C. Crispin*	$3.95 Canada $4.95
☐ ☐	54732-2	HERE ABIDE MONSTERS	$2.95 Canada $3.50
☐ ☐	54743-8	HOUSE OF SHADOWS *with Phyllis Miller*	$2.95 Canada $3.50
☐ ☐	50722-3	IMPERIAL LADY *with Susan Shwartz*	$3.95 Canada $4.95
☐ ☐	54754-3	RALESTONE LUCK	$2.95 Canada $3.95
☐ ☐	51678-8	WHEEL OF STARS	$3.99 Canada $4.99
☐ ☐	54750-0	WIZARDS' WORLDS	$4.95 Canada $5.95

Buy them at your local bookstore or use this handy coupon:
Clip and mail this page with your order.

Publishers Book and Audio Mailing Service
P.O. Box 120159, Staten Island, NY 10312-0004

Please send me the book(s) I have checked above. I am enclosing $ _____
(please add $1.25 for the first book, and $.25 for each additional book to cover postage and handling.
Send check or money order only—no CODs).

Name _____
Address _____
City _____ State/Zip _____
Please allow six weeks for delivery. Prices subject to change without notice.

FANTASY ADVENTURE
FROM FRED SABERHAGEN

☐☐	55343-8 _55344-6_	THE FIRST BOOK OF SWORDS
☐☐	55340-3 _55339-X_	THE SECOND BOOK OF SWORDS
☐☐	55345-4 _55346-2_	THE THIRD BOOK OF SWORDS
☐☐	55337-3 _55338-1_	THE FIRST BOOK OF LOST SWORDS
☐☐	55296-2 _55297-0_	THE SECOND BOOK OF LOST SWORDS
☐☐	55288-1 _55289-X_	THE THIRD BOOK OF LOST SWORDS
☐☐	55284-9 _55285-7_	THE FOURTH BOOK OF LOST SWORDS
☐☐	55286-5	THE FIFTH BOOK OF LOST SWORDS
☐☐	51118-2	THE SIXTH BOOK OF LOST SWORDS
☐☐	50855-6	DOMINION
☐☐	50255-8 _50256-6_	THE HOLMES-DRACULA FILE
☐☐	50316-3 _50317-1_	THORN

Prices:
- THE FIRST BOOK OF SWORDS — $3.95 / Canada $4.95
- THE SECOND BOOK OF SWORDS — $3.95 / Canada $4.95
- THE THIRD BOOK OF SWORDS — $3.95 / Canada $4.95
- THE FIRST BOOK OF LOST SWORDS — $3.95 / Canada $4.95
- THE SECOND BOOK OF LOST SWORDS — $3.95 / Canada $4.95
- THE THIRD BOOK OF LOST SWORDS — $4.50 / Canada $5.50
- THE FOURTH BOOK OF LOST SWORDS — $4.50 / Canada $5.50
- THE FIFTH BOOK OF LOST SWORDS — $4.50 / Canada $5.50
- THE SIXTH BOOK OF LOST SWORDS — $4.50 / Canada $5.50
- DOMINION — $3.95 / Canada $4.95
- THE HOLMES-DRACULA FILE — $3.95 / Canada $4.95
- THORN — $4.95 / Canada $5.95

Buy them at your local bookstore or use this handy coupon:
Clip and mail this page with your order.

Publishers Book and Audio Mailing Service
P.O. Box 120159, Staten Island, NY 10312-0004

Please send me the book(s) I have checked above. I am enclosing $ _____
(Please add $1.25 for the first book, and $.25 for each additional book to cover postage and handling.
Send check or money order only—no CODs.)

Name _____

Address _____

City _____ State/Zip _____

Please allow six weeks for delivery. Prices subject to change without notice.

SCIENCE FICTION FROM
L.E. MODESITT, JR.

54582-6	THE ECOLITAN OPERATION	$3.95
54583-4		Canada $4.95
54584-2	THE ECOLOGIC ENVOY	$2.95
54585-0		Canada $3.75
50348-1	THE ECOLOGIC SECESSION	$3.95
		Canada $4.95

FANTASY BESTSELLERS
FROM TOR

☐	55852-9	ARIOSTO	$3.95
☐	55853-7	*Chelsea Quinn Yarbro*	Canada $4.95
☐	53671-1	THE DOOR INTO FIRE	$2.95
☐	53672-X	*Diane Duane*	Canada $3.50
☐	53673-8	THE DOOR INTO SHADOW	$2.95
☐	53674-6	*Diane Duane*	Canada $3.50
☐	55750-6	ECHOES OF VALOR	$2.95
☐	55751-4	*edited by Karl Edward Wagner*	Canada $3.95
☐	51181-6	THE EYE OF THE WORLD	$5.95
☐		*Robert Jordan*	Canada $6.95
☐	53388-7	THE HIDDEN TEMPLE	$3.95
☐	53389-5	*Catherine Cooke*	Canada $4.95
☐	55446-9	MOONSINGER'S FRIENDS	$3.50
☐	55447-7	*edited by Susan Shwartz*	Canada $4.50
☐	55515-5	THE SHATTERED HORSE	$3.95
☐	55516-3	*S.P. Somtow*	Canada $4.95
☐	50249-3	SISTER LIGHT, SISTER DARK	$3.95
☐	50250-7	*Jane Yolen*	Canada $4.95
☐	54348-3	SWORDSPOINT	$3.95
☐	54349-1	*Ellen Kushner*	Canada $4.95
☐	53293-7	THE VAMPIRE TAPESTRY	$2.95
☐	53294-5	*Suzie McKee Charnas*	Canada $3.95

Buy them at your local bookstore or use this handy coupon:
Clip and mail this page with your order.

Publishers Book and Audio Mailing Service
P.O. Box 120159, Staten Island, NY 10312-0004

Please send me the book(s) I have checked above. I am enclosing $ _____
(Please add $1.25 for the first book, and $.25 for each additional book to cover postage and handling.
Send check or money order only—no CODs.)

Name _____

Address _____

City _____ State/Zip _____

Please allow six weeks for delivery. Prices subject to change without notice.